RESIDUE

RESIDUE

Nitasha Kaul

RAINLIGHT
RUPA

Published in RAINLIGHT by
Rupa Publications India Pvt. Ltd 2014
7/16, Ansari Road, Daryaganj
New Delhi 110002

Sales centres:
Allahabad Bengaluru Chennai
Hyderabad Jaipur Kathmandu
Kolkata Mumbai

ISBN: 978-81-291-2485-2

10 9 8 7 6 5 4 3 2 1

The moral right of the author has been asserted.

Printed at Replika Press Pvt. Ltd., India

Still divided between the joy and tear
Of those that be and those that are

Contents

1

Named For Trotsky

What kind of a name is Leon anyway? Especially for someone who grew up in Delhi and doesn't care much for politics. But I guess I was fated to live out the irony. Or maybe I am a revolutionary of some type. Only, it has been over two decades and I just haven't found my purpose in the grander scheme of things.

The academic year at Delhi University starts in the month of July. The year I joined, it was to begin on the 15th. I had finished my school-leaving exams after a long period of intense study. The Science and Commerce stream guys that I hung out with were forever telling me how easy it was to be doing the so-called 'Arts'; it was merely words. Also, what guy studied Arts & Humanities? It was a line of inquiry fit for girls, who lap up the sentimental bullshit; us men ought to excel in Commerce and Mathematics and Physics, the hard and analytical stuff. I couldn't care less, though, true to this stereotype, most of my classmates were girls. In fact, there was not much 'scope'—a word that every teacher and parent parroted non-stop, and which irritated me beyond belief—in wanting to graduate in a soft subject like English Literature.

'So, Leon, what is your plan after twelfth standard?'—this had unfailingly been Uncle Siraj's opening line in every phone conversation for at least two years before I was due to finish school. He would call Ammi and ask her too, 'Albeena, what is your son up to in life? You must keep strict control over young boys these days. Fatherless boys are always prone to go astray.' Ammi generally stood up to her brother, saying that I had never given her any cause for concern. Still, she would be visibly strained after these taunts. Ammi was a fastidious mother, prudent, and by no means lenient. I never got pocket money in school. I was not allowed to go on trips away from home. I hardly ever missed classes.

It was quite funny that I actually turned up at school on 7 December 1992.

Half the class was absent, and after roll call, the Principal summoned me and sent me home escorted by a peon. He rang Ammi, 'In this environment, we cannot take responsibility for your son's safety,' she should not send me to school until things calm down. Barely a teen, I was thrilled about the bonus holidays.

It wasn't funny actually; it was sad.

Throughout my growing up years, Ammi pretended we were regular people, but we were not. Wherever we went, we were Muslims. For an entire winter in 1992 and early 1993, because of the Babri Masjid demolition fuss and the Bombay blasts and riots, Ammi did not let me watch TV. Her excuse was that since the Cricket World Cup—Oh! that amazing final where Pakistan beat England by 22 runs—I had spent way too much time in front of the tube. I needed to concentrate on my studies. She had a weird way of protecting me. When we had leaflets about Kashmiri Hindu migrants shoved under our door, and I tried asking her why we, as Kashmiri Muslims, did not even visit Srinagar, she snapped back that she would not discuss Kashmir. As I grew older, I got a better grasp of topics that could not be broached with Ammi—'Father', 'Kashmir', 'Politics'—and to these I added some of my own—'Career' and 'Home'. It was a Catch-22; I yearned to run away from home, but without a career, where could I go?

I was selfish, I admit. But with a missing father and a suffocating mother, it did feel like having a chip on my shoulder. And it isn't like I did not love Ammi. She and I were close, at least until I joined university.

I understood that Ammi had made a lot of sacrifices for me. Though she did not go on about it, I could see that being a single mother in Delhi was tough. Her relatives and our neighbours were ever ready to pass judgement; the smallest actions would provoke comment.

Ammi taught History at a nearby secondary school. In later years, she gave private English tuition to children in the locality. There were always enough takers. People knew that Ammi had been abroad (to 'Oh England!') at one point in her life, and this was a never-ending positive attraction. Despite the bonhomie, we were marked, being the rare Muslim family in our colony. We lived, if not in fear, then in constant awareness of our actions and behaviour. Ammi, being husbandless and with a child, kept her head covered and wore bland clothes, never speaking to men in the absence of their wives.

As a small boy, I used to have an Imaginary Father. For our safety, Ammi had put out a story that her husband worked in the Gulf. I had been drilled not to let anyone know that I had never seen my father: 'Not a word about it, even if they offer chocolates!' I had to say, 'I have a very loving father, my Abbu, who lives abroad.' If probed further, I should reply that I met Abbu in Dubai last winter and that he gave me lots of presents. I was under five at that time.

When we moved to another flat with a longer-term intention, my instructions changed. The story about my Imaginary Father would be difficult to keep up as I grew older. So, here, we just pretended that my father was dead. He had died suddenly from a heart attack in England when I was very young, and my mother had not remarried, preferring instead to live as a widow.

In truth, my father, Mir Ali, was neither working in Dubai nor dead in England. Depending on the day, I could tell myself: He went missing. He disappeared. He abandoned his wife Albeena when she was expecting me.

Albeena, for that was Ammi's name, grew up in Srinagar in Kashmir. She was born in a village, where both her parents had succumbed to a cholera epidemic. She and her younger brother Siraj were reluctantly accepted by an aunt on the maternal side of the family.

They moved to Srinagar and attended school there. Uncle Siraj helped in the family shop and developed a good head for business, skills that came to good use when he expanded and set up base in Punjab. Ammi managed to complete a BA Pass course, juggling her studies with the onerous household chores. Soon after, she was married to Mir Ali, an engineer, a communist, a firebrand activist.

The marriage to Mir, it was universally admitted, had been a big mistake. Mir Ali had deserted Albeena in England and vanished when on a visit to Berlin before my birth, never to be found again.

'How were we to know that he was going to run away like that? We thought he was a good catch, educated, what with his engineering degree and all. We hoped he would make Albeena happy,' Uncle Siraj would opine.

I'd heard this narrative so many times, I knew it by heart.

'We were thrilled—nay, overjoyed, to hear that he was given the opportunity to go abroad; a posting to England of all places! We were so happy for Albeena. In fact, even the distant cousins were jealous. How lucky is Albeena, they would ceaselessly repeat, her husband is a blessing. Pregnant directly after going to England to be with Mir, everyone was green with envy.'

'But,' they lamented, 'it was Allah's wish.'

'Us mortals cannot understand how these things are supposed to work. It was a buri nazar, someone's evil eye, that ruined her life. Poor Albeena! To be left alone in a strange country with a newborn and no husband.'

Beyond that, Uncle Siraj, and everyone else, felt that the right and proper course of things had not been followed. They had plans for Albeena which included her giving me up for adoption, being remarried to a good man and forgetting all about the past.

Ammi, however, had stubbornly refused.

She had decided that she was going to bring me up on her own and support herself by working as a teacher. She began on low wages and did her BEd part-time through correspondence, before securing a lifetime job in a government secondary school. I was admitted to a private English medium school nearby. In the mornings, we both left in the same rickshaw. She would drop me off at my bus stop and then continue on to her school. I recall the uncomfortably rickety morning rush. I was horrible at getting up early, but other than that, I tried not to give her too much trouble.

Uncle Siraj never approved of Ammi living on her own with a child. According to him, I was spoilt because of her indulgence and lack of discipline. In my childhood, when we visited him and Aunt Shama in Chandigarh, I would climb the guava trees in their front garden while he forced his children to take a siesta. I scampered off to the yard, picked grapes from the vine. He thought I was a bad influence on his kids. As I grew older, he deprecated me for other reasons. If you ask me, he just plain hated my guts. Basically, he had four daughters and no son, so he never let up any opportunity for telling me what to do with my life. I did not pray or fast at Ramadan. I did not want to go and study at Aligarh. I did not like listening to repeats of his hokey 'tale of a self-made man' or show an interest in his 'violence and politics of Kashmir' sermons. I was Westernized. I was insolent. Freedom to do as I please and cricket were all that mattered to me. He was certainly right on this last count.

He and Aunt Shama had wanted us to visit during the Eid festival of my Board exam year. I could not make it as there were extra classes at school. Plus any free time I got, I would spend reading as many out-of-syllabus books as I could lay my hands on. It might come of use in being able to name-drop impressively in the papers. But Uncle's family had made it a point to let us know that since I was studying 'Arts', they could not understand why I needed to be so bothered about the exams. Ammi had been nervous. She thought that I could be overconfident about my academic skills. What a surprise it was, then, when I came out on top of the Humanities section in my school and received a congratulatory letter from the Principal himself! This was the man who thought that I was not driven enough: 'Leon Ali—studious but lacks ambition, liable to lose focus,' my report card at school had previously noted. It was a special joy to see his signature on the letter of commendation.

Once those dreadful school-leaving exams were done, I was relieved to get back to sports and life as usual. I was a topper all right, but I wasn't a nerd! In the weeks before, I had hardly been out and had cut down on playing cricket. I had even secretly smoked due to the stress. It had begun as dares and fun, trying to inhale and exhale without sputtering, in the lunch break conclaves behind the water cooler. Then, one girl gave me a couple of Marlboro packets which belonged to her ex-boyfriend, 'I can't keep fags at home and it would be a shame to waste them. You can have them if you like.' It was a pity she wasn't hot or I would have tried getting her to blow smoke with me. I said 'thank you' and walked away. At home, I smoked during the prep hols when Ammi was at work. Soon, she knew I had, from the smell in the corridor that I could not banish despite the deodorant. She was furious and I quietly reconciled, inwardly pledging to hold back till I joined university.

She also disapproved of my playing the stereo music loudly. 'Who can listen to the *Top Gun* anthem tune without turning up the volume?' I shouted, saying that I needed this to de-stress after the study sessions.

'De-stress? Distress, more like,' she determinedly argued back. 'How would it seem to the neighbours? What if a man came to argue with me at this hour? What would our reputation be? We need to be mindful of our reality!'

I lost my temper even more at this.

'How ridiculous is that!' I remember exclaiming. 'Your son can answer any guy who turns up at the door. You don't need to worry. Why do you want to spend all your time living in the shadow of other people's fear and censure? Are we criminals? Why should I live like the fearful condemned? Because I am fatherless and Muslim? Every other guy in the colony plays his music loud and you know that.'

She silently walked away after this outburst of mine. I realized my mistake. Next morning, I went out and bought headphones from Connaught Place, even though it was not the same thing at all. I hate listening to music over the headphones; it makes the process artificial and I can't immerse myself in the music in that mode. I need to hear it loud and clear, thumping through everything around me, so that I can really feel it. But it didn't matter; I couldn't upset Ammi. I was all she had. I said 'Sorry Ammi' thrice before she acknowledged it and spoke to me again.

Career guidance was quite an alien concept in those days. Had someone said, 'See a counsellor about your future life choices,' I would have laughed in their face. I was not going to graduate from Delhi University to get a job or make money, though I knew dozens who had precisely that aim. Of course, I would get a job and make money, eventually and somehow, 'but why think of that now?' The boring adult stuff could wait. My youth, the only one I would ever have, would be a period of exploration, self-discovery, experimentation. In my imagination, I would go to university, make stunning friends for life, discover new freedoms, set performance records effortlessly, and find the women of my dreams.

I'd gone enthusiastically with friends from school and filled the admission forms for the select North Campus colleges, feeling ready for the big world outside my school, outside my neighbourhood 'colony', outside my city haunts. The North Campus crowd was further split by the Stephanians' elite disdain for the Hindu, Kirori Mal College and Ramjas types, and the latter's caricature of the Stephanian 'pseudos'. I had wanted to be at the hallowed and elite St. Stephen's College. Hindu, Hansraj, KMC might do if the entrance mark for admission was unimaginably high, but I knew that I would get into English Honours at Stephen's with my results. This was the first time I had been so excited in my life. It came from a feeling that I could be a success at anything.

'Leon, is this the right decision? Are you sure you want to study Literature?'

'Ammi, English will never go out of fashion in India, I assure you. Even if it does, I could always run away to England. They'll love that I'm stamped from Stephen's!' I joked.

Surprisingly, Ammi humoured me, 'Yes, England is your birthplace after all.'

'Trust your son.'

'How can I not? I trust you and pray every day for your success in life.'

I had vague ideas about becoming a travelling man of words, maybe a journo. I had done well in the Board exams, getting above 85 per cent in the 'Best of Four' subjects. My worst score was in Geography, but even that had been decent. I was delighted to see Ammi's eyes when I came home and told her my result. She had tiny tears in them as she looked over my shoulders into the far unknown distance and smiled contentedly, but also sadly. We both knew what the moment was missing.

Since that time, and especially until I got busy with college, I often surprised her out of a trance. 'Ammi? Ammi?' the sound of my voice would startle her from pensive isolation and leave her slightly confused at her surroundings. We never spoke about it but I tried to imagine what she was pondering over. Did she think of how life might have unfolded had my father been around? Had she secretly hoped for his return all these years? No, I told myself immediately, that is simply beyond belief, yet could she really have? Perhaps she was thinking of my upbringing and how I had made her proud by my results. After all, so many unheard-of relatives had called when the news spread that 'Leon did well, he topped in school'; it must have meant, in however small a way, a societal approbation of her parenting, even as a lone working woman. I foolishly assumed that the exciting transition in my life from school to college was affecting Ammi the way it was affecting me.

With hindsight, I see how mistaken I was.

During those years, we, my mother and I, drifted apart. While we had never been very communicative, during my childhood we had shared a deeply felt sense of togetherness in our identity against the world. Her interest in the minutiae of my school life—home assignments, exams, uniform, mealtimes, habits—was central to her and to me. This was redundant now; I could come and go when I wanted, I preferred to choose my own clothes, my studies were beyond her, I mostly liked to eat outside. I didn't really need her. It sounds callous, but she seemed boring and backward. She needed me, of course. But when did I have the time to realize that? I had plenty of distractions. There was the heady freedom of a fast-changing age, my posh friends at college, the old cricket pals, a part-time job on weekends at a specialist video shop in Khan Market where I developed a passion for out-of-the-way movies, added to which there was the time spent on the phone. Most importantly, there were girls. Girls! There was so much to learn in life!

I should have wondered why Ammi got cable TV installed when she had been against it for years. In front of the *Tara* and *Shanti* tele-serials, she sat knitting and stitching. I would see her taking more time than before in praying and cooking. I was not keen on elaborate home food—a sacrilege for her that I chose burgers over rogan josh—so she would send covered dishes of delicacies to the neighbours, those among them who would eat from a Muslim household, that is. In return, they would send those bowls back with Punjabi chole, dal makhani and chutneys.

Getting back home unexpectedly early one afternoon, I was greeted by a tutee of Ammi's—two beribboned oily plaits, downy upper lip, thick glasses—a dork who lived next door.

She answered my 'What are *you* doing here?' by swiftly disappearing behind her bulky textbook. A shy lass.

'I teach her and help with her schoolwork,' Ammi broke in.

'Really! Since when?' I could not help exclaiming.

'Six months.'

Had we been living in the same household? I came to know

then that my mother had been offering English language tuition to the neighbourhood kids.

'I could do a few extra hours at my weekend job if we are short of money,' I idiotically persisted.

'It's not about money, Leon.'

'Would you rather I spent more time at home? I am sorry, I know I'm never around, but you know I can't bring my friends here, and also these days, computers are very important, and I...well, I will—' I genuinely felt like a rubbish son.

'And what would you do sitting here? Help me explain the present continuous tense or the figures of speech to sixth graders, or mark bundles of exam papers with me? You have a life ahead of you.'

'So do you, Ammi.'

'Have you eaten?'

'Ammi, don't change the topic.'

'Have I ever said anything to you? You are a good son. You pay the bills, do well at college. I am proud of you.'

'I take *your* money to the utility office, Ammi! You know what, this year on Mother's Day, I'll get you a wonderful gift! How would you like one of those new gadgets...a cellphone?'

'Don't even think of it. What notions exist in your head! Mother's Day! Cellphones!!' she was earnestly worried that I might spend a load of money.

'Relax! I can't afford it anyway. I was kidding, miserly Ammi,' I teased her.

'What in the world would I need a walking phone for, anyway? To call the Prime Minister of India?!'

'Yes, call him. Say I'd like—' I stopped. The hell I knew what I'd like. To be famous? Rich? Abroad? Never to be called 'Kattu' and 'Mian'? 'Some food,' I lamely ended. 'I haven't eaten. What have you cooked?'

Often, seeing her conversing with the housewives on the staircase landing of our apartment block, I felt better, assuming this was woman-talk about ornaments, food prices, whatever. She did the groceries herself. I ran certain routine errands, paying the telephone and electricity bills in person at the crankily functioning government offices. I made myself packets of Maggi noodles or an omelette in the middle of the night when I kept odd hours. Otherwise, I had my own world of things and people. I rebuffed her attempts to get me to speak about my friends and college life, and she had stopped recounting her experiences at the school where she taught. *Our* world no longer existed. It is the way things shape up sometimes. We unintentionally let people fade. Ammi gradually came to just be there. I did not know any better. The influences of youth can be intoxicating.

My heart sank the day I saw a large crowd of people gathered around our flat. It was evening, and as soon I turned the corner to our block, I felt a massive premonition accompanied by a heavy thud in my chest. What had happened? Why was everyone conspiratorially looking at me as I walked towards them? Had there been a robbery? No, no, shove the bloody thought out of my head! No murder. Nothing bad. Nothing. Nothing. Nothing.

A policeman materialized out of the crowd and asked me menacingly, 'Are you the male member of the family?'

I stammered. Authority could terrify me.

'No, I m-mean yes. Ammi, m-my mother, is the head of the household. Where is she?'

'We have been waiting for you. You must come to the police station with us. We need to do some paperwork.'

'Why? What is this? What have we done? Where is my mother?' Recovering myself, I was getting enraged at the crowd and reddening in the face.

'I'm going to the van. Your mother is inside. Speak to her and then come with us.'

I ran up the stairs and dashed into the room where Ammi sat on the worn-out sofa. Her head, covered as always, was bent low, tears streaked her face. Two women consoled her.

Seeing me, she broke into sobs, 'Leon, son. How, in the name of Allah, can man do this to fellow humans?! Look how they have disgraced us! What can they get out of such malice?'

'Ammi, who hurt you? I will kill the bastards. Tell me, honestly.'

'In mercy, peace be upon Him, I am not hurt. But we will move away from here. We will go somewhere else.'

'Your mother will be fine, son. Some people made malicious complaints against you at the police station,' one of the other women spoke.

'What have we done?' I almost screamed.

'Leon, they said we steal electricity from the meter. They cut off the wires downstairs. They say we are thieves. We are illegal because we are subletting.'

'Who? Who the devil is behind this? I paid every single bill. And we are not the only ones subletting government accommodation!' I was frantic.

'Someone with a grudge, the police aren't saying who.'

'What right do they have to humiliate us like this without proof? We have legal rights. Human rights. There are laws and courts. I will—'

'Leon. Just plead with them. Don't take a stand. I called Siraj the moment they came. He says there is no point trying to assert our rights. We will be persecuted even more.'

'Damn Uncle Siraj! What does he know? We are educated citizens, not illiterate pushovers. We can—'

'Leon, in the name of Allah, swear by me that you will not be arrogant with the police. You are young and hot-blooded. You don't understand. They can do anything. We must remember who we are. I already showed the police copies of the electricity bills. They need you to write an application and we must vacate the flat this month. Siraj has also spoken to them about the subletting.' She wiped her tears. 'Leon, are you listening?'

'I will not disobey you, Ammi,' I stomped out to where the van stood.

By the time I got back from the police station, it was nearly midnight. They made me wait for hours. Our landlord, a Malayali gazetted officer of the postal department in whose name the flat was allotted, was summoned from the other end of Delhi. Uncle Siraj called from Chandigarh and spoke to the Inspector at length. An acquaintance of his came to the station and held a private talk with the Station Head Officer—to pay a bribe. I sat like a moron. Fuming. Cursing. I rang a college course mate with political connexions, asking for help. He made vague promises and pretended to be in a rush for a birthday party. I wrote a long letter full of cruel satire at the way Ammi had been treated, hoping to irk the unjust establishment with my prickly remarks. The Inspector filed it, without even a glance, in the middle of dealing with a petty lout being brought in by a constable, only asking me, 'Leon Ali. Is that your full and real name? On your mark sheets and other documents?' 'It is,' my voice rose. I could kill him. With brutal force, I shut myself up to refrain from saying anything else.

Those were black days.

After years of living in the same locality, we were rendered homeless due to a vicious and purposeless complaint. For three weeks, I did not attend classes as I went from area to area of the blasted city trying to find us a flat to rent. The replies I got ranged the entire spectrum of prejudice and bigotry:

'Mohammedan, I see.'

'No father also.'

'She is a teacher but you are still a student, you have no real job. Oh.'

'Kashmiri? But why did you need to come to Delhi? Didn't your folks drive out Hindus from the Valley?'

'I am sorry, we only rent to professional couples or families.'

'Your mother living here is fine but we can't have you. We have unmarried young girls on the upper floor.'

'We would like three years' rent in advance.'

'Someone just let the place today morning, or I would have said yes to you.'

'Do you need police verification? How do we know that you are not Pakistani or a Kashmiri terrorist?'

'Why did you leave the last address you lived at?'

'Sure, what age is your mother?'

'Why don't you try looking in Old Delhi? It would be easy for you there with your own Muslim people.'

Every response made my blood boil. I considered trying with a false name and identity, but that might lead to complications in the future.

Ultimately, Ammi got a letter of recommendation from the Principal at her school—a respectably surnamed Mr Joshi—'Mrs Albeena Ali is a widow in dire circumstances. She has been a loyal and faithful government servant for many years. She bears a good moral character. She is solvent and has a service pension. We cannot allocate her accommodation because of our waiting list. We would request you to do the needful in helping her.'

My college Administrative Head had the steno type on letterhead paper, 'Leon Ali, who is enrolled in English Honours, has an excellent academic and attendance record. He is a personable young man and a credit to our institution. We recommend him to you without any reservations whatsoever.'

A Sikh family agreed to rent us a flat in a private media employees' housing society complex in Mayur Vihar. It was a long commute from Ammi's school but there was a direct chartered bus from there to central Delhi, which made it quite convenient. The Sardar and his wife were nice friendly people relocating to Malaysia. They wanted us to move in quick and it suited us. The rent was not exorbitant and they held a mere six months' deposit.

'Why can't we buy a place of our own?' I asked Ammi, as the Bihari workers lifted our scant belongings onto the truck hired for the moving day. When some sympathizing neighbours had conveyed their farewells and left, I repeated, 'Multinational banks offer home loans these days.'

'Siraj also said the same thing. The problem is not arranging a loan. I have saved enough money over the years; it is all yours. I want you to be comfortable. I am not going to be here forever—' The strange faraway look was on her face again.

'What comes over you, Ammi? Why can't you understand? I don't want anything. I was thinking of you.'

'Are you going to marry soon and have kids if I say so? Settle down and give me grandchildren to raise?'

'No way! I don't know what I want. I definitely don't want to marry!' I protested.

'See. This is what I mean. After your graduation, you may get a job anywhere. I may retire into an ashram. I have done my duty as best I could. I need to devote myself to the Maker's orders at some point in the future.'

'*Arrey*! Careful! That is very precious,' I cautioned a man carrying Ammi's antique Qur'an stand.

'Ammi, I am not going to get a job *anywhere*. I will work where you want me to work. And you can't go away to any ashram. Don't worry me with that talk.'

'Leon,' she directly responded, 'Everyone has their life. And I don't mean to worry you. Nevertheless, you know I am not given to impulsive statements. I have been thinking on it for over a year now.'

I was flabbergasted.

She quickly said, 'Anyway, this is not the time and place for such a conversation. We can speak of it another day.'

The topic didn't come up in the succeeding months.

It was, soon, my final year at college. Most people were deep into their preparations for the IIM-MBA entrance exams, others crammed for GRE and GMAT, some for the IAS, and some just got ready to travel abroad. Corporate firms commenced their campus recruitment exercises. I wasn't into any of this.

College for me had begun on a terrifically pretentious note. During freshers' ragging, a minister's niece informed me with a supreme air, 'Do you know what Kashmir is, Leon? Kashmir is a Led Zeppelin song. Now, sing it for us. And be sure to mime the guitar plucking, okay?'

It was rousing to be surrounded by the rich smart set. The endearing mannerisms and cool lingo was catchy; I enjoyed the 'hot sams' and the 'g-jams' with friends from the 'Rez'. Idly, I watched the 'ShakeSoc' fellas do their rehearsals out in the open. There were people who went to 'Cal' for holidays. Word games in the corridors were fun.

It was as if I'd always said hot sams, g-jams, Rez, ShakeSoc, Cal for samosas, gulab-jamuns, Residence, Shakespeare Society, California.

A new girls' hostel had opened in Allnutt South Block of the Rez. I had no trouble getting casual girlfriends. I was quite a prize, apparently. Special because bright, I thought at first, but realized that it was mixed with special because Kashmiri Muslim and exotic.

I understood the different categories of girlfriends. The Miranda girls scoffed at the wannabe-ness of behenji-turned-mods, or BTMs, from Daulat Ram and Indraprastha colleges. The 'cool lingo' and the fundamentals or 'fundas' changed every year and every season, along with the fashionable clothes and accessories. My confidence levels soared. I regularly featured in the gossipy tattletale *Spice*, got involved in the music scene of 'Krosswindz' celebrations. I smooched a girl, partly on the strength of my brother—imaginary, of course, but hush!—being a fighter pilot. A gay teacher even hit on me. I dressed casual and crazy, smoked to show off, carried must-read novels, learnt avant-garde movie titles from my Khan Market job.

It was quite a charade; good while it lasted.

I tried my level best to maintain the fantasy. I socialized with the prominent names. I ignored their vacuous and petty talk, consoling myself that once I was admitted into their select soirées, I would be privy to the forces that mark the chosen on their ways in the world. I faked an interest in their drink parties and their lifestyle, which wasn't such a blast given that I was perpetually short of money.

But status is like pee. It can be detected by smell.

In time, people put two and two together. I never gave lavish treats. I never arrived by car. I didn't live in GK, GP, Def-Col, NF-Col (that is, Greater Kailash, Green Park, Defence Colony, New Friends Colony), nor in Hauz Khas, Vasant Vihar, Mehrauli, Jorbagh, Chanakyapuri. *Sorry, where do you live again?* My dad wasn't a senior bureaucrat, a politician, a diplomat, a businessman, or a Brigadier. I definitely wasn't Old Money or Family Friend. Come to think of it, no one in my family had been to Stephen's before. *Oh Wow! Really?!* As for being a Muslim, the Kargil war with Pakistan happened, and I had better stress my patriotism, above all.

With predictable comeuppance, I rejoined the common crowd. I was essentially uninteresting to those whose company I longed for. I did not have a desirable address, contacts or family. I was no great risk-taker, mostly sidestepping alcohol, drugs and random sex.

By the end of college, the bubble had burst. I came to see the futility of my endeavours at fashioning myself to the caprices of others. Growing up, I had successfully created for myself an illusion that I was one of the entitled, that luck was going to be mine as soon as I could break free of the bondage of school and childhood. Why did I believe I would have a future devoid of the commonplace worries? I don't know.

My life in Delhi was an exercise in trying to successfully live with the stark reality that stared me in the face, no matter where I went. Me, of uncertain provenance in the eyes of the world. Me, the child who grew up without a proper family. Me, whose father had abandoned him even as an unborn. Me, the son of a man who had bailed out on his wife in an alien land. Me, the stranger in every neighbourhood in Delhi that I lived in. Me, the one people spoke about and then hushed up as I entered the room. Me.

Only during the time I spent with Maya, my love, things were different for a while. I no longer felt aberrant. Yet, I fucked it all up in a big way. She was the centre of my waking thoughts and my fantasies. This was after I'd started mingling with cricketers from her college across the road. With her, I could be secure in the knowledge that life had other plans for me; not just an absconding father. I suppose I could have gone on and married her, made her happy, and repeated none of the mistakes of the other adults in my life. I could have gotten a job at some corporate firm after my graduation.

The turn of the millennium wasn't such a bad time for educated young professionals in India, and I could easily have passed myself off as a normal wholesome young man from a good family. I had the stereotypical Kashmiri features: brownish hair and the famous sharp nose. I was reasonably well-built and healthy. I smoked in moderation and played decent cricket. Okay, granted, I did have a degree in English Literature, which was not seen as having much 'scope' in India, but even that was no insurmountable handicap to getting a middle-level management job in a private firm or bank, to begin with. In the couple of campus interviews I'd cursorily given, people had seemed pretty impressed with me. They had been taken in by the accidental facts of my life, such as my being born in 'Oh England!' or that I had a 'name like Leon'.

I was in no position to take credit for achievements like these, but I could, with effort, substitute my life with that of someone else: the suave upper middle class educated son of a government official or senior executive, complete with a doting mother who painted glass with acrylic and bought crafts at 'Expo' events and state emporia. I could even invent for myself a sister that I always wanted but never had. Someone beautiful, with a hint of fragility, like one of those Pre-Raphaelite heroines I adored. Preferably an elder sister; I hated being the firstborn. Then, I could periodically tell my colleagues at the bank or firm about this highly capable elder sister of mine, who, no doubt, worked for a publishing firm or media outlet. And she would have a completely normal name, unlike mine. Something that would fit right into the Delhi middle classes, like Ritika or Reena, and I, too, would change my name by deed poll to something more normal and Hindu, like Rahul or Rohit. I would be part of an imagined normal family and enjoy its happinesses. I would not be marked out as different.

Maya wasn't the sole person I'd hurt, either. Life is lived in gradations. Nothing is perfect. And shunned as I often was, I was equally capable of honouring the pecking order when it suited me.

I am thinking of that time I had been rotten with a guy who probably considered himself my friend. I'd met him in a cricket coaching club during my secondary school years. It is perhaps a bit grand to call it a 'cricket coaching club'. Most guys from our locality played either cricket or football, inexpensive games we could play anywhere. A few of us occasionally used to go to a nearby stadium after school where a retired sports teacher, whose son played with us, would teach us some moves. There was minimal payment involved as between the thirty or so of us, the stadium fee was a small amount. It was good practice, at any rate. I befriended a guy there. His name was Dharmendra, after the handsome Hindi movie star whom he resembled not the slightest. He was way poorer than the rest of us, his father being a dhobi who made his living cleaning and ironing soiled clothes; his mother washed dirty dishes and mopped floors in other people's flats for a monthly wage. He could not speak any English and had studied under the National Literacy Mission scheme till fifth standard in a Hindi medium school.

For all that, he was a genius on the pitch! He bowled better than the best. Facing the batsman, he would come into his own. I particularly remember some of his deliveries. He would squint with concentration, perspiration on forehead, fingers gripping the seam with an assurance to match any. Taking his moment, a micro-moment really, he would look straight at the batsman and inwardly *do* something with his mind. From then on, it was a scene to watch in slow motion. It was as if he was propelled by invisible strings that guided every inch of his body into the exact right point in space, and his fingers deftly twisted this way and that as he released the ball and spun his skill. It was sheer joy to see him concentrate and then deliver like that. I absolutely envied him. Once or twice, I wanted to walk up to him, there and then, right in the middle of the game, and pat his shoulders. Attaboy! The batsman's successful deflection here and there meant nothing; all of us, even the coach, knew that this guy could bowl. Oh sure, I might love the game, but our pal Dharmendra had it in his bones.

However, the fact that he did not look like a cricketer's pin-up poster or the namesake actor did matter. He was short, stocky, dark, and with a stubby broken nose. Not the type to hang out with in public. For one thing, apart from cricket, we shared zilch. Outsider as I was, this guy was very low on the societal scale. Dharmendra's world and mine were poles apart.

Years later, I ran into him again. He was working as a caterer at my college festival. That evening, I was with a group of elite types.

Dharmendra, uncomprehending of the social distance between us, came up to me with a plate of nibbles, blabbering enthusiastically, 'Hello! I am so happy to meet you again! You, my cricket pal!' His countenance was lit up with joy.

Immediately, I remembered who he was, but kept a poker face.

'You don't recognize me? The stadium...,' he trailed—perhaps something in my icy stare had intimated to him the fact of my pretence—turning to offer the mini kebabs on the tray to those standing with me, and then left our sight with the slow tread of a shackled prisoner.

'You know him?' the glitter-mascaraed girl leaning on my arm softly whispered.

'Me or my twin!' I retorted, biting into the meat with a smile.

It was my mean streak, a capacity for wanton cruelty.

I graduated, and for want of a better option, decided to continue with postgraduate studies.

That autumn, shortly before my twenty-first birthday, Ammi announced to me her decision to withdraw from the world-as-we-knew-it.

She asked me to pull up a chair, and while I sat, she remained standing.

'Leon, the time has come for me to devote myself to a larger Cause. I'm going away for the greater good.'

'What, Ammi! Why? Why all of a sudden?'

'Don't you remember what I said when we were preparing to move here? I have thought on it for a long time. I wanted your degree to finish first.'

'I might as well have flunked the year!' I was nervous. 'Don't go, Ammi,' I pled.

'Listen, son. My prayers will always be for you. I am always here for you. You are my darling. Think of it as me going to live in another city.'

'This is why I hate religion! It leads people to—'

'Enough! May Allah forgive you,' she flared for a moment, 'I am going to enrol in a Gandhi ashram in Maharashtra. It is a rural social service organization. My induction training will be at the central office in Delhi, and after six months, I will move permanently to the ashram near Pune.'

'What will you do there?'

'They run village-level projects on education, sanitation, women's health, and disease prevention. If someone had done this in my village in Kashmir when I was a child, my parents might not have died in that blight.'

What could I say?

'You are young, there is still time for such work,' I tried to reason.

A bitter look briefly passed over her face, and she turned to me with brimming eyes, 'When age did not matter all those years ago, why should it now? I have fulfilled my duties. I feel that the time has come for me to live for myself, and age has nothing to do with it.'

'It is because of me, isn't it? You feel distant. I see my mistakes.

I hate the college and those people now. I can spend time with you now.' I felt burdened by a guilt.

I had no idea what it must have been to live a life like hers.

'Leon, banish such thoughts. I have always said you are a good son and I am proud of you. Don't you want to see me happy?'

I reached for her hand. 'I am sorry, Ammi. I am being selfish as usual. I hope they will let me visit you there.'

'That's like my son! Of course, you will visit me. How else will you show me your girlfriend's face?' She ruffled my hair lovingly as she said those words.

This gesture was a throwback in time.

As a child, I dodged situations where my parents might need to be called to the school. For this reason, I avoided extra-curricular events and did not interact with more than a couple of people. I was boisterous at home but reserved in school. I would rather not be in charge of anything. I wanted to put my head down and play by the rules. Basically, I detested attention. I tried my best not to get into fights or scrapes.

Still, I got bullied a lot in junior school. I would take it silently, shedding tears behind walls and in corners. The worst period was when I was harassed and abused repeatedly in the bus on the way back from school.

Miss Rawat, a new class teacher in charge of my section, had forcibly entrusted me with disciplinary responsibilities. She praised my handwriting and my obedience in the class on several occasions. That was 'it' for the bullies. I was taunted, called names, spit at, shoved about, and once, my shorts were pulled down. This one guy called Narayan was especially nasty.

'Go back to Pakistan!' he would jeer.

Following it up with, 'Kashmir belongs to us!'

'Loser boy! Loser boy! Has no-o-oh fa-a-ther,' they would heckle and pinch me.

I tried desperately to resist those jerks, but in the spring of 1990, I was a total ten years of age. They were much bigger than I was, and more united in their intentions. My friends chickened out, leaving me in Narayan's hands. That sadist monster!

One such time, I got off at the bus stop in the afternoon with my shirt torn and hanging over my belt, hair tousled, hot tears flowing freely on my burning red cheeks, biting my lips.

It was nearly the start of the summer holidays. As the school bus snorted and sped away, I was blinded by the exhaust smoke, the physical pain from the blows, the excruciating humiliation. Everything on the road was lined by a shining dust in the blistering heat. I sweated profusely and was disoriented, ready to faint. Suddenly, Ammi stood in front of my eyes! She had meant to surprise by being there to receive me. A buzzing dark anger coursed through my body for being the person who could not be stronger. I hated to be the cause of the anguished look on her face when she saw me.

With shock and consternation, she asked, 'What happened?'

I was tight-lipped and refused to say anything or even move my eyes from the ground.

My shoulders were hurting from the straps of my bag bursting with textbooks.

Sensing it, she unloaded it off my back and held it in front of her.

Then she guided me to the shade of a tree, and for several minutes, gently ran her fingers through my hair, smoothing and ruffling it in turns. I felt like a bovine animal. Slowly being placated. Calmed. Treated.

At length, she took a few steps to where the water-seller's trolley stood. I remained fixed to the spot and watched. The battered aluminium trolley on wheels had a waterspout at the top, which sat atop a cuboidal base structure that was painted with the red and yellow picture of a figure resembling the Air India Maharajah, complete with turban, long achkan jacket and a twirled-up moustache. He was bending with a smile in anticipation of being delightfully hospitable. Next to the painted Maharajah was inked in large letters, '25 paise Glass', in English and Hindi. Seeing a potential customer, the seller, lounging on a bench nearby, trotted up to where Ammi was, and grabbed one of the smudged common drinking glasses. Ammi motioned him to stop, unscrewed the cup cap of my empty water bottle, and held it out to be filled. She was particular about hygiene.

I drained two large cupfuls of refreshing cold water. She waited for me. I was numb to sounds around. Dazed and stunned, I stared at things around me as if I was seeing everything for the first time: the bowing Maharajah painted on metal, his shoes like his moustache curving upwards, the trolley shining in the fierce sun, the thin cotton red and white check-print gamchha around the neck of the water-seller, and across the road, the pedestal in the park where a stone warrior on a horse brandished a sword.

As we walked home, I slowly began telling her of what had been happening and how I was being bullied. She wore a salwar kameez and a long mauve dupatta, with one end of which she periodically fanned me. She sheltered my head with her palm.

'Never be afraid of those who are cruel to others.'

'I have faith in you. You can be a brave and strong person, able to pity those who need to make others suffer for their enjoyment.'

I am not sure I understood, and I am sure I did not internalize, all her lessons. But I believed her promise that it would get better. I trusted her. As long as she was there to see after me, I would be fine.

Less than a year after she decided to leave for the Gandhi ashram, I gave up my postgraduate studies in Delhi. I was only nominally enrolled in my degree anyway, spending my time being depressed and loitering about trying to figure out what the hell I was to do with my life.

The millennium bug had come and gone; no apocalypse would deliver.

I'd bought a New Year diary. In the 'Personal Memoranda' page at the start, I noted my name and my blood group; in the blank space next to 'Home' I wrote 'Never Had Any'.

I could not be bothered with anything anymore.

In 2001, I moved to England, the accidental country of my birth.

2

Flâneur Abroad

*S*oon after I came to England, the world started to fall apart. Landing at Heathrow Airport, I was impressed by the clean floors, absence of unruly crowds, large halls and walkways. I was glad that the queue for UK passports was moving much quicker than that of foreigners. It felt strange to be in a different queue than the many Indians on the other side. When my turn came to pass through the checkpoint, I also held my new red British passport open for display, the way everyone else around me did.

I was about to walk past, having flashed my passport, when I saw an outstretched hand.

Instinctively, I reached out my hand for a handshake.

The officer's hand registered a slight movement in response, then he immediately withdrew his arm and said, 'Can I examine your passport please?'

I felt like an utter idiot. Of course, he hadn't wanted to shake hands with me! What had I done to deserve a welcome greeting? He was asking to see my passport. Embarrassed, I gave him the document. He directed me to another desk and continued to wave other people on across the post.

'Leon Ali, is this the first use of your UK passport, which was issued overseas?'

'Yes Sir, it is.'

'According to your passport, you were born in Britain. Have you come here to settle permanently?' a white immigration officer queried. Another bespectacled older officer stood looking over his shoulder.

'I don't think so, Sir. I am here to satisfy my curiosity about my place of origin,' I gave the rehearsed reply, accompanied by the most charming smile I could muster. I wore trendy gaberdine trousers and a sweatshirt that had a Union Jack embroidered on the front. It wasn't the most comfortable outfit to spend eleven hours in—the indirect Air India flight was via Rome—but I didn't want to take any chance of being refused entry.

'Young man, your place of origin is India. England is your birthplace,' he held the details page of my passport against some light on his desk.

'Are any of your parents British?'

'No Sir.'

With his gimlet eyes fixed on me, he complained, 'I wonder how they thought of issuing you a passport. You haven't lived here in your childhood and neither of your parents are British.'

'The British High Commission in India have all the documents.' What else could I say? Because I was born in England, the issue of the passport was a discretionary matter, according to law.

'What made you think of coming to Britain?'

'Well, Sir, my father is no more, and my mother has joined an ashram, something like a nunnery. I have no siblings. I am educated in English Literature. It seemed—'

'So you intend to work in the UK? I see that your English is very good.'

'Not sure, Sir. I have financial guarantees and savings.'

The elder officer behind him intervened, 'You Asians are very good with money, aren't you? Soon, you'll be running a corner shop,' he appeared cheered up at his own words.

'I am not keen on money or a shop,' I meekly protested, not wanting to contradict him outright.

'I have money in the bank, Sir. Here are the statements. I also have a letter of financial guarantee from my mother's bank, and a letter of recommendation from my college, and there is a letter confirming my accommodation agreement in London, and a copy

of my insurance policy.' I even had my toddler photos with a row
of Victorian semi-detached houses in the background.

'Hmm,' the desk officer entered some data into a computer,
then said, 'Tell you what, you are a very organized fellow. Let me
have that file. I shall be back with it soon. You wait over there.'
He indicated me to a bench against a wall, and walked towards an
elevated glass cabin behind the immigration counters. Nothing inside
this hi-fi cabin was visible.

The man standing behind him replaced him on his seat. I sat
on the bench next to some black women.

I had been planning for this crucial ordeal for months. I had
made Ammi dig up every paper from her London days: my birth
certificate, the 'Missing Person' UK newspaper cuttings for my father
Mir, the letter from a London MP supporting Ammi's appeal to stay
in England for a while after my birth on compassionate grounds, her
old passport with British visa stamps. The British High Commission
in Delhi had interviewed me several times and sent the papers to
England for approval. Ultimately, I was issued the passport. Now, it
was the moment of truth.

After a long wait, during which I agonized over whether I had
given the best answers possible, a woman officer approached me.

'Waiting for an interpreter?' she asked.

'No, I am waiting for the officer. He has my papers.'

'Oh, you are being processed. All right.' She turned away, then
having second thoughts, swivelled on her heel, 'Why don't you go
through the health check while you are waiting?'

'Okay, Ma'am,' I stood up. 'Why is it taking so long for my
passport verification?'

'I don't know, dear. The systems may be down today. Like I
said, you could go to that room and have the X-ray screening for
TB done while you wait. It's up to you.'

'Thank you.'

She punched in a code on a wall and went away.

I joined the queue for tuberculosis screening. Many women

were being asked to confirm that they were not pregnant. My X-ray technician wore lots of gold jewellery. I noticed, because she asked me to take off any chains that I might be wearing around my neck.

'If you was British, I don't think they want you to be screened?' She was not sure if I was required to undergo the procedure.

I didn't know either. I said, 'If they need it for newcomers, they might. It is my first time ever here.'

'Jus' now, you said you was born here,' she reminded me.

'Sorry, I meant first time as an adult. I was being particular.'

'To be fair, I can't see why they would. Never mind,' she emphasized, 'you've got nuthin' to hide. Take off your shirt then.' The machine came on.

I was healthy.

I was also quite bored by the time another official brought me my passport, 'Mr Ali, here you are. We were wondering where you went. We've checked your details. You are fine. Please proceed to the baggage area.'

I heaved a sigh of relief. I was 'in'. I could begin another life now. Start anew in London.

Like me, London had a funny name. It was 'phallic' in Hindi. The moment I stepped out of the underground tube station at King's Cross and set my eyes on the city, I realized this is where I was destined to be. I had the freedom to become anyone here. No one cared who I was. It was brilliant. Masses of people were going about with a purpose, 24/7; I might find one at an intersection!

There was a blue summer sky above. Bloody blue. Not yellow and scorching like Delhi where there would be dust storms at this time. Just a bluer than blue dome above the leafy trees and the solid stone buildings that proceeded on a geometric grid. People—so many people—walked about, chattering in different languages, or with headphones donned, doing their own thing. Gorgeous women wore halter tops and short shorts; still no wolf whistles or stares! It felt like being in the cyberworld, or the movies, or the future. Wow, it was quite something. Traffic stopped for pedestrians at the zebra crossings, there were lanes marked for cycles—for cycles!—the cabs were big and black, I saw pink limos! The pavements were broad; a pram for twin babies moved comfortably along one. The red double-decker buses and the red telephone booths gave you the feeling of being in a toy town. People were not crammed and hanging from bus doors like the Blueline buses in Delhi. The bus doors even opened automatically. I felt excited and adventurous. I had a map with me and I spent entire days walking, painstakingly charting a different route every day. Places flew past as if in a dream, there was so much to see: names I'd heard of—the Big Ben and Houses of Parliament, Westminster Abbey, Trafalgar Square, Leicester Square, Buckingham Palace, St. Paul's Cathedral, London Bridge (initially I thought the blue-gold Tower Bridge was London Bridge); and names I hadn't thought of—Covent Garden, Soho, Greenwich, the newly constructed tall giant wheel which was called 'London Eye', the Millennium Dome which looked like a big tent with pins sticking out of it, and to get to which I took the overground Docklands Light Rail, which was fun, the snaking riverside paths by the Thames river where Shakespeare's Globe theatre still stands (if only I could send a postcard to my college ShakeSoc!), barges and squares, steel, chrome and glass city towers.

When tired, I'd relax with a sandwich or a McD burger on benches in the many parks all over the city. Strange people speak to you in parks sometimes; I had old men ramble on at me, once a drug-addled fellow asked me why my shirt was so white!

I took photos like a tourist on a three-day visit.

London was great. The world came here to do things.

I visited MCC where I splurged on a Lord's cricket keyring, a little patch of the pitch embedded in a glass paperweight and a real leather ball. It was awesome, really. I wished I was gifted enough to be a famous cricketer!

After some weeks, when I had walked the marked routes and visited the major places, I went exploring the city randomly. I'd get into a bus without a specific destination, decide to get off at the fourth stop, then walk three intersections, cross a road, find the next tube station, and head in a transversal direction from there, reaching wherever that led me. It was a construction site on some occasions; a public toilet, an utterly ordinary residential street, and a shopping arcade on others. I threaded my way through Whitechapel and Camden, Notting Hill and China Town.

When I wandered about at night, I noticed how neon-lit the whole city was. Every pavement was ghosted by murrey shadows that slid across the fancy black grills often marking the Georgian façades of houses. Unlike in Delhi, there were parking enforcement officers constantly on the prowl, examining every car and white van.

Once, I stood peering at a tiny image on a sticker in the rear window of a parked car on a road near Hyde Park. It was a map of India, but it looked odd. Kashmir had both its ears lopped off.

'May I help you?' a uniformed security guard appeared behind me.

'No,' I said, and continued squinting at the boundary markings.

'You can't loiter about here,' he said forcefully.

'I'm not loitering,' I countered curtly.

'You've been on this street since 11.10 p.m., and in the vicinity of this building since 11.30.'

It was true. I had lingered watching the operation of a rubbish collection van. I turned around, shocked. 'How do you know? Are you following me?'

'We follow everyone. Look, there is our camera,' he pointed right behind me, 'and there and there.' I was at that moment in the frame of three cameras!

'Amazing! Is this street special? Why are there so many cameras here?' I was puzzled.

'Don't you know?' he laughed, 'every bit of London is on camera.'

'I didn't know that!'

'Look, those round, black, berry-like things, and these tubular ones, and other kinds also. We always know what people do. Got to keep the city safe!'

'I'm leaving now, didn't mean to loiter,' I said, walking away. I felt very conscious all at once. On my walk back that night, I could not help surreptitiously glancing up at these weird devices all around me. Wow, this really was bizarre, and different from Delhi, for sure.

So many cameras. But they didn't stop people from behaving like lunatics! In Soho, I saw a dwarf one Saturday night. He walked proudly amid the gay crowds, barefoot and with his head held high. Clothed in threadbare dungarees, he had the two edges of a bedsheet tied in a knot at his neck. The entire length of the dirty long cotton fabric trailed behind him like a King's coronation cloak. I couldn't take my eyes off him, though I'm not sure anyone else paid any attention.

After a month and a half, I decided to move lodgings. I had paid for my bedsit in advance, before my arrival in England, and the landlord had faxed me the confirmation agreement. The building was advertised and recommended on the Internet, in a good location, and called by a quaint name, 'Good Inn'. It was also cheap, and unfortunately, too good to be true. It turned out to be a run-down hole: the roof leaked, the heating pipes sang all night, there were no windows, the telly was broken. The neighbours were up to nasty stuff that I didn't want to know about. And every day, every single damn day, I knew that the cleaner rummaged in my belongings. Once, I'd even come in unannounced and found him rifling through a drawer. There was no point complaining to the owner. He had refused to let me leave before the agreed six weeks. I had reconciled that I'd been cheated by a fraudster, and so, I spent most of my waking hours wandering about town.

As soon as I could, I cut my losses and found accommodation in a flatshare with a Turkish student called Turan and a plumber from New Zealand called Ron.

This was a much better place. To pay the bills, I found work in an art and photo studio-cum-café in Mayfair. It had a very chilled-out clientèle and we were supposed to multitask. A Scottish man was my senior there; he was quite capable and made life easy at work. The day I got my first salary, I bought an Accurist wristwatch for Ammi and posted it in a carefully bubble-wrapped package, along with a photo of Gandhi's statue in Tavistock Park that I'd taken with my own camera. Coming out of the Post Office, I did an unusual thing—I walked into a Starbucks café. I'd seen the green logo at every street corner for months, but never been in one. I spent quite a bit of money, making nothing of a Tuna Melt Panini, a Rocky Road, a bag of crisps and a very large Mocha Frappuchino. I shook the crumbs off my shirt and wiped my lips on the paper napkin as I left.

The air was nippy that night. I felt light-headed and happy. The July evening was glowing in the skies and digital colours flickered past each other on the panoramic rim of the BT tower that watched over the city.

On an impulse, I called Ammi from a red phone booth using pound coins, instead of buying a phone card as I normally did. We ended up having the same conversation every time: she was well and so was I; she had sent a letter and I promised to reply; my concern over her health and her worries about what I was eating. Calling from the phone booth was not such a good idea, after all.

I stood there for a few minutes after hanging up, my eyes latched on the surrounding sexually explicit images that acted as barbed reminders of my virginity. The women in the photos wore corsets that were untied at their breasts, or else, stood bending with their legs open wide and feet in stilettos. The words 'Hot Blonde', 'Kinky African Mama', 'Submissive English Lady', 'New Japanese Doll', 'Asian Chic' assaulted me. What a democracy of desire in this red London cage! Kicking aside the crushed green plastic Sprite bottle and a banana peel that lay on the messy floor, I pushed the phone booth door open and went into a newsagent's. I bought a chilled can of beer and a lads mag. Back in my room that night, I had my first taste of Heineken and wanked to glory in the company of the pornographic images. It was heaven.

My flatmates were no trouble. Ron, the plumber, was a dull ex-seaman, generally never home. Turan was always with his German girlfriend. I watched cricket on Sports TV, emailed and web-surfed, ate beans on toast, listened to music. On my day off from work at the studio, I woke up late and lazed around.

One night, I was jolted out of my sleep.

'You fucker!!! You son of a bitch! You bastard! Why did you call them?'

'Whatsthat, you slut? I hate you. Serves you right.'

'Shut up! Call them back and say you were lying.'

'Make me. You can explain it yourself.' A *loud* thud—something shattering against a wall.

'You can have your precious things and get lost.'

'I never want to see you again. You can go to hell. Your Tubbish Hell.'

'Whatsthat, thick woman? Can't even speak properly. Vat iz ze matter? Had enough kebab?'

'Rotten kebab. I can't imagine why—' a crying sound, a loud blowing of the nose at intervals.

The shouting match went on. Poor them. I am glad to have escaped women. I would never get into a relationship, I affirmed to myself. They're a nuisance.

The morning after he split up with his German girlfriend, Turan came to my room to apologize for his behaviour. He had bloodshot eyes. We went out to a pub together that weekend. We became sort of friends. He was a research assistant on a five-year project study of European Integration. I didn't really want to talk that boring stuff with him, so we kept work aside. His love of beer from growing up in Germany was infectious, unlike his habit of regularly asking 'whatsthat?' I'd tease him for the way his speech was unnecessarily peppered with whatsthats. But we broadly kept our distance, never talked personal. It was better that way.

I was getting familiar with everyday life in my new country. The tube was a pain, and the weather was miserable, and it was expensive, but it was still London.

With effort, I was trying to dim my memories of Delhi. When I'd told people I was going to leave for the UK, people in India said, 'What? This is the best time to be in India. It is booming. On the way up.' Maybe. I saw a dug up city littered with construction projects and a people that hated Muslims. I was the worst kind: a Kashmiri Muslim. Because of my looks and the 'Ali' in my name, I had been asked nasty questions. I could not read the newspapers or watch the news on TV without hearing a tirade against Kashmiri Muslims, or coming across reports of people being killed there. The country was breaking apart. There had been a big earthquake on Republic Day, killing tens of thousands of people. It was depressing. England was mild. The British general elections the summer I arrived happened without violence, vote fraud or vigilantism. I was glad to have escaped to this blessed place where a novelist politician being corrupt was the biggest news on some days.

Turan was also an unorthodox Muslim like me. When he found that I was Kashmiri, he didn't ask awkward questions. One day we were at the café in his campus and a group of people sitting at the next table said hello to him.

'They are Kashmiri like you,' he commented.

'Really?' I don't know what came over me; I went to their table and addressed them in Kashmiri. They could not understand a word of the language!

Nonetheless, they were excited to meet me. They expanded on the plight of Kashmiris. After spending some time chatting over coffee, I realized that they were Mirpuris from Azad Kashmir. Their food and their language was different, but I didn't want to say that aloud. They asserted repeatedly that they were Kashmiris who had set up a Society with the explicit aim of propagating the cause of Kashmir. Would I, as a Kashmiri Muslim, come to their meetings?

I wanted to say, 'Honestly, you are not Kashmiri.' I bit my lip.

'I'm sorry I'm not into politics. Anyway, it's rather late and I should be going now,' I was abrupt.

'You Indian Kashmiris are like that, sellouts and spies,' a woman said as I got up.

She was most vocal in insisting that I admit—I didn't know what she wanted me to own up to—something. I lost my temper, 'Well, you are not Kashmiri. You are Punjabi. Or Pakistani. Or whatever. I am not an innocent Briton. My parents grew up in Srinagar. So I can tell the difference.'

'Have your relatives grown up in Azad Kashmir? Been displaced elsewhere?' she spat.

'No, I have not been to Azad Kashmir. I have not even been to Kashmir since my childhood,' my voice rose.

'Okay, enough. That's fine. Let us not frustrate each other,' a man intervened. Turan, who had been typing on his laptop, immediately came over and pulled me aside.

'C'mon man! Relax. Let us go. Take care, guys. Khuda Hafiz.'

I felt an idiot for having been so worked up over the whole thing. Ammi was right, politics was crap. That night, I spent hours on the web chat forums posting random rants.

One feebly sunny Tuesday afternoon, I had a half day off work and decided to buy myself a new mobile phone. I flipped through a handful of the free advert magazines, and went to a Phone Warehouse near Tottenham Court Road. I was toying with the idea of going for a movie later at the Prince Charles cinema, the cheapest in the West End. That was all the entertainment I could afford, having recently bought a new futon, duvet and a Nintendo. I whistled at a billboard advert for a book charity and walked into the shop. I hadn't read a novel since my English degree, preferring to watch *The Simpsons* instead. How England was changing me!

The buxom redhead at the counter was diligent, and I listened carefully to her advice on which phone package would suit me best. I was almost ready to make the purchase when her manager came up and took her aside to say something; he was looking deadly serious.

For a moment, I wondered if the deal I had been offered was too good. Was the poor babe going to be ticked off for her generosity? Her face had blanched. She came up to me, offering to complete the transaction if I could decide instantly. Slightly annoyed, I chose a phone. She apologized in a faltering voice, saying that they were very sorry but they wanted to close shop early, probably for the day.

'Why?' I asked, perplexed. 'Is something the matter?'

At the same time, a man brought a crackling radio from the 'Staff Only' door behind her. They did not have a TV in the shop. Everyone's attention was distracted.

The antenna pointed to the customers like a long silver finger of accusation.

The redhead whispered, '50,000 people are rumoured to be dead. Something has happened in New York and other places.'

Attacks. Fear. Shock. Was it the start of World War the Third? I felt tossed up, unable to grasp the news, distanced from everyone around me. Better get home, people seemed to be saying and sensing, en masse. I left the shop and ran headlong into a homeless man who wagged his finger and cursed at me.

Invisible needles of panic pierced the air. People were rushing about, and those who did not yet know were continually finding out. I went straight to my room and bolted the door. I switched the TV on and flipped from one news channel to the next, addicted. The angry face of the homeless man had stuck in my head, and around his curses swam the images of the towers being hit. Once. Again. And again. The planes ram into the twin towers. Everything felt unreal. I had no friends in America. I also had no enemies in America. I was scared witless.

I called Ammi and placated her fears. I assured her I was all right, and gave her my new direct phone number which would become functional soon. That night, the Scot colleague from the studio called. There was no need to come into work the next day. They would remain closed for a couple of days. I stayed awake much of the night. At 3.00 a.m., I had a panic attack. I was hyperventilating.

What if we all die? What if everything just dissolves? What have I done with my life? The TV was still flashing scenes; words like 'Al-Qaeda', 'Afghanistan', 'Muslims', 'Islam', 'Bomb', 'Revenge' were piling up like explosive debris ready to be ignited. I drank glasses of cold water, breathed deep, and knocked on Turan's door. He was not in. I was alone in the flat. I had no medicines, not even a headache pill. I covered the duvet up to my nose and tried to banish the day from sight. I shivered with an indefinable anger. An impotent anger. Struggling, I didn't realize when I fell asleep.

That Tuesday onwards, things went downhill for me. I did not regain a sense of happiness or sanity for a time to come. I felt confused by what I saw and heard and felt. What the hell was happening? What exactly was being engineered? Swiftly, Islam became the focus of every news broadcast. I was a Muslim, wasn't I? People I worked with and met, constantly asked me: What did I think of the happenings? I was furious beyond words. I had come to England to escape the marking that had followed me all my miserable neighbourhood existence in Delhi. Fatherless son of a woman, a Muslim. Circumcised, Pork-avoider and Teetotaller, and they added up: Jihadi and Traitor to boot.

And now, when I had opted to lose myself in the crowds where no one knew me; now, when I had developed a taste for beer, wine and whisky; now, when I ate any meat without a question—Now, suddenly, I was Muslim again. Fuck it, I was a latent fundamentalist! I felt angry at the collapsing bloody world. I had never bothered with politics or religion, never voted, never had an opinion on these monumental topics. I just wanted to be left alone. Why did I have to be so singularly marked now? Why did the loony madmen who ruled and resisted the system have to choose the cusp of my adulthood to do this? Could they not have done this another decade, another century? People always kill each other. The harrowing. The heroic. Go gorge on your slice of history. Choke on it. I blamed the whole lot of them. I almost felt forced in conversations to take up a point of view—either I was a fallen infidel Kashmiri who did not care for his Muslim brothers and sisters, as a preachy religious old goat admonished me in Trafalgar Square one afternoon, or I was a filthy Paki scapegoat, or I was a token needing rescuing.

I am a Nobody, I wanted to scream out in their faces. I don't know any of you. Left or Right or the sinking stinking Middle. Just let me be invisible! I don't want to be marked. To conduct myself under scrutiny. I want to be free. I have no illusions about the world, its politics, do-gooders, resisters and maniacs. I am just a young man of twenty-two with a name I did not choose: Leon Ali is of no religion, race, ethnicity or belief. I am male. I am alive. I like sports, movies, games and TV. I am unfortunate, but no more hysterical than the times I inhabit. I wanted to do what I had done before. Escape. But this time, there was no faraway birthplace called England to escape to.

In the following months, I kept my head down at work. I stopped going out late after 'Arab Pig' and 'Paki Terrorist' were hurled at me in a night bus. I avoided certain areas and roads. I cut down on the web after stumbling across blogs and chat rooms that glowed with hatred of Muslims and Islam and the infidels. Who were these people? How could they be so vituperative? At intervals, I went out with Turan, but it wasn't like before. Neither he nor I really wanted to say anything about the unfolding events, and that silent elephant in the room ate up all the joy.

I thought of visiting Ammi, but the idea of air travel spooked me.

I tried understanding the politics bulletins on TV, but realized I didn't want to. I tried playing ridiculously juvenile games on the console, and watched so much of *The Simpsons* that at nights I would be slumped on my bed in the dark playing the electronic tunes and title song in my head, over and over again, trying to get every nuance right. It still was a rubbish substitute for facing up to things.

I stopped taking photos in the city after being questioned more than once. I used to take random arty pictures anyway, the sort that when taken by famous people, hung on display in studios like the one I worked at; manhole cover patterns, and pipe networks along a wall.

I experimented with going to the big Borders bookstore every evening and reading books till closing time. I found myself immediately averting my gaze when I came across the mushrooming books on Muslims: my life under the regime here or there, my time in the West, my experience of being a fundamentalist; what Allah wants, how Muslims think, why Islam is violent, is the clash of civilizations imminent?

'Ammi, Ammi, can you hear me? Are you all right? Are you safe?' In the summer of 2002, Gujarat was Riot and Rape Central. India was torched with communal hatred.

'I am praying. We are praying here at the ashram. Allah will save us all,' Ammi wept, and I listened.

The whole world was on fire. And Iraq hadn't even been officially invaded yet.

Somewhere, in all of this, I stopped watching TV and books re-entered my life. This time I didn't need them to name-drop impressively in an exam or to win the approval of my elite college peers. I registered as a member at a local council library and began borrowing literature that had to satisfy one important criteria: it must not be directly relevant to, nor must it remind me of, the world around.

With the sounds of Aphex Twin on a CD player and the gritty glowing teeth of the convector spewing hot air at me, I read Dostoyevsky and Dante, Kafka and Kerouac, Huysmans and Hamsun, Aretino and Apuleius, Flaubert, Baudelaire, Goethe, Mishima, Nabokov, Proust, Prevost and Petronius. They filled up my mind. I began to model myself on a dissatisfied ideal stitched together from centuries of words.

I would read books by as obscure authors as I could find, hoping every time that the Council librarian would finally be lured into looking up from her thick impermeable glasses lodged halfway up her swollen nose, and say something to me about the outlandish authors I was reading. 'What kind of a man are you? What do you find interesting about stuff that no one reads? Oh, I see, you are a

Mr Ali. That is Muslim, is it not? Are all Muslims weird that way? Why can you not be normal?'

I waited for her to defy me like this every time she selected the dates on her rubber stamp carefully and stamped the inside flap of the books. Then, when she would be baited thus, I would deliver loudly and clearly my unrehearsed but superbly coherent speech—detailing the larger dissatisfactions of the foul times and my own screwed-up expectations of myself. Serve it like a stew, the poison brew. She would be bewildered, and everyone else would turn around to listen. After concluding, I would not hang around for their response, but coolly fling the book on the counter and walk away, without the slightest betraying change of gait or timorousness.

Breathlessly, just like that!

Then, outside, I would exhale a serene and noble sigh. I had answered back perfectly to the world and established for myself, once and for all, all my freedoms as an intelligent adult man and my inalienable right to live as an unmarked and unidentifiable individual.

The librarian never bothered with me in the slightest. I doubt that she ever read the titles of the books that she was issuing. I never had any chance to make my grand speech about identity.

I realized that my identity was a terror. If mute, I could have tried passing myself off as European, integrating into the unquestioned crowd, but my accent was certainly Indian. I couldn't safely be Crown Brown British.

The circus went on around me, a photo of Blix sweating, Karzai in a magician's cloak, a photo of Sir Galahad the gallant bastard, Tony blaring Bush, Osama tapes, crooks with hooks bent on incitement, milling protests; it was like reading a cartoon strip. I stood for nothing, denounced nothing.

I lived in the mad times—by refusing to live in them—in my own way. This was one answer. It deserved to be recognized. I spent the next three years like this. Pigeons ate time off my window ledge, clocks sprang forward and fell back with changing daylight hours; I was in a carapace, working and saving.

Sometimes, I reminisced about my Delhi life, usually after speaking to Ammi. One time I rung her and she was unwell. I became worried although she insisted it was a routine viral that several people were suffering from, 'Leon, I am not incapable. It is a change-of-season illness. I will be fine.'

Despite the bravado, her voice had been weak and defenceless. My lovable obstinate Ammi. So far away. And impermeable. Why? What had made her fear vulnerability so much? Even in front of me, her son, she never let down her guard.

That night, I could not concentrate on the book that I was reading. I couldn't stop thinking about Ammi. About this woman Albeena. Why the hell did she refuse to talk about my father, Mir? Why did I not know anything except the little old chestnut of his mysterious disappearance in Berlin? Why had he bailed out on her, married and heavily pregnant? Who exactly did I carry in my blood? Who was this father of mine?

I went to sleep speculating. And no matter how much I tried to banish this thought, it doggedly followed me around the next few weeks, during which I lost my virginity with a Slovenian girl I met at the library and never saw again. Sex had been absolutely uneventful, but it had unlocked a trigger.

I stopped going to the library or borrowing books. Mir was the name of my misery. I thought of him non-stop. He even popped up in the middle of masturbatory images once—my father, an indistinct face, appeared astride a pair of heaving breasts. Insane! I lost my erection and sat naked on the broken chair, pushing aside the tattered magazines. I crumpled balls of paper that crackled in my fist like dry autumn leaves, aimed them at the bin, unsuccessfully. I could not understand myself. I had not felt like this in ages.

I must know who he was. It felt foolish to be thinking of this now. I was no kid at school with everyone asking me who my father was. Who the hell cared who fathered me? I was far and free. To a large extent. But this obsession to seek him gripped me as a developing fever. I started to see a project and purpose in it. It was a new escape. I noted that I was an average creature of genealogical curiosity, with a temperament for obsession.

The monomania held me and I could not rest till I had made up my mind to go to Berlin and try to trace him. When he faces me, what would I ask? But no, I would not find him after all these years, so there was no real worry about how I would confront him. If I did not succeed, at least I would have worked through this manic urge. Shortly after I resolved upon going to Berlin, I saw other changes in me. I was filled with hatred. With hope. With hatred of hope. I was recalling the past far too much, becoming sentimental and lachrymose. This was terrible. I settled upon giving myself a month of industrious seeking in Berlin to cheat this obsession of its denial.

It was a shameful regression. I was neither too young nor too old, and thus, not ripe for memory. I consoled myself that, if nothing, I could take pictures in Berlin, walking about the streets and alleys. Turan would be useful to get an idea of where to stay. I would not tell Ammi any of this. She was bound to have her ways of dissuading me, even if I could never do the same with her. I would call her as usual from Berlin.

Behind my clever word barriers of a casual indulgence, sincerity was coalescing into my thoughts and desires. I did not really wish to find him. But. But, what if I did? What if I found something that I was better off not knowing? No, that was impossible. I should not allow myself to dwell on that. I was doing the bidding of a curiosity that would not let me be in peace.

I arrive in Berlin.

'Lay-on Allee, Are you British?'

'Yes Sir.'

'You have a return ticket for London?'

'Yes Sir.'

'Good.'

He swipes my passport through a machine and hands me back

the red document that secures a part of my freedoms for me.

I wait an extra moment. He waves impatiently at the person behind me in the queue.

That was it?! I expected a grilling, so I am naturally surprised as I leave the counter. I suppose a shaven face and a fixed address do come in handy once in a while.

I take out my wikipedia city info print-outs and check the underground routes. I have travelled abroad after years. Flughafen Schöenefeld, the airport I am at, sounds exotic. The German signs and sounds around me feel beautiful because I can't understand them. I, too, want to say something guttural and baring. Play the guitar like that Goth at the S-bahn station, have a girl like his girlfriend listen to it. Then I remind myself that I am here for a mission; I must focus and be serious. I get into the train. I don't know. I look out of the train window and murmur, Bayleen, Bayleen, Bayleen, trying to copy the voice on the announcement system. Bayleen, I say aloud. No one hears or looks at me.

Turan had given me the contact details of a Dr Jutta Schlaf, saying she might be willing to rent me a room for my stay in Berlin.

'I hope she's okay with me being a man and a foreigner?'

'Whatsthat mate? Don't you think of stuff like that. She's very nice.'

'Just being particular.'

Jutta is helpful. She agreed the rent and dates over the phone, apologizing that she could not receive me at the airport when I reach, as she has to be at her medical practice.

'Take the S9, change at Alex, then take the U2 to Senefelder Platz. It's a short walk from there to Kastanienallee and the house is just off it,' I was told.

Alex is a confusingly big terminal going by the name of Alexander Platz. I see that Berlin is a young and edgy city. Many youngsters on the U2 line to Pankow have keffiyehs around their neck.

I discover that Jutta is middle-aged and speaks passably good English. She spent her formative years in England, she tells me, as she shows me my room.

'I won't trouble you. You can come and go as you wish. You can use the kitchen. The number of my Handy is on a paper at the table. There are also maps and brochures.'

It is a three-bedroom flat on a side street in Prenzlauer Berg, not far from the hub of Kastanienallee. Two rooms overlook the inner courtyard of the building; one is her bedroom, the other a store, where her cat, a ginger tabby called Klip, dozes in the corners. I have the room with the big window facing the street, a view from the fourth floor. The wood furniture is large, and on the walls of my room hang several posters, none of which I recognize or am drawn to. They are by Klimt. I am told they were left behind by the American woman who had the room before me.

I am in Berlin on a Mission, I tell myself.

I get busy from the first day. I imagine that I have to write an exam on a subject called 'Missing Mir'. My search takes me to libraries, archives, newspaper offices.

I take a blank notebook and divide it into three sections:

Things I know about Mir

Things I've thought about Mir

Things I'm discovering about Mir

Under 'Things I know about Mir', I write 'FACTS' and underline the word, adding in brackets '(from Ammi, Uncle Siraj and other relatives).'

Mir, my father, was a communist. He wrote poetry. He trained as an engineer. He grew up in Srinagar and gave fiery speeches at the university there, which denounced both India and Pakistan and called for an independent peaceful Kashmir. It was thought he would eventually become a full-time politician. He was employed by an Anglo-German collaboration that was a major partner in large-scale technological projects in India. He married Ammi of his own will. After his marriage, he was posted to England for two years. When this contract was extended beyond the initial period, Ammi joined him. It was there that she became pregnant. A month before she gave birth to me in a hospital on the outer edges of London, Mir was called to Berlin on official business. He had decided my name: Leon, after Trotsky. If it was a girl, she would be called Rosa. A committed communist, he continued to have links with the Left. He had once been on the verge of being sacked for his radical politics. But, as he was exceptionally bright, they retained him. He went to Berlin as normal, did not say anything out of the ordinary to Ammi before departing, but never returned. Ammi and the relatives had frantically searched for him, placing ads in newspapers of the time and writing letters to all and sundry, but he had vanished! Neither German nor the British or Indian authorities could trace where he went. After the requisite seven years, he was declared legally dead. The company he worked for became bankrupt and stopped existing years ago.

There are a few theories: (a) a neutral conclusion was that he had met with an accident, possibly without any identity papers on his person at the time, and hence, was untraceable; (b) something more involved was at work. He might have become part of the political underground in pre-1989 Germany. His official trips were to West Berlin, but he had definite connexions in the East. When I pressed for more details on (b), the relatives got taciturn and said they did not know. It was all in the realm of speculation; maybe he was kidnapped. 'In any case, what is the point of asking that now? What can we do about the past? What is done is done. It was Allah's wish that it should be so.' At this point, the particularly Kashmiri tone of resignation, an emphatic sighing and whispered grace, ended the conversation.

Under 'Things I've thought about Mir', I write 'IMPRESSIONS'. In my childhood fantasies, he was a Hero. He was a secret superman. He had invented a magic formula that evil empires wanted, and when he refused them, they kidnapped him. He was still in a prison somewhere. When I grew up, I would find him and rescue him.

In my adolescent years, he was a Revolutionary. When I read

about the fall of the Berlin Wall at school, I imagined him being involved in the heroic effort against the Wall in East Berlin, fighting for freedom, but then realized I had my politics wrong, mixed up the Left and Right.

He had grown up in the Kashmir Valley between two hostile powers and disappeared in a European city divided by two ideologies. As an adult, I don't know what to think of him. I am curious.

I have never seen a picture of him. No, that's not correct. When I was very young and Ammi and I told everyone the Imaginary Father in Dubai story, we did have pictures of him on the walls of our flat. They were black and white. One had him speaking on a stage in front of a crowd, another showed him reading a book with his head resting on his arm and a shaft of sunlight behind him. The final one had him and Ammi standing together. I was tremendously attached to these pictures and asked Ammi questions about him all the time. When I was a bit older and didn't stop asking, Ammi destroyed them. I had shouted myself hoarse and cried for hours upon getting to know that she had burnt them on a kerosene stove in the kitchen. 'You have no father. We won't ever speak of him.' It was awful of her. So I have vague memories of what he looked like, but no actual photograph.

I was enraged with Ammi. I saw her dump the ash from the burnt pictures into the plastic bin. I could not speak about Mir to anyone. So I took revenge upon both of them in my own way. I used to maintain a secret notebook for a while in which I drew portraits of Ammi and Mir. On purpose, I sketched them differently on each page. On some pages, she was a coiled snake with fangs and he was shaped as a lamp. On others, he was a huge gorilla and she was a mountain. They were both clowns on some pages, and in one sketch, they both had perforated bodies from which blood spurted in a fountain-like fashion. I did not do it to hurt them; I never let Ammi know about this copybook. I just wanted to draw them grotesquely and terribly.

Under 'Things I'm discovering about Mir', I write 'BERLIN'.

It is true, I am becoming an expert on the dark chapters of this city: Nazism, Holocaust, Liberation, Division into four sectors, Early fencing, Wall construction, Checkpoint Charlie, Intrigues, Unification. Like a piece of gneiss rock, layer upon metamorphic layer of solid history have accumulated here. When not at the Landesarchiv or the Neue Bibliothek, I squander days in the Zentrum für Berlin-Studien on Breite Straße. People occasionally give me inquisitive glances. Studying some records at a documentation centre in Bernauer Straße, I read about the radicals, including an Indian student who was involved in making tunnels under the Berlin Wall. There was another Indian fellow who declared a satyagraha, spearheaded marches, and vociferously argued for freedom in early 1960s Berlin. Wasn't this the time of the Indo-China war? How could he be so bothered about alien issues? Heroes and Revolutionaries. I am reminded of my adolescent fantasies.

I try to get appointments with officials. It isn't easy. I have few proper facts and no official background. I am not a professional researcher. I am knocking at the doors of institutions asking about a missing non-German father; I have a story in a city where everyone has one. Not many want to speak about the past anyway. I come across amiable people in the most unexpected places, in the offices of the former Stasi, they help me however they can. My heartbeat quickens when I find a small pamphlet by an author called 'M'; it is titled 'Lebenslüge', the life-lie. The librarian provides a translated copy. A brief three pages long, it is a political manifesto listing the injustices around the world and making brave statements about the importance of resistance. It was published from an office in Fasanenstraße in West Berlin in 1980, an address that does not exist anymore. It could be any 'M'. Is it Mir? There is no suggestion about the nationality of the author in the grand words of a cosmopolitan world citizen.

I am clutching at straws. I read voraciously about the city, locked in a struggle to devour its past as it has done mine. I have a thick new register full of handmade notes on the subjugation, liberation, partition, division and reunification of Berlin, the plans and agreements, the political parties, the length and height of the Wall, the crossings, the chastening of the dissidents, the surveillance society. I spread the photocopied pages on the table, go over my notes. No picture emerges from any of it.

After three weeks of giving it everything I've got, I have conclusively failed. I am dispirited and spend a couple of days indoors. Until now, I was eating my meals in cheap cafés, abundant in Berlin, or picking up snacks from Imbiss stalls. For the last two days, I have eaten microwaveable ready meals. As I go to the kitchen to get a glass of water, I see Jutta making tea. She invites me to have a cup with her. I am not sure how to refuse, so I join her at the table. She pours me a watery liquid with rice floating in it.

'It is Japanese,' she says.

I sip it. Klip jumps on my lap.

'How have you been? I noticed you are at home yesterday. Is your projekt finished?'

I dither. I do not know what to say. 'Jutta, I am not here to do research on any project,' without a conscious decision, I bring up the truth. 'My father disappeared in Berlin before the Wall came down. I have never met him and came here to try and see what I could find.'

'Oh,' she utters. Is it that matter-of-fact for people to vanish here?! I don't know what reaction I expected; I give Klip a nudge.

'Was he German?'

'No, from Kashmir.'

'My parents went there once.'

'I hope you don't mind, but Germans are not polite like English. Can I ask you, is it possible to find someone after that long?'

'Not him. But at least what happened to him,' I say, sounding unconvinced. She is right. What was I thinking in coming here?

Klip meows and leaves the room.

'I am sorry that it is difficult for you.'

I remain quiet. How could she understand?

'Can you see the people in that photo, there, above the rack?' she points to an image of a couple—dressed in old-fashioned formals, smiling—framed in gilt. I go up to have a closer look. He seems equable and she skittish.

'Are they your parents?' Jutta resembled them.

'Yes. I tell you something. When I was six and my brother Julian two, my mother was playing tennis one day and had a stroke. A stroke which affects the brain. She never recognized us after that day. Not even her husband.'

'It could not be treated?' In the Hindi movies, good people always regain memory or sight after accidents.

'Not in her case. You can show pictures and souvenirs, talk for hours. We did that. She will remember for some time, but if we went out to get water or use the toilet, she would forget everything again.'

I feel distrait. 'I didn't know. I am sorry.'

She does not hear me. Her fingers turn the silver cross on the chain around her neck.

'We lived with it.' She slips into German for a sentence, and then gaining her composure, wryly adds, 'Everything has an end, hmm?'

'Is this the flat your family lived in?' I ask.

'No, no. We always lived in a nice flat in Charlottenburg. Then we sell it three years before when my parents move to Hamburg. Even after the Wall came down, I never came here to the East. Today, this is my home,' she says calmly, contemplating her surroundings.

Back in my room, I return to the stories we exchanged. Berlin has so many pasts that mine pales in comparison. It feels commonplace enough to not have seen a father, and wretched to not let go of the fact.

I switch on the TV but can't find anything absorbing to watch in English. I splash my face with water, look at it in the mirror. My departure is in two days. 'You are going back to London,' I tell myself. I pack my belongings, stuffing the notes and papers from Berlin underneath the clothes.

I cannot sleep well that night. Is my search meretriciously cast? No, I do want a clearer past. My mind is seized with images: Mir my father as deadwood, having lost his memory, his speech, and what else? Jutta's mother as Miss Havisham in her dim room, the veil, the wedding cake endlessly rotting, and spiders spinning hope from bitter threads. A child's memory, but with Pip I tremble at the horror and agony of witnessing a past that is neither dead nor alive. To bear with things, like Sisyphus, the spectacle of his toil. When the boulder rolls down the hill, he claps to cheer his failed effort. His fate is not a punishment; it frees him from having to think up treacherous schemes, there is happiness in repeating the same task to the same results. Sisyphus would be worth knowing the day his boulder wears down, eroding his fate and his purpose.

The next day, I go out briefly to buy a calling card and call Ammi from Jutta's phone. I tell her I am in London and everything is fine. Now I have about twenty-four more hours to kill in Berlin. I don't want to sightsee. Jutta has already bid me goodbye. She is going to Hamburg for the weekend and I am to leave the spare key under the doormat. A bohemian-looking neighbour in his fifties, dressed in overalls and purple-rimmed glasses, who lives in the flat below and paints cityscapes, has come and taken Klip away.

An afternoon silence hangs about the flat. I wander about the living room and look at the picture of her parents again. Then, scan the bookrack which has a lot of medicine books. The fiction is in German. I am about to give up when I spot a translated *Elective Affinities* by Goethe. I had always thought of this as a strange title for a novel. It sounded like a chemistry book! I take it out, dust it, and settle on my bed. I am transported back in time. It is fascinating and much better than Goethe's account of Werther's sufferings which I read in London. When hungry, I pour some boiling water into a cup of noodles and slurp it standing at the window, from where I can see the loud Saturday night revellers pass below. When I finish the book, I notice that the cover has a painting of an egg in a cage. The back flap says it is 'Les Affinités Eléctives' by René Magritte.

I slake my thirst and slump into a deep slumber.

I wake up late and with a start! Fuck!!! Today is Sunday, my flight!!! I'd forgotten to set an alarm on my mobile. I jump into the shower, wear whatever mismatched clothes I can grab, and rush all the way to the airport. The plane could be delayed, couldn't it. Couldn't it? I run into the terminal, panting: no use, the flight is closed. 13:52 on the blue and white screen announcing departures. I have missed a plane for the first time in my life! I queue up at the ticket desk, prepared to lose the complete fare.

I notice a group of hip backpackers, one connecting his iPod to the plug point next to a bench. When my turn comes, the woman at the counter informs me that I can change dates or destinations for a fee and fare-difference, either in person or on the web. However, there is no seat that I can afford on the flight to London for the next few days. I mull this over for a minute. I ask her what other destinations I could go to, thinking of connecting flights. She taps into her computer and recites adenoidally, 'Athens, Prague, Bristol, Barcelona,' then turns the screen towards me, saying, 'There are lots of destinations, Sir, so it's better if you book over the web, it's also cheaper.' I leave the queue and wander out, strangely relieved. My journey is not over then. I walk back to the S-bahn station, dodging the red and yellow construction tapes, my luggage trolley trailing behind me. As I descend the steps into the earth, it starts to rain.

I try hard to picture her, but I don't remember seeing anyone else at the airport. All the same, that evening I get a call on Jutta's landline from an Indian woman with a winsome voice and a compelling name: Keya. She wants to hand me my phone back. It is then that I realize losing it at the airport. I arrange to meet her in a café at 6.00 p.m. the next evening.

3

Crossing Paths: Keya & Leon

Two things happened halfway through the flight to Berlin, just as the air steward began collecting the sandwich packet leftovers: the dense clouds underneath parted, and the person a seat away addressed Keya. Both these things took place at the exact same second, as though one brought the other on. Keya had barely noted the uneven terrain below when she heard a question.

'Have you been to Zhe-mon-ay before?' she heard.

Quick and accented it was, 'French, definitely French,' she thought as she took in the details: a well-dressed man, sparse hair, compressed lips, tanned.

'Yes, I am an academic, so I travel quite a bit. I've stayed in Berlin for work before. How about you?' she said.

They were interrupted by the screams of a jumpy little boy in the front row; Vee-day-hall-lall-lahh, he trilled unstoppably.

The man responded, 'Me? I have not been there before. Strange, because I wanted to see Berlin, but it never happened. It is a very special city,' ending on that enigmatic qualifier 'special'—did he mean historical, different, interesting? Keya wondered.

He spoke haltingly, thinking in another language.

The child was now loudly declaiming that the other distant plane in the sky was small like 'me, like me. I am small, an' look Mumm-ayh, the montain is tiny too. Evythin' is tiny. Evythin' is tiny. Boom, Boom, I can catch evythin.'

'Do you like Germany, the Germans?' Hedging his question behind a smile, he was obviously keen to hear an opinion expressed.

She obliged. 'I speak German and enjoy Berlin. I also think there's an earnestness about the people. I find them sincere.'

He sized her up, diagnostically, as if to ascertain a mysterious stress in her words.

Last week in Bristol, she had gone to a supermarket to get a kettle descaler. When she asked an elderly shelf-stocker for the location, the woman returned a testing glance, nakedly assessing her ethnicity, language, authenticity. Keya had made an extra effort to smile ingratiatingly. Upon this, the shelf-stocker, whose name badge read 'Komal', gave her the directions in Hindi, 'Wahan hai.' Everyday social interaction could be a minefield for Keya who, as a specialist in culture and nationalism, could not stop thinking about these situations. If she had first addressed the supermarket employee in Hindi, would she not have been stereotyping Komal into an ethnic box? Equally, by not having done so, was she denying their commonality as Indians, maybe seeming arrogant due to her privileges?

At the university where she taught, everyone generally treated everyone else as good indistinguishable liberals. But nuances arose in classrooms, 'Are you a Brahmin?' a Home County student might ask her. Or at one of the many 'Raj' prefixed or suffixed Indian eateries that were abundant in provincial England, 'Do you have permanent settlement in the UK, Madam? I still have many years to go,' the Bangladeshi waiter might casually say. Even on the telephone, the telecom sales call centre woman from India might unaccountably veer into an exaggerated American accent upon hearing Keya's voice confirm her UK location.

Musing on the way stereotyped signals classify us, rightly or wrongly, she blinked and queried, 'Do you?'

He answered with the expected 'Ah yes, it is a straight country. Commo—' he searched for a word, 'Solid. I don't understand the mindset. But we have a long history.'

Thinking perhaps of his school texts: Alsace, Lorraine, the world wars, football, the EU, who knows what, Keya lowered the stakes by asking the innocuous; where he worked and what his name was.

Alain was from Provence and worked as a manager in a French defence company. Having recently holidayed with his wife in the Caribbean after a long assignment in England, he was going to Berlin to see some friends who had moved there last year.

'But why? Why can't I open the windouw? Where's Jermany, Mumm-ayh?'

Alain had to increase his pitch to be heard.

He usually vacationed in the south of France, in Porquerolles. 'C'est formidable! A superb island with stars, cycle routes and a clean sea for swimming. Not like the English beaches,' he laughed.

'You are Indian, no? From Bom-bye?'

'Yes, not from Mumbai but Delhi—and originally from Kashmir, though I haven't lived there,' she always felt compelled to add the qualifier. She had studied in East Anglia—'where?' followed by 'in the east of England, not far from Cambridge'—where she had completed her doctorate and was now a lecturer in Bristol; a practised self-deprecating smile at his surprise that she looked much too young to be a Professeure.

Then, when they had acquired this information about each other, abruptly, the conversation stopped.

Keya thought of mentioning to Alain her love of French philosophy, but desisted. He didn't seem intellectual and may not know. Besides, the French philosophers were no more his than hers, in terms of belonging and love. She sipped the rest of her watery tomato juice, regretting not having asked for Worcester sauce. Alain grew drowsy.

'Mumm-ayh, can I get it when we reach, when we reach Jermany?' asked the boy, quieting down.

As the plane gradually descended, clouds blanketed the wing, and deceptively close, there was land below.

'We are going to land in less than ten minutes. Please fold away your tray tables and pull your seats forward,' came the announcement from the cabin.

Travel done, here begins the journey, Keya thinks.

In spite of spring, the radiators are on in the shed-like airport; passengers chuckle derisively. The uniformed guys at immigration take their time with her Indian passport, but do not meet her eye or speak to her. She has handed the document to them opened at the page with her German Schengen visa, but it is never any use. *Every official at every port goes through every page, just-in-case.* Partially concealed behind a large glass counter, they check her face twice, then scan several pages of her passport into a machine. This scrutiny at airport crossings makes her feel counterfeit and embarrassed.

'You are not smiling,' an American Immigration officer had once pointed out in a serious tone when taking an image of her iris.

'My lips aren't in the photo,' she had said in a smart-alecky way.

'According to the invitation letter, you are going to a feminist conference, are you one of those Feminazi types?' had been the question another time.

She read in the newspapers about bio-political tattooing, DNA databases, electronic cards and codes; it is scary the way technology is numbering people and making them uniquely individual.

Finally, she is handed back her dark blue passport.

Swiftly walking towards the baggage conveyor belt, she maps out her schedule for the days ahead. Keya has a PhD degree on the subject of 'Artistic Subjectivity and the Experience of Exile'; she is now finishing a follow-on case study looking at Indian artists in Berlin before 1989. This is to be her last trip to Berlin for this work; most material gathering and interviews have been completed.

Agnes Michael is a principal subject who still needs to be interviewed. During Keya's previous trips here, Agnes was away in India, on an extended visit to her son who had relocated there as part of his global investment firm's Asia expansion. An Indian who has made Berlin her home for forty years, she calls herself 'Agni', not Agnes, in the written communication and questionnaires with Keya.

She searches for her bag. The conveyor belt is in motion and people are clustered in anticipation around the rubber flaps of the hole in the wall from where the luggage appears. Seen from behind, this is a quirky sight, it seems they are eagerly awaiting someone on stage; the cinema of travel, she reflects.

She waves to Alain as he leaves, then yawns and remembers to turn on her phone.

It beeps up instantaneously. She has received a text message some hours ago, probably after she had switched the phone off at Bristol airport. It reads, 'Hi Keya, cant meet this wk. If u r alrdy here, v. sorry. 4give me? Pls. call & I'll explain, Agni.'

A departure gate is announced; Keya regards the flurry around her and eyes the ceiling studded with metal beams and cameras. No one understands her frustration at this moment. She kicks her bag with her right foot and curses under her breath, 'Offohh! What a holy mess!' This will need to be sorted before anything else. She walks over to a snack shop in the arrivals area but there are no free seats. Before she can swear *Shiese!* a tall blonde girl leaves, pointing Keya to the chair. She says a quick thanks and after depositing her bag under the table, comes back with a double espresso safely in her palms. Touching her cheek with the warm cup, she dials Agni at her home. No answer. Then, the mobile. Someone passes the call.

'Hi Agni, it is Keya here, the researcher from—' she is interrupted.

'Of course.'

'Not at all.'

'Oh! I am sorry about that.'

'Please don't worry.'

'It is totally fine.'

'Please don't bother, Agnes, er, Agni.'

'I would, naturally, include you in the study. There is no question about that. I would love to. From what you have written in the questionnaires, I would be delighted to meet you.'

'Sure.'

'Yes, I shall probably. That's right. Re-do the trip.'

'Certainly, I will call.'

'Yes, the same number as before.'

'That's fine, and take care. Get well soon, Bye!'

The coffee is a trifle cold. Agni is in hospital. Shortly after coming back from India, she had severe chest pains and is currently under investigation. It is unlikely that she would be discharged before the next weekend. This means five days of wait, assuming Agni would be well enough by then. While sorry for Agni, Keya is sore with herself for not keeping the phone on for longer at Bristol airport. Another fifteen minutes and she would have received the text before boarding. She could easily have come to Berlin later in the week.

'Then again,' she tries to brighten up, 'what would be the point of everything going to plan. If I was in Bristol, I would have had to attend two faculty board meetings tomorrow.'

Keya often consoles herself with the 'I have no shoes, but someone has no feet' kind of thought process; there are worse alternative possibilities. One ex-boyfriend, who used to be a psychologist, had classified this habit of hers as a 'cognitive dissonance reduction mechanism'.

It does work though! Agni's interview or not, she feels a relief to have escaped the Programme Board and Module Board university meetings. These events involve endless quibbles over the same old questions, where the same old lines get drawn between the department oldies and the newbies.

'Should we award an extra mark to Matsuo so-and-so in relation to his performance on the other modules?'

'But it might mean considering Sarah so-and-so for another mark.'

'However, it must be remembered that the extra mark in each case, while being the same mark, would be the cause of change in two different degree classifications. While Matsuo will progress to a first, Sarah will achieve a 2:1.'

'Should the case for extra marks not vary according to the classification under view? If not, let's consider Martin for his 2:2 as well.'

'Also note that the modules studied by Matsuo and Sarah differ significantly. Matsuo is on a joint programme with more quantitative modules, which means there is a fair chance at getting deserved marks, while Sarah has largely descriptive modules in her degree mix, and that can produce bunched assessment.'

'Moreover, she had verified extenuating circumstances on one exam at least.'

'She has been a bright student who has pulled her weight in the staff-student committees.'

'On the other hand, these external circumstances should not count, because they depend on subjective impressions.'

'You are right, they might be biased. People tend to favour and promote those most like them.'

'Come on, this is lip service to political correctness. We need to address the question of student welfare, and in attending to their needs, some subjective impression is invariably part of the process.'

'Then why have anonymous marking of exams and assignments?'

'Well, perhaps the Faculty ought to bring in a set of guidelines where the scope of mark reconsideration is removed at the Board level.'

'Correct. This is a good idea because it reduces the say, in general, of those who have not taught the student directly, as will inevitably be the case with every student going through this process, for we cannot have individually taught everyone we consider.'

'And apart from that, it will make the job of the administration and the note-taker much easier!' chimes in the veteran secretary.

Grins all around, a guffaw.

'Okay, guys, let us draw back to the present. We must decide on this as Peter has to leave the meeting early, and we need to discuss the changes to our Master's provision, and ways of clawing back our Faculty money from the Centre as it is being used to cross-subsidize this other department.'

'I can't think what the university has in mind with this cross-subsidy; does the Chair know if the Dean has an opinion on this? We could better spend it on overseas publicity of our programmes which is crucial, since our recruitment is currently mainly home student based.'

On and on.

Having taught undergraduates since the first year of her doctoral degree, Keya has attended over five years of these gatherings, more than once a term. She does not have to try, it mechanically flows through her head: the room, the Venetian blinds, the chairs in a long rectangular formation, the doodles.

What a poker-faced send-up it often was; everyone taking themselves a little too seriously!

Being in Berlin is definitely better, she smiles.

An old man a few tables away smiles back, verging on a leer.

Without realizing it, she changes the tone of her face to the 'greet stranger, look away' mode, then rises to leave.

Outside, the sky is patchily sunny, the car park full, and construction has begun on a walkway to connect the arrival and departure terminals to the train station underground. The red and yellow plastic boundary-marking tapes appear festive when taken with the rusty orange machine at work near them. Whenever in Berlin, Keya has seen ongoing construction everywhere. It is right. Cities are akin to people, and as with people, one needs a vision for them, a project, without which they have the danger of sinking into an all-too-easy nostalgia. She admires the new and risky architecture in glass and steel, with angular shapes that slash through the skies and reflect pink clouds on warm evenings. Old solid garlanded baroque buildings decorated with passion stand side by side with hungering frames that are coldly beautiful and insanely fragile. Walking through this city a few times, she has loved it for its buildings.

'Well, I have the evening to myself here'—she can only return tomorrow, at the earliest. 'But, wait! I have not changed my ticket, and it is better to do it in person at the airline desk here; availability might be an issue later,' she thinks, and goes back into the terminal where, typically, one of the two counters is closed and five people stand in the queue ahead of her.

She does not see the other four.

He is striking. She knows him! How? She has never seen him before. Hasn't she, really? She must know him. She tries to move her eyes away from his profile, and fails. It must be that colour yellow in his clothes, she tells herself; look how effortlessly he wears it, brightly magnetic, and how his shirt collar is reversed, a sartorial flaw, adding to the intrigue; how he stands tall, even leaning with poise, his legs crossed like long bold strokes on a canvas. His face too, his face, so clearly defined, so flawlessly captivating; he is a photograph.

Yes, that is what he is! He is a beautiful photograph that has come alive. He has aroused her fancy without even looking at her. If he turns back in her direction, she might smile, her fail-safe dimples acting as the vortices of her desires. But he does not. He surveys a group of travellers charging their iPods. Then glances at his wrist where instead of a watch, he wears a stylish band. Upon realizing this, he quickly puts his left hand back into his pocket and shrugs gently, as with the other he pulls out a mobile phone. What time is it? Keya can ask him as an excuse to make contact, but it strikes her too late when his fingers return to the bag strap clung diagonally across his handsome chest. He is second in the queue and steps up as his turn comes.

She hears him speak. His English is her own, though the passport he casually holds in his palm is of a different colour. It occurs to her that languages cannot be shared in a vacuum of sentiment, where words lead, lives follow. He is from India? Could he be Kashmiri? He is young, younger than her? A student—he has missed a flight, she hears—from England? 'I am drawn to him,' she admits with a shallow breath.

A cleaner mopping the floors asks everyone to step aside, and they do. Except him at the counter. The other four people, she belatedly notices, are a couple of American girls discussing hostels, a woman texting intensely, and a middle-aged man in a suit reading a leaflet on the terms and conditions of airline carriage, which he has picked up from the counter.

Again, she regards him. He is sexy in an edgy unsettling way; a figure in a photograph that might step out of the frame and disturb your certainty. The male man-child, eternally inviolable, beguiling yet passionate, vile. The two girls leave the queue. Keya can listen better. The woman at the counter is turning the screen towards him and saying that since the airline flew to various destinations, he should change his ticket online. He has a choice of 'Athens, Prague, Bristol, Barcelona and more', names of cities scattered over the map, in the middle of a sentence, conveying to Keya the irresistible phonetic allure of a foreignness that is out of reach. Maps of the world rustle in her ears, sepia parchment and slick pixels conspiring up a cartographic—oh graphic!—geography of desire. A frisson courses through her body, and her gaze abstracts as she tries to focus on something other than fleshly images from Michelangelo.

'Him so gorgeous and his freedom so attractive! How free he must be. To be able to travel like that, without a specific destination in mind'; doing this has forever been Keya's fantasy. Being an Indian citizen, she knows her limitations. The visa requirements put iron chains on her fanciful wings. Even during the lastminute.com boom, she has never known what it is like to buy a ticket 'Last Minute', unless, of course, she was travelling to India. Because she is not from a 'white-list' country, she has to plan and book her travel months ahead, call premium rate automated lines to get appointments, travel down from Bristol before dawn to queue in person for hours outside the embassies in London, get processed by the degrading bureaucracy, checked and rechecked at every stage of travel, line up in separate queues for 'Non-EU citizens (excluding Swiss, EEA nationals, etc.)', which at some small airports are attended to only after the EU queues have ended. She endures all this not as a visitor but as someone who has made England her home for years! She has been unable to get to conferences at times. The situation is no different in the Third World, where she is never seen as a tourist even when she is one, or in India, the name of her birth-boundary, where she is again valued less than a white foreigner.

Reading the tales of Western explorers and adventurers as a

child, she had insisted on getting her first toy compass, and pinned a colour-coded political map of the world above her study table, preparing to discover continents someday, never imagining that she would fall short not on fortitude but on visas. Her travels, especially in Europe, frustrate her.

'Well, thank God I was not born in Saudi Arabia, Pakistan, North Korea, or Iran.'

He has already left when she emerges from her meditations. Treacher. Treacher.

The deceit of a fleeting dream! He has uncannily impressed upon her senses.

Keya arranges his memory in her mental 'must forget' folder, carefully labelling the unknown. The texter is quick, but the suit man takes a long time with his pecuniary enquiries, and with no one behind her, she is the queue. Her change of plan is marred when they say availability to Bristol and back in a week is impossible with her ticket type. Her already rented studio in Berlin will have to do, she figures, and decides to stay an extra few days. She will email the Department head, and with the teaching over, it should not be a problem.

As she bends down to retrieve her bag and slip her ticket into a zip pocket, she notices a mobile phone. Gleaming trendy silver, it lies on a narrow shelf underneath the front end of the ticket desk. Evidently, someone has forgotten it behind. The woman at the counter calls the security guard; he radios around, but the lost property manager is not in his office. Can they not ring the owner? The guard is called elsewhere.

'No problem,' says Rhianna at the desk, and tries to locate the address book on the tiny flip screen. She laughs nervously as she makes clumsy attempts at working 'these gadgets'.

'Should I try?' Keya offers.

There is no entry called 'Home', so she calls 'UK Me' and gets an answer phone: 'If you are trying to reach me, ring in Berlin at landline 004930255961112'.

The accent is unmistakeable; the voice is his! She represses a spontaneous joy. It is an unmixed excuse to know more about the stranger who caught her eye.

When Keya tries the Berlin number, the phone is out of credit; the first call has been international to the UK. She then uses her own phone but there is no answer to the rings. Obviously, he has not reached wherever he lives, if he left that counter less than half an hour ago.

Rhianna notes Keya's details in case someone enquires, relieved that she has taken the responsibility of returning the phone.

More people have queued by now and she thanks Keya exaggeratedly for the trouble before turning to serve them.

Keya passes herself off as the Good Samaritan.

She even tries to convince herself that she is doing it for the peculiar gratification of returning to people their lost things; she is only after a kind of validation. Some people in the world do, after all, commit random acts of kindness, don't they? They repair unknown old graves, send stray letters on their way, drop passing greetings down a deep well.

Lies! Her pursuit is none so altruistic; she wants to see him again, she is keyed up and curious. With a slight spring in her step, she walks out of the airport terminal. She lights up a roll-up and inhales. Sehr gut. Even the light rain is not going to detract from her feeling a hint of pleasure. Lifting a strand of tobacco from her tongue, she hums Ella Fitzgerald. In her ears swirl soft jazzy tunes with deep voices of women, rising and falling, falling and rising, reaching forward from an opulent past, a past of furs, jewels, smoke and sound. The rain becomes part of her soundscape, with the voices of the jazz women, the rain, too, keeps a rhythm, it doesn't just fall, it rises back up and falls down in adjacent strands, a continuous movement of water-drops up and down invisible air strings—beat, beat, beat...Night and Day...a schizophrenic rain...It Had To Be You...a percussive rain. The S-bahn into town takes an hour, its rolling wheels adding to the orchestra.

Keya stops at Kaiser's to pick up food and reaches Keithstraße. The flat she rents whenever in Berlin is located at the intersection of Tiergarten, Schoeneberg and Wilmersdorf. Minutes from the Zoologischer Garten and the Wittenbergplatz station, it is excellent for the subway connexions both to the East and the West of the city, and handy for the Indian embassy in leafy Tiergarten. The envelope with the keys is in the letterbox. This is going to be her last stay. Anticipating this, the studio radiates intimacy. The pull-down wardrobe-style bed, working table, comfy leather armchair: none are hers, yet she has spent months here in the past. Heinrich, the landlord, has replaced the TV since her previous visit. A Nokia decoder sits atop it, serving an unclear purpose, the channels are mostly scrambled anyway. On tuning, she gets about five German channels, and then BBC World after a laborious positioning of the antenna.

Grocery in fridge, slippers off, freshly showered, she tries the stranger's number. The Ponds Dreamflower talc on her neck and the green tea on her tongue spell delicious. But there is no answer. She decides to laze with the TV on.

Big mistake.

The headlines are enough to make her feel miserable about everything. The state of the world—the sheer state of it! The universe is a terrible joke; how else can you make sense of the violence? There is a darkly absurd comedy to our lives, whoever we are, sincere or not, we can be assured of appearing, in the end, ridiculous. Love of others, as of oneself, may be the big hope. A small voice in her head repeats – The Big Hope – and the words sound stretched and concave, rebounding back onto the coloured screen in front of her.

The European Union is being reported; a politician talks about Turkey like it is the oriental plague! Then, there is an item about the Americans and their PR debacles in the Arab world. The Guantanamo situation is depressing. It is easy to feel that nothing would change anyway, so why bother? People dying in Uzbekistan, people dying in Somalia, people dying in the Tsunami, people dying from the unrest in Iraq, people lying in America, people lying in offices of the government, everyone accusing everyone of being ideological, and the well-heeled suited-booted commentators giving 'expert' opinions on everything with poker faces. The seriousness of the news is interspersed with the commercial updates; fly Qatar Airways, use OCRA services to avoid paying taxes twice. 'I cannot take any more or I will dream in BBC land tonight.' She changes to comedy on a local Berlin channel. Bored, she turns it off.

To occupy herself, she cooks and innovates, making monj haak, a soupy green kohl-rabi with leaves. This vegetable is a Kashmiri delight, available in Berlin but hard to find either in Delhi or in England. After dinner, she takes a chair out to the small balcony lined with wooden planks. She is barefoot and the cool of the planks is balmy on her soles. Without thinking about it, she redials and he picks up. 'My phone?' he clearly has not missed it until then. He sounds relaxed, in no hurry to get his phone back. They arrange to meet the next evening. She suggests the Sommerfrische café and he agrees. 'At 6.00 then.' Hanging up, she feels apprehensive. Will her instincts lead her to a disappointment?

The key turns noisily in the latch on Monday afternoon. Jutta is back with Klip in her arms.

'You didn't go?'

I tell her about the missed plane. Klip circles around me, 'Meow, Mee-oww!'

'So I hope it's okay that I decided to extend my stay for a while,' I finish recounting.

'No problem. I don't have anyone coming for the room. If I'd known before, I would leave Klip here. He gets stress from moving to other people's place.'

In the evening, I walk my way to Oranienburger Straße. It is a lively place, even on a Monday. I see trendy and expensive eateries, wondering which kind Keya has chosen for us to meet.

I reach the Sommerfrische café a few minutes early and go

inside to avoid the pedestrian rush on the sidewalk. It is a basement place owned by a chatterbox, who ambles past and tells me that after celebrating his father's birthday the day before, he has drunk a lot and hardly slept. 'I am foggy,' he cheerily explains.

I order a beer. I forgot to ask this Keya what she looks like; maybe she is here. When this thought occurs to me, I survey the room. One single woman at the bar—but she is elderly and arguing in German with the bartender. No one looks remotely Indian. I wait. A few minutes later, someone comes rushing in.

She's dressed in an unbuttoned cotton coat over a camisole top, a printed scarf, curls of hair touching her temples, red in the face. She scans the room and finding me, she says with a dimpled smile, 'Hi! I'm Keya Raina. I am sorry I kept you waiting.'

I stand up and we shake hands, 'Good to meet you, Keya. I'm Leon Ali.'

'You won't believe it but I am never ever late for anything! I am chronically punctual. I've broken a rule today by making you wait.' She takes the chair opposite me.

'I arrived a second ago,' I lie barefacedly.

'Karl must have become super at serving if he got you the drink in a second,' she catches me.

'Sorry I ordered. I walked my way here and was thirsty.'

'No, please don't bother with formalities. I was just joking.'

She asks for a fresh fruit juice and busily stirs the ice in it.

'Keya,' she looks up as I speak, 'Keya, your name, does it mean anything?'

'That's a very Indian question to ask,' she remarks. 'It is a kind of flower in eastern India. In certain Native American legends, it refers to a turtle with the connotation of carrying the weight of the world on its back. My mother named me for a novelist she liked.'

'I didn't mean to be nosy. Why is it an Indian question though?'

'Because, in India, names are supposed to be a significant influence on a child's life. You know the way in which priests assign auspicious alphabets by which to name a child when they write the horoscope.

People often choose names with good meanings, and rhyming names for siblings. Also, so that the child is always called first on admission lists, names that begin with A or closest to A are especially common.'

'Are you by any chance a name specialist or something? Given you know so much about it,' I can't help but smile at her detailed reply. What does she do for a living? Talk?

Totally not getting my comment, she explains, 'I am a cultural studies specialist. Nations, nationalisms, cultures are my thing. I think about such stuff.'

Coming from most people, that would sound pretentious. She actually looks perplexed and all tied up as she says it. Bemused.

'It's a beautiful name.'

'Well, I used to be teased Kya?—What? in Hindi, at school,' she sighs, 'School with its picnics, "best-friend" arguments, slipping on polished corridors, punishments, awards. It's a pity we get to be adults.'

'I like being an adult,' I instantly say. I don't know why.

Her eyes widen. 'Really! Why? We should switch lives. I wish I could have childhood back.'

'Well, mine wasn't tremendously joyful, I guess. I got bullied and had it tough being—' I want to say a great deal, but I finish 'a shy kid.'

'I've never been shy. I wonder how that feels.'

I notice that she has kohl in her eyes.

'You grew up in India,' I say neutrally, tone between a statement and a question.

'Yes, I was born in India, though I have lived in England for many years now.'

Then she adds, 'I am actually from Kashmir, but I grew up mostly in Delhi. You?'

'I am from Kashmir too, though I was born in England. Like you, my city has been Delhi.'

We realize we are Kashmiris who grew up in Delhi and live in England.

'So we are both from the same state in India, grew up in the same city, have connexions to the same country, and now meet in Berlin. That is some coincidence!'

We laugh. Freer.

'Were it not for our different religions, we would be twins,' she jokes, then immediately gets serious, 'Sorry, I didn't mean to be presumptuous, I assume Ali is Muslim, isn't it?'

'It is.'

'I must say, I think what is happening in the Kashmir Valley is not fair. Of course, the insurgency was badly handled. Why should a community have to leave their homes and feel unsafe? But the Indian government has not helped itself by the huge presence of armed forces there. Both Muslims and Hindus have suffered. As a Kashmiri Pandit, I feel for the plight of my cousins who became refugees, but that should not make them intolerant of Muslims, which they are becoming. I can't even talk to some of them; they are blinded by hatred. Women in the Valley have it worst; they've lost husbands and sons, are raped. It's so grim.'

'You do research on Kashmir?'

'Funnily enough, I don't. I write and think on many areas, but I avoid Kashmir. It's so…so involved with sentiment. Kashmir for me is in the memories of a dead fatherland narrated by a father who is now dead. I am not sure how I could ever approach it analytically.'

'You have a way of expressing yourself. I am stilted. I avoid Kashmir too. But I do it because I hate being marked.'

'And here we are talking about it. Let us talk of something else then. Something European and *nice*.' She stresses the end of her sentence.

'Kashmir is a Led Zeppelin song,' I echo from long ago.

'It might be,' she says tersely, changing the topic nevertheless.

'I'm glad we met, what does your name Leon refer to?'

'Trotsky, the communist, he was—'

'I know. A Bolshevik Leninist. He fell foul with Stalin. How nice to be named after a revolutionary figure.'

'Why? He made many enemies and died with an axe in his skull.'

'He was a handsome man.'

'You think so?'

'Not as good-looking as you, maybe, but...' she teases me. I must confess I feel cheered up.

I ask hesitatingly, 'Keya, would you like to have dinner with me? I don't know what your plans are, or how long you'll be in Berlin, but if you are free.'

'I'd love to. I'm here for a week, at least. It would be good to meet again. Call me—oh, damn!—I forgot. I'm supposed to give you your phone back. What a dolt I can be!' She hits her forehead lightly in mock exasperation.

'We might never have met, had you remembered your phone.'

Our glasses are empty. Karl sidles up to the table. I ask for a Heineken and she gets a fresh brewed coffee.

She hands me a small paper bag; the kind they sell museum postcards in.

There is a quote from Goethe on it.

I grin, amused.

'Tell me.'

'I mustn't need the phone much if I didn't even miss it. I do need all the Goethe I can get.'

'Might be good to have both.'

'You study till there's nothing left to know/And in the end you let things go,' I read the words on the envelope.

'Do you like him very much?' she asks, after a pause.

'Who?'

'Goethe? Who else?'

'He deserves his fame. I missed my plane partly because I was up till late reading *Elective Affinities*. Have you read it?'

'No, I wish I got more time to read fiction. But between teaching, research, administration, supervision, it's a bit tough. That's not an excuse though.'

'It doesn't sound like one.'

She smiles. 'What's it about?'

'*Elective Affinities,*' I repeat, 'the title sounds scientific, like a chemistry book. It sort of questions whether we can really say that our affinities to other people are chosen.' I rub my chin.

'I think I like where this is headed. Say more.'

'The plot of the novel involves four people; basically, the idea is that passions are like chemical reactions. Once you bring together the chemicals, they have no choice but to react.'

'Hmm. I'll get a copy asap. Are you studying Literature?'

'Not studying. Studied. I did English from Stephen's. Then a year of postgrad before coming to England.'

'What do you do now, these days?'

'I wander. Wonder. Take pictures. Loaf,' I give a dishonest reply. It's more like what I *want* to do.

'Sounds fabulous. How do you pay for it?'

'Oh, that! I'm squandering my massive inheritance,' I try humour. Then, 'I saved enough over three years to do this for a few months. When the money runs out, I'll do something again. Unless I make it big as a photographer by then.'

'Do you have a website to show your work?'

She is definitely more ambitious than I'd ever be.

'No, but I mean to get one up soon. I am lazy. Or I'd be Cartier-Bresson,' I joke.

'I'm poorly read and you're lazy, that calls for a slice of cake.'

'Go right ahead. I have a sweet tooth.'

'What type of cake would you like?'

'Any.'

While Keya goes to the counter to order us a slice of cake each, I can't count my fibs. Sweet tooth?! Come on! Why did I say that? I haven't been tempted by a cake in months. And what is wrong with saying I work at the studio?

I lean back in my chair. We've been here for over an hour. The place is filling up. One waiter asks me to move my chair forward a bit, so he can go past behind me to turn the music on in the corner. The Beatles' song 'I am the Walrus' starts to play.

'Thank you for the cake and the phone and—'

'Save it, Leon. I'm enjoying myself.'

I get a chocolate cake with layers of chocolate goo; she has what looks like a flapjack.

'Are you in Berlin for work?'

'Yes. I have been interviewing Indian artists who have lived here for decades. I have to finalize some things. I did my PhD on artistic subjectivity and exile, and—'

'Wow, you have a PhD!'

'Anyway, so exile fascinates me. A lot of artistic creativity is the result of enforced exile. The pain of being away from your homeland. But even voluntary exile can be fertile. Not as going away in order to get away, but going away in order to go away. A kind of conscious derangement. It is as if there is a pain of knowing that a return is always possible, and all escapes are contingent. And what this does to a person, to the scheme of their desires, their work, their life. Do you follow?'

What can I say? I am not smart enough? She is pedantic?

'Sort of,' I muster.

'So, although there are many scholars who study the economic and political reasons for exile, I am interested in the experience, the feeling, the autobiographical narratives of exile, especially where they lead to what we call Art.'

'You find runaway arty people and interview them?'

She bursts into uncontrollable giggles. I am being serious but she is all mirth. She laughs till her eyes water. It is somewhat humiliating.

'Ha ha! Leon Ali, what a wonderful summary.'

'I wasn't being funny. I hate the Big Issues. And Big Words.'

She looks at me with incredulity, 'It's not just words. It's people's lives.'

'They speak to you about it?'

'Not always, and not instantly. But largely, yes. I am drawn to people's stories. They become a part of me. I make sense of them in the larger context. Looking at Indian artists—and I mean dancers, poets, writers, all sorts—in Berlin before 1989, also tells us about modes of resistance, their politics—'

'Did you ever hear of anyone by the name of Mir Ali here in Berlin?' I eye the cake crumbs on my plate.

'No, I don't think so. Why?'

'Nothing. Just someone I was trying to locate but I've lost his details.'

'Mir...Mir. No, I'm sure there isn't a Mir in my notes. Did you try the city council registrations? If he's an Indian, the Embassy could help.'

'I didn't think of the Embassy. I went to libraries and newspapers.'

'Is that his full name? Does he have a pseudonym? Some artists did at the time. What kind of an artist was he?'

'Yes, that's his name. Mir was an escape artist, Keya. I'm his son, I should know.'

Her fingers involuntarily close the coin clasp of her wallet. It snaps on her skin. She winces. She's thrown by my abruptness.

'Are you hurt?' I ask.

'So, Mir Ali is your father? And he's been missing since the 1980s?'

I shrug a yes.

'Will you tell me more?'

'Perhaps,' I inhale. 'Can we go somewhere else? I feel hemmed in with the music and people.'

We summon the server for the bill.

Once we are outside, she asks me, 'Where would you like to go?' her voice mellow.

'Isn't that an Indian flag?' I gesture over her shoulders to a fluttering saffron-green-white cloth on a pole across the road. She follows the line of my finger, but isn't surprised.

'I didn't see that before. There must be an Indian fellow among the squatter artists; either that or someone who has been to India.'

'What building is that?'

She tells me it is the Kunsthaus Tacheles, an art centre. 'The building is occupied by a diverse group of artists. It used to be a department store in the past; now, colours run on the walls inside, installations, cinema, workshops. A very creative mix.'

I am intrigued.

'We could go there now,' she suggests.

I hesitate, 'I'm not sure I want to meet people.'

'I'm not going for interviews! If I run into anyone I know, I'll pretend you don't exist, all right? I insist, because the place is worth seeing.'

'Let's go.'

'Leon, I think this is the beginning of a beautiful friendship.'

She mimics Bogart. She is quite good with the copying. 'You plagiarist,' I rib her.

'I prefer Impressionist.'

'Kashmiri, isn't that author, what's-his-name?'

I cross the road, but she steps back from the oncoming traffic. 'He is too,' I hear. A passing car honks loudly.

'You cross the road like a madman,' she exclaims.

Once inside the building, we wander. I observe metal sculpting in the workshop; fountains of fire glitter as the machine blade cuts and welds the metal into statuettes. Then I go upstairs to the cinema on the first floor. Lights come on, there are occasional cheers and whistles, laughter, people call out names, messages. I find Keya on the landing, and together, we saunter towards the left wing of the building where there is an isolated run-down flight of steps. 'Maybe we can reach the roof,' I say.

We start climbing the stairs unhurriedly.

We are near a glass window embedded in rough concrete.

'I'm sorry to offload this onto you. You liked stories, you said, so here's mine,' I purse my lips nervously, speak with pauses and emphases, tell her the tale of what I've really been up to in Berlin.

'Mir Ali, your father, was a political activist married to your mother Albeena. He disappeared in Berlin before you were born

and you are trying to trace him,' she says, 'but why do you refer to
your search here in the past tense?'

'Because I have a pile of dead-ends to show for it. I am useless
at trying to access information. Plus, people treat me suspiciously.'

'Leon, I don't know what it's like to be a Muslim, I am not
related to any activists, and I know what killed my father, so I don't
know what to say. I can understand. Try to. And I can certainly help
with the search.'

'Keya, I don't mean to trouble you,' I am focusing on the
silhouettes of the buildings in the distance.

'I want to help. I have some free time. And I know how you
feel. Closures of some kind are essential.' She lifts her elbow off
the concrete, blinks. 'I witnessed my father's untimely death as a
teenager. It was painful to lose a parent, but, you know, I also lost
a home, homeland, at the same time. I could never go back to
Kashmir with him. His stories were the bridge to my homeland.
I can't agree with the business of pretending that we do not live
under the shadow of mortality.'

I want to convey the feelings, our bewilderment, the confusion;
all that as it was. But I don't know how to express this. So, I whisper,
'Life is a residual phenomenon.'

'We must plod on. I can definitely help. I am not sure how
useful it would be, but I could get you access. I know many people
at research centres and archives here.'

'Thanks,' I lightly touch her sleeve with the back of my forefingers.
Then say, 'It's getting chilly. My fingers are numb.'

Someone shouts. We look at each other. It's a bit raw. The moment
quietly slinks away, and it seems incredible that we have just met.

No one has traversed the stairs during this time. The doors on
each landing that connect to different floors in the main building are
locked. After climbing a few more steps, we reach the penultimate
floor.

We are startled as someone calls out, 'No, you cannot go any
further.'

Taken aback, we peer over the broken railings.

A corpulent man sits by the wall where the stairs turn the last corner to the roof. From where we are, we can see the upper half of his body. I go a couple of steps further, and then retreat. His leg is badly damaged and swollen to huge proportions. He is suffering from serious trouble. His attitude does not betray any of this.

Jovially, he starts to sing, 'The roof, the roof, the roof is on fire! The roof, the roof, the roof is on fire!'

Keya looks at me quizzically.

'It's a song,' I say.

The large man hears me, adding, 'From Bloodhound Gang.'

A German, the man speaks English with relish.

'I'm Bernard, German Bernhardt.'

He swigs from a bottle containing buff-coloured liquid.

'Are you all right up there?' she asks.

'Oh yes, I am fine. It is milk.'

He's from Bremen; he was born there.

'I am not here,' he concludes with these words a long soliloquy describing a recurring theme of 'six years.' It takes a while for me to work out that the 'six years' refers to the Second World War.

'Shall we go?' I nudge Keya.

'No, let's hear him.'

I have no choice.

I stay and hear her speak to him. What does she do with so many stories?

His uncle owned a cinema after the war, where as a kid, he had seen a movie about 'Three days in the Isle (which he called Ayezel) of Wight'. 'Oof! Hendrix, Jethro Tull—' 'David Bowie—Oh!'

He isn't making much sense.

He sings this song which I can barely make out. He's lived for a while in the '70s in Neukolln.

'It was cool, I mean,' is his favourite refrain. I remember Turan's whatsthat.

Now and again, he pronounces some words in a way that

makes them vibrate; 'boongkerr,' he says boomingly, describing his grandmother going into a bunker during the bombing in Bremen.

'One day during those six years, she decided to take shelter in a high-level boongkerr instead of underground.'

'She sat still in a—what's the word for this?' he asks dazed, showing us again and again an L with his arms— 'a corner,' we chant in unison.

'—corner, and someone saw bombs fall.'

He adds, 'Because it was normal at the time.'

'It was normal,' he says; then, with a barely perceptible pause, 'It was crazy, I mean.'

His surname, he explains, is 'Ewelts', which between the alphabets E and S has the German word for 'the world'.

'That's pretty cool,' I speak for the first time, in his own idiom.

He speaks of bombed out Coventry, Rotterdam, Bremen.

'Do you think he means Dresden?' Keya whispers confidentially. I shrug.

His grandma's house 'is the last on the street'. He emphasizes, 'After this is the port—I mean, there is a railway line and then the port, but this house is the last one on the street.'

'Bombs fall from the sky in the raid every day for some minutes.'

Inexplicably, instead of the history book pages, my mind flashes up scenes of the twin towers being hit, Baghdadi women ululating, bombs and death.

'I mean, did Benjamin Britten write the *War Requiem* for the Battle of Coventry?' he asks.

Keya replies, 'I think so.'

'I mean, did he write it for Coventry?' he repeats.

I assent that I also think so, without actually knowing.

He says that it is probably so because his mother told him this when listening to the requiem in a concert.

He has been visiting Tacheles since 1992. 'Oh no! I am like you. Here to wander. To see. But every day,' he replies when Keya asks him if he knows any artists here.

She enquires about his leg.

'Everything in my life is just a little bit rotten—like my teeth, or my sleep, or my leg, my morals, just a little rotten,' he evades.

Then he starts to tell us a potted history of the building we are in. He talks of a company in Cologne, of doctors and dentists, offices. Of those 'six years' reiteratively. At last, his words ease, and we leave.

Downstairs, someone is saying, 'You have to let me win. Because I always lose. You never lose? Never? You have to play.' It's quite right for this place that the person who unfailingly loses wants to win by insisting the person who never loses play with him; let me win.

We come out of the building. Bernard's nostalgia has been a mood spoiler. The lively hip road feels weird.

'You want to catch dinner?' I ask.

'I have a meal already cooked at home. I don't know if you'd like to join?'

'Not tonight, thanks.'

In awkward silence, we continue for the length of the street. At the corner, we exchange numbers and details.

'Leon Allee,' she reads my writing aloud and smiles. 'You sound like a German Street.'

'I'm surprised I didn't see you at the airport.'

'I'll ring you soon after I have called a few places for access.'

'I'll be waiting.'

We hug and part ways. Keya is aiming for the bus stop on Unter den Linden and I have to walk back.

Some hours later, Keya stands on the balcony of her flat, as a tame dry wind blows seeds off the lime trees. In the fluorescent lights of the street, the seeds are dancing like frenzied dervishes, pivoting in the air, around and around as they touch the ground below. A few reach her. She thinks of Leon, of the day. His story has struck a chord in her. He hasn't been able to mourn Mir. She recalls her life in another country, her own prisons of time in India.

4

Homeland From Afar

The 1980s have spread themselves as a plain horizontal strip of time in Keya's synaesthetic memory. The '70s slide downwards and the '90s ascend towards the millennium, but for the decade in between, the years align themselves like symmetrically arranged books on a shelf, neatly bounded at both sides by bookends titled 'home' and 'school'.

Keya's growing up years in '80s Delhi were marked by a slow proliferation of colour TVs, colourful fridges, washing machines, videos, Maruti cars, touchpad phones, school computers. The news bulletins were ten-minute long monologues by deadpan presenters and hardly any pictures, the sole All India Radio channel closed at night, there was no TV transmission for much of the day, 'trunk' calls were unreliable and expensive, and the yellow-green DTC buses ran innocent of any schedules. People adored the Appu elephant mascot of the expensive Asiad Games 1982 in Delhi; celebrated India's Prudential Cup 1983 cricket win on the streets at night; saw a PM being assassinated; were shocked at the Union Carbide industrial leak, the Bhopal Gas tragedy; complained of Muslim appeasement in the Shah Bano case; moaned about the omnipresent corruption and Bofors scandal; deplored the killings in Punjab, the Northeast and Kashmir.

When Indira Gandhi was shot, Keya's parents lied to the mob to protect their Sikh neighbours in the 1984 riots. Keya's school took her on guided educational trips to places like the Campa-Cola factory. All these snapshots of the past floated randomly in her mind, failing to sediment. Delhi in the India of those days. The reality of those routines.

Keya was a student at St. Vincent's Girls' School. Like several good schools in the capital, it had a Christian name and affiliation, it was English medium, had a hefty fee, and the Principal was an elderly Anglo-Indian woman. Unlike some other institutions, at St. Vincent's, the non-Christian students were not required to attend church services, and all festivals were celebrated. The bottom line was that the students would become good missionaries of universal values—spreading light, joy and goodness.

When Queen Elizabeth II visited India in November 1983, she walked through a part of the school where it was reputed that Mahatma Gandhi had previously strolled. A day before that, Keya, along with students from dozens of other prestigious Delhi schools, had lined the procession where Her Majesty had been carried in a palanquin through a large green park. From a distance of over two hundred metres, the small children had watched a moving spot and imagined that they had been waved back at. Under the specially set-up marquees, each child jostled for a better view as they all waved two painted flags, a Union Jack in one hand and an Indian tricolour in the other—white chart paper squares that had to be coloured at home with crayons and fixed onto a snapped stick end of an Indian broom, approved by the teachers as being accurate and the right size.

When the *India Today* magazine carried photos of the event, every parent, including Keya's mother, had proudly pointed to a pixel saying, 'There, look carefully in this corner; that, yes, that is my daughter greeting the Queen of England!'

School rush began at 6.00 a.m. and the return home was at 3.00 p.m. There was always mountains of homework to do: sums to practise, poems by Tennyson and Sarojini Naidu to be learnt by heart, there was the marking of states on blank political maps of India, answering exercise questions on the water cycle, learning in detail about continents and oceans—the educational coverage was encyclopaedic—except for nothing contemporary on neighbouring states like China, Nepal, Sri Lanka, Bangladesh, Bhutan and, most importantly, Pakistan!

Everyone in school understood that fluency in English was the most important ingredient of success. For many years, students were discouraged from speaking in Hindi at any time except during the Hindi class. If found chattering in any other language but Hindi, there was a reprimand and the threat of a fine.

With time, changes filtered in. The central government brought in a National Anthem policy and a National Integration policy. At St.Vincent's too, during the daily morning prayers, it became compulsory to sing *Jana Gana Mana*, the national anthem, after reading from the Psalms and singing 'The Lord's my Shepherd'. It also became necessary to study a 'third language' in middle school. At Keya's school, the school nurse was a Keralite from South India and she got the additional duty of taking Malayalam classes. This extra coursework was not assessed, and the parents moaned that their kids were having to learn a useless language when they could be studying a language like French or German or Spanish that would open doors for them. Keya had once pleased her juniors by pretending to faint in the middle of a sports drill, so that the Malayalam students could rejoice in getting a free period as the nurse rushed to the sickroom.

The cemented stone stage in the grounds of her alma mater was the setting for extra-curricular events. It was a beautiful solid stage, forget the rumour about it being built upon a graveyard. Keya had, on many occasions, gracefully stood there to play the Bard's Lady Macbeth, Fagin from Dickens and Milton's Satan. Secretly, she had wished to play the part of the blossoming Juliet who sat atop the elevated back of the stage and with lilting music beheld her 'Romeo Romeo, wherefore art thou Romeo', but she was not light-skinned enough; as an unstated rule, the beautiful actress parts generally went to the fairest girls.

She understood later that it was a colonial colour hangover, characteristic of the entire nation that craved 'tall fair brides' in the newspaper matrimonial pages. 'Damn the lot!' she would curse, after unsuccessful auditions.

Colour and beauty were a bother at home as well. In those days, when cosmetics were primitive and rare, on weekends, her mother would cajole and compel her to rub lemon rind on her skin, massage egg whites into her hair and wash it with boiled soapnut water, apply gramflour paste to her body. It was torture.

Like an ant, burrowing and hoarding, Keya had saved up insignificant details of other lives too; she had collected ordinary stories with the anthropological passion of a friendly and observant child, storing them patiently, etching them indelibly in the scrapbook of bygone times. From her study table or the bed, both of which faced the windows, she would spectate for hours on end, a consummate voyeur, witnessing the goings-on outside, feeling implicated in the lives of those she watched.

Before daybreak, the temple woke everyone up with the neighbourhood pujari ringing the bell. Many women in cotton or polyester sarees, with their heads covered, would walk over to say their first prayers. A few men in crumpled white kurta-pyjamas went out for their morning walks, often exercising in the common park where the temple stood at one end. Dogs barked and squealed; small, fluffy and mostly white Pomeranians bouncing around their masters, who called out their names like Lucky and Bobby in authoritative stentorian voices usually reserved for the chaprasi peons at their offices, the security guard, house servants and, occasionally, the wife. On their bicycles, the paperwallahs, the newspaper delivery men, went around pitching rolled-up rubber-banded issues of *The Hindustan Times* and *The Times of India* with perfect aim into balconies on the higher floors.

This typical dawn in a central Delhi 'Type IV' officers' colony also included those who got up at 4.00 a.m. to get fresh milk for their masters. These were the fetch-men who lived in the garages and servants' quarters of the colony residents. In the hazy light, a colossal elongated lorry would come to deliver the transparent polypacks with the blue Delhi Milk Scheme, 'DMS', logo emblazoned on them. With some clatter, the crates of milk would be deposited in a ramshackle booth near the multi-storey buildings. From a restricted hatch, a sleepy designate would hand out the milk-packs in return for exact change. As some residents strolled at sunrise, they could be sure that their children were being dressed for school and fed breakfast by the servants.

Keya would see the line of marker stones outside the booth in the evenings—it was a weird ritual; how did the fetch-men know which stone was whose when they came to claim their queued place in the wee hours? The servants busily worked at odd jobs for the rest of the day; she saw them bringing water in colourful plastic buckets from communal handpumps during summer shortages; taking shoes for polishing to the mochi, the cobbler, who sat underneath the large banyan tree; getting cigarettes from the paanwallah, the betel-nut-seller, behind the bus stop; buying bread and butter, shampoos and conditioners for their employers' guests or bars of handmade soap for themselves from the provisional wooden stall in the locality.

The servant-boys washed and shined the cars that their fathers drove for their bosses; the girls cleaned utensils and clothes twice a day in the flats; their mothers waited at school bus stops to receive the officers' children in the afternoon, carry their heavy bags, hold their hands firmly when crossing the roads. The housewives and teachers among the master-class would greet their bundles of joy themselves, but others had to be ferried through the dangerously accelerating vehicles by the maids as safety could not be taken for granted—a junior schoolmate of Keya's had been run over in an accident.

In spite of this multitasking, the community legend of the middle classes suggested that good servants were hard to find, tough to keep, the maids never arrived on time for work, asked for pay in advance, and took too many days off. The younger workers being prime suspects, households preferred older and sturdier females. Sometimes, even they turned out to be unreliable.

Santosh, a kitchen-maid much in demand, had one day been exposed as Zahira; she was a Muslim woman disguising herself as a Hindu with a false name. She had played a clever trick to get the jobs. The master-class was outraged; they had trusted her with touching their food utensils—shock, horror, imagine! There was much tattle. She was immediately dismissed from all but one or two homes.

Some fetch-people's children attended state school and studied in Hindi medium until a certain age, after which the boys got co-opted into informal professions and the girls were married off. Underage marriage was less uncommon than the laws and official stances might suggest. Manju, a young and vivacious girl whose hair had turned golden from malnutrition, and who occasionally played with the children of the colony folk, suddenly vanished after a ceremony one night to reappear many months later, pregnant and starting to resemble her mother. Why did anyone not stop this?

Because it was said that 'they' have their own rules, it was useless to intervene. Keya wrote a letter to the editor of a national daily expressing a small girl's outrage, but it was never published.

Manju is leaving her home, as she has to one day, said her tired parents and their friends, and look how comely the decorations are for her marriage. She looks old enough to be married, they said, she has other sisters who have to be thought of. She is clever enough to manage married life. She might be a victim of circumstances if her maturing youth is spent living unmarried in the colony garages. She is betrothed to a man who lives Jamuna*paar*—on the other side of the city's rapidly shrinking Jamuna river—and works as an electrician in a hardware shop; he will earn good money for her. Her in-laws are nice people who will treat her well. She will have her own shed there to live in, rather than sharing a garage. She will not have to immediately consummate her relationship, but it is good to be settled with her in-laws. She wants to be married for the sake of her parents and their honour.

What a comparison to a rich classmate of Keya's who also

married underage at sixteen, invited people to Chelmsford Club for the ceremony, and went to Sharjah with her businessman spouse afterwards. When Keya interrupted Jaspreet's pompous announcement of her forthcoming wedding in the school canteen by pointing out that it was illegal to marry before turning eighteen, Jaspreet sneered that nobody could prove anything, she had proudly failed all her exams and was quitting education.

Jaspreet glowed, but the pregnant Manju had a wilted face when Keya last saw her.

This story was similar to others, but there were variations on the theme. There was the much-mentioned tale of a driver's daughter who was studying for her BCom degree. Her family rented two garages across from the sabziwallah, the vegetable-seller, at the far end of the neighbourhood. Some middle class women deliberately chose that route for their evening walks to go and view this specimen of a poor girl, who had managed to study so much while living in a cramped six-by-six feet cubicle underneath a building. You could barely fit an LML Vespa scooter in there. The mother of that girl would lament to those passing, 'My daughter is sooty black and wears spectacles; with her degree, who will marry her in our class? She cannot work in gorment like you babu-log. What is the use?' The daughter went about her chores within earshot, but kept silent. Keya had never heard her speak.

And then there was a harmless lunatic who consistently hung around, but lived who knows where. He had no money for a roof or skill for work, they said. He had not even a proper name. He used to wander aimlessly, muttering to himself, smiling or talking to bushes, trees and metal electricity poles. He would perform insignificant errands, mainly for the local shopkeepers and the kabadiwallah, the scrap-seller, like getting their glasses of tea. At intervals, he would prune communal hedges, help with moving heavy objects or clean rubbish in return for loose change or food.

The reason he was a special part of the landscape was because he was fair and tolerably good-looking. People initially speculated why a fair-skinned man like him had to be in this unfortunate position. Surely he was not born like this. It was common practice to associate fair skin colour with 'good caste and genetic stock' and 'class'.

Later, it became known that the wretched fellow had been through the Bhopal Gas tragedy in December 1984, losing his family and his mind. He did not know his name or his past, remembered Bhopal and nothing else. He was often seen talking about Bhopal to the metal pillar mounted upon three concrete circular steps in the centre of the colony park.

From this pillar, too, was unfurled the national tricolour every 26 January and 15 August for the Republic and Independence Days. Ordinarily, it was a perch in the evenings for the young daughters of this middle class neighbourhood to sit and dream about their futures.

Years later, Keya had visited that same colony in Delhi. Her father was now dead, her mother had moved away, and she herself had been living in England for a long time. 'What a transformation!' Keya marvelled; how it contrasted with her recall of the insulation of an earlier age. She saw that the hedges were overgrown, boundary walls had sprung up, the temple had expanded to take up the entire park, and the colony buildings were under repair. The place had an air of decay about it, as the centre of Delhi was shifting from Connaught Place and associated areas to the south and to Gurgaon and Noida, where the new luxury apartment blocks—with names like Charmwood, Magnolia, Belvedere—and the multinational corporation offices were mushrooming. There was ethnic chic in Dilli Haat, malls a dime a dozen that sold branded merchandise to consumers hungry for a taste of the West.

The pace of change had been remarkable. There were mobile phones everywhere; young men and women working for foreign BPO firms earned skyrocketing salaries. Summer jobs were common, often in the call centres that operated on British and American time; it was unremarkable for girls to be out at 3.00 a.m. Cable TV was booming and there was a choice of multiple twenty-four hour FM channels. Middle class children amused themselves with video and computer games; when older, they attended private universities where the high fee was matched with easier entry and opportunity to network with wealthy scions.

The green neighbourhood area where Keya had played hide-and-seek, chain, or badminton with her teenage crush, a Bengali boy by the name of Shantanu, was an encampment of impoverished migrant workers from Rajasthan; they were building a wall to comprehensively encircle the colony. Someone boasted about the high level of 'security' enjoyed by the residents. The servants now need a valid entry pass to come inside the colony, the garage fetch-people are all 'gone', shortages are rare, and the Residents' Welfare Association is a hive of activity.

Security and religion are the prime concerns of the rising rich— hence, the towering boundary fence and the encroaching expanding Hindu temple. In her old flat, whatever view of the starry skies she might once have had would be blocked by the tall grim wall.

The city itself appeared stark and brightly garbed. The loud billboards and the keen corporatization of every domain of life was inevitable, given that globalization had sunk its teeth into the national flesh, regurgitating elites, and spewing NGOs and Incs that promised dreams for profit at a discount.

Keya sighed.

The crooked tree in the park, where she and Shantanu had reclined talking, from whose branches she had rescued a scared stray cat, was a mere rampike. The peculiar slanted S shape of the smooth bark had become a lopsided L, with the central portion sunk into the earth. How deviously were those pictures set aglow with a vast and generous light, that on second view only seem meagre, diminished and struggling. 'Nothing lasts forever,' said the boy who had kissed her for the very first time in her life. He had meant the Guns N' Roses song 'November Rain', but it had sounded portentous.

The nameless Bhopal Gas mumbler was nowhere, and the only

person who recognized Keya after the span of those years was the mochi. Surrounded by the selfsame tools and implements under the same old tree, the cobbler had aged significantly. Speaking through paan-stained teeth, he had delightedly recounted that she was the daughter of the Kashmiri family, wasn't she? He asked after her mother, commiserated again about her father after so long. He had insisted on polishing her shoes, red ones from Clarks across seven seas—the same to him as the black leather school shoes of her schooldays. How could she return the largesse of his concern? She had paid him in money and shared his reminiscences. Of course, everything changes.

People in Delhi had vaguely exotic ideas about Kashmiri Pandits. Kashmir was an imaginary place on an imaginary map. Keya's family were the sole Kashmiris in the colony, and somehow, their Jantri calendar meant that they were celebrating the same festivals on different days than their neighbours. As Kashmiri Hindus, they celebrated Shivratri as Herat a day early, Janmashtami a day early, and several North Indian festivals not at all. Keya's parents did not allow Holi; the powder colours were toxic and it was an excuse for inappropriate behaviour by the opposite sex. Diwali was the only concession; even though it meant nothing to them as Kashmiris, the world around erupted in fireworks and gaiety—they too, lit candles, did puja and wore new clothes. Their own Kashmiri rituals like Gada Batta, Pan Dyun and Khaiyach Mawas were unheard-of in Delhi. In any case, for Keya, Christmas at school was the real event of the year.

It was difficult to explain to her classmates why she had two birthdays in the year, at one of which there was the yellow Teher rice in her tiffin; why, if they were Brahmins, did they eat meat; and why their new year or the Navreh came in spring—the day she woke up to the sight of a thali with flowers, coins, inkpot, pens, curd, grass, rice, sugar, salt, walnuts and the Jantri book.

At junior school, students would gather around her during the lunch break and question if she was really Kashmiri.

In reply to her 'yes', they would ask her about the Kashmiri language, did she know it?

'Please, please recite some.'

'Suna,' 'suna naa,' they begged in a Hindi chorus.

Sometimes, she would be peeved and retort that the language is 'not a poem that I can just recite'; at other times, she humoured them with titbits—Keya wasn't a fluent speaker herself—which they gleefully tossed around their tongues: the compressed sounds, the diphthongs, the intonation.

'Do you truly drink tea with salt?' she would be asked, even into her college days.

'Kashmiris do. I don't like the Ksheerchai or Noonchai. It's pink and tastes funny.' She would, instead, elaborate on the other kind of Kashmiri tea, the nice golden brown Koshur chai 'without milk and with sliced almonds, the Kahwa, you should try it'.

In the gatherings of her relatives or at Kashmiri Pandit functions, the adults talked of Indian tea, or Lipton tea versus Kashmiri tea, and of 'Kashmir' and 'India', or this or that side of the Jawahar Tunnel. As a child, Keya did not understand why these distinctions were made, if, as the government and everyone else said, Kashmiris were a part of India. She had seen men and women in her extended family marry late, greet with hugs, and play cards with each other on occasion, something that many North Indians saw as being too liberal, bizarre. Before the wave of 1989 Kashmiri refugees, they were hardly known, and were a difficult fit in the environment of Delhi.

It was only when the armed insurgency in Kashmir gained momentum in 1989-90, and waves of Kashmiri Pandits were forced to flee the Valley, that Keya properly realized that her homeland was a fraught place that she might never know. She met several cousins and uncles and aunts for the first time. They arrived with their boxes and bags at the refugee camps in Jammu, in Delhi. They lived in ramshackle conditions, out of jobs, away from home, dependent on a monthly refugee allowance. In Jammu, the native Dogras complained that the Pandit migrants' children were taking up all the seats in colleges and offices. In Delhi, Kashmiris were too few to matter. People in the capital were already preoccupied with rioting over the Mandal Commission reservation for the 'Other Backward Castes'; young men were immolating themselves publicly to protest against the caste-based affirmative action.

Keya's school admitted Nancy, an uprooted Kashmiri girl from Srinagar. That year, a tele-serial called *Gul-Gulshan-Gulfam* was broadcast on prime-time Doordarshan national TV. It was set in the houseboats of Srinagar and it captured the imagination of Indians at large. The caption song was lyrical and Nancy was constantly requested to sing it during the lunch break.

'Why did you leave Kashmir?' children would pester the more authentic arrival from the Valley. She was fair with chestnut-coloured eyes, long nose and a bashful manner. If they could, her classmates would pick walnuts and apples from her very words.

'Because of Toorism,' she would say.

'Tourism? Why?'

It was discovered that she was trying to say Terrorism. Her kirket meant cricket, she said neighbourer for neighbour, and mispronounced her own name as Nunsee—common mistakes for a native Kashmiri speaker. Her English didn't get better, and after a few months, she withdrew and went away.

At home also, they had a new visitor, Sheetal, an older cousin of Keya's on her father's side of the family. Sheetal's parents were living at the refugee camp in Jammu, and she was sent to Delhi to appear for the medical entrance exams. She was to share Keya's room. Sheetal was the kind of girl who won hearts; she cooked well, studied day and night, recited Kashmiri verses in the evening, and she was beautiful.

Keya hated her.

Sheetal could speak in perfectly fluent Kashmiri with Keya's father; he would then exhort Keya to learn by Sheetal's example. Keya was talkative, naughty, dissipated. Sheetal was quiet, mature, sensible. Sheetal was cultured and polite. She had faced adversity bravely. She was the centre of attention and received much sympathy.

Keya's mother occasionally intervened on her behalf when Sheetal was praised, to Keya's detriment, by her relatives, 'Her family claims the refugee benefit twice by cheating on the residence proof. They get it in Delhi and in Jammu.'

Keya tried taking petty revenge on Sheetal. Sheetal would stay up late studying and have tea with fen bread, a snack which she kept on her table wrapped in newspaper pages. Once, Keya replaced the bread with a sanitary towel in an attempt to humiliate Sheetal. It got no reaction. The next morning, Sheetal smiled at Keya as always. She did not report it to Keya's parents either. At another time, Keya secretly spilled a bottle of ink over a stack of Sheetal's notes. The poor girl quietly wept. When Keya's parents enquired, she lied about having accidentally destroyed her own notes. Keya could not understand. Sheetal seemed unreal. It was a relief when the year was over and she left, having secured admission into the medical college at Bangalore.

'But doesn't she get in automatically because she has the migrant quota? Her brother must have found a way of giving them the capitation fees.' Keya had gossiped with her mother.

Some seven or eight years later, Keya learnt that Sheetal, now a doctor, had been excommunicated from her family because she married a Muslim from Srinagar. Sheetal had moved back to Kashmir to join her husband Shahzad, a horticulturist. 'Sheetal is a shameful disgrace. I always knew her façade of goodness was a front for her cunning,' everyone averred. No one had good words for her any more.

Keya's parents were both professionals. In her school bag, she carried a duplicate key to the latch-lock of the flat to let herself in on weekday afternoons. An old maid would prepare warm food, feed her and leave. Keya would settle into a private time groove until the early evening, when first her mother, and then her father, returned from their offices.

After finishing her homework, she scoured the bookshelves for reading material. In addition, she was a member of many libraries—at school, the Christian Community Centre, the British Council, the American Centre and the mobile vans of the Delhi Public Library. She would wade through dog-eared biographies of explorers, scientific inventors, discoverers, famous heroes, and browse the current affairs periodicals.

At about five o'clock, her mother arrived. Just before seven, her father would ring the bell. Usha, and only Usha, opened the door to Veer in the evening. Once or twice, Keya had tried to welcome her father and been told not to. For people who were not demonstratively affectionate so far as Keya could tell, this everyday ritual at the door had a momentous significance. Usha opened the door and took Veer's briefcase as he came in. That was all. A while later, they would sit in the large balcony and have tea or glasses of red Rooh Afza. The three of them would talk of their day. After dinner, they would watch the Doordarshan telecast on a four-legged Weston TV set that stood in a corner of the drawing room, its blue screen veiled behind shutters like a coy mistress. Prior to bedtime, Keya had to rinse her teeth with $KMnO_4$ crystals mixed in water, and briskly walk a minimum of fifty to-and-fros in the corridor 'for good digestion'. Later, she would go and wish her father goodnight; he worked late in his study, hours past her mother retired to sleep in the main bedroom. Once a year, they went on the LTC, leave travel concession, holiday to hill stations. The same routine ran for years without a break.

Usha and Veer were Kashmiris hailing from two different contexts. Usha came from a family in Uttar Pradesh that had migrated out of the Kashmir Valley decades ago; Veer had grown up in Srinagar. Usha had completed her studies in Hindi and worked in the National Language section of the Human Resources Ministry. Veer could barely speak Hindi; his language of thought was Kashmiri, and of work, English. Growing up at home in Delhi, Keya spoke all three.

Keya's knowledge of her father Veer's life in Kashmir before he came to Delhi was a patchwork of stories and anecdotes that she coaxed him to relate during wintry evenings and summer night power blackouts. The texture of darkness would thicken with personal histories narrated in a mix of Kashmiri, English and broken Hindi.

Veer's father Shankar was a wealthy contractor in Srinagar. He had been married early to Veer's mother Shanta. Keya had never met her grandmother, but knew her to have been a pious woman who ran a large household, toiling endlessly. There were several children, but only four survived—a daughter and three sons, of whom Veer, being the youngest, was the favourite.

Despite being illiterate herself, Shanta wanted Veer to be educated. She would feed him sweets and baked breads while he studied. Being mischievous, Veer enjoyed fooling her. He imitated learning by rote from his books while actually repeating aloud the literal text of an advertisement—S-U-N-L-I-G-H-T; SUNLIGHT, S-U-N-L-I-G-H-T; SUNLIGHT, SUNLIGHT WASHING SOAP. Sitting cross-legged on the charpoy, he swayed back and forth to the alphabet sounds as if memorizing a formula! Impressed, she would shower him with kisses.

From early childhood, there had been father-son clashes, and it was Shanta who used to intervene on behalf of her son, protecting him from his father's tough love. The old man had a ruthless business ambition and wanted his son to follow in his footsteps, but Veer professed his desire to be an architect. Shankar did not think that this was a sensible vocation and would not have any of it. He apprenticed Veer in the business of a friend, so he could learn the ropes. That culminated on the day Veer forgot to lock up the safe and shutters properly, because he was engrossed in reading a feature about monuments. Goods were stolen and much social muck heaped upon the careerless, careless, bookish son and his temperament.

There was a big showdown, other elders arbitrated, and Veer

eventually enrolled at the Engineering College in Srinagar. He was not interested in his studies and had an average result. What was more, his close friendship with Muslims was the talk of the community. Shankar and Veer's relationship never recovered from the setback of those youthful years in Srinagar. After his degree, Veer spent a few barren months in Shimla trying to get a job of his choice.

While in Shimla, he learnt of his mother Shanta's death. As part of a religious fast, she had taken a dip in the holy river Vitasta and caught pneumonia. Without telephones, by the time the news reached him, she had already been cremated. Locking himself up in his room, he refused food for days.

A week later, he went to visit his father.

He was surprised to see Shankar distraught. This lion who had never expressed emotions was helpless without Shanta. He padded about the rooms, lacked concentration in transactions and looked ill-worn. Veer's going away was not discussed. He himself did not know that this would be last time that he would see his father alive.

The winter snow was melting on the eaves of the wooden house. Veer had decided to leave for Shimla the next day. In Shanta's absence, the place did not feel right. He was not the capable son Shankar wanted. Veer went to the Kheer Bhawani temple on foot and returned at dusk. Upon coming back to his room, he found a large fruit bowl laden with oranges on the table next to his packed luggage. He stared at the big ripe oranges that were heaped on the carved pannier; they were an incongruent sight to his desolate grief-stricken heart.

'Hussein? Hey! Hatay! Hussein? Come here, will you?' Veer opened the window and leaned out over the courtyard, calling for Hussein, the family servant.

His sister who was carrying the firewood, looked up. 'What happened? What is it?'

'Lado, where is Hussein?'

'He is out. Why?'

'Who placed the oranges on my table?'

'Oranges? What oranges?'

'A whole heap. Send Hussein upstairs when he's back.'

As he pulled the window in with force, a gloppy patch of snow from the roof slid past his arm. He was cold and moved to the bukhari fire.

Hussein finally came in and revealed that Shankar had himself gone out to buy the oranges for his son. 'I have never seen anything this strange. Shankarji did not haggle! He asked the seller for the price and paid. Even carried the bag back himself.'

Shankar was known to be curmudgeonly and stingy. That he had not haggled for the oranges was extraordinary. What is more, he had arranged them on the table himself.

Veer was not sure how to go to Shankar's room.

He stood hesitating at the doorway, one hand upon the knob and one foot on the threshold.

A crouching Shankar pored over accounts as he sat enveloped in the warmth of a fur cap and a fire-pot kangri burning coal underneath his large grey pheran. Veer lightly coughed.

The old man beheld him wordlessly from above the rim of his spectacles.

Veer entered and sat on the edge of the divan.

Before he could open his mouth, his father said, 'It's all right.'

'Would you like anything to eat or drink? Should I ask Hussein to bring some peeled orange sections?'

'I am fine. I had tea a moment ago.'

'I am leaving tomorrow,' Veer managed to make the declaration.

Shankar looked long and hard at his son, 'May God go with you.'

For the first time in his life, Veer had felt a mix of guilt and tenderness towards his father, the tamed tyrant.

They sat there in silence for some minutes until Shankar mentioned some auspicious dates from the Jantri for the year; before Shanta's unforeseen death, he had received a marriage proposal for Veer from their gor, the priest.

Veer faintly resisted; he did not want to spoil his going away by protestations.

He had warmly shaken hands with Shankar when departing the next morning. He was sure that he would be able to refuse marriage once he was out of sight. Within that year, Shankar died. Shimla did not feel right anymore; getting contracts was a burden.

In need of a job, Veer turned to the heat and smoke of the vexing metropolis Delhi, heartbroken and anguished. Severed from his ambitions, he was lucky to find a well-placed position with the central government. In the alienness of the city, the language, the climate, he had struggled.

Relatives soon pressed upon Veer for agreement on the marriage that Shankar had approved. In the beginning, he had been strongly opposed to matrimony. But then ensued a protracted bilingual epistolary courtship during which Usha and Veer, who lived in two different cities and were unable to meet, unchained their emotions, his letters in English and hers in Hindi. They had both needed dictionaries to understand their lover's turmoil. Families on either side could not wait much longer, and after a year of words in various inks—blue and red and black and green—flowing back and forth in his rounded well-spread letters and her angular close-knit paragraphs, they had been married.

The bridegroom's baraat party had travelled on North Indian Railways to reach Usha's town, getting robbed on the overnight train. This misfortune was put down to a woman having crossed their path when setting out; the ill-luck of a woman's 'bad leg', Zanan Zang. They reached the large bridal haveli, where no expense had been spared for the event, without the jewellery, the gifts or the fine clothes. Usha's trousseau was all. Marriage ceremonies were conducted with some delay in this confusion, so it was never certain whether their anniversary ought to be the 18th or the 19th of January.

For Keya, the distance between her parents resonated with ungraspable suggestions. Only once had she seen them kiss. Like other couples, they periodically differed over their daughter's upbringing, relatives, finances and housework. Usha was vocal and articulate; unable to keep up with her Hindi, Veer would whisper and then be stilled.

They also argued about the Kashmiri language. Veer resented that Keya would never be fluent in her mother tongue for her mother's tongue was Hindi. Usha did not understand the particular way in which Veer belonged to Kashmir, and Veer could not understand how Usha could see herself as a Kashmiri. For Usha, Kashmir lived securely in her surname, in the large round holes pierced in the skin of her upper ear for the married woman's dezhor, in the memories of her summer vacations in Srinagar. She was a Kashmiri who had grown up outside the Valley and without speaking the language familiarly. For Veer, Kashmir was the yen for his dead mother who he had been close to, the breads she baked with milk, and the extra meat she hid under the mound of rice in his plate when he sat down to eat with the other boys and men in the large household of forty-odd members who lived in the carved old house with many rooms and floors in an alley by the banks of the small Kuttukol stream of the Jhelum. His Kashmir was in the language of his thought and in the childhood shouts to his friends while playing truant from the local school. It was spoken to his mother on the long walk to the Tulmul shrine at Kheer Bhawani where she prayed numerous times in the year.

The three of them could not share these fragments of Kashmir during much of Keya's adolescence, since the insurgency in the state meant that they could not even visit Srinagar as tourists.

So Keya and her mother would listen to Veer describe the elaborate wooden houses, the bridges on the Jhelum river, the lot of the poorer Muslims, the centuries-old divine poetry of Kashmiri women mystics such as Lalla Ded, Arnimal and Habba Khatoon, the various kinds of food that stewed in pots all day long for flavour, the glowing kangris, the preparations for festivals, and the dogs that chased a prophetic madman, Nanna Mot, who had once foretold the end of Sheikh Abdullah's reign in his very own court by turning his chair upside down. In the many registers of fact and fiction and legend, Keya heard these stories, grasping at them as precious fragments of her authentic identity.

She leafed inquisitively through the voluminous books written by Englishmen and other European travellers to Kashmir over centuries. In the yellowing pages of these library reference tomes, she saw black and white photographs of houseboats on the Dal, women in exquisitely embroidered pherans, apple orchards and royal entourages. Crushed silverfish would land on her lap as she read the mannered descriptions of the 'Valley People and Customs', authoritatively provided by the imperial surveyors who generalized the 'fair-skinned mountain natives'.

One Sunday, her father taught her to make a papier-mâché box, a renowned Kashmiri craft; she painted it with green and golden Chinar leaves. The lid did not fit, the green Chinar leaf was smudged, but the small box was virtually bottomless—it held ancient yearnings in its depths.

As the school years progressed, Keya no longer had time for these sessions; she had to study Defoe or Organic Chemistry, or revise differentiation and integration for her Mathematics exams instead. Usha was increasingly busy with her double burden of home and office. Veer too toiled longer hours on projects, his health suffering from exertion and overwork.

Keya idolized her father. On some days, he was the psychoanalytic myth, a firm but dappled shadow without any essential entity, but one that was going to forever be beyond her reach. On other days, he was an ordinary man with thwarted dreams who had lived in alien places and functioned in alien languages. On still other days, he was a loving but unsettled parent, trapped in a sickly body and a job that demanded a lot out of him.

When he was no longer there, Keya would often think of all the conversations that she could have had with him. She might have led a different life if he had lived on. Might she have studied medicine if she had not seen him die? Might she never have come to England nor developed a fetish for nostalgia and exile?

Assailed by these questions, Keya stands in the bathtub holding the hot water pipe that connects to the broken shower-head in her Berlin flat, washing her hair. Weary of watching the lime seeds pirouette, she has decided to shampoo at night; she might not have time in the morning. Eddies of water form around her feet as she twists to soap her back. The evening with Leon has welled up a flood of memory—she remembers, and as always, she wants to forget that which she wants to remember most: her father's death. The death of a loved one makes no distinction between the opposites of 'want to remember' and 'want to forget'. She hiccups.

She glances at the splashing transparent water that slides off the translucent curtain; shining traces that contract as soon as the drop starts its inexorable descent, feeding its fascination for gravity. Here she is, her body and the room, the warm water and soap, smells of magnolia and camomile, halogen lamps embedded in the ceiling overhead, and the sideways mirror by the door getting slowly misted.

Yet, in her memory, she can see herself on the other side of the world, being pushed into a small stark bathroom with slime around the drain block and an unshielded bulb overhead, a bar of Lux soap and a towel hastily thrust into her hands by an older woman asking her to shower, the water cold, the weather warm, and in a room nearby, the dead body of a man, her father.

'Daddy, daddy, you,' the shoe, the Jew, I do, the uuu—reverberating sounds of jazz also hounded Plath's poem; the uuu-uuu-uuu had so many uses.

Keya can see herself standing near the window netting in the hospital corridor a little way from room number nine in the new building ward, looking out at the muddy evening sky. She was seventeen, the fingers of one hand clasped the two-by-two inch wire squares, and her eyes sought to crystallize what was before her—the sun setting, a haze of smoke, the rough shrubbery and the dusty open backyard with the shanties behind the hospital, children shrieking like sea birds—young boys of fourteen or so flying kites. The papery kites valiantly rising in the sky, the boys manoeuvring to cut each other's threads; excited skirmishes. The bleat of goats, the cries of hawkers, the shuffling of feet behind her. She is framed in this picture: captive to that death, those kites. Subsumed in the parallel currents of the living and the dead. The image would never leave her.

In subsequent years, whenever she inked billowing kites or balloons, their sinuous threads spanning the skyscape were broken. There was always a gap, a place where she had lifted her pencil or pen and left a blank where a thread should have been. This essential discontinuity had come to mark her existence, the thought of death drove a rude wedge between every present and past.

That summer day, he would breathe his last. What he had not said or seen would remain suspended everlastingly. And there would be no bridges.

He had died. But slowly. With life sucked out of his brittle yellowing frame each day; in inches and centimetres, at last, he had been forced to give up. He maintained his vitals, battling the illness for sixty days on a hospital bed. Initially, there were promises of palliatives and cures. The doctors had held out hope; Usha had worshipped at the Kali temple. On a seer's advice, she had visited the Sikh gurudwara daily for forty days, fasted and prayed, prayed and fasted. Taken good care of him, shuttling between hospital and home.

Keya was kept away. From a distance, she saw her father's epic suffering and her mother's torment. Veer did not want his daughter to be at the hospital every day. She was in the middle of Board exams that would define her life chances upon leaving school. While he was still able to, he had held Keya's hands in his and told her to be brave and make him proud. He did not want her there, he said.

'Why?' she had cried.

'You are my intellectual, my lovely darling.'

Did he know that the brooding child could not handle blood, gore, bedpans and the sight of creeping death, or did he not want his best friend—for that is what he called her when they shared their special handshake—to see him in that incomplete and incapable state?

One day, when Keya arrived at the hospital, he was particularly weak and afflicted. With the cooler malfunctioning, the 48°C temperature of Delhi summer was making him insane with discomfort; he wanted his mattress to be laid down on the floor of the room, right under the ceiling fan. The nurse and her mother achieved this with some effort, but as soon as he was settled there, he wanted to be back on the bed.

Usha's patience was breached by the lack of sleep, the stress and the turmoil. She had gruffly snapped at him to make up his mind. Keya saw her father say nothing; a tear had rolled off the corner of his eye.

Standing in a corner of the room, she had felt lumpen, viscous, null.

'If I had the energy to leave this bed and crawl to a window, I would jump out of it,' Usha had heard Veer say these helpless words towards the end. She comforted Keya that death, at least, was a respite for her father.

From his first collapse onwards, there was no agreed diagnosis; the inexact professionals had buffeted him relentlessly with tests from barium meals to bone marrow examinations, transfusions and procedures, finally misadministering an injection, causing a toxic ferrous reaction in his bloodstream—sudden acute liver failure.

The medicine-men in their white coats had killed him.

The countdown had begun: he bloated yellow, lost consciousness, gazed skyward through the slits in his partially shut eyes, gurgled as his voice would not issue forth from his sputum-blocked throat, sweat dripped through the growing facial hair, was brain dead. Relatives gathered around his bed, waiting. He was a spectacle of decay. No one should have to die thus. Blessed amulets from shrines chafed his skin and sanctified Ganga-jal from the river was sprinkled on his brow, but he was beyond rescue.

The hospital file recording his treatment was promptly misplaced by the institution, hours after his death certificate was signed. 'If you were very rich or politically connected, this would not have happened,' people whispered in the ward; the worth of a life was variable.

Keya's father was considered beautiful. In dying, he was again all that. That night back home, in a room made bare, when his body lay tightly wrapped in white cotton sheets on a slab of ice, the natural proportions had returned and his face seemed alive. An earthen lamp burned near the corpse. To Keya, his lips might have spoken, told her of his childhood, of his first love, of his voluntary exile, of his dreams and realities in imagined far homelands – she could try to understand – how he had felt being out of Kashmir, living in the festering urban melt of Delhi, and speaking in English and Hindi.

She had mourned and remourned.

Today, when Leon spoke of the search for his father, a part of her wanted to say: let it go. She who could never herself let go, how could she ever measure a death against a disappearance? Leon's father might still be alive; he could be an ordinary businessman and a loving father to a daughter like her, a traitor and a spy, a mercenary, a madman in some asylum, a beggar, a bar owner; or back in India, a solitary miser in some small town, an artist and a recluse. He could be anywhere. In a mortuary unclaimed—did they keep unclaimed bodies that long? And what about dead letters? Did they keep bodies as long as letters? Which one was kept longer? Leon's father had possibilities other than the ultimate. Leon could have an imaginary father in every stranger; her flying kites would always have strings broken in the middle.

Keya can see very clearly now who she is.

She is a girl of seventeen who has returned after weeks of staying with her relatives. Her written exams are over, but she does not aspire to be a doctor anymore. She will study anything but medicine. A cousin has dropped her home, where there is no one, the main door is locked, and a doleful song from a new release is playing at high volume somewhere in the building. Mother has taken to living in the hospital and the flat is abandoned.

She lets herself in with the duplicate key. Tomorrow, she will visit her dying father.

It is night and she thinks of her mother, who has started carrying a handful of dried red chilli powder in her purse in case she is threatened as she runs about the markets and medicine shops near the hospital at all odd hours, buying vaccines, capsules, tonics, oxygen cylinders, units of blood, food, water—pepper sprays, mobile phones, the Internet, credit cards, lollipop ladies, patient rights legislation, are things unheard-of in this place and time where accidents, deaths and events roll on.

The flat has cast off traces of its inhabitants. The walls and furniture exude an aloofness—do they know her? Has she laughed and played here? Family? What family ever resided here? They are purged clean of memory by the dust and dirt that has settled on everything. Lizards live here. In scores. She is terrified of these reptiles that surround her. They have asserted a summer sway over the flat. The way the lizards run freely about—jute-brown and plump, with ringed flicking tails, pellet eyes—chasing each other, snaking, gliding, slithering, slipping—'plop'—it seems humans have not dwelt in this place for decades.

Keya has to spend the night here as an emergency. She reaches her old room and pulls a single box bed away from the wall on which the tubelight is mounted; insects gather in abundance near the fluorescent light. She lies awake on the bed waiting for the night to pass. Hours confer with each other at ease and slowly part company at the corner of a circular walk. At 4.00 a.m., the phone rings in the other room. She looks at her wristwatch and wonders. Cautiously, she climbs out of the bed, and as she makes her way through the corridor, she is stopped in her tracks, stunned!

She cannot proceed. She cannot move. She feels nauseated.

She wants to vaporize into the air, un-see, un-be, eliminate this moment from her consciousness.

The phone is continuously ringing. A soundtrack to that gruesome sight—there is a mad revolting frenzy of two lizards on the floor in front of her; they are dancing around each other, a dreadful cavorting, around and around, on the polished cement floor, spotlit by the light filtering from the room behind her. The mouth of each is under the tail of the other, and they form a repulsive ghastly circle of flesh inches away from her. Are they copulating? With their moist slimy flesh, they wreath the moment. The O formed by their bodies swiftly moves and frolics, coiling, recoiling: O~O~O death-blood-sound—she is a lizard too; they will gird her, flesh for flesh, clamp her close, shackle and never loosen the bond. She feels them inside her mouth; she stifles her scream and runs back to the bed, keeping her eyes shut till the day breaks through.

In the morning, she leaves for the hospital. She is wearing the same clothes from yesterday, and there is kajal liner smeared over her eyelids. She does a sudden about-face at the staircase landing near room number nine, and goes to the tap trough one storey below, remembering to wash the eyeliner off. In better times, her father had admonished her for using potentially harmful chemicals. It does not matter anymore, for he cannot see her now.

She cannot see him dying either. There is an assortment of relatives planning for the hour. 'Poor girl,' they say. They mean it precisely. She is not just a poor child about to lose a parent; she is a poor girl who is more helpless because she is a girl. No one expects her to do anything. Had she been a boy, things would have been different. She would be her mother's bulwark, doing all the running around, liaising with doctors and chemists; as a boy, she would have a good number of active, helpful male friends who would do whatever they could, day and night. In the present context, even if she tried doing these things, she would not be taken seriously, girlfriends would be useless, and a new headache of keeping her safe would arise. They pity her. She resents it. They are reconciled. She hates that. She believes that her father will be all right—she has been told he is brain dead; still, she believes.

All afternoon, his throat makes rasping noises, what is he trying to say?

She sits by the bedside holding his hand, sees his face, pale, sweating, and grown over with the beard. She notices the long and complete line-of-life cut into his palms. 'His love of her isn't allowing his soul to leave his body. He is worried for his child,' people say. Her mother and others tell her to whisper in his ears, Go away, Papa. I'll be fine. We'll all be fine. End your misery. Leave this body. Go away. She does not want to perform in front of the solicitously ogling crowd of relatives, colleagues, well-wishers, couples, old people—everyone without their children; children must be kept away from tragedies—garlanding the edges of the rectangular room. She wants to shoo them away. It is not a circus, vultures. She does not want to ask him to leave his body. She will not whisper. But she does. She does. Leaning over his swollen, comatose, brain-dead body, she says something in his ears. She loves him.

Someone says his clothes need to be changed, the oxygen cylinder needs to be changed; clothes first, then the cylinder. She goes outside to the corridor and stands by the wire-mesh window for an eternity—those kites, that death. Some men play cards on a bench nearby, a stainless steel multi-compartment tiffin box sits in the middle as if arbitrating. There are other patients in other rooms.

Then she is called to the room. Urgently. Tenderly. He has died. Mother asks her to kneel at his feet. She rushes to place her hand and then her ear at his chest—he is not dead! His heart still beats! Look! Hear! She runs in search of a doctor. He arrives. Place it here! I can hear his heart beat! Hear that! She is told that she is mistaken. The sea closes up to explode over her head. She bows at his feet, an entirely new gesture fit for sacred death. Handshakes, hugs, kisses were for living bodies.

People become busy with organizing things: priests, lamps, ice, flowers, incense, food, and then later, certificate, accounts, applications. They flock with condolences and there begin weeks of grieving ceremonies. Who knows who drops in, and outside the flat, there is a congregation of shoes and slippers that any newcomer to the mourning has to walk through, one arm on the railing with peeling brown paint, avoiding the dying potted plants and stepping through the deluge of footwear. Inside, the furniture is cleared away and people sit on the floor with their backs to the wall. Old women who have never been there in seventeen years wail as if they have lost a dear one. It is ritual, she realizes, since they are not shedding any tears.

A gaunt Usha reads the *Bhagavad-Gita* by her husband's body that night. The cremation is to be the next morning. At dawn, the first monsoon shower breaks through the months of torrid heat, the plants and trees are a glabrous chartreuse green; Keya wants to be a tiny new leaf, the topmost in the tallest tree.

Then, the sun appears. Only the males are allowed to accompany the dead to the cremation ground. She does not challenge this betrayal of her father's explicit wish that his daughter light his funeral pyre. She cannot forgive herself.

5

Stories In Berlin

Sunbeams upon her eyelashes, Keya wakes up to a new morning. Where is she? This is not her room; she casts about in confusion. Is she still in the grip of the sandman and Queen Mab? Oh no, she is awake. Then she realizes that she is in Berlin. Upon meeting Leon yesterday, she had recalled her years of growing up in Delhi, and Papa's death. Isn't that why she was so moved by Leon's search?

She jumps up and makes her way to the adjoining kitchen, puts the kettle on to boil, and searches her bag for the bottle of mouthwash.

'I've got to help him,' she says to herself. Her hair is frizzy from not being blow-dried after the wash. She busies with getting ready, putting on a cream polo-neck over khaki trousers, then adding a black cotton jacket. Black pearl earrings complete the outfit. The hair is lightly gelled and tied in a ponytail. She creates a ringlet of hair on her temple by curling it around her index finger.

Switching on the radio, she hums along a love ballad playing on Berliner Rundfunk FM station while getting her laptop bag ready for the day. Meine Musik, Meine Stadt, the jingles come on. She takes out a Kamps Oliven Seele bread from the cabinet; buttered and warmed, it makes for a tasty breakfast treat.

She plots the day ahead: she will first make some phone calls to try and arrange archival access for Leon, then go to the Embassy and thank the people there who were helpful during her last visit—it would be good to re-establish contact and she might casually ask about Mir. Even though he disappeared a long time ago, someone there might have a lead. From the Embassy, she would head to meet

Professor Shivakumar, a retired East Berliner of Indian origin who was active in the 1980s. Before she can plan any further, her phone starts belting out the 'William Tell Overture'. She excitedly reaches over to see who it is.

It is Agni—the main reason for Keya's Berlin trip having gone awry—calling.

'No, I am still in Berlin.'

'Are you back from the hospital?'

'That is good news.'

Agni is sorry. She had panicked at the initial medical response to her chest pains. A session with the doctor-in-charge has confirmed that they will not keep her under observation after all. Stress from her trip to India might have been responsible for her feeling unwell. Her results are fine and she will simply need a check-up a week later. Therefore, she can see Keya at any time now.

'Thanks for this, but are you sure it is okay to meet? Do you feel up to it?'

'Good.'

'Today is difficult since I have a few things lined up. And I have to help a friend.'

'Yes, tomorrow is great.'

'Don't worry about food; I'll probably be there in the afternoon.'

Agni insists that Keya bring an appetite anyhow. They say bye.

Next, Keya dials a research centre. Her contact there is an American man, an amiable fellow who remembers her.

Upon first meeting, he had introduced himself with a handshake saying, 'Bill Gold,' with an impish smile, 'shining, ya'know, same as Bold or Fold but with a G. Some Britishers say it like it's Billy Goat.'

Bill with the droll sense of humour was in charge of the document section at a private library. Interested in Keya's research, he had asked her how she came to be working on this topic of artists in exile. A mix of her cultural studies training and a liking for people's stories, she had speculated.

While he hadn't a clue about Indians there, he knew a lot about the divided city before the Wall came down.

How did he come to his job at the library? Keya had asked in turn.

'I used to work with American officials in those days. But the city was packed with spies,' he said. 'They were everywhere.'

Hearing him speak was like being in the Berlin that now survived only in books and museums.

'There was a listening post on the top of that hill,' he had pointed in a direction.

'The embassies and missions were full of people who worked for one side or another. I just got tired of it.'

With his golden hair and twinkling eyes, he looked younger than his densely spent years, for it was clear he had seen the world.

Bill belonged to that class of which Keya increasingly knew many—a long-term expatriate, more at home in a foreign land. He had lived in Germany for decades.

'Potsdam is my home. It's beautiful, though when I initially moved there, I saw swastikas on the bus stop. In a few hours, they'd cleaned it off. It's illegal.'

If Bill had anecdotes, he also had a large body of useful information about the city; where to go and who to speak to about a certain area or period.

Keya could not help but think that, at least, some of this had been acquired first-hand. He had mentioned the thousands of spies on the East side who became jobless overnight when the Wall came down. When the Stasi ended, they were incorporated into other assorted state jobs, or worse. She wondered if Bill's distaste for the world of espionage stemmed from personal experience.

It is not an unlikely conjecture, she thinks, as the receptionist transfers the call, 'Hello. Hello! Dr Keya. How are you?'

He is on duty. Keya mentions Leon's difficulties in trying to get information about his father who went missing in the 1980s.

Bill doesn't sound optimistic; he says the search is tricky given the length of time that has elapsed. On hearing that Keya's friend is a Muslim from Kashmir, he warns that security clearance will be required.

There is no way around the procedures, but he can try to expedite matters. He gives a fax number for the documents, and his office details for Leon to visit.

She rings a few other places, then calls Leon to report the result. He sounds as if she's woken him up. It's 10.30 a.m. Belying the obvious stupor in his voice, he pretends he isn't in bed. She dictates the details of the places where he'll get access.

'I can't believe you are taking this much trouble for me. Keya, I owe you.'

'Friendships are accountless,' she shoots back, 'unaccountable and accountless.'

'You have me there,' he says.

She hangs up, reminding herself not to read layers into every phrase of his.

The Indian Embassy is in Tiergarten. It is a beautiful walk along the Lützowufer and Keya chooses the side of the canal densely lined with trees. There is a tourist boat anchored near the metallic arch of a small red bridge. The trees are greening and there is a family of swans gliding on the waters: two adults and three young ones__sssSS__a bright white troupe. A galaxy of petals scatter where an extravagantly flowering bush weighs spring's soul on its tender arms. A bird drops diagonally from a branch in front of her, chirping. The tiniest cygnet opens its beak for an instant. Keya feels unexpectedly joyous about her present. Why had she been crying last night over the miserable past? Her contemplation is halted as she arrives at the building.

There are a mere three people queuing in the visa section that she passes on her way upstairs. She has an appointment with a senior officer acquainted with her research project. It is a courtesy call, to express her gratitude for their help—'I'll thank your office in my published book and send you a copy.' Welcoming her, he speaks of the historic connexions between Berlin, Bristol and India—Max Müeller, Raja Ram Mohan Roy, Subhas Chandra Bose.

On her way out, Keya stops by the office of a clerk who has served there the longest. After enquiring about his health, she asks him if he knows anything about an Indian man by the name of Mir Ali in the 1980s in Berlin.

'He was an activist, used to come here from England where he was posted at the time.'

'And you say he just vanished?'

'That's right. Searches at the time yielded nothing.'

Mr Ramnath, the bent and balding bundle, mulls over the details. He drums his fingers on the table, rocks back and forth, then abruptly recalls something. A glimmer of recognition is evident in his bearing.

'Was this man, this Mir, from Kashmir?'

With trepidation at this unbelievably quick conclusion of Leon's search, she replies, 'Yes, he was from Kashmir. We must be thinking of the same person.'

At her eagerness, he closes like a crab, 'No, I must be mistaken. Excuse me, I was thinking of someone else.'

She is a little surprised. 'I felt sure you had an answer a moment ago.'

Ramnath fumbles, 'My memory is beset with age and confusion.'

Keya tries a mellower tone, 'Are you sure you don't know anything else, Sir?'

He is adamant he knows nothing.

'Well, please do tell me if something comes to mind,' she persists.

Softening, he says it is a remote possibility. 'I'll answer if I can—some day, if I remember.'

It is a pity Mir Ali was not a professional artist, Keya thinks. With her contacts among Indian artists in Germany, she would definitely have been able to trace more.

Potsdamer Platz is abuzz with tourists.

There are people taking pictures, sitting in the cafés, sauntering on the streets.

There are also a few motorized rickshaw-pullers, the pedicab drivers: young and able-bodied blonde European men ferrying excited sightseers around under the brightening sky.

What will the rickshawallah from Berlin say to the rickshawallah from Delhi, if they ever meet? They will probably have only the rickshaw in common, not the language, not the skin colour, and not the social status, let alone the money or worth of their labour. The guys here drive what they call Velotaxis—It is fun! Environment-friendly transport! And as operators of these vehicles, they are treated decently by their customers and the police. The scrawny Delhi rickshawallahs, like the ones all over South Asia, come from small provincial towns and villages, sleep in the slums and communal renbaseras, and earn petty cash in return for labouring in the searing summer sun and winter freeze. They have mere cycle wheels, no motor, and their legs do the hard work as they bob up and down, standing upright on the pedals to make way through the honking unruly traffic. The police, when they have a chance, beat these men mercilessly for the smallest of offences, and the city folk who depend on them, nonetheless, largely see them as pests.

The tall Sony Centre and surrounding high-rises gleam like delicacies in the sky. Loud music plays in a shopping arcade. One cute girl, possibly Brazilian, asks Keya the directions for the Brandenburg Gate and the Siegessäule. Her friend hangs behind and emits an unfriendly vibe; she appears unsure whether Keya, being the skin she is in, would know. Keya explains the route, marking it on their fold-out hotel map. When they say thanks, Keya responds by asking the sceptical girl, first in German and then in English, whether she likes the city.

'What if I had grown up in Germany and still faced that look from a tourist?' Keya thinks, as she makes her way into the underground U-Bahn to Spittelmarkt where Professor Shivakumar has his home.

She has not visited him before. He lives in a tall grey building that is one of many such structures lining both sides of a rather broad and busy avenue. The ground floors of these residential apartments are occupied by shops selling knick-knacks, Chinese restaurants, pizzerias, photo studios, hair salons. In the neighbourhood park, people are out with their dogs on leashes, some carry grocery bags, others lounge about chatting. Children play boisterously. Large billboards sit atop the roofs of the buildings; an especially remarkable one announces 'Coca-Cola!' in gigantic coloured lettering. She might as well be on the set of the movie *Goodbye Lenin*. A makeshift stall sells Marlboros in what would have been sometime East Berlin and East Germany; a GDR that made efforts to manufacture pride over Club Cola and f6 cigarettes! Keya smiles, considering that she is the least likely candidate for ostalgie, a nostalgia for the East, but she knows she is heading to meet someone afflicted with it.

Professor Shivakumar has lived through communism, and published on the East Bloc achievements in addition to his biology textbooks. In his correspondence with Keya, he mentioned that he misses the world that he was used to.

The downstairs door to his building opens with a discordant buzzing sound after she announces herself on the intercom. From Slovenia to Poland, ex-East Germany and many places else, these Panelák Plattenbauen type of prefabricated blocks were the functionalist architectural form that had sought to provide large quantities of affordable low-cost housing to as many as possible. It is concrete and grim. The hallway is cluttered with letterboxes, and the narrow cell-like lift opens with a creaky double shutter and moves with a loud clatter. Despite this, Keya thinks, it is convenient assembly-line housing, not to be scoffed at, especially in view of the shivering Parisian and San Franciscan homeless who sleep every night on pavement hot air vents, around the corner from the swanky diamond, leather and fashion shops of Champs Élysées and the Union Square.

The Professor is in a good mood.

'My wife Lydia is away at our dacha these days,' he says, as soon as they shake hands. 'Here is a portrait of us done by a Soviet artist who was a childhood friend of hers.'

As it is an unstructured interview, he speaks at length and keeps returning to his favourite themes and historical moments, avidly sharing copies of his earlier publications.

'The Wall was necessary, every country needs a border.'

'People of GDR liberated themselves. It was their consciousness.'

'The intellectuals crossing over to GDR of their own will is downplayed.'

'Our trouble was mediocrity, bureaucracy, and an inability to deal with pluralism—but this inability is a wider European problem of Leitkultur, isn't it?'

Quoting theoreticians of bygone eras, he stresses on the merits of the communist era, in particular the artistic achievements of the East Bloc, and their pro-Third-World attitude. Keya marvels at his devotedness to an ideology that has been near-universally derided.

'Did you never feel censored?'

'I faced prejudice, but that was because the system did not work properly at the end,' he replies, referring to the events in the run-up years to 1989. 'Our system could have been corrected; it was not necessary to dismantle it. The capitalist mode of production will collapse, there is hope in the future. Have you seen what they have done at Checkpoint Charlie? It is a rip-off, so blatantly self-congratulatory.'

The interview ends with a rhetorical flourish. He quotes, 'Which society is more wrong—one which is wrong a lot every day, or a little for a long time?'

When it is time to go, she casually asks, 'Did you happen to know, or know of, a certain Mir Ali in the 1980s? He was a communist activist.'

'Activist? I didn't know any activists. Communism is first achieved through ideas in the head; we still had not perfected that. I had theorist friends, philosophers.'

He comes to his balcony to see her off, waving till she is out of sight.

Keya decides to spend the rest of the day back at the flat. She types up her notes and works on an article for a magazine special issue on 'Multiculturalism in the face of terror.' Connecting her laptop to a wireless network, she checks her university email. Even though she is on leave, there are bound to be students emailing for references or extensions, and maybe there are comments circulating after the Faculty Board meetings.

Logging out of her completed session, she realizes she is starving. In no mood for cooking, she changes into a denim skirt and sweater, taking care to wear matching earrings, and steps out. She is going to Nollendorfplatz, the stylish gay heart of Berlin; an Indian restaurant there serves spicy flavoursome food.

The evening is vivid and the walk long. She sees a fabulous fish-shaped pink cloud against the lilac sky. As she passes a glass-fronted bookshop, she recollects Leon's mention of Goethe's *Elective Affinities*.

The sibilant *ffffs* of those chemical-passionate affinities ring in her ears. She finds herself unmoored and lingering at the distant doors of fantasy.

She can't buy the book because the shop is closed, she can't call Leon because…well, because she would rather he call her, so she distracts herself by running through the number directory on her phone. The highlighted band of colour shifts from one entry to the next; she is uncertain who to call. At last, she dials her mother Usha, the safest bet.

'Hello, Mother, is it late for you?'

'No, I am in Berlin this week.'

'Yes again.'

'How did your doctor's appointment go?'

'Any other news?'

'Wow! Some people will not get a hint, huh?'

'They said that?'

'Well, tell them it's not a vegetable market, and anyway, it's not their problem. Do they really want to take responsibility for arranging it? I'll live however I want.'

'Who cares. I mean, let them. I am what I am.'

'Fair enough. What?! This year? Yes, maybe.'

'Fine then, take care, love you too, bye.'

Her mother told her that an aunt was suggesting a groom for her. Apparently, since Keya was living alone abroad, she was bound to be morally lax. So it was fortuitous that a divorcee computer programmer based in Silicon Valley had, out of pity, agreed to communicate with her with a view to a possible match. What pretence! Keya cannot stand the idea of these shenanigans called Arranged Marriages. Column upon column of newsprint in the Classifieds—with categories such as 'Brahmin', 'Scheduled Castes', 'Manglik', 'Agarwal', 'Handicapped', 'NRI and Settled Abroad'—where every kind of prejudice was honoured in the name of culture and tradition. In the West too, the brouhaha about the colourful, joyful Indians celebrating middle class marriages, Bollywood style, had captured people's imagination. It was frustrating indeed: the Indian woman is a paragon of virtue trained in oriental docility and family values; she and her man dance around mango trees when in India, and speak terrible English when they step off the boat in the West.

At the eatery, Keya takes a table under the tarpaulin awning and sips a mint julep. Taking time to study the menu, she orders a vegetarian meal. A rose-seller from the street comes up and offers a cellophane-wrapped red rose. She says, 'No thanks.'

'Why? You look so kind, won't you help a poor lame man?'

'I have no need of roses.'

'You are from England?'

'Yes, I live there. How did you guess?'

'I'm from Bangladesh. My brother is in England. In Bradford. I went to see him once.'

'What do you do there?'

A waiter asks Keya if she is all right, presumably trying to help in case she is being bothered.

'I'm fine,' she says, then turning to the rose-seller, 'I teach.'

'How good. My son also teaches in a madrasa in Dhaka. He began last year. I am proud of him.'

'Do you have any daughters?'

'No. By the grace of God, I have four sons.'

'Your wife is in Berlin?'

'Oh no. She is with my family back home. It is very difficult to get legalization papers for them to join me in Europe. Inshallah, some day, I will go back with enough money so I never have to come back here again,' he sighs.

'Is it tough here?'

'I live in a hovel with other Bangladeshis; we need to stick together in case of difficulty, like if a dead body needs to be sent back home.'

'Will you like a glass of juice?'

'Daughter, that's very generous of you. If you like, I can.'

'I am Keya. What is your name?'

'Ruhul Amin.'

Keya beckons the waiter and asks for an orange juice.

'Give it in one of the plastic glasses,' Ruhul requests the waiter.

'Can you do me a favour? I have a pound coin that one Englishman gave me some time ago. Can you change it into euros for me? The currency office don't change coins, they said.' Saying this, he takes out a two-pound coin and offers it to Keya.

'Absolutely.' She checks her purse and hands him a five euro note in return for the coin.

'Isn't that too much?'

'No, you gave me two pounds and I've added a bit extra, that's all.'

Ruhul takes the juice, explaining, 'The plastic glasses are reusable. And I can take it away so you are not disturbed any more.'

Keya smiles.

'Thank you, daughter. Here is a rose for you. It is my gift.' He leaves a rose on the table and hastily departs.

'Take care,' she calls after him.

Keya regards the flower that lies aslant on the pink gingham tablecloth. In a minute, her phone sings.

It is Leon.

He says that he has been to the library and will chase the remaining leads. He has not found anything on Mir but, 'Perhaps'.

That 'Perhaps' followed by no other words reminds her of Shantanu, her first boyfriend. He would call her from a payphone PCO—there were no mobiles in India then—and when she asked him something difficult or when they reached a sticking point, he would slowly whisper, 'Perhaps,' and fall silent.

'Where are you?' Leon asks.

'In Schöneberg. About to have dinner.'

'With company?'

'Yes, a rose-seller from Bangladesh, but he just left,' Keya laughs. A pause. 'Great. So, we meet tomorrow then?'

'As you like, I'm free in the evening. Where?'

'Let's see. You know Berlin inside out. I know Alexanderplatz. How about somewhere there, in that area?'

'No problem. Have you seen the Neptunbrunnen fountain in front of Rotes Rathaus. It's not far from Alex.'

'Umm, is that the fountain of the four giant women?'

'Exactly. That's it.'

'Okay. How about at five?'

'Perfect. At five, you can find me near one of the four.'

'I wonder which,' he quips, as they say bye.

Eating her naan and alu gobi masala, Keya recalls the conversation with her mother. She has promised to visit India this year. Keeping the academic term in mind, August is the only viable option, she concludes. Skipping dessert, she briskly walks back to the flat and has an early night.

The next morning, she wakes up to the sound of a screeching tyre on the street outside. There is an underground car park across the road.

She has a late morning in bed with her laptop, while she browses the web for news. Still in her satin négligée and slippers at ten o'clock, she makes a cup of breakfast tea and calls Agni to fix a meet at noon.

A few minutes before the designated time, she reaches Agni's lush residential street. Though Keya has corresponded with Agni in the past, she wonders what kind of a meeting it will be. Each encounter is unique. The way in which people prefer to make sense of their life is reflected in their choice of storytelling mode, mien, physical environment, attire and behaviour towards Keya herself. With some interviewees, she has to keep asking questions; with others, she needs to be aware of their efforts to take charge. People often want to emphasize specific aspects of their life and work, balanced by a much greater reluctance to disclose the rest. It is like being a biographer of many people's lives, all incomplete, all fragmented. She never feels she can do total justice to the many layers of expression she is presented with.

Keya raps on Agni's door before she notices the well-concealed bell under the paperwork decorations that hang outside. Under a count of three, Agni opens the door wide and apologizes for the wait, welcoming her in warmly. Keya finds herself in a flat that resembles Professor Shivakumar's in size, but the set-up could not be more different. Shivakumar had been in equal measures relaxed, cautious, enquiring, judging and peremptory. Agni is spry, enthusiastic, trusting, and maybe even apprehensive about how she is going to come across in the story of her life in her own words.

Keya enquires after her health. 'Much better,' Agni says, as she leads the way into a well-furnished living room decked with framed stills from her theatre and film days. There are autographs of Indian movie stars from the 1950s, and a picture of Agni in a group of dancers with the then Prime Minister, Nehru. As Keya studies these images from Agni's youth, her host excuses herself, returning with cups of green tea and roasted crackers.

'Those were the glory days. I was famous,' she says, setting the tray down. 'I used to be interviewed weekly at that time. All that attention from boys and men—Madam, please, I love you—what a nightmare!' Agni does a comic impersonation of a star besieged by fans. Keya joins in the joke, trying not to think of scenes from *Sunset Boulevard*. They sit down.

Keya's opening question is about why Agni uses two names. The

Agnes is for the Germans and the Indians she does not know much. Also, for those she does not like. It is the Oriya Christian in India part of her. Agni is fire; it is her spirit name and descriptor, her name as an Indian artist in Berlin. She speaks theatrically, on stage in perpetuum. She is casually but carefully dressed, and attentive to every inch of her svelte, if aged, body. Radiating emotion, she talks about her experience of being an artist in exile, and Keya listens. When she repeats, 'My life is nothing short of extraordinary,' she is hardly exaggerating.

As she takes notes, Keya begins to perceive that the diminutive and effervescent old woman sitting opposite her has lived an immensely colourful life. Undaunted by the social mores, Agni had trained in dancing and chosen to act in films in an era when doing this was considered unthinkably 'bold' for girls from good families.

'My God, that journey from Cuttack in the East to Bombay in the West to give my first screen test for the talkies. I still recall it vividly. My mother almost got a heart attack. It seems only like yesterday.' A producer who smoked foreign cigars as he went about in large convertibles selected her on the spot. 'I had a screen presence,' she bubbles; instinctively, her fingers caress the rugose cheeks, 'but breaking into stardom was not easy.' She played second lead in a few movies, the vamp, the siren, the sister.

Keya can understand how meaningful those early achievements must have been when she sees a file of the newspaper cuttings and certificates from the period. Agni had received accolades for her melodramatic performances in the golden age of cinema in newly independent India.

'I would have become a proper heroine—as it is, the audience loved me, but,' she exults, 'I was swept off my feet by the love of a German man. So I quit and came here. Ahh! My exile.' She married her lover and moved to Berlin to find that she could do nothing to please her domineering mother-in-law, who liked her son to hold on to her apron strings. They had a child, but split up before long. She could not go back to the movies in Bombay as a married mother, and there was no Indian theatre or cinema in Germany. Agni set up from scratch a classical dance and theatre company, from which she had recently retired after an active involvement of decades.

'Dance did not need language; it was universal. And I got to meet some men who knew how to use their bodies,' she winks. Agnes became Agni, the dancer who brought Indian culture to the West German island of Berlin in the Eastern part of Germany.

When she first arrived in the city, there had been no physical partition. But within years, the lines got drawn ever more rigidly, and she gradually lost many friends who lived on the East side of the city. She wiped from her mind the memory of the East, including their ideology, politics and reasons for the Berlin Wall. She had seen it go up and come down, and been profoundly affected by it.

For Agni, the Wall was a blank and dark fact that ominously sprung up one night when she was celebrating her wedding anniversary. 'We were eating, drinking, making merry—when we heard the shouts, the shots; turn on the radio, someone said, turn off the lights, someone said. I blew out the candles on our cake and collapsed. When I came to, I was hysterical and frantic.' She drinks daintily from a glass of water before continuing, 'I had come here from a continent partitioned in two on the eve of my adulthood, to a city sliced in half on my anniversary,' she declaims, 'I am an artist, I used the pain; this theme of divided lives was the basis for a dance-drama we performed; 'Moiety' it was called.' She shows Keya a programme brochure.

'What were your experiences in establishing yourself as an artist in a country where you were not born?'

Agni speaks of the language barriers, the historical circumstances, the painstaking process of getting the resources to set up her dance and theatre school. 'There have been many battles along the way.'

Going over dear memories, her eyes flit like a bird glancing around to muster the various viewpoints. Intermittently, her chain of thought wanders, and she ends up talking about something completely different, repeating things to keep them alive.

They take a break and Agni asks Keya to have lunch. She is not hungry, 'it really is not necessary', but they end up having asparagus soup and Zwiebelbrot anyway. During this interlude, Keya enquires if Agni has ever known or heard of anyone called Mir Ali in 1980s Berlin. She is dunking a piece of onion bread in the soup when Keya asks, and she pauses to think long enough that the bread falls into the tureen.

'Mir,' Agni finally exhales.

Then she says she is not sure, she might need to look at some old documents, a friend of hers may have mentioned him. She divulges no more. In the next part of the interview, the focus is on Agni's cultural métier and how that has validated her sense of existence. She speaks at length and there are printed memoirs from the period. Keya gets restless as the evening approaches. She assures Agni that she will be back the next day and excuses herself.

A policeman brusquely wags his finger at me, 'Mister, step back.'

I take a step back and wait on the pavement for a cavalcade to cross on the main road. There are at least thirty security vans and the police have completely cordoned off the area. A cyclist who has stopped at the signal guesses aloud, 'Maybe it is a Hollywood star.' When the roadblock is lifted and the go-ahead given, I overhear a local man nonchalantly tell a tourist, 'It is some important minister from Israel. We have to be careful; there was arson at a Jewish memorial outside Berlin a few days ago.'

For my rendezvous with Keya, I reach the large fountain adorned with beautiful bronzed sculptures. At the centre is the martialist sea-god Neptune with his trident. Surrounding him on a circular parapet sit four towering women, equal spaces apart. I walk around the fountain slowly, deliberating her choice. The first statue I pass reclines with grapes and a large fishing net on her lap. She looks regal and wistful. The one after her holds a pitcher of water, posing to peer over her shoulder, pensive and lost. The square is teeming with people. Before the next one, I pause and wait for tourists who are taking photographs of each other. They ask me to click them together; I consent. Then they move away and I see the third statue of a woman leaning back with a skinned animal in her lap, gazing sadly and dreamily at a vessel. The last figure stares ahead with one leg folded; she holds a sickle and a branch of an apple tree laden with fruit. She seems vaguely to hope and expect. They are all nearly naked and astonishingly alive, despite their larger-than-life size. Keya does know how to select meeting spots!

A dog barking fiercely at a short distance diverts my attention. It is a funny sight; a tiny intrepid terrier is desperately trying to provoke a dog five times bigger. It rushes and lunges at the large dog who maintains a studied calm. The owners chortle merrily as they try to get them apart. Onlookers are amused; I film a few seconds of the encounter with my camera.

Catching sight of Keya, I steal upon her from behind and utter the words, 'So you were unable to choose then.'

Startled, she smiles. 'They are beautiful. I could fall in love with every single one of these four statues.'

'Are you always this generous with your affections?'

'Not always, only when I feel happy around certain people. Leon—'

'Could I—' I speak at the same time as her.

'What?'

'Sorry, you were about to say something. You go first,' I say.

'Nothing significant. I was just wishing I knew who built this fountain or what the statues represent. Let us try to find an information plaque around here.'

I am delighted to have done my preparation for meeting a curious researcher type. I say, 'Keya, they depict the four rivers in Germany, and a sculptor called Begas made them.'

'From the nineteenth century?'

'1891, to be precise.'

'I suppose you know the names of the rivers too?'

'Guilty as charged. The Oder, the Rhine, the Vistula, and uh-oh! Damn, I forgot the last one!'

'Better luck next time. Did you say the Vistula? How like our Vitasta it sounds.'

'Hmm, to be honest, I'm not so crazy over rivers.'

'You are awesome, how do you know though? When we spoke on the phone yesterday, you barely recognized it as the fountain of the four women.'

'What a difference a day makes! Your exactness is inspiring me to know my Begas from my Degas,' I jest.

'Good for you. Now tell me what you were about to say.'

'Ask. I wanted to ask if I could take some pictures of you.'

'Here?'

'Yes. That golden light of the setting sun is my favourite colour.'

'Ah-an. How should I pose?'

'Don't. Be yourself. I'll do the rest.'

In a coral red dress against the flaming sunset, she glows. I take photos of her, adjusting the lens and stepping around, cocking my head, kneeling, pretending I am a total professional. When I finish trying the fancy angles, she borrows my camera and takes a straight shot of me in close-up.

'Don't forget to send me a copy of my skilful shot,' she instructs.

'I can even arrange the original to be delivered in person.'

Why am I flirting? I have no clear idea. But I am. There is a bond. We banter back and forth. Pick up the threads of words and take them further, spinning, seizing upon connexions. Walking and talking, we start towards somewhere.

I ask how her day has been. She actually tells me in unnecessary detail about a woman she met and had a long conversation with. I do not press further. We cross the road and wander into gardens with delectable names like Lustgarten and Kupfergraben; they open treasures when Keya details their meaning.

Couples of all ages stroll by, groups of people laugh, a pair of Frisbee-playing lovers kiss. Keya turns her head to follow a poster on the side of a moving double-decker bus that goes past, and signals me to her returning glance; I see our shadows behind us.

She says, 'Look, two elongated outlines that take on the matter and form of whatever they cross.'

'Yes, it is strange that our shadows never desert us,' I give a ludicrous reply.

I like how I feel. I haven't felt this light in a long time. I say nothing about my reasons for being in Berlin. I sense that she, too, wants us to consciously act like two people who have just met in a new city and have a lot to talk about and discover.

I apprise her of my wanderings in London. I have taken hundreds of photographs; I could show them to her someday. 'Not hundreds!' I promise.

Keya enlightens me about a director whose movies I have heard of, but not seen: Tarkovsky. Movies such as *The Mirror* and *Nostalghia*. 'They are terrifically visual. I watch his films, and while watching them, I forget that I am watching them, you know what I mean?' Her shoulders move to the emphasis of her words. 'It is like I see the screen, and then, when I return to seeing the screen again, I realize that I have been watching the screen all this time, but without realizing it, I have been watching another story, my own images have been placed on the screen before me.'

I nod.

'Anyway, if I go on about the politics of cinema by exiles, it'll bore you. It's too sentimental,' she reflects.

'I'd love to be a bone-dry cynic and I try, but I can't resist sentimentality,' I offer.

'Sentiments are not in fashion,' she casually replies.

'Owning up to them is not in fashion,' I retort.

'Sentiments are the stuff of cinema, literature and music. Who wants to shed a tear over art when compared with the actual sufferings around us?'

I cannot deny that, but I press on, 'Actual sufferings?'

'Yes, like when people die and starve, get killed.'

'Unlike the fabled sufferings of love,' I conjecture.

'Hmm. Unlike love, because it is self-inflicted.'

'I disagree,' I state, 'We cannot choose when or why to suffer.'

She smiles at my naiveté, 'We choose to inflict love. But when a fatal illness strikes, we must die.'

'Right. In an illness, we may die. And we suffer. In love, we suffer, and sometimes die.'

'You are winding me up,' she says perkily.

'Sorry,' I reply, sparkling. 'Can I buy you dinner as a peace offering?'

'You don't need to. But go ahead.'

Going past a building, we see enticingly enlarged images of produce—fresh carrots with leaves and traces of earth on them, water-splashed tomatoes, peas in pods agape on the stem—that whet the appetite. We go in for dinner at this crowded self-service restaurant. It is a popular joint, she tells me, pointing out a large dandelion clock painted to cover an inside wall. The atmosphere is incredible.

'Get me anything. I am flexible,' she says.

Carefully decoding the labels, I pick Bratwurst with Sauerkraut and Kartoffelsalat for myself, and Kasespaetzle and a slice of Stollen for her, while she stands on alert to grab any table that might be vacated. We get two good seats at the back and tuck into the hearty fare.

In between mouthfuls, I tell her how I came to be interested in photography. It was a passion that replaced playing cricket when I moved to London.

'What is yours? Gathering stories?' I hazard.

'So it is,' she answers.

'How come you're not a writer then? Or do you write in addition to doing your university work?'

'It is difficult to get the time. Anyway, writers tell stories. I'm not sure whether it is the telling that I am interested in, or the collecting.'

'But what can one do with gathered stories instead of retelling them? With photos, I can store them in albums or on files. Don't the stories you collect make you want to share them?'

'I don't know…I kind of like holding on to other people's stories. They start to become a part of me, and then I feel I am living lots of lives instead of just this one.'

'How vicarious,' I comment, 'in a beautiful way.'

'Why beautiful?'

'Mm, it's like writers are people who write books, then there are people who get written about in books—the former make stories, the latter are stories—and then there are those who live life like it was a book.'

'I live in a storybook world?'

'Don't you? The way you nurture other people's stories, make them your own, as you just said.'

'Do you know deconstruction?'

'Only the name Derrida. It's academic philosophy, isn't it?'

'It is. And I have a feeling you might like some of that work.'

'Yes teacher,' I mime.

'I know. It is an occupational problem. I have to guard against being advisory. I don't mean to patronize.'

As I speak, my gaze falls on a dog under the table next to ours. It is staring at us with spaced-out eyes. His owner sees me and says, 'Hello!' We respond to his greeting.

'Are you young people enjoying Berlin?' he affably asks.

'Yes. You?'

'Oh yes! I've been in Germany for twenty-five years. Twelve in Berlin. It's good.'

'Your dog is very quiet and well-behaved,' Keya compliments.

'She likes listening to you smart people!' he chuckles good-humouredly. 'Her name is Lollipop. Lolly, Lollo, Lola, I call her. I don't like Lollipop so much.'

He extends his hand, 'I'm Tsehaye.'

'Keya.' 'Leon.' We shake hands, and falter in trying to repeat his name correctly.

'Tse-ha-ye. It means sunshine in Ethiopian language. You know Ethiopia?'

Before we can reply, he prompts us on 'Haile Selassie. Rastafari.'

'It's also the setting for *Rasselas*,' I say.

'And there's the tragic Ethiopia-Eritrea conflict in the news,' she adds.

'Right on. Good man. And lady. I've finished my food, I'll go now. Lola here is sleepy. I carry her around in my bike basket. She's lovely. Come, Lollo, we'll let these people enjoy themselves.'

'Goodbye. Have fun!'

'And you.'

It is late when we leave the eatery; the night sky outside is silvered by a slice of waxing moon shining above the trees and behind the buildings. Dressed up groups of young men and women are shouting, laughing and going to clubs. We toss between going for a coffee or a movie, then decide upon neither. The warm food and the conversation has put me in another universe; it's the kind of universe where lovers and good friends and old friends dwell; a generous universe where I can forgive with ease, smile at little things, see pleasant hidden meanings, and grope forward. We walk aimlessly, our hands touching, our bodies close.

By and by, we are in a cobblestone street near a pub with green doors. Keya reads the German sign and tells me it's been in existence for nearly four hundred years. 'We need to have a drink here then,' I say. We walk into the Zur Letzten Instanz and passing the diners, go to the bar. Seated on high stools at a polished table in the corner of a room where everything is preserved in a rustic old style, we down shots. 'Tschüss!' she whispers, looking into my eyes. 'The German cheer,' she demystifies. 'Tschüss!' I reply, 'It sounds like a kiss.' Pleasantly tizzy, we toddle out after some time. The barmaid gives us souvenir matches as a departing present, 'Have a nice night in Bairleen.'

Keya scat sings a jazz tune as we pass by a gazebo. Standing above the neon lamplights embedded in the ground in the midst of a park square, we desire to know more about each other, to know each other more. I feel it, for sure. It is a pleasantly blurred moment and neither of us is sure how it would end. Our fingers lattice, shoulders comply, noses touch. We kiss for a time: lips meeting in quick succession at first, and then exploratively. When I am all afire, she pulls away without a reason, retreating. It is unbearable. We are running back into our selves like coltish children and playing safe. Then, like magnet parts, our bodies draw together, interlacing again. For several seconds, we hold each other close, silently, without making any movement.

'What's your favourite flower?' I ask, my lips grazing her earlobes.

'Calla lily,' she says.

'I've never seen it. Describe it for me. Please.' I catch my breath.

'It… it's a folded spiral flower, um, a curving st… strip of petal… long stemmed. Enclosed. Around a centre column, cream coloured…'

'Tell me more.' I want her to keep speaking; the words are helping me tide the rush of sensations.

'I see a field of calla lilies and—' she is breathless too.

A clock chimes midnight. A peal of bells rings through our bodies.

'The subway will close,' she is sobering, 'Let us go.'

She mouths goodnight and touches my lip in a final kiss before walking away.

As I stand glued to the spot, I see her break into a run, her shadow getting longer as she gets farther from me.

I curse the universe.

Then, in a magic coin of a moment, I see her slow down as she reaches the road. She turns back—yes, back—and walks determinedly in my direction. Step by wonderful step. I stay rooted till she is a few paces from me.

'Leon, do you want to come with me to my flat?' she asks.

'Yes, Keya,' I advance with docility.

I am surprised by the rapidity of it all, but certainly am more than kicked about it. In a state of arousal, I have no desire to pause and deliberate. I let my body lead; in fact, to be honest, for the most part, I let myself follow Keya's lead.

On the silent night bus ride to Keya's home, we stand closer than warranted by space. Surely she can feel my hardness but does not move away. Good, otherwise, it would have been an embarrassing sight for the other passengers. I barely hear Keya's constant flow of words as I resist the temptation to kiss her savagely and tear her clothes right there. If only the world around us could freeze for a moment, I'd take this woman here and now. Fuck her mercilessly. But all I can do is rub myself against her slightly, nuzzle at her neck. Gosh, how does she manage to continue speaking while all this is going on? I control myself as we say thank you and goodnight to the driver and walk towards her place.

I steady somewhat, not sure where exactly we are going to end up.

As soon as we enter her flat, she stops her monologue and turns to say something to me softly. I lean into her and my ear is bitten hard. A shiver of pain and pleasure runs down my spine. I had forgotten how my ears were so sensitive that a split second of bite could make me hard as a rock. Keya the cerebral transforms into Keya the uninhibited.

I don't actually tear her clothes, nor do I fuck her mercilessly as I was fantasizing in the bus. But my hesitation does not stop her from unbuttoning my shirt with a demanding urgency, from snatching away my belt, leaving me to take off my jeans immediately. I stand naked while she has everything on. Her eyes reflect a mix of surprise and adventure. 'I have never seen a circumcised one before,' she utters, almost conspiratorially, as if she were talking about someone else. But, unlike the sex with that woman in the library, I don't feel shy about being exposed. I enjoy the lust in her eyes; she ogles at me as if she is a child who gets the candy she has been demanding. Another discovery for me—Leon the active man rather enjoys being devoured by a woman. I let her savour me, consume me.

As I move to unclothe Keya, she stops me, opens the fold-down bed, but instead of lying on it, she pulls the mattress down to the floor and closes the bed frame. My clueless expression merely makes her smile and she pushes me down on the mattress. She dims the light, takes her clothes off in an excruciatingly slow manner, deriving a high from my torture. She leaves her bra and panty on. At least I get to do something! As she sits on top of me, I pull her down and kiss. In the heat of the moment, I am not sure we have touched lips since leaving the park. She lets me. She lies on top of me. With a feverish intensity, I snap open her bra, cup her boobs, knead them as if it is my sacred duty to do so, kiss and suck them. While sucking the firm nipples, I sense my hands sliding down and fingers pushing under her G-string. She does not resist as my forefinger and thumb reach a spot of wetness and enter it, as if it is the only natural thing to do. I push open her mouth with my hungry tongue. I sense her shaking and shivering and I almost lose myself, but her expression remains one of control and she stops. She abruptly gets off me and fumbles inside her bag. For a condom. As she throws the packet at me, she removes the last vestige of cotton from her body. I untie her hair and she sits on me again. Grinding slowly but surely. I feel myself engulfed by a hot tightness which only ends when it has extracted every drop of me. I see why she had put the mattress on the floor.

She collapses on me, our bodies wet and sweaty. Suddenly, Keya the confident becomes Keya the vulnerable. I hold her in my arms. I stroke her back. She coos, and soon, dozes off. I get up, go to the toilet, remove the used condom, pee and look at myself in the mirror. There are love bites all over my body. I come back to the room and observe her while standing, silent, still. She has a great body and even more hot moves. Why had I not noticed this before? As I watch her, she turns over, exposing her entire body. I am erect again. Usually, after I masturbate, I don't get hard-ons so soon. Well, this is a night of new discoveries about myself.

I lie next to Keya. I cannot resist playing with her lips, very gently to start with. As she wakes up and before she gets the chance to analyse everything, my finger movement becomes more urgent and rough and my other hand goes down. A healthy doze of porn and my teenage fumblings with Maya, rather than actual sex with that other woman, have given me better and more graphic ideas. I find her clitoris, play with it, rub it and she squirms. Very soon, my thumb moves to and fro inside her. The image of tens of thousands of inked thumbs pressing down on sheets of paper in lieu of signatures flashes inside my head. She remains eagerly passive as I enter her. We make love again, leisurely this time. Our hips involuntarily move in unison to let us probe each other even more. I want to touch all possible nerves inside her. I last longer than the last time. By the end of it, we are drained. We smile like two cats who got the cream.

Meanwhile, Another Part Of The World,
A Few Decades Ago

6

Shula Farid's Unwritten Autobiography

Both my parents are like unwavering straight lines in my imagination. They had a simple approach to life that included settling into their environment and doing their best under the circumstances.

Baba and Ma had married late—he was forty-five and she was thirty-two when they met, and by that age, they had outgrown the ideals that may have surrounded them in their youth. Zealous patriotism was rampant in the decades after Indian independence, and the world at large was shivering through a million crises in the 1960s, but my parents were happy in their small world of earning a living, keeping house, and wishing their neighbours well. I grew up blissfully unaware of anything beyond idyllic Santiniketan.

Baba was, first and foremost, a Mathematics Professor—he was appointed a Reader, though everyone always called him Professor—in the department at Bengal's Visva-Bharati University. The son of a village schoolmaster, he took great pride in his educational achievements. A confirmed eccentric, Baba lived in an abstract parallel realm of outlines and forms in space.

My childhood memories comprise instances where he would shout urgently for me—'Shula! Come here quickly, child'—and when I would reach, running in from the outdoors with dust in my hair and under my nails, he would ask, 'I called you, did I? Oh yes, here, look at this. I made this paper toy for you. Run your finger along this plane, it is straight, but see how strange it would be if we were to make an oval from it.' I'd hesitate to show him my muddied hands, but he would not even notice my griminess.

'Here, Shula, do you see the cowlick on my head?'

'Where?'

'This, here——,' he would point to a tuft of hair, 'See, the hair here stands up because it grows in a different direction to the rest. If I sketch it on paper, you can see two kinds of radiating spirals— imagine them as mirror images of each other. Yet, when we rotate this shape—'

'Ma is calling me,' I'd make an excuse and hurry back to my dolls.

Seating me in his lap, Baba would try to make me listen in to fervent discussions on topology he had over cups of tea with his keener students. The sole striking fact I vividly remember from these conversations is the theoretical conclusion that at any given time, some point on the earth's surface is windless.

He would, in his spare time, try and explain to me the connexions between objects, and the significance of holes in solid surfaces. These erratic attempts at my education gave him profound pleasure, for he would pat my head and tell me of the day when I would become a great scientist like Jagdish Chandra Bose. Saddled with a child's distractions, I would remember very little of what I heard. Many years later, when I discovered the artwork of Escher in Europe, I wished that I had paid more attention to that strange knowledge of objects and mathematical impossibilities.

Baba was often out teaching. In this unique rural university founded by Rabindranath Tagore, classes could be an informal affair, going on for hours under the shade of large Peepal trees.

I liked spending time with Ma. She and I would play treasure hunt around the cottage. A porcelain doll was the treasure in these games. I'd hide her and with a piece of chalk draw arrows for clues. As Ma tried to find the doll, I'd goad her by taunting impatiently, 'Khoje-cho? Khoje-cho?' To this short 'Did you find it?' she would jokingly call out, 'Ay-khune naa, maye'—Not yet, girl. Her weird accent was different from anyone else's manner of speech in the town; I loved hearing it.

I thought Ma was the prettiest woman in the world, even though she dressed sloppily and spoke queerly. She was an outsider in the community. Her family were Jews from East Europe; none had survived the Holocaust. She had moved to the Soviet Union and worked for years in a garment factory. The one time that my father travelled outside India, he went on a government-sponsored trip for young scientists and mathematicians to the USSR. As part of the project on industrial mathematics and statistics, he was taken to a garment factory to study the stretching ratios of threads and the slippage of materials. He had met my mother there. She had a hard life and wanted to escape from the country. My father was able to get her admission to a course at his university. She arrived in India on that pretext, and some time later, they decided to get married; or rather, my father decided that he could imagine a life with someone else. She moved in with him at the cottage and I was born soon after.

Over the years, she acclimatized; she had learnt to speak Bengali and could manage broken Hindi and English, she tied the saree tolerably well, she dyed her light brown hair into jet black, and she cooked great food.

When she would seat me on the red stone floor of our bungalow and, from the chair behind me, braid my hair in the evenings, my mind would bristle with questions about her past. In asking them, I would forget even to wince at the sharp bursts of pain when she tugged hard at my oiled serpent-clustering hair that sat weightily on my head.

'Ma, what was your childhood like?'

'Did your mother oil and plait your hair in the same way?'

'How far is your mother's village? Is it even further than Calcutta?'

'Are there swings there? What about mosquitoes?'

'Does a train go there?'

'Why did your family die?'

These questions about the fabric of a life were infinitely more exciting to me than the holes in imaginary surfaces that preoccupied my father. Ma would give vague answers that did not satisfy my curiosity, or her statements would contradict each other, or change if I repeated the question. I'd feel cheated and respond by pleading. Cleverly distracting me till my hair was done, she would finish with, 'Shula, let yesterdays be.'

I would sulk and she ignored me until the smells of her cooking drew me to the kitchen against my will. Then she would wipe her fingers, clap her hands on my shoulders, and kneeling, look into my eyes, tenderly calling me 'Shul! Shuli! Shula! What will she get for dinner today? Hahn? Something she likes? Or not?'

When it was something I did not like eating, such as spinach or other leafy vegetables, Ma would force-feed me by trickery.

'Shula, this is a special morsel. It looks like bitter gourd and rice, but when you put it in your mouth, it will turn into fish curry and rice. Truly!'

She would eat some and pretend it had changed into tasty fish in her mouth.

'Silly girl, try it for yourself and see!'

I would. 'It didn't, Ma. It's still horrible.'

'Very well, let me check.' She would examine the plate.

'Shula, the rice says you need to eat five more morsels before it'll change gourd pieces into fish flesh.'

'I won't.'

'Yes, you will. One for Ma. One for Baba. One for the bird outside. One for your porcelain doll. One for—'

There were enough things to keep me busy. I danced in front of the mirror, blew soap bubbles, and played with the trees and shrubs in our garden, calling each one by its own name.

When I went to play at my friend's place, I would see special corners, or even small rooms, where the deities were worshipped. There would be images of a fierce-looking woman in a black blanket dress who wore a necklace of decapitated heads, her red tongue hanging out, or of sagely men and women in flowing robes. Upon asking who these people were, I would be told names like Goddess Kali, Ramakrishna Paramhansa, Vivekanand. We had no altar in our home. There was an alcove in the wall where a picture of Tagore hung near the ceiling, and underneath it was an old table with a tubular wooden box that had a handle on the top. It contained a Singer sewing machine. I had seen Ma stitching clothes on it and I longed to be old enough to operate this enchanting contraption. The shiny black body was shaped like a small elephant and it was decorated with intricate yellow patterns; to one side, there was a wheel with a handle that had to be turned. When she was sewing, Ma turned the crank handle in circles, and a needle at the other end went carrying the thread up and down, up and down. It was magical to see it work. I would lie on the red stone floor and close my eyes, the mesmerizing khatt-ticc-khatt-ticc-khattticc-khattticc-khattticc-khatticckhatt-ticc sound from the machine was the music to a fantasy. As she stitched, it got faster and faster, then slowed, then stopped as the bobbin thread was replaced, then began running fast again. And at the end of it, I would get a lovely new frock to wear!

Gradually, I realized why we were often not invited to the neighbours' festival pujas. My parents were godless and odd. Baba was an atheist and a Muslim, I understood. He was seen as a cranky old professor with his head in the clouds, looking for the shapes he loved. Ma lit candles on an elaborate candelabra a few times, but had no statues of her God either.

Monsoon was a forceful event that brought a few days of holiday every year when the school building got flooded. One such day, when I was in the final year of senior school, I was walking back home with a friend. I casually complained that my parents were not helping me decide what I should do after school. She immediately whispered in a conspiratorial tone that was meant to make sense of my life for me, 'Don't think about it, Shula, we all know that your parents are older than anyone else's. Old people can be very strange sometimes, and they are not originally from here, which is why you can't properly belong with us either.'

As she uttered the last part of her sentence, I almost slipped in the slimy mud; it was raining and I held an umbrella against the August skies with one hand, and with the other, I was gathering up the front folds of my cotton saree as I readied to jump over a gutter in the wet earth. I recall flinching at her words. There was a confusing sensation of trying to gauge the rivulet, and at the same time, seeing myself drowning in its shallow reflection, thinking, am I really not from here? Is this how removed my friends see me? I gave her a side glance. She had not realized the gravity of this nugget and went on nattering.

That evening, I had come back feeling unwell, my stomach cramps and period pains were severe. I went straight to the kitchen where Sankuri the servant was making tea. Going right up to her, I asked, 'Do you think I am from Bengal? Do I not belong here?'

Sankuri was a wizened old woman, short of stature, with a gleaming dark skin and an unimaginably thin frame. She had very few teeth and claimed to be working in the area from the early days of Thakur. Looking at me with her shining timeless eyes, she asked me in her sing-song voice, 'Whyy do you wannt to beelong, Shoola? Mm-hmm?' I was struck by her words, not knowing what to say. The lone servant-woman who had lived all her life in the nearby village had asked me the question of a lifetime; why had I wanted to belong—why indeed?

Grinning toothlessly, she told me to hurry up and get out of my wet saree; otherwise, I would catch a cold and He would get me—this is how she talked of death. She laid her dried and knotty hand, marked with a network of wrinkles, on my head and said, 'The iiimportant thing is to be gooodd,' as she handed me a cup of strong tulsi tea. Inwardly, I resolved that I would not search for belonging. I did not need to belong. Wherever I was, I would make myself happy. In subsequent years, I repeated these words to myself like a charm, and tried to hear in them that conviction and hope they first embodied.

Finding one's own path is easier said than done.

Never was this truer for me than when I had to choose what to do with my life. It was clear both to me and to my parents that I would not be married off immediately. I decided to go to Calcutta and study at the university there. I wanted a taste of the city—its variety in food, clothes, sights—something that, until then, I had only experienced on rare brief vacations. Baba probably wanted me to study the sciences; Ma just wanted me to learn anything, so long as it would enable me to get a job easily, if I ever needed to. I ended up satisfying neither of their wishes.

I was not hard-working and I did not care much for results. I passed my exams every year. Throughout school, I was drawn to fairy tales and had an instinctual fascination for art, poetry and music. I loved to sketch and stencil from fairy tale books the princesses and their fabulous palaces, the flying winged chariots that took them to forests, the witches disguised as animals, and the castaway princes that rescue from spells. These magical yarns were mythically relevant to me, for in those pages I could be the romantic heroine who is errant but good of heart, and eventually things turn out all right for her. I should have studied the creative arts; certainly, that was my plan when I left Santiniketan.

Calcutta was a confusing place that accused and challenged my dreams; I was simultaneously attracted and repulsed by it. I had not seen such wealth or so much desperate poverty before. Yet, I could never judge which direction the city was pointing me in. On the one hand was the allure of make-believe, and on the other was this need to understand what I saw. I was torn by the need to do something with my studies so that it might address my unease at the misery and pain of the people I saw everywhere.

Reading the newspaper one day, I saw a detailed article on

the economics of the five-year planning process and how this was helping to develop India into a new and prosperous nation. I went up to Baba and said, 'I want to study Economics.' He gaped at me in bewilderment without saying anything. My marks were not satisfactory, but he may still have hoped I would take up Physics. The Calcutta relative, Baba's cousin at whose place we were temporarily staying, thought my declaration peculiarly bizarre, 'Why make so much effort to learn about money? You have to get married, better study something practical.' I replied that I was going to understand economics not to make money but to eradicate poverty and make people happier. In front of Ma-Baba, he remarked that I was, after all, the strange daughter of strange parents.

I had announced my decision with a finality that one can best entertain in youth, and so, I was enrolled into doing three years of Microeconomics, Macroeconomics, Economic History and Public Finance. I lost interest in most of this very soon, but was stubborn enough not to let others think that I was going back on my word. In my twisted moral universe, I rationalized that I should let myself suffer for my bad decisions and carry through with the projects that I start. I somehow endured the serene lecturers, who all talked and dressed alike with their starched shirts and black-rimmed glasses, speaking in their booming sonorous voices of the importance of demand and supply and the new theories that were coming from England, America, the Soviet Union, and 'our very own' India.

I took notes when I could, but for the most part, I stared outside the windows; the grass-cutter labouring in the midday heat: what is the effect of capital-labour ratios on the life of a man single-mindedly tackling the grass with his scythe, ceteris paribus? I read some controversial books that I found in second-hand stores on my weekend trawls of College Street: Keynes adapted for Indian readers, Joan Robinson, Henry George and a bit of Marx. That 'bit of Marx' was his lines of love poetry to Jenny von Westphalen. How utterly romantic that this bearded and moustachioed serious figure from the theories of surplus value should also be the darling bud of amorous rapture!

I realized that economic theory was like Baba's Mathematics, if you forgot that the formulae and symbols referred to real people. It was a mountain of abstractions and I couldn't ask why we needed them. The senior-most Economics Professor had already told the classroom, during our introductory lesson at college, 'Economics is about what is, not about what ought to be.' All the lectures began with the example of an imaginary rational person who knew everything, made complete calculations and perfect decisions—whether he was buying or selling. There was no place for people like the beggars on the roads, the homeless, the poor, the sad. I could not imagine what recompense there was in studying Economics, unless one did want to make money. And when I looked around at the people who had made a lot of money, their faces showed the strain; it seemed to be a tiresome business.

To me, studying Economics felt like a punishment that I must endure for being rash. After all, I used to think, why did I not seek opinions and advice before announcing to the world impulsively, on the basis of one newspaper article, that this is what I wanted to do with my life? I ought to suffer, and suffer I did.

My solace in those days was spending whatever free time I got in the bazaars of Calcutta. I wrote letters to Ma-Baba once a month. I was staying with Baba's maternal uncle and his wife, an elderly couple who lived in a roomy antediluvian house in Maniktala. He went to his club every day and she was a homebound invalid. Their two sons lived abroad and they had servants to take care of them. As long as I came back before dusk and did not worry them, I could do as I pleased.

My previous freedoms in Santiniketan had consisted of doing things like sitting out till late on the weather-beaten porch steps and watching the million and twenty-four—this is the count I used for the night sky of my childhood—stars in the pitch-dark sky, or wandering about the relatively large garden trying to catch fireflies in washed and cleaned Chelpark Royal Blue Ink glass bottles. Or I would take my favourite poetry books and walk up to the edge of the lotus pond behind the houses and sit there under the shade of trees, memorizing verses like Jibananda Das's 'Banalata Sen'. I would grow restless reciting Victorian and Bangla poetry to the sounds of nature around me.

In spring or in the late afternoons of early summer, humming Baul tunes, I would lazily trace images on rice paper. My saree edges tucked in place, I would settle on an unfolded mat—for the grass was prickly and the insects crawling on the ground could bite—and follow the movements of dragonflies with diaphanous wings hovering over the stagnant waters, or look at the distant line of houses and trees mixed with animal sounds, smells and the colours green, yellow and blue. I would imagine a hundred and twenty-four realities then—for this is how many there were for me—and wonder if I could ever feel body-less in the manner of the breeze sswwizzlingg through the trees.

At these times, I wanted to reduce myself to imagination, and touch things with thought alone. I would close my eyes and fancy running my thought over the curling surface of a slightly hairy and soft broad green leaf~~~~I wanted to compact myself into an idea, as a part of the universal mind, and exist merely with my voice, my body having dissolved itself into an ephemera of anti-matter, finer and more invisible than the finest sugar powder Ma used to coat her sweets with.

Looking at the sky, I would think that if the whole universe was only the image of a potter making different kinds of pottery—on rows of shelves these lay, some glazed, others not, some fine, some painted, some broken, some beautiful, some unfinished—then I would not want to be any fragment of the pottery at all, the potter, or even the wheel or the clay. I wanted to be the idea in the potter's mind from whence it all came. Perhaps I just wanted to be free of everything that I could not understand about myself.

In Calcutta, I began experiencing my freedom more communally. I used to go with a group of women friends to the famous Bharat

Café. We would climb the grimy stairs and sit around those formica-topped tables in that huge hall on the first floor, where sounds of people, plates and fans filled the dimly lit space above our heads all the way to the very tall ceilings. The surly unhurried waiters would bring in orders, while people talked animatedly about movies and politics, gossip, theatre, books and their work or love troubles. We would sit and chat for an hour or more, and I was starting to see that the world was verily full of my hundred and twenty-four, and more, realities.

A large and changing contingent in the smoke-filled café was made up of those who were studying for their civil services examinations. These young men would board in Calcutta as students at the university, while they studied for the prestigious national examinations to become civil services officers. Of the UPSC crowd (as they were called), some were our seniors too.

I had seen Abhilash before on campus. He spoke to everyone, but avoided the overly political types, who were the most visible presence in those turbulent days. He was an Economics senior, a reasonable and good-looking fellow who paid me attention. My friends teased me about his stares, but we had scarcely talked. He was usually in the library digging into books for the UPSC examinations. I thought his face had an intelligent look about it, and he was the kind to say the right things at the right time. The teachers consulted him at the entrance to the staff room, and he was never seen without an academic book on his person. A young man assured of a brilliant career, in other words.

We talked for the first time in the café one morning when a bearer put an extra chair at the table where I was sitting with two friends. We were in the middle of coffee when this old waiter suddenly and inexplicably added another chair to our table and walked away nonchalantly. Maybe he was rearranging furniture in accordance with some table-chair tally, but at the time, we all laughed at this strange gesture and I mirthfully waved my hand in the air with a flourish, as if to summon an invisible guest joining the table! At the same moment, I happened to see Abhilash a few seats away.

He had seen the gesture and my joke and was smiling through the smoke. I smiled back. He walked up to our table minutes later and asked if he might join us. The other women were studying languages, and Abhilash found things to say about the curriculum that only he and I shared. Soon, he confessed that he found me strikingly attractive. I blushed. I had gratefully received my looks and figure from my mother, and compliments about my prettiness did not faze me; I accepted that I was a beautiful curvy woman. Yet, Abhilash had been the first man to say so directly into my eyes.

After that, we met for coffee or went on walks several times. Once or twice, he accompanied me on my visits to the bazaars, but it was clearly not for him. He would be at a loss while I perused the displays of paintings and crafts. When we visited memorials or parks or Chinatown eateries, I would indulge him in turn and hear his discourse on the state of the nation.

Abhilash was not interested in poetry, but we had ways of connecting. I showed him my sketchbook and even did a portrait of him that he cherished. Once, I said a line aloud from Shakespeare, 'It is the east and Juliet is the sun.' He picked up on the way I had intoned the words, and we made up a game to pass time as we waited for a friend. It consisted of alternately saying, 'It is the east, and Juliet is the sun,' placing different stresses on the syllables and exhausting all the ways it can possibly be said:

It is, the east, and Juliettt is the sun

It is the eeeeasssst, and Juliet (sigh) is the sun

It is the east and, Juliet, is the sun

It is the eastttt and Juliet is the sunnn

And over and over again, we said it with playful emotion and emphasis.

We played another game where we would have to make up three nonsense sentences so that there was no connexion allegeable between them in word, structure or thought.

'The sky is blue'

'I like milk'

'The main cities of Morocco are—'

And here, Abhilash paused to think before adding, '—Marrakech, Rabat, Casablanca, Fes and Tangier.'

We spent a lot of time together. In the next eight months, matters had progressed to his sedulous declarations of love for me.

He cleared his written UPSC exams and we decided to wait for his interview results. During these final weeks of preparation, I saw very little of him. His name was among the top ten candidates when the results were announced and we were overjoyed. I was duly introduced to his affluent merchant family, who, although they were not keen to have their one son and sole heir marry me, at the same time, did not want to offend him. Whatever arguments they had happened behind closed doors and Abhilash spared me the distress of it all. My parents had given up on me doing what they wanted, so this came as no great surprise to them.

After Abhilash's return from training at the diplomatic academy, we were married in a small cheerless ceremony attended by very few people. In the surviving photographs, we are the only two with beaming faces; everyone else looks sombre and abstracted. Over the years, I have come to think that perhaps they knew better.

7

Shula Farid's Unwritten Autobiography—Life With Abhilash

It is easy to betray oneself in the quicksand of intimacy. I was discovering this each day of my married life, quietly but surely.

'You are beautiful, Shula, I will die before I stop loving you,' Abhilash said, his chin nestling in the arc of my neck, his lips sowing a field of kisses upon my nape, our bodies locked in a nervous unchaste embrace. We had returned from an evening out on College Street, our first time there as a married couple.

It was before 15 August; loudspeakers boomed patriotic songs, a shy sun had followed the rain, illuminating the bookstalls and the trams with a sandy light; I had worn a frangipani pink saree, a gift from Abhi. Before he could reap the crop of his kisses from my lips, there were footsteps up the stairs. We had stolen our moment from the company of friends who had accompanied us back to dinner at our new flat in Calcutta.

'Ssh, don't say that!' I hastily put my finger to his lips, extricating myself, while he continued to pull the front buttons of my blouse, breaking one.

We had laughed together at the meal, and as we saw our guests to the door, Abhi had even put his arm around my shoulder in their presence.

Days were rosy, and each night glorious, then.

Abhilash was handsome, intelligent, successful, and he loved me.

He remembered to bring me flowers back from places. If there were no bouquets in his arms, there would be laughter and jokes about the closed-down florists.

I was going to be an artist. Failing one of my final year exams, I had abandoned my degree, deciding that I had studied enough. Why should I torment myself with Economics when I did not need to? Abhi did not mind my dropping out—'I don't want you to work anyway.' Carefree, I would go to the bazaars, paint at home, listen to music and read poetry. I had it all. Abhilash had been the find of a lifetime and I was going to be happy.

Happy on a much larger scale than my parents, who lived by an old routine: teaching and cooking, content eating fish and rice, their window netting to keep out the mosquitoes, stars in the dark sky, Baba's lines and curves. How did their world shrink to be so small? I would wonder. I wasn't going to be settled like them. I would make my rules; invent them, if necessary.

Why should I assert my freedom by slaving over textbooks, getting weak eyesight and many useless degrees? What need was there to attest my worth as a modern woman by filling application forms here and there, working under supervision, going to office every day? I did not need to earn my living to prove anything to anyone.

I was free, I would see the world, I would travel with Abhilash every holiday, speak to barefoot beggars and smile at people and things, leave large tips at restaurants to make the servers ecstatic. I was, after all, the wife of an IAS officer. Unchained from provincial concerns, I would realize my dreams of doing everything. I would chase the poetry of spring with its far wind and the little bird. I would run by the seaside with Abhi my love. I would cut red ribbons at ceremonies. I would ride a horse in the hills. I would be the mistress of his heart.

Abhilash loved to take the initiative in things; he would plan our evenings, outings, holidays, well in advance. His office diary chronicled his day by the hour. He forgot no meeting, missed no engagement, offended no one, his precision was admirable. Suave, polished, impeccable, not a hair on his head was ever out of place. At the same time, he was indulgent of my behaviour. We were different, undeniably. I barely managed to be ready for parties in time, he would call to remind me, aware of my carelessness. When I mislaid the wedding ring, he did not chide me, but ordered a replacement from the jewellers the next day. I could not fault him—he was sincere at work and tolerant at home.

One evening, he announced that we were going to Darjeeling. He had some work there, following which we could take a longish break. This was our first proper holiday since the honeymoon: a glowing memory of a cottage in Mussoorie where we had hardly gone out, had trays of gourmet food delivered at our doorstep, and were treated like royalty owing to the caretaker's arrangements. Now, in Darjeeling, I was determined to be out and about.

We travelled by car from Siliguri onwards through the winding roads in the scenic mountains, going up from the mist-clad Teesta river. Abhi's subordinate, who was from the area, pointed out to us the passing potato farmers, basket grass carriers and wood gatherers, brooks gushing through the rocks, gashes where the land had slid, forests of trees shooting vertical and long, road-building workers, children sharing colourful umbrellas walking arm-in-arm wearing school uniforms, 'fooding' shops in tin-roofed hamlets, a hen crossing the road cautiously, moving away from a garbage pile set on fire. We stopped to have a cup of tea at an altitude of 6,800 feet.

I was enormously excited. I tried to snuggle closer to Abhi in the car, but he rebuffed me. He was playing the role of an officer capably in command in front of his driver and junior officer. I thought he was being fussy; they sat in front and had not a smidgen of interest in watching us. I forgot the snub. When we reached the circuit house, there was a hot bath and a sumptuous meal ready. Later, we went out for a walk.

I looked at the hills—they were the testament of a mad god's wild imagination, the way they went up and down, and up and down, and up and down, all around us, running amok, wild and unburdened. I wanted to be free as they were, shining, with their body a green riveting shade of life itself. I expressed some of these feelings to Abhilash.

His response was crushing, 'You should mind yourself in front of other people.'

'What did I say wrong? Don't you like the undulating land?' I reached for his arm.

He paused and said in a level voice, 'Don't play the fool. I meant before, in the car. These people are my subordinates. Can't you act dignified in front of them?'

I could not understand why he was taking this so seriously. I tried to divine what had actually put him in such a crabby mood.

'Are you feeling well?'

'What kind of a person are you?'

We were silent; a peanut-seller approached us, Abhi barked at him. Before stepping aside, the man met my eye. I pitied him; he was poor and old. I wanted to buy some of his roasted peanuts. For the first time, I realized how Abhi treated those who were of an inferior status. He was ideally mannered, but only so long as you were within or above his class circle, or if you had a purpose for him. It was astonishing that I had never noticed it before. But there it was, my first major realization about the man I had married, a gleaming cold truth—instances flashed in my mind. I heard him shouting at the removals man, losing his temper with the cook and the typist, satirizing the fawning supplicants and the approachers. He had never been anything but nice with me until that day, so I had not noticed his attitude towards others.

'That peanut-seller was poor. Why did you take your anger out on him?'

'I'll buy you a ton of peanuts, my silly, my lovable.' His voice was familiar again.

Warily, I stepped closer.

He immediately gave me his arm and said, 'Come here.'

His transformation was so sudden that I wasn't sure whether

he was the same man who had spoken tersely to me and growled at a poor stranger minutes ago.

Shortly afterwards, we came upon an open horse-riding ground. The sight of those shiny brown manes ensorcelled me. Horses are mystical and magical, like creatures from fairy tales, or from another era.

'Their faces have a secret knowledge of deeper peace. They are—'

'—long-faced!' Abhi was tickled at my rapture.

'I want to ride one.'

'Are you sure?' He seemed not to believe me, until I beckoned a keeper and asked for the price.

The man named a paltry figure. Abhi looked askance at me, 'Are you really doing this?'

'Didn't you wonder why I had bought these boots before this trip?'

He ignored my question, and signalled to the man to help me get saddled.

When I was all set, the keeper tugged at the bridle. 'Please leave the horse alone. I want to ride unaccompanied,' I instructed him. Instead of doing what I had said, he gaped at Abhilash, who in turn answered me.

'Shula dear, you could get hurt if you do not let him accompany you.'

'I'll be an equestrian treat. I'll fly over the hills, Abhi. You watch,' I said with a flourish, reaching to hold the reins in my hands.

He was about to say something, when I added on an impulse, 'I won't ride unaccompanied anyway because you are riding with me on that other horse.'

'I am doing no such thing,' he said, stepping back.

'You didn't take a second to say "No". Abhi, please! Please let us ride together. It will be romantic. You and I, these hills—'

'Don't drag me into your tomfoolery,' he said in an affected voice.

'Please, Abhi. For my sake. You know I don't ask you for things every day. Just this once.'

'I am uncomfortable on a horse. I don't like it. You go ahead. I'll wait here.'

'Are you afraid? Because if that is the reason, I won't insist.'

'I am not afraid. I just don't want to get on a horse.'

'Why, Abhi? I said please. I want us to. At least, give me a reason for not wanting to.'

'Shul-*ah*, I said "No". My "No" should be reason enough. Must you always behave like a child?'

'My wishes don't mean anything to you, do they? What if I also say "No" when you want me to do something, or want us to go somewhere, without giving a reason.'

'Do whatever you like.' Saying this, he turned around and strode over to the car.

I debated whether to get off and follow him, or go ahead for the ride.

As I held back my tears and pulled the reins, I saw him talking to the driver. In another moment, he was gone.

What a horrible day to start such a long-awaited trip! First, his behaviour in the car, then on the walk, and now this—what exactly was I doing so wrong today? I had lovingly entreated him to ride with me. Was that worthy of such offence?

I dug my heels at the sides, the horse obliged, and I trotted off. I had always dreamed of riding a horse in the hills, it meant so much to me; now that I was actually doing it, it was no fun at all. A group of men stared at me in an openly lecherous manner. It might have been better to dismount and go after Abhi; I would be humiliated but not jeered. I loosely sheathed my body with the ends of my stole. 'This is no fun,' I said aloud, when I was sure that nobody but the horse could hear me. 'Well, never mind. I have this ride with you, my horse. Can you understand my husband? See, neither can I. Aren't lovers supposed to pluck the stars from the skies for the ones they love? And he refused to ride your friend for no reason.'

I knew I was being stroppy, but wasn't it important that I would never be able to picture myself riding into the hills at sunset with

Abhilash? If I had been childish, he hadn't been much of a man either. Did I have to go and marry someone as unadventurous as all that? Why, he was like Baba! Bowed down by reason and sense. Even Baba was better. He had, at least, been eccentric enough to dream outrageously, if only of Mathematics. Agreed that I had been insistent about his riding with me, but what was the point of intimacy if I could not insist? It was essential to tug and pull and nudge on the emotional chords. I cannot insist with strangers; insistence is an emotional demand with my intimates. It is an ask that shows me that I can insist.

The horse's keeper had been paid in advance, so when the ride time was over, I trudged along in disappointment to the car. One dream of mine ruined already.

The driver sat relaxed, smoking beneath the cap that sat askew on his head, his feet crossed at the ankles and an arm hanging limp. Seeing him, one would think I'd be here a million years. I knocked on the window. He leapt up, stubbed out his cigarette, and scuttled to the other side to open the door for me.

'Madam,' he said obsequiously, 'I am sorry. I was waiting, and then I lit a beedi. I am sorry.'

'Don't worry. What is your name?'

'Roshan Subba, Madam.'

'Well, Roshan, drive me to the circuit house, and fast, please. Has Sahib gone back?'

'Yes, Madam. He left when you were...er...horse-riding. Nice horses. Good sport.'

'I agree.'

'Madam, did you see the mountains, our Kanchenjunga?'

'Not yet.'

'You should see that and also the toy train.'

He tooted the horn at a group of children chasing a dog across a bend.

I thought I saw him fleetingly observe me in the rearview mirror, before he said, 'Madam, if you don't mind me asking, are you a foreigner, like Anglo-Indian people?'

'Why?'

'Nothing, Madam, sorry. My wife Rani met an Anglo-Indian lady last week, from England; she was very kind. I am from Nepal. I went to Delhi once.'

'I am from Calcutta.'

'Oh. My people are Gurkhas, but I don't mind Bengalis. They are also good, Madam. I have seen Mithun Dada in movies.'

'Do you drive many officers and their families?'

'Yes, Madam. I have seen many Sirs, from Bihar, Bengal, UP, Orissa, Meghalaya, many, many states. Nowadays, we are not so peaceful. Many government officers come for meetings.'

'I have two sons, Bunnu and Jatin. Bunnu will start school soon. You don't have children, Madam?'

'No. Here, take this. Get some sweets for your children.' I handed him money as the car pulled into the circuit house gates.

The double-storey building was bathed in lights that had been switched on too early. There were cars parked outside. I had to pass through the living room on the way to our bedroom. It was alive with chatter; there were three guests. As I entered, Abhilash was the first to see me. He was putting an LP record on the gramophone. Setting aside the paper sleeve, he acknowledged me, then smiled beneficently in front of the others, pointing, 'And this is Shula, my wife,' suffixing, 'what a voice this man had'—referring to K. L. Saigal whose song 'Main Kya Jaanu Kya Jaadu Hai'—What do I know what magic this is—had started playing. 'Thank you for picking this music, Mrs Nath.'

The couple on the sofa greeted me, the woman said Namaste and the man partly stood up; another man moved a few steps forward. He held out his hand. I said Namaste, and in response to the third man's, 'Hello. I am Bhowmick. Krishna Bhowmick,' I said, 'Hello. I am Shula Farid...uh...Shula Basu. Pleased to meet you.'

The servant came in carrying a tray loaded with bone china cups, a teapot, pakoras, pastries, Crax and Bourbon.

'We are Mr and Mrs Nath. We have not met you before. I am a colleague of your husband and this is my wife Aarti.'

Aarti instantly said, 'I really like your name, Shula. Is Farid your father's name? We used to know a Mrs Mirza at my husband's last posting.'

I pierced to the heart of her question, 'I have not been married long enough to forget my original surname, so it slips out. I am half Muslim, daughter of Professor Farid from Santiniketan. You can think of me as Mrs Shula Basu.'

'Oh no, Shula. I was just curious. You don't seem very Bengali. I mean your eyes are almost green. Umm...I...,' she simpered.

'My mother was a foreigner. Is,' I offered.

'Yes, yes.'

Abhilash joined in, saying, 'Shula has a wonderful heritage. She is also a very good singer and artist.'

'Great. You must sing us something, Mrs Basu.'

Before I could respond, Abhilash quipped, 'She is probably tired from her horse-riding today.'

Why did he say it like that? I was irritated. A slight silence ensued, before the song 'Jab Dil Hi Toot Gaya' scattered the plaintive notes of a broken heart across the room.

Abhilash's remark had drawn everyone's attention to my outfit, which was certainly out of place. Mrs Aarti Nath was dressed in Banarasi silk, and here I was, the hostess, in black trousers, collared kurta and boots. Before the conversation could progress further, I left to change. In front of the dressing-table mirror, I looked at myself. I was dressed kookily for guests, but Abhilash had not told me that we were to have company. I did not embarrass him on purpose. I always dressed properly in sarees, even used the vermilion sindoor in my forehead parting, and wore the mangalsutra necklace. And why not? I was Mrs Shula Basu. But I was also Shula Farid. This was my holiday too. Did I not have the right to live and dress the way I wanted to, on some days? I can't help it if Mrs So-and-so sees me like this, or finds me strange. My eyes, green or orange, are mine. I would not change the person I am for anything. Abhi married me for love. He ought to know.

I returned downstairs in a cinnamon and gold embroidered saree. The blouse for this had been stitched in a hurry before leaving Calcutta and the tailor's new assistant had not done a good job of it, especially at the sleeves, which fitted loosely. I was not entirely comfortable in the clothes, but I confidently assumed the role of hostess as the dinner-table was being laid.

Abhilash was busy discussing the Nehru-Gandhi dynasty over food and a nightcap. I was stuck with Aarti's gossip bulletin that chronicled the ins and outs of the Officers' Wives association, its functions and fundraising. I demonstrated a moderate interest in her monologue about the last charity event she organized. I was grated. The men droned on: strategies of the officers, the capers of the politicians, the latest round of selections for the Delhi posting that Abhilash had applied for. On other days, Abhilash might involve me in the parleys, but that day, he did not address a single word to me throughout the meal.

When everyone had left, he turned to me as if nothing was amiss, saying, 'You should not have exerted yourself if you were not in the mood for a get-together, they would have understood.'

I did not reply.

'Shula dear, you must not let people misjudge you.'

'What are you trying to imply, Abhi?'

'You did not seem to like the guests.'

'Why do you think that?'

'What do you mean, why? It was quite obvious from the way you behaved. You did not act normally, your defensive attitude about your name made them feel unnecessarily bad. They apologized to me after you had left to change those clothes.'

'Do you think it was polite of her to inquire into my private life, my name? If they felt bad, it's their problem. Maybe they should.

I did not take any extra effort to be withdrawn. In fact, it was a strain to tolerate such boring company.'

'I cannot choose my colleagues to suit your tastes.'

'I cannot suit my tastes to make every colleague of yours feel liked. Have I given you any cause for complaint in Calcutta?'

'I am not complaining. In any case, we had better go to sleep soon, it is late.'

'You brought it up. Not me.'

'Can we postpone this discussion till tomorrow?'

'No, we can't. What has come over you today? I need to know. Why did you leave me at the riding grounds? If you were coming back to meet the guests alone, you should have said so.'

'Look at you. Theirs was an impromptu visit. What did they say that was so upsetting? Don't take it out on them. I didn't ride because I do not like being on horses. I have never liked it. I have never liked *be*-ing around animals. I feel *un*-easy,' he spoke exasperatedly, stressing words excessively to make his point.

'I am not taking anything out on anyone. But it is not the horse alone. You have been off since we arrived. In the car—'

'As I told you, I do not like my wife to act undignified in front of others.'

'I am undignified?'

'I did not say that. You are putting words into my mouth. I said I do not want you to act undignified.'

'And how did I do that?'

'Ask yourself.'

He had changed into pyjamas and rang for the bedtime glass of warm milk. I went to the bathroom to undress, continuing to speak from behind the door, 'I know. You do not need to explain things to me like I am a fool. I can see now that you do not like horse-riding. That is precisely the point. It was a silly romantic demand that I made of you to do something that you do not like, because I want you to do it, because it would mean a lot to me. But, never mind. And I am sorry for it. Can you see what I mean?

You could have tried something new with me. Who knows, you might have liked it even.'

I heard him say, 'All right.' He did not say anything further.

When I returned, he was resting against the headboard on the bed; the glass of milk was empty, there was a newspaper in his hands.

I got in beside him; he was warm to the touch. Still reading, he casually thrust his hand under my red and black nightie. Laced with tiny bows, it was his favourite.

'Abhi, did I look ridiculous today?' I asked, pulling the paper out of his hands.

'As a matter of fact, you looked really nice in that saree,' his hand halted.

'And not in the trousers? You did not comment on the new boots or trousers the whole day. It was meant to be my surprise in Darjeeling for you,' I pressed on.

'Well, what can I say. I like you best in sarees.'

'Do I look fat in the trousers?'

'You are not fat, my darling.'

'Then?'

'I am glad you broached this topic. I did not know how to, this afternoon. Please refrain from such experiments. I don't like women who can't be women.'

'Abhi. What you are saying is that you don't want me to wear trousers and shirts?'

'Yes.'

I considered his words. 'Oh, so this is the cause of everything! This is why you were off today. This is what you have been referring to all day, and I did not understand. How slow of me!'

'Shula, you amaze me,' he said sarcastically.

'I know I am amazing. But Abhilash, you told them on purpose that I would be tired from horse-riding in order to draw their attention. You wanted to discomfit me, punish me. You are no less amazing.'

'I did do no such thing. You can imagine what you want. If

I had not spoken, do you think they would not have seen your tomboy clothes and those...those...boots you wore?'

'I like those boots.'

'You want to know? The pant-shirt was not becoming, nothing is left to the imagination in those clothes. They are tight. The outlines of your ample breasts were bursting. The boots made you look like you were out of a Wild West movie. All you needed was a whip.'

'And that's not sexy?'

'No. That outfit and those boots are for hunters, not women.' Saying this, he folded the paper away.

'My dear orthodox husband! Aren't there women hunters?' I hinted saucily.

'There must be. You want to be a cowboy in the hills? Go ahead. Don't expect me to be by your side.'

'Abhi, women today are doing everything alongside the men. Is wearing pants such a big deal?'

'It is, to me. I want a graceful wife.'

'You'd rather prefer ill-fitting full-sleeved blouses and covering up sarees?'

'I would rather prefer you did not continue with this unprovoked tirade.'

I was quiet. In his place, I would have been so different: adventurous, open-minded. Unlike Abhi. But could I have taken the civils examination? Could I have put in those hours single-mindedly studying? He had his merits. I would have wanted variation and colour.

He bent over to my side of the bed to turn off the lightbulb. I blocked his arm and held his body to me, rhetorically alleging, 'Abhi, you do not find me attractive.'

'Shul-*ah*, please stop behaving like this. If I did not find you attractive, why would I have married you?'

'How would I know?'

'Let us sleep now. Please.'

Does he not understand me at all? I want him to want me right now. What's wrong with him? Why can he not see the desire in my eyes? Why should I bottle it up? I asked myself these questions.

'Abhi, I love you.'

'I love you too, Shula,' came back the rapid-fire response, but his arm remained where it was; he was waiting for me to let him switch the lights off.

'Abhi, what can you see in my eyes?'

'Everything that you want me to see,' he was playing along.

'Well, then why can't you see the desire in my eyes right now?'

Straightaway, he was serious. 'Because, Shula, it is not desire for me that I see in your eyes right now. What I see is a desire to be desired. You want to be worshipped and you want me to pretend that I am aroused by your desire for your own self,' he explained cagily.

'And what's wrong with wanting to be desired?'

'There's nothing wrong with wanting to be desired. There is something not totally right, however, with wanting to be desired just for that reason itself. Because it means that you want to be desired. Period. By whom, it does not matter. I happen to be here next to you right now, and the person that you happen to be married to, so convenience would dictate that you want me to desire you, but I don't want to be a placeholder for your fantasies. I would love to make love to you when we desire each other, and not when you want to be desired by anyone nearest who can witness your flesh in all its beauty.'

This was cruel and untrue. I had wanted to be desired by him. He was acting out of a jealousy and spite that he did not want to admit.

I let go.

'Goodnight, Shula,' he said.

I thought of what the day had taught me. I had married Abhi, but not understood him. The three nonsense lines game of our courtship came back asudden: Peanut-seller, Horse, My desire to dress and be desired. Three lines of sense about him I had learnt that day. He was an amphibian, reverting between treating people respectfully and meanly, depending on who they were. He could not bear to be in an unfamiliar situation where he did not have control. He could not tolerate me taking the initiative in some things; he liked me passive.

I can't say which one of us went to sleep first. In the darkness, it was difficult to make out as we slept with our backs to each other.

The next morning, I behaved as if I did not care. It was raining outside. Abhilash sipped his morning tea with the papers in the covered balcony, and I ransacked my suitcase for something to read. I found a book of poems by Wordsworth. Holding it aloft, I too sat in a cane chair next to him, one leg swung over the other, reading. First, it was 'The world is too much with us, late and soon', then, I turned to 'Ode to Duty', and with the second cup of tea, 'She was a Phantom of Delight', after which I clapped the book closed and went to dress. On my way to the almirah, I saw a photograph of us lying on the bed. It must have fallen out when I was rummaging through the suitcase. I picked it up and examined our faces inside the oval frame, behind the thin glass, a made-for-each-other couple on honeymoon.

I put on an indigo coloured saree with a broad silver border, taking time to do my eyes. Abhi was getting into his suit in the same room. Careening into the mirror, eyes popping and jaw dropping as I applied the mascara, I thought of myself as Abhilash's wife. His wished-for graceful wife. Could I live up to this all my life? I would have to, what else could I do? What did I want anyway? Fairy tales were for children. I thought of the lip-liner and the crimson nails I would do next, and sighed. Abhilash's parents had been conventional, and charming as he was, he would not compromise on his definite sense of the aesthetic.

True, we had loved each other; the romance had been the first for both of us, and we had wed. There had been no real obstacles. I had never resisted him either. Maybe that was a mistake. It was resistance that bore passion. I pouted to inspect my self-intuited handiwork. There, beneath the frosted glass cupola, I felt like the oldest actress in the world. I was playing a part. He was playing a part. Yet, for all its limitations, my present role was empowering when compared to my insular growing up years. I was making my world come into being in the theatre of my everyday life. Wasn't I? Life was teaching me. I had far to go. I would make my own mistakes. Why think of mistakes? Marriage to Abhilash was not a mistake. First mistakes are granted, overlooked. But if I erred at each new thing once, it would add up to a lifetime of errors. I finished my make-up as the rain ceased—there'd be puddles outside. 'An all too easy muddle,' I thought, suspiring.

Abhilash came up behind me as I sighed, and placed his hands on my shoulders. Our eyes met in the rust-flecked mirror. Some things were said and understood, but neither of us knew what or which. He told me that I was attractive. Was he making up? Or approving my countenance because it fitted his ideal? How could I let him know that I was still angry about yesterday, without actually saying it? Did he think that my dressing in this way indicated an unimpeded acquiescence in his unfair restrictions? I said nothing to express any of this. He drummed his fingers on my clavicle, and proceeded to tell me of the plans for the day; we were going to Kalimpong and were also invited to a tea plantation; we needed to leave soon. So then, his comment had only been a prelude to get the factual domain back in working order. He summoned the driver. I hastened to the car.

That trip had broken us in. From then on, we were judicious about the demands we made of one another. We began the process of accumulating grudges, learning things about the other, saving these insights for maximum impact in arguments. The camouflage of undefined love that had lingered on from the courtship days could not conceal our incompatibility. Time rolled on.

'What about that?'
'Well, I think it is a good idea, Abhi.'
'It is foolish.'

'Why can't you see what it might mean?'

'We won't have that. We don't need it. And we won't get it.'

'Why do you always diagnose?'

'Excuse me. Diagnose?'

'Yes, don't you notice how you always judge, and never suggest or propose.'

A pause.

'Shula, you never understand what I mean, and distract by getting up on the semantics. It is part of your agenda to misunderstand my intentions.'

'Spoken like an analyst, but did you hear what I said about your tendency to judge rather than suggest or propose?'

'As in?'

'You react to people, or me at least, by saying things like "that's because you have X", or "you are Y", or "you do this in order to—" You don't say "I think" or "it may be", or "what about" or "why not" or "don't you think". It is as if there are no realms of possibility open. Your word is final.'

'You are doing this on purpose. Gnawing at me.'

…

An earlier argument:

'Come on now.'

I made no answer.

'I said, Shula, will you stop being cross?'

I wanted to, but did not say—I will not stop being cross until you think back to what started this in the first place, and remedy the root cause. Just because you said sorry, or some time passes, does not mean that the point of the argument has vanished. And please don't wait for me to tell you all this. It should be obvious. If I tell you it and then you do it, there's no point, because then you are only addressing the problem because I told you to, and not because you wanted to remove that which hurt me enough to cause this argument.

He waited for an answer from me. While I pondered my unsaid, he vented, 'At least, I am trying to get things right between us.'

'Trying how?' I blurted.

'Trying by asking you to forget about the quarrel. Come on.'

I had another unspoken thought in my mind—he does not see life as a feeling continuity. He cannot see that which is obvious to me: that one can only set things right from the point at which they went wrong, and not by pretending that they did not go wrong at all.

...

'When did you first realize that?'

'When? I don't know.'

'Try to remember. At what age?'

'I don't think it is important anyhow. Sometime in the past. Why should it matter? How can it?'

'Abhi, I remember exactly when I saw the first picture of a person where the face was not sketched out but left blank, and when I first saw a play where the story did not end as it should but ended vaguely. I can still relate to how it made me feel. It is wonderful to know when we first learn something new, that's why.'

'Maybe for you.'

'Yes, for me, and if we share our emotions, it creates a connected universe where things have their points of origin.'

'Well, Shula, I have a job to do and many things to think about. I cannot waste time on peripheral recollections. You and I are different people.'

'But, *our* domains can also exist, Abhi.'

When I look back to those early years of our marriage, I conjure up the image of fish in an aquarium being fed tiny scraps of food. The glass enclosure of our lives like a coffin of mossy waters, artificially lit. As fish, Abhi and I swim around and around, blindly moving our lips that utter soundless words as we lurch and search. Sometimes, the fish gets a morsel, sometimes, the fish passes it by, and at other times, both the fish and the fragment float apart, right out of reach. This randomness was the essence of my communication with Abhilash—we drifted, unable to be generous, unable to make sense of each other.

Initially, we had arguments, but later, he began to adopt a purposeful silence as a shield against my petulance and my passion alike. He did not want confrontations, demonstrations and remonstrations; he wanted a pattern, orderliness and a sanity that I could increasingly not provide. My whimsical spontaneity, my impulsiveness, my inability to remake myself into the image of his ideal wife drove him further away from me. His actions would remind me of my parents with their solidity, so full of holes out of which it was carved, but of the worst parts of it. I wanted to be water and air and fire, to fly, to flow, to be, to blow.

Abhilash wanted to explain myself to myself all the time, a consistency that I could never achieve. I wanted Abhi to understand me, to share my thoughts, to let me live the way I wanted to. He thought I was not brought up in a cultured household, was given to impropriety; hence, we never visited Ma–Baba, rarely made love, and seldom communicated beyond the necessities. In the midst of our awful silent phases, I would set up an easel and begin painting in the afternoons. Abruptly, as I was colouring a scene, my hand would freeze in the middle of a brushstroke; I would be hit with unhappiness. I'd go and collapse on the sofa, depressed. In that half-awake state, I would see myself plummeting to the bottom of the ocean, the weight of charcoal water, miles of it, engulfing me, pressing me down. I did not know whether I was alive or dead, dreaming or awake. My breathing would slow down as I descended into the depth of the rocky underwater craters. I was unable to live my life, to find my happiness.

'Let us drive there ourselves. Just you and me.'

'The driver can get us there faster. The road is not properly marked. If I drive, we might get lost.'

'So what? It would be interesting.'

'Interesting? We could be stuck.'

'And?'

'It is not safe. I would rather not.'

'You would always rather not.'

'And you would always try to do something different, just to amuse yourself into thinking that you really are different.'

'I don't care.'

'You never do.'

'You are afraid of adventure. You are a bore.'

'Enough. I am not telling you how irresponsible you are, am I?'

'Oh! And what else?'

'And frivolous, and pretentious, and uncultured, and improperly brought up.'

'Don't bring Ma-Baba into this.'

'Why not? They have not taught you the basic attributes of being a good woman and good wife.'

'And what a good husband you have been!'

'In what way am I not a decent husband? Do I not provide? Do I hit you? Do I not bear with you? Do I pursue other women?'

'You provide. You do not hit me. You bear with me. And you are not a womanizer, Abhi. You bear with me, but how? Ask yourself, do you love me?'

'I am sorry that I married you. That things have come to such a pass between us. Every-single-day, it's the same. I hate arguments, tension, explanations. Why can't we stay silent? Keep out of each other's way?'

'Because I want a life, not a compromise. If you married me, it's your problem.'

'Look, I didn't mean that. I married you and I don't regret it. I am sorry. Now get up and get ready, Shula. Please don't create a scene.'

'Why not? One sentence and that's it? I should dance to your tune. Be at your command. For you, things cancel each other out. The positives and the negatives add up to nothing, and one word sets everything right.'

'It's better than your world where the positives and the negatives just haphazardly pile upon each other, and nothing is ever resolved.'

'Wrong again, it is easy resolutions that I find unbearable. The papering over that you are so fond of. The shallowness of it galls me.'

'I'd rather be shallow than deep as you, and deeply miserable too.' An outburst. My face was covered with tears.

'I am miserable because I am tired. I am tired of this life. Tired of everything in it. I wanted to be free. I wanted freedom. I wanted the world. I wanted a million sense experiences. I wanted to really live my life. I thought you did too. We never do things together. I hate the get-togethers that you are so fond of, all that flaunting, vaunting. The staid uptight people and their stuffy opinions, their ironed-out lives, their consecrated aims, their holier-than-thou comparisons, their opportunistic sucking up...You have no idea how I feel inside when we sit and watch those slides. I think of corners and I think of edges, and colours running into each other. I think of the slide projector as a big black cake, and while you watch the screen, I am already slicing and apportioning that cake. I am eating that cake, Abhi-*laash*, do you understand? I am eating that cake, I am eating that darn venomous black cake. I am sad and furious and I feel maimed—'

'Please don't be so histrionic.'

'I am a hysterical woman. Fine.'

'I didn't say hysterical—'

'I know what you mean. It's the same. Abhi, I am sick. No, listen. I am tired of this. I want to be something too. I want to do something too. I could have been an artist, done something creative—'

'Did I ask you to study Economics?'

'Did you encourage me to work? Do you ever see me as anything else except your wife? When I wanted to enrol for the part-time Art degree, did you let me? When Mr Gupta wanted to consider my work—'

'That man has a reputation. He corrupts women.'

'What about my paintings that you took off the walls? That you won't let me exhibit?'

'Can't you draw anything except naked figures? You used to sketch lovely pictures, faces, flowers. I had one on my desk even. Others can call it art, but I won't have it in my home. I can't have my wife behave like an immoral woman painting lewdness.'

'I am your wife and nothing else. You want to bridle me. And even then, you do not lovingly support me. I could, at least, be your muse. Your inspiration to strive afar and anew. I want to be interested in. I want your attention, Abhi-*laash*. I want your love. I wanted your love.'

I sobbed.

'Ever wondered what I wanted? I wanted a quiet and decent life. I thought I had the makings of it when I met you; you were innocent and beautiful, capable of making me happy. I loved you as best I could, but it was not enough for you; you want the trappings of love, not love itself. I wanted a comfortable house. I wanted a loving wife, not some self-obsessed maniac. I wanted a regular life. I wanted children. Completeness. And a home and a life.'

He spoke mildly. Effectively. I sat down and paused. With some shock, I said, 'Children?'

'Why is that such a surprise? Am I the first man in the world to want children from my wife?'

'No, not if you put it like that. But you had never said this before.'

'It is not easy to say things to you.'

I stared fixedly at the furniture around me. The sounds of Calcutta poured forth into the silence between us.

'I am not sure I want children, Abhi.' I had forgotten my tears, the argument, my creative frustrations.

'Well, I do,' Abhilash mumbled.

There was a blank into which eternities tumbled; my mind was mixed up. There was no point. Was there a point? My thought processes had jammed and stalled and were producing nonsensical thought-strings: child—children—Chilled Run—Chilled RUN—plural—babies—wings—love, to love, to give—gift of love—complicated—shaft-door-wire-rope machinery—Like a circus in a narrow underground—Butcher—.

There was really no point. 'All right, maybe you're right, Abhi.' It was a sweet victory for him. Everything else was forgotten. He held me in his arms. He was not an unkind man. So this is what it was that he wanted.

'We will be happy, Shul,' he said. 'I will try and pursue that posting to Delhi again. They didn't accede to my request that time; I have a greater chance now. We'll be in a new city. We might even go abroad.'

I nodded through the drying tears. I wanted him to wipe away my tears; I wanted him to drink them up with his lips. I did not say so. I dabbed at them with a tissue. We made love. It was not remarkable, but it seemed right.

Abhilash kept good on his word and tried every network he could to make his case for the transfer. It was approved, but initially, as a temporary move. I was calmer. Although I did not want a baby, I did not know how to go about what I wanted; he, at least, was certain of what he wanted. This was my warped logic for going ahead with pregnancy. My poetry moved further along the shelf to make space for books on women's health and childcare. I did miss my periods soon. A urine test at a private lab confirmed the news that delighted him and sunk my heart a little. All being well, we were to be parents.

He started bringing me flowers once more. We must relocate to Delhi soon, he said. He would move first to take the new job assignment, and I would follow after the allotment of a family residence. In the meantime, I should visit Ma-Baba. He showed uncharacteristic emotion towards his in-laws, 'Because of me, you have not seen your parents for some time. They must be missing you. Go stay with them in Santiniketan.' I agreed to do this, and Abhi left for Delhi giving me lots of advice and instructions. As his train chugged away, I felt strange. Now that he was trying to be caring and nice, giving me attention, I was not sure I loved him anymore. It was a travesty. But I didn't know why I was standing there at the Howrah station platform, pregnant and married to a bureaucrat, a lifetime of motherhood and housekeeping ahead of me. I cringed. This wasn't what I wanted to do.

Abhi had been right, I was improper and incapable of making anyone happy. My lying to myself must cease, yet I did not want to step forward or go back. I did not know anything. I felt faint; worried that I might pass out, I bought grapefruit juice from the food stalls. With deliberately slow steps, I walked my way out to the car, taking care to avoid the rush of people and waving off the beggars and touts. It was all a mess.

That evening, I went straight to bed and woke up late. I did not immediately rise, and remained looking at the squares of light on the ceiling as they marked another morning with their blurred penumbras.

If two colours met at a corner and you didn't look carefully enough, you'd never see the world at the edge. Because there *is* a world at that edge. Where you could live as you want to live. Stand by the shore with a handful of wet sand, clutching it for dear life, and spend your whole life standing by that sea, holding that sand. Lie on your back on the tender green grass and feel the rain on your face and body, the drops, one by one, all at once, always; and to spend your whole life there—to never get up. I wanted to go out, walk the longest route possible, walk through the rain, the thunder, the dust storm, the scorching heat, and reach the absolute centre of the world. And then standing there—still, at the centre say, I don't agree with your universe, I will make mine.

I slowly got up and called my parents. They had recently installed a phone at home. Ma had been gardening and Baba was at class. They sounded just the same, old and content. How was their health? Fine, some check-ups for his prostate, nothing serious. Ma congratulated me again, asked me how things were going—they had received my letter—when was I planning to come over? I said that I had reconsidered my plans, I was thinking of staying on in Calcutta.

'On your own? In Abhilash's absence?'

'Yes, on my own,' I replied. 'I will be all right. There is no need to worry.'

'In Maniktala—'

'Don't inform them, please. I am perfectly fine. Servants come daily. I have good neighbours in case I need anything. I will also move to Delhi in a couple of months, at the latest. Abhilash will visit before that.' Some lies did not hurt.

'Is he very busy?'

'So busy, Ma. He's trying to get a posting abroad; being in Delhi will help with that.'

'Oh, good. Have you started thinking of names? Do you want suggestions? Your Baba was saying—'

I interrupted her, 'Ma, I do not want the baby.'

She was silent. 'Don't say such things.'

'I am serious.'

'Then why, Shula? Why?' she stammered.

'I don't know. I do know. It is a long story. I was broken. I want to be someone, to do something, Ma.'

'Why don't you want the baby?'

'You won't understand.'

'Make me.'

'I don't love Abhilash anymore.'

'Poor man, what is wrong with you?'

'He is no poor man. He blames you and Baba for all my faults. I don't want to live with him any longer.'

'Is there someone else?'

'No! Ma. Why can't you understand? I don't want this life.'

'Stop dreaming. Where will you go?'

'Can't I come home?'

'What will happen to you after us? Don't make yourself unnecessarily unhappy, rey.'

'You are telling me I should not be true to myself?'

'It is difficult to be true to yourself.'

'Ma, I will kill the baby. Abort it. I will say I had a miscarriage. Don't tell Baba. Abhi need not know.'

'Shula, I don't want to hear this.'

'Then don't.'

'Shula?'

'Shul? Shuli, Shulaa. Shun…Shun na! Don't be rash. You can't have everything. No one does.'

'Why should I be afraid and unhappy? I am sure I want to do this, Ma. If I mother his child, I will never be able to let go…Say something. Tell me I am capable of breaking free.'

'What can I say? What you want is not good for you.'

'I know. But I do not want to have a baby. Not now, not with him, probably not ever.'

'Shall I come to Calcutta?'

'I forbid you, on my life, to tell anyone or to come here. Swear! I will do this myself.'

'How?'

'There are special clinics. Someone I know knows a good lady doctor.'

'Shula? Shula—'

'What, Ma?'

'Just be sure.'

'Yes, Ma. Don't tell Baba or anyone else. Don't cry. Don't think about it. Swear.'

'Swear, Ma, please. If you don't, terrible things will happen to me.'

'Na, don't say that! I swear. You be brave, my poor angel.'

I choked my tears and hung up on her quivering voice.

The next few days, I did not keep a specific track of time. I got up and slept when I felt like it. I took out my old sketchpads. I painted furiously. I resolved to be more regular in my diary-writing.

The vegetables and milk were delivered at the doorstep. Servants attended to the chores. I did not go out. When acquaintances or friends called, I made excuses, got out of prior engagements, and fastidiously refused to attend anything. I wanted time to myself, and I was going to have it. Within a week, I had settled into a routine, where I ate when I felt hungry and slept when I was tired. I scribbled poetry that came into my head, painted an outline of the city that I could see from one of the windows. Still-life scenes suggested themselves to me; once, when books from a shelf fell onto the bed, I sketched them instead of clearing them.

When my hands trembled from working on the canvas day and night, and my body was covered in stray pigment stains, I took a long shower and rubbed myself everywhere. I decided to go out alone; nowhere in particular, just somewhere. I asked the driver to take me to the other side of town. We were stuck in a jam. The city was damp and dilapidated, its buildings like old men with rheumatic joints, covered in mould, and the air was charged with smoke. I thought of what Calcutta had evoked in me before I had met Abhilash. On the rotting streets, the lepers and the beggars were still there, the cart-pullers, the destitute. Near the sickle-and-star posters, crows ate dirt. How naïve had I been in thinking that one could understand poverty! Wish it away! I thought of the afternoons by the pond in my childhood when I had sat and dreamt. Where had all those years gone? What had happened to all those dreams?

I considered my life. How do I pursue my happiness? Love was an intense yearning, a losing madness—had I felt that with Abhi? Love was privileged communication—did we have that? What did I know about him?—the way he talked, his opinions, the way he liked his tea and his kiss? I could leave him. But should I not stay and suffer for my mistakes? And the whole prospect of 'if not Abhilash, then what?' daunted me. Where could I go? Going back to Santiniketan was not an option; Ma had said as much. I did not have any specific skills or qualifications. Perhaps it was better to stay where I was. We might weather it out.

A grave sentiment is carved in ruins. So there were tears in the fabric. Every tear released a new thread. And every thread wove the pattern of the fabric. We feel. We stop feeling. It is the story of our lives.

Whatever happened, I became determined not to bring another human being into this loveless marriage.

Is that how marriages fail, friendships collapse, love dries up? I felt lost. I expected this realization about my marriage to come during a quarrel; a large and loud argument, at the end of which I would grasp that I hated Abhilash, and could not bear another second with him. I never expected that I would come to this realization, so quietly and anticlimactically, on a soaked winter day, stuck in a traffic jam. No fireworks heralding the end, a mere dogged simpering realization coming into being out of nowhere.

Abhi would call on the phone. I would placate his worries. Hearing his concern for me, I suffered, because I had once loved him. He couldn't understand and he couldn't be blamed. The fault was mine alone. I was the fault.

'When we meet, Abhi—Abhi, do you miss me?'

'Don't start again. Are you taking care of your health? Eating properly? All the balanced food groups?'

'Yes.'

I dreamt of a lover's passion and intensity; a sense of awareness in me that he feels me, that he burns up inside for those moments when we can experience the soul of one another; for him to look into my eyes, deeply, and with his palm on my chin, turn my face up to his so that we are looking at and into one another, and then breathe some poetic words that reach into me; words that make my insides churn, words that suggest heaven and earth, words that implicate me into him—that make me, pull me, to belong to him, and him alone; that command, that demand of love which is apparent even in the choice of emphases.

'Why are you silent?'

'Nothing,' I answered.

'Are you upset over something?'

'Abhi, do you know I wrote a poem today?'

'Good. Send it somewhere. Publish it. You should make use of your poetic talents. It would be good to see your name in print.'

'Don't you want to know what it is?'

'What is it?'

'The title is: "The World is an In-between Place—Hold Nothing Dear".'

'Yes.'

'It starts with these lines:

Between floating embraces of cloud and land,

Casting nets to capture lost thought,

The secrets of riverbeds when—'

'Shula, I'll hear it when we meet. I am at work and I have to go for a meeting. I will call later, I promise.'

Abhi rang the next day, but forgot about my poem.

While I waited to hear from him, a storm brewed in Calcutta.

After two more days, I went one afternoon to have the abortion. It was not easy. I felt scarred. I had finally reached the one windless spot on the surface of the earth that Baba used to speak of, and I had become stuck in that unique windless place. Suddenly, it was not a future possibility. It was real. I had killed a baby. Taken a life that I could not give. I wanted to stitch myself together again. I was incomplete forever. I dreamt of being heavily pregnant, and then giving birth to nothingness. I thought of a name for a girl that I would have had—Shunyika.

Back in the flat, I sat staring at a potted money plant and listened to the sounds in the building: the violent battering of wet clothes as they were being washed, the puffing momentum of the pressure cooker, the hawkers' cries, and the remote whooping squeals of children. I asked the maid to take away my canvases and dump them. I could not create. I can't lack something I was never able to acquire.

The phone rang. Abhi asked me if I was well. I have been through a storm, I said meekly. He did not understand; the connexion

was not clear. I told him to call again. He did. I let him know that
the baby was lost.

'Gone.'

He was stupefied. He asked about the miscarriage. He did not
imagine that he was married to a murderess. How did it happen?
When? Was I all right? Weren't my parents with me? He would
take the next plane or train and try to reach the soonest. I said I
had bled and the clinic had prescribed medicines.

He was over the next day. He saw the sheets of paper spread
around me everywhere as a sign of the general state of disorder,
and he treated me as if I were a mad child. He took leave from
work and stayed with me. I felt I could let go. I slept under several
covers to bring down my high temperature. He gave me pills, and
castigated himself for agreeing to my insistence upon staying alone. I
was his duty. He tried to be nice. Nice. Weeks passed in the carousel
of time, days that expanded and contracted at will.

As the winter progressed, one Sunday in December, there was
an unusual amount of fog. It was cold and I wore a knitted sweater
with baggy sleeves over my salwar kameez. Kneeling in a corner of
the second bedroom, I tried to tune the big box radio. The hanging
sleeves were interfering with my task. I blamed the fog for the sub-
par transmission of the All India Radio station.

There, amidst my futile efforts to tune the radio clearly on a
foggy winter afternoon, Abhi walked into the room and told me
some news that he had just heard informally, 'We are going abroad.
I have been posted as an officer at the India Office in Berlin.'

'A new life,' he announced.

We moved to Berlin.

Abhilash did well and kept busy with his work. He was capable,
unruffled, and he attended to everything with ease. In front of
others, he treated me kindly but not gently, nicely but not lovingly.
He had hardened since the baby was gone, and there were mutual

compromises. I made no demands on him and he did not restrict my freedoms. We fulfilled the charade of social expectations.

In the evenings after he went to bed, I would crouch in a corner of the living room. Despondent, I stared at walls. I would try to sketch. I thought of poems from my childhood. But nothing sang anymore, it was all dead. I felt stifled by the years. By my faded hopes. Was this how it was meant to be? In the garden when I wanted to run after the fireflies and Ma-Baba would force me to come indoors, should I just have run away very, very far into the night, chasing after the fires of the soul? Would I have become different then? Would my soul have sung of the passions of life if I had been braver? For hours together, I asked these questions of my self.

I did not want this—his house, his life, his dream, his reality. What did I want? Why did I not find myself?

All this because I could not bear the thought of poverty! Because I was afraid of dirty beds, cold nights, bad laws, and men who might, what, rape me? Fear of disease, of want, of hunger. My fears are why I am in Berlin today. Why did I not search my art? The life I wanted. Baba and Ma would have given up on me. So what? Who knows, a cousin or an uncle might have done worse. And the police. With no money, how could I have been an artist? Who would I have stayed with? Yet why did I not find a struggling artist to live with? I must have seen some, met some. No? Why did I not live with a struggler, a straggler, a random lying cheating thief? But someone who would understand me, love me as I want to be loved.

Anyone, so that I would not be facing this beige carpet! This lampshade. This framed gilded picture on the wall. This invitation card. This respectability. This bloody bourgeois brandy whirling in the air around me.

Abhilash the respectable. Abhilash the clever. The diplomatic. The successful. The persuasive. The careful. Yes, careful never to cross a line, use a wrong word, or express what he really feels! The negotiator. The excellent husband. The dutiful son. The perfect diplomat. Why? Abhilash the chameleon. The amphibian. The narrow-minded. The greedy. The narcissist. The smug vain contemptible surface-ridden man! The wearer of endless masks. The doer, the calculating dreamer. When did I last see him sigh? Does he sigh?

Look at the way he avoids discussing my failures. He is careful never to address this despair right at the centre of me. He only visits the edges in comfortable sanity. He has hardly ever spoken of the baby in all this time. And why should I ask? I will never tell him that I killed the unformed mass of flesh that could have been my smile, his finger-shape, my eyes, his voice. Something that was Ours, as a child. He has not expressed his disappointment even once. He is beyond lowering himself by expression.

But, see, when he sleeps—he never snores, his brow slowly losing its day's crease at midnight, looks gentle—I think, why are we thus? Why can I not simply whisper into his ears, wake him up and say, Abhi...abhi, abhi abhi. Calling him into the moment of now—my abhi, my forever present—and without uttering another word, I could walk hand in hand with him to a place near a river or a fire, and then we will commune with our every thought. We will realize we are the saddest yet happiest people on earth. We will bare our inmost. Not having the baby would not matter.

Everything would be forgotten, but because it could be spoken into endless memory. I will go back to a small house with a patch of plants in the village, sing the Sangeet, welcome the dark starry evenings on the porch. We will live again in another universe, where our selves will not spike and lash at each other in frustrated expectations. I will paint. Do something. It does not matter what. He will teach little kids. Read poetry to me. Smile at me in a dark room, and I will sense it without seeing it.

Na, na! He will never give in. I will never ask him to. We will wound each other with words and, even more, with silences, every day. His ambition will hunger for promotions, for better postings, for more networks, for his niche in the world of the diplomat. The new year cards on time, the dinner engagements. I will act normal at the gatherings. Dress up and feign happiness. And no one will know. We will continue this play and encroach ever less on each other's turf. He will not make unreasonable demands and I will not impose on him. We will know our limits. How terrible that is! We will know our limits. Within these limits, our drama of intimacy will be conducted. Why am I in this life? Where shall I go from here?

8

Finding Mir

Keya dreams of bridges. They pop into her mind in the middle of an orgy of sentiments, and locate themselves solidly square, spelling out loud, bridges, b-r-i-d-g-e-s. A visual collage of all manner of bridges passes by. She watches this procession, awed at the construction, the engineering, the beauty and the fear of bridges. When awake, she thinks, is it about relationships? Death, sex, and connexions?

Leon left the flat at dawn, saying he would call. Keya has no hangover from the drinks last night. She does not feel any moral scruples, or issues of rectitude, in sleeping with someone she didn't know a week ago. Why? Sex with Leon had felt natural somehow. It was devoid of relationship paraphernalia; there was no scheming involved. She probes herself to make absolutely sure—there must be clarity, or things become diabolical. She feels a gentle care for him. That's all right. Anything else?—No? Sure? Well, maybe a niggling feeling that he is capable of subsuming her. Really? Why? She has almost willed him into being, marking him out in the airport queue, then that meeting and his search, her involvement. She is uncertain; she feels an intensity, but she does not need to resolve it, only be aware of it.

Keya's back is sore from sleeping with her mattress on the floor. Post shower, she has a big brunch, smokes a roll-up on the balcony, slings her bag over the corduroy shirt and worsted trouser combination. Stepping into flat-soled sandals, she likes the red-grey mix of her comfortable get-up; it is a nice colour contrast too.

That day's session with Agni is marked by a most surprising revelation.

In the middle of showing Keya some old press cuttings from German newspapers, Agni—she insists Keya call her that—abruptly quizzes her: the Mir Ali she was asking about, was he an Iranian accountant by any chance?

'I used to know a Mir Ali and his family; they lived in Kreuzberg in the 1980s. He audited for a German friend's business.'

'No. The Mir Ali I am interested in was from India.'

'And you say he had no other names. So he could not be Mir Ali Baig from Pakistan.'

'His complete name was Mir Ali and he was from Kashmir.'

'So, what do you know about Mir Ali then?' Agni put the ball right back in Keya's court.

'I don't know anything about him. That's why I asked.'

'I spent a day thinking about it. And I've decided that I am going to tell you what I know,' she adds.

'I'm all ears,' Keya leans forward.

'But dear, please tell me why you want to know about Mir?' Agni's eyebrows rise and fall, her palm cups her chin. She is every bit a dance drama actor.

Keya is taken aback at the sudden sally.

'Oh, that. Mir Ali, you see…Someone is looking for him.'

'Actually, looking to find information about him, to be more exact,' she amends.

'Someone?' Agni asks. 'You knew him?'

'Not me,' Keya quickly answers. 'His son. I recently met him. I know him,' she cannot think of anything else to say.

'I didn't know they had a son, but it has been so many years now,' she replies.

'His name is Leon,' Keya informs her.

'Really,' she states, with not much expression. Then looks at a picture of her own son on the mantelpiece, 'I don't know where Mir Ali is. We don't know anything after he and Shula left. I can tell you of the times before that.'

'Shula?' Keya repeats the name. Agni's words make her feel the force of a returning wave.

It is the first time she has ever heard of someone called Shula.

'You don't know the story then?' Agni brows rise and fail to fall.

'No...But I would be very grateful if you could tell me it,' Keya does not want to press too obviously, and she cannot withdraw from being so near to unlocking a mysterious door.

'It's a very filmi story. Shula Farid was married to a man. A good man of society, his name was Abhilash. But she was so...umm...' Agni searches for a word, 'restless,' she spits oratorically.

'I knew the first time I saw her and Abhilash together, at a celebratory function after our dance event in the diplomatic mission cultural centre, that there was something not right with their relationship. They were too formal for their age, and very expressive in their politeness towards each other. Not like a husband and wife behave. I had been through marital turmoil myself, so I knew. Moreover, I had seen many women like her in the Bombay cinema industry—'

The allusion to the diplomatic mission cultural centre rightaway makes Keya think of Ramnath the clerk's evasiveness that time at the Embassy. 'Would this be the Indian mission centre?' she interjects.

'Yes, classical dance programmes are held there,' Agni says simply. 'Shula was the wife of Abhilash Basu, a Foreign Service man, bureaucrat of high order at the offices here. I admired him,' she breaks into a laugh, 'but no one succeeded in seducing him! He was an upright pillar of society—urbane, measured and ambitious. He made his point persuasively. Like I said, I admired him.'

She continues, 'Shula was an unconventional pick of a wife for him. Singular. Everyone thought so, and I must say there was some truth in it, even though I liked her and was almost a friend to her in some matters.'

'You said they had left. So you mean Mir and Shula went away? She left her husband for Mir?' Keya asks to make things clear.

'I think that is what happened. But with issues where officials are involved, things are not spoken about openly, so one doesn't know whose side of the story to believe. I would trust Shula.'

Keya cannot be certain whether Agni is implying more than what she is verbalizing.

'Why was she singular and unconventional?' Keya persists.

'Did I say that?' Agni is caught off-guard. 'I don't mean it in a bad way. I like rebels and non-conformists. I've broken many rules, as you know. But people just weren't sure what she was rebelling against, with being married to a sensible man like Abhilash.'

'When was this?'

'In the '80s, but when...hmm...let's see; Leena's wedding, Shula was still here, because she had looked stunning in her outfit. We had all asked her to stay longer, but she had left urgently—I later knew why. This must be some years before 1989, around 1987, I think.'

'What did you find out later? You referred to something a second ago.'

'What a tale! Hah. I was a part-time Cupid. I was drafted in to help her.' Agni pats her hair. 'Abhilash had briefed the drivers and Shula's activities were under close observation. I was one of her only remaining friends and I used to help them meet. I mean Shula and Mir. Before that, there was a time when Shula could not communicate with Mir at all. I knew it was adultery, it was bad and wrong, but she was so miserable, even though Abhilash...I don't think he could be a bad husband.'

Then, out of the blue, Agni whispers, 'Can you imagine, at one point they used the Wall as a noticeboard a couple of times?'

Keya is agog, 'You mean The Wall?'

'Yes, The Berlin Wall,' she underscores, 'Lovesick fools! I kidded Shula about this when I was trying to cheer her up once. I said, here is the Wall that grows up inside the best moments of my marriage—our anniversary when Christian and I were still happy, and before his mother became such an issue—and the same Wall is your easel of love. Of all things. Mir would leave some codes for Shula scrawled on it, I suppose telling her how much he loved her,' Agni recalls with a grin, 'Anyhow...And so she would, during one particularly bad phase, go and scan it from the road to see if he had left any agreed or special marks for her—'

'That is so unusual!'

Agni sighs affectionately, 'It is, isn't it? Those were crazy times. People and politics and love, it was mixed up. We were so sure. All of us. So sure.'

'What was Shula like?' After reaching thus far, Keya has to continue digging.

'She was strikingly beautiful. I mean, really! She should have been in the movies. She had green eyes, good skin, long dark hair and a lovely curvy body that was like an apsara's. Dressed up and smiling at the social events that she attended, she looked ravishing. We envied how she managed to be so beautiful. She knew it too.'

And then, 'It wasn't a surprise; she had the best of both worlds. Her mother was from Europe, and she settled in Santiniketan with her professor husband. Shula was an only child and could be quite opinionated about her parents and her heritage. She was herself Muslim, I suppose Farids are, even though she married a Basu.'

'You remember much,' Keya remarks.

'It's true. I did covet her life. She had a marvellous husband, beauty, and she was poetic—'

'Oh.'

'—even though she was reticent about her artistic abilities. She spurned invitations to recite and did not send her poems for publication. Later, when I started helping her meet Mir, she opened up and showed me her poems and sketches. When you got to know her, you saw how talented and lovely she was. At the time, she was childless.'

'I'm quite surprised that her name never came up in connexion with my Indian artists in Berlin historical project. I never picked up anything about her from anyone,' Keya wonders aloud.

'I'm not surprised in the least. People are sensitive to power. As I said before, where senior officials are involved, things get hushed up. Shula's husband was an influential man.'

'You're right.'

'Also, Shula was a closet artist. She never put her paintings or poetry out in public. I know, because I was a friend and an artist myself. I have to perform for the applause, for training others. I can't imagine having a talent and wasting it like she did.'

'You said she was childless. Did that worry her?'

'I don't think so. She never said anything about it to me.'

'What about Mir? Did you meet him?'

'I wish I had. I was curious. But the closest I ever came to seeing him was when I dropped her off near a bridge where he was waiting for her in a car. I could not find a place to park. She was late, there were vehicles behind me, and I could not stop to see him. I did not have a driver,' she titters, 'I had to drive myself.'

'So you know nothing about him?'

'That's right! You wanted to find out about Mir, and I have been going on about Shula! Let me try…She had met him here in Berlin. He was a poet, but single, I think. So you see, he did not have the problems that she had with being married. They wrote a lot of poetry to each other. Met a few times in the old Krantzler café, over near the Ku'damm, but usually, they would go for day trips lasting hours. Then, one day, we heard they had both gone away! Eloped. After that, people in the circle shunned this topic. Later, we heard Abhilash had gotten himself a transfer. People lost interest. You know how it is with such things! News today, forgotten tomorrow. I made efforts to find her, but I was quite hurt that she never wrote after leaving, so I gave up. I've not been in touch with either Abhilash or Shula since then. I just hoped, and still hope, that they are happy, back together or wherever they are.'

Mir and Shula had eloped. But Leon had said Mir was married to his mother Albeena when he vanished. Had Mir lied to Shula about his previous married life? Did she return to Abhilash afterwards? Or, had Shula lied to Agni about Mir being single? Keya is in a tizzy. She must try and trace Shula.

'I'm sorry to bother you, but before we resume our interview, can I ask if you have any address for Shula? As a last favour,' Keya entreats.

'Address, address...umm...I don't have any address for her. Other than the one she scribbled on a note that time; you see, I had to go to India in connexion with a theatre performance of my students, and since I was visiting Calcutta, she gave me an address,' Agni empties the contents of a manila envelope, then looks through her concertina file. At last, she extricates a yellowing sheet of paper from a transparent holder. She holds it out to Keya, 'Here it is, but it is Abhilash's family address.'

'Thanks ever so much.'

'Shula was from Santiniketan; I think I already told you that. A year before I was to go to Calcutta, her parents died in a train accident in Bengal. It was so tragic. She was distraught when she spoke to me about that, but she kept her outward pose generally,' Agni trails off. 'Oh yes, that is why I do not have her Santiniketan address, otherwise, I would have met her parents at their house.'

Keya thanks her again, copying the address of Mr Abhilash Basu in Kolkata. She writes down Shula's name too, carefully checking the spelling with Agni, 'S-h-u-l-a F-a-r-i-d,' and casually observing, 'Shula is an unusual name for an Indian.'

'You don't say,' Agni fires with hilarity, 'What about Agnes or Keya?! I am Christian. What's your excuse?'

Keya replies she was named for a novelist her mother had adored.

'Shula might also have been named by her mother. She was part Jewish, I think,' says Agni.

'We could resume the interview now. It's a nice segue as well, since I want you to talk about how your belief in your religion has affected your conception of an artist and your relations with people in your adopted country,' Keya begins.

'Before we go back to that, tell me, why is Shula's son, this Leon, looking to find information about his father Mir? Did Mir leave Shula? Is she back with Abhilash now? I am curious.'

'Leon is not Shula's son. His mother's name is Albeena. Mir

had a wife, but left her when she was pregnant. Leon has never met his father.'

'Oh dear! I am terribly sorry to hear that. I am sure Shula said he was single when she met him. So, because of Shula, he left a wife he had! May God pardon me for helping them. The poor son,' Agni's eyes are watery.

Is she emoting?

'Don't blame yourself. Mir left his wife some years before he knew Shula. If the years you remember are correct, Leon was already born then.'

'It is quite tangled. I don't know about Shula and Mir, but I'm glad I was never in such complicated relationships.'

'Hmm, thanks for all your help.'

'Don't think of it. Please. To come back to answering your question, I am deeply religious in a spiritual way—'

Agni cuts herself short, 'Wait, let me refill those cups with tea, and then we can continue talking.'

When the interview is done and Keya is ready to leave, she hands Agni a thank-you gift for her time. There is no monetary remuneration for the interviewees' time, so when she can, she tries to give people a symbolic token of her gratitude. For Agni, she's chosen a carved replica of an African tribal mask and a fountain pen.

'Keya, my car has a dead battery, or I would have given you a ride back to your place.'

'Thank you for that thought. Please don't worry. It's a lovely evening, I like to walk.'

They agree to communicate via letters—Agni does not use email—if there are other questions or things needing clarification. Keya bids her kindly host goodbye.

She doesn't take any transport and walks the hour's way back. She has copious notes from the interviews. She needs to use a library to get copies of some German government publications from that period: the relevant ministry papers on cultural policy and funding in the 1980s. The photocopies would have to be authenticated as well, but she thinks she can wrap it up with a couple of days work in Berlin. She can head back to Bristol over the weekend.

She has been skirting the revelation. Nonetheless, it plays on her mind. The running green man symbol, the Ampelmänn, in a traffic light, prompts her to cross the road. Yet, Keya stands defiant on the pavement. She finds herself interested in Shula's story. The ravishing closet artist adulteress eloping with her lover; she must know more. Can it be that Agni had dramatized her? Or the story?

Keya immediately checks her watch. Yes, not yet 5.00 p.m. She takes out her phone and calls Ramnath the clerk at the Embassy. She leans on a pillar, staring down at her sockless feet in sandals, as she tells him, without revealing the source, what she has found. Ramnath directly corroborates the truth of the story, saying he did not want to let her know earlier because there had been a scandal and a cover-up following the event. 'I am still in service, so I can't leak anything. I hope you understand.'

She hangs up feeling a mix of relief, gratitude, trepidation, excitement and fearful anxiety. How can she tell Leon this? Should she tell Leon this? How will he react?

Upon reaching the flat, Keya boils water in a kettle, then pours it in a pan—choosing a short cut—and drops two handfuls of conchiglie pasta in it. Eating it with microwaved tomato and mascarpone sauce a few minutes later, she reaches a conclusion about the Shula and Mir revelation. She will tell Leon what she's found out, but not the first thing when they meet next. She will couch it amid other things and make it seem spontaneous.

I chase the remaining leads at a documentation centre. There is a copy of a 'Passierschein,' a pass permit, in the records of Berlin Wall crossings, which mentions Mir Ali by name, but nothing else. Anyway, it dates from the time that Mir was in Berlin, to Ammi's knowledge.

I am impatient and unsure where this is headed. I don't like to sit in offices in front of people I don't know—like that American guy Bill today—and reiterate my story every time. They enquire about so many things before they'll agree to help. My life feels bogus when I try to sum it up. Every place I tell the story, I lose something of me. It is different if the person who I am talking to has a genuine interest—I didn't feel fake telling it to Keya, or even Jutta. But when it is an office, there just isn't a human angle. I feel recorded.

Enough! I am going to give up this charade and go back to London! I miss my life there. The familiarity of my room, the city with a language I can understand, even the rain. Berlin was a bad idea. I'll never find Mir. Ammi is right—when I spoke to her the morning after coming back from Keya's place, she said I sounded chirpy—there is a reason behind stuff that happens.

I dial Keya's number.

'Hi! What are you up to?'

'Not much; web surfing.'

'How was your day?'

'So-so. Yours?'

'Ditto. But I am upbeat.'

'Hmm. I'll fly back over the weekend. It'll be good to get a week in Bristol before teaching starts after Easter. How long are you here for?'

'Not much longer. I haven't a job that needs me desperately. I'm a free bird.'

'Well, free bird, don't rub it in,' she is the teeniest bit stiff.

'Keya, do you want to meet up?'

'I hope I do not have to choose a statue at the fountain again.'

I am kicking a round pebble on the ground in front of me.

'I couldn't make you do that,' I bounce back, 'I know you love each of those four women. It's too much love going astray. You choose a place.'

'What about Kreuzberg somewhere? There's this road, I like the vibe there, Bergmannstraße. Will you be able to find it or do you need directions?'

'I have a map. Let me check. Hold on a sec.'

My pebble went gambolling into a thicket. I was outside a tube station.

'Okay, in an hour?'

'Oh no, Leon! I had no idea you meant today. I've just had loads of pasta and am all ready for bed.'

'It's 7.00 p.m.!'

'Remind me to repeat that when I call you in the morning at 10.30 a.m. and you're in bed.'

It is uncomfortably intimate. I am nervous.

'I'm sorry, Keya, I should have clarified first. Would you mind meeting me tomorrow, same place?'

'Leon, don't switch into such a formal mode, please.'

'I'm ever your blithe pal.'

'Great. Why don't we meet at…let's see…the Mehringdamm station about 6.30 and then walk from there? My turn to get us dinner.'

A butch girl in a parka is pasting |System of a Down| music posters on fibreboard panels that are part of a scaffolding. I make way to let her pass.

'Sure.'

'Bye for now.'

'Keya? Hello?'

'Ya, go on.'

'Bye, and by the way, I've something to tell you when we meet,' I tantalizingly leave this in the air. I want to tell her I've found my peace with the search. And that it's because of her.

The next day when we meet, I notice that Keya is wearing a black suit. She seems severe in that outfit. I try to get the lovemaking image of her out of my head.

'Wow, you are dressed for a business meeting!'

'I had to meet a ministry official today. And people do judge books by the cover,' she grins, before continuing, 'I thought we could have dinner at a proper sit-down place.'

'If they'll let me in.'

She gives me an up-down look, 'Why not? You're always dapper.'

She is preoccupied in crossing the street with care.

I feel odd. Is she being brusque?

When we are on the other side, she turns to me, 'You know, Leon, I've always been insecure about my looks. I grew up surrounded by the 'fair is beautiful' shit. If I went to social gatherings dressed in certain colours, people would immediately say, you should not wear that dull colour. It does not suit you. It makes you look darker than you are. It was a while before I could wear black and not feel it was wrong.'

I didn't know what to say. 'What do people know, you'd look good in anything if you ask me.'

'Thanks. That's called fishing for a compliment. Hmm...Do you feel like French?'

I kill the first resonance of her words in me. 'I'm not fussy. I eat American food. British food. Ping cuisine. Anything.'

'Let's have something nice in this cosy place.'

'Sure.'

Walking in, we sit facing each other over the lit candle on the table, but it's not the same as when we had that romantic evening by the fountain last time. I feel in her a dynamic energy, like she has a goal, she is efficient. I guess meeting important people and being successful requires that.

'Keya, will you excuse me a minute?' I quickly make my way to a florist outside and come back with a jaunty step and a bunch of white calla lilies.

'They're bewitching. It's so wonderful of you. Thank you!'

As the cocktail apéritifs arrive, and we raise our glasses to a cheer, I bet the people around us think we are schmaltzy lovers.

It is syrupy and fantastic.

I am on a high, as if I have discovered something new.

'Tell me,' she asks, 'what were you going to tell me? You referred to something on the phone yesterday.'

'I was thinking how I miss London,' I say, 'even more than I missed Delhi when I left it. I will leave Berlin soon.'

She appears strangely cheered up, 'I think that's a good idea.'

'Mir might be dead. In fact, he probably is dead. If he was alive, I would have found something.'

'Hmm...Could be.'

From her reaction, I sense that she doesn't want me to talk about this, so I change the subject. There's no rush, I can find another way of telling her how much I value what she's done in freeing me from the past. I like her.

'So, I thought of London a lot yesterday. I had this imperious urge to eat a biryani—a proper Hyderabadi biryani.'

'You should have said. We could have gone to an Indian place instead.'

'Why? I am enjoying it here.'

'Can you find proper Hyderabadi biryani in London? Because you sure can't in Bristol!' she laughs.

'You can, in London, if you try hard enough, if you know where to go.' I recall my first days in England when I ate canned food from a shop run by a Pole. 'Otherwise, it is faux food, and the oily taste of Sylheti curries carried away at midnight in takeaway foil packs.'

'I've always experienced that Indian food here in Europe is better than in the UK.'

Our order arrives. The ratatouille and artichoke risotto are yummy. As we begin eating, she tells me about the herbs involved in Provençal cooking.

I am not interested but I want to appreciate her knowledge, so I say, 'You can function so capably in European places—you know the language, you know what food to order, you are talented at work.'

'What are you trying to say? I am inauthentic?' I am caught off-kilter at the defensive words, but when I look up at her, she has an innocent twinkle in her eyes and a smile dimples on her cheeks.

'No, no. I meant that you can be very European.' Shit, it sounds wrong and judgemental.

Luckily, she does not take offence. 'I like Shahrukh Khan movies. I grew up in a Delhi locality and I played typical desi games as a child, where friendships are made and broken with the thumb and lip gestures of Abba and Kutty.'

I have stepped on her toes somehow. 'I didn't mean to doubt your Indianness. How can I? Who am I?'

I am relieved when the waiter comes to refill our glasses.

'When did you come to the UK?' she asks.

'Before 9/11. You?'

'Before New Labour.'

It is not funny, but we giggle like we are sharing a joke.

'What's the goofiest thing you've ever wanted to do?' she asks another question.

'Me? I was born goofy. Let me think...I'd love to be in the 1960s, free love, hippies, the open doors of perception. I did pot in my postgrad year. It speeded up time. In London, one day, I was reading Huxley's *Doors of Perception* on a bench in Tavistock Park, when a fellow man, a down and out British Asian, came up to me. He saw the title of my book, my clean shirt and shoes, and said, "Man, wass dat you reading? Your shirt is so white, it making me blind. Do you wash it in DAZ or what. You so good, not like me. I am in the dumps. I do, like, drug advising."'

I do an impression.

I don't know why, but I can't stop talking.

'How did you respond?' she asks.

'Not very well, I'm afraid. I was new to the city at the time. Scared shit of everything.'

'How did he react?'

'He was too sloshed to mind.'

'Park benches in London, that could be an entire realm of gathered encounters. Hey, Keya, you like collecting stories, don't you? Why don't you collect all those stories of accidental conversations on London park benches—or park benches anywhere—and call them—'

'Please Mind the Gap,' she completes. Sighs. 'Yes, why don't I?'

I'm not sure how to interpret this, so I say, 'Did you read that Goethe book?'

'Not yet. It's a scarcity of time thing. It flies.'

'It does,' I echo.

Then I ask her, 'My turn now, tell me what's the goofiest thing you've ever wanted to do?'

She bats straight out, like it was waiting to be uttered, 'To be a man for a while.'

'What?...Why?' I am surprised.

'I want to be physically a man so that I can see the world from that body. To be free like men.'

'Wow!' I wonder which exact freedom she lacks.

'It is a limitation. A boundary I cannot transgress. It enrages me the way men have infiltrated my imagination.'

I am about to make a wisecrack, but I see the sententious look on her face and stop. She is serious.

'Men of the myths, the heroes. Since I was a child, I've read these tales of adventurers and explorers and doers and big dreamers, people who've changed things, and they're all damn men. I've got a Madam Curie, an Indira Gandhi, Mary Wollestonecraft, Catherine the Great, Amelia Earhart, Jhansi ki Rani, and others, I know—I do know. But it's not the same. Women are fewer, they need to be recovered from the pages of history. Anyway, I don't want to be Florence Nightingale.'

'Joan of Arc?'

'That's it. To break the mould, you need to be mad or heretic or be called a witch, or be more manly than the men—I'm thinking of Thatcher—or take the soft feminine road, be a muse or beloved, or be self-effacing, which is not wrong at all. It's just that—'

'But it is. It is wrong to sacrifice and suffer.' I find myself faced with Ammi's life.

'You think I am ranting?' she tilts her head.

'No, Keya. I think you are right. When I was in college, it was quite an experimental time for me. I used to try so hard to be cool, to be accepted. So, I'd carry Camus in my pocket, watch Guru Dutt and Satyajit Ray movies. When I came to London and after 9/11, I was depressed. I'd read outlandish books. And it's funny that I think of it now, all those characters I admired—they're all men! It is bizarre! I saw them as people, universal people.'

'You, Leon, totally get my point,' Keya beams.

'Wait! So, I sort of agree with your point. Because I've also wanted to be these people, these boys and men, the seekers, the courageous souls. This character who is in search of something true, something he cannot name. But—'

'But what?' she prompts. 'This character is always a man with the freedom to travel.'

'But, apart from the heroes of history—and honestly, I don't care about the Big Picture in that way—to be free, you have to have acceptance which comes with money.'

'Money can't buy respect.'

'Can't it?' I think of college, with resentment. 'People judge a book by its cover, as you said.'

'You are right; social class hierarchy hasn't gone away. And religion.'

'Having been a status-less Kashmiri Muslim man in India, I have to agree.'

'At least you are British! I saw your passport at the airport,' she sounds irked by the fact.

'My life would have been very different if I hadn't been born by an accident of personal history in ye olde England!' I say.

'Leon, it's not you alone I envy. I envy the unfair privilege that a passport confers. Though I suppose it is an improvement if passport colour beats skin colour when it comes to prejudice. It can, at least, be changed!'

I smile, 'I get questioned, too, sometimes. The trick is to be very polite, say Sir and Madam, and endure.'

'Be submissive to injustice, you mean,' she exclaims.

'Partly injustice, partly their job.'

'That's not good enough. I want to belong to the world. And I am willing to learn things in different places. Yet I cannot. I feel insecure that despite all the degrees, education and the job, I am treated like some fool or cheat when I travel. And why should that be fair? Especially when I look at the Euro-American free domain over the world. Come to think of it, I am enormously privileged. People die of dehydration on ocean rafts, suffocate in lorries, face fierce dogs, prison walls and inhuman insults—why? Because they want to earn a living or escape violence, and they were born on the wrong global latitude and longitude, imaginary lines that dictate real fates. What a world!'

She is emotional, opinionated, and totally unable to see that everyone in the world is not like her. I don't want to anger her further.

'I know what you mean; well, I can try to imagine,' I offer.

'I don't mean you, Leon, because you probably have it rougher, being a Muslim.'

'Sorry, I am not a fun person to dine with. All right, I'll shut up with my passport-envy now,' she traces her finger over a napkin.

'Keya?' I repeat her name.

'What?' she enquires.

'We should all revolt,' I wink mischievously.

'How?' she speaks up, running her finger cursively on the tablecloth spelling h-o-w.

'Here's how…If one day, all the people around the world were to refuse to produce their passport upon travel—just refuse, on principle. Hide it or burn it or something, and say, we do not know, we want everyone to have the same paper of identity, wherever they are.'

She's excited at this silly spontaneous idea of mine. What a babe! I want to kiss her.

Jocular but impressed, she adds, 'Fabulous. The systems would not be able to cope with such civil disobedience. Passport bonfires, non-cooperation and boycotts until people are treated better! How Gandhian! The strategy has worked before.'

I like it, so I continue, 'Let's make a manifesto.'

She giggles.

'Keya, careful,' I gag, 'you are bringing out the Leon in me. The Trotsky, after all!'

'Shhh—lest some Stalinist stab you!'

A couple look at us pointedly.

We simmer down. The world passes us by outside the glass shutters.

After a quiet moment, she says, 'I'll have to do with the animation genre till the big revolution.'

'Hmm?'

'Some Japanese animation and other fantasy games have girls and women do everything. I don't need to think of being a man watching them.'

'I won't be able to see Lisa Simpson without thinking of you.'

'How cute,' she satirizes.

Our plates are being cleared.

She gently sets the calla lilies to one side, and reverts into her serious face from earlier in the evening. I can't decipher it.

'I want us to be good friends, at the very least,' she says, her voice level.

'Sure.' I feel nervous, like an exam were to begin.

The dessert menus are placed on the table.

'I am not sure how to say this, and I still don't know if I should, but I have something to tell you too,' her preface exacerbates how I feel.

My first instinct is to get up and run away. Whatever the hell it is, it doesn't sound good, and I am in such a nice place after so long that I don't want to be hurt with anything again. Please, don't tell me! I want to warn.

'Go ahead,' I drop my gaze.

She settles the bill and pays in advance for a liqueur and coffee, then adjusting her voice to suit the Provençal décor of the café, she begins storytelling.

This strange woman who is trapped in so many people's stories. Yes, this beautiful naked woman I fucked, this bluestocking who belongs everywhere, she cruelly rips apart my delusion of peace with the search. When I had reconciled to theory (a) from the diary— Missing Mir died in an accident, she tells me she has proof he was gallivanting with an adulteress seven long years after he was gone.

Maya's face flashes before me; when I had jilted her, she had cursed me with ferocity, 'You loser, you swine, it is in your genes to desert women—I am sure your father left your mother for another woman! You've inherited the blood of cheats.' She was right. The bastard Mir had screwed my mother over for a woman.

I am thunderstruck. I listen with an intense surrender. Keep my eyes fastened on Keya and ask no questions. To torture me on purpose, she is being as detailed as possible. At the end, she even indicates the availability of an address.

I request to see it, as she expects me to, for she immediately dives into her bag and draws out a yellow square of Niceday notepaper.

I hold it up.

She looks at me as if I am a mix of chemicals in a tube with a reaction about to happen.

I will not please her with a display. No more additions to her storybook on my account.

'But this is your handwriting,' I remark.

'Yes, I had copied out the address.'

'I wanted to see how she—Shula Farid—wrote,' I manage to say.

The bitch Shula Farid. Could she not even have asked Mir to keep contact with his ex-wife and son? Damn beautiful fickle women! I'm glad Ammi is plain.

'It's strange how we met, and now, it's as if I've known you. Whatever I've learnt about Shula and Mir—' Keya is still talking.

I feel bitter and mad at her.

'I had made up my mind that I would keep to myself what I had learnt from Agni, but then I thought you should know what happened. That he may not be dead. I hope I did the right thing?' she breathes out.

'Yes, you did,' I give a tired reply.

There is nothing more to say to this woman Keya, the deus ex machina, the devil in an angel's garb. I am woebegone.

'Are you all right?' she asks.

I am sinking in a well. I am puke-ish. I hear her, muffled.

'I am exhausted. I want to go back to my room and sleep,' I speak like an automaton. I stand up suddenly.

She jumps up, and we leave. As we part ways, she hugs me, I think. I am not sure. My body is inert, my hand limp. She says something as I trudge away. I do not look back.

I pull myself around the corner and feel an old unhappy Leon resurgent in me. I curse volubly.

I wish I'd never met Keya.

My head hurts.

The road is full of people. Gaudy early weekenders are celebrating. Am I in a carnival? A carnival where only those with happy faces can go? I miss the underground station.

The food rolls about in my stomach. I feel sick and vomit by the bushes. I am fumbling in my pocket. What am I looking for? I have an urge to shout. I tear up a poster on a lamppost. Good. I should tear up everything in sight. Why should I care? I have him in me. He doesn't care. I don't care. I don't want to care.

A beggar; I don't want to listen to anyone's sob story. I have no loose change, and even if I did, I would throw it on top of passing cars from an overbridge! Yes, I will glower, as much as I want.

Here. Here is the station. Get on the line and go home. Go Home. Ha ha. Home is not a place. Home is a fucking state of mind.

I need the spare key. Jutta is asleep early. I wish I could sleep right now. I cannot bear to face the mirror. Who will I see there? Me; the one face in the world I would rather never see again, because who knows how much of it is him? I hate my face. My face—of which probably the eyes and the nose and the chin and the cheek are all due to him. Albeena and him. Mir.

The man who...No, go on, say it the way you wanted to say it the first time. Say it the way you have been wanting to say it every time that you did not have him there. When you realized at school, when friends at college pitied you silently and oh-so-discreetly for being the one with a chip on his shoulder. Say it the way you wanted to say it all those times. Say it the way you wanted to, in that overdone French place in front of Keya.

I should have looked up and said, Keya, that man was a bastard. Don't you understand? I am a bastard. Say it to the sky...Mir was a bastard who left his pregnant wife for some beautiful adulteress. Damn it. I, his son, don't know his whereabouts because the beautiful adulteress can't take on so much baggage? Because she wants him and him alone? Because he wanted her so much that he could not even care enough to let anyone know where he was going with her? Because she was his muse? His damn reason for a cause, or whatever it is, whatever it's supposed to be. I am tired. Do you hear? Leon Ali is tired. Leon Ali is a bloody coward who cannot face up to the fact that he was abandoned.

What happened? Have I been staring at the sky for the last half-hour? Air, I want some air. And cigarettes. I shall smoke a whole pack of them. The largest and the strongest I can find. Pity, I cannot be drunk here in this room that is not mine, where the Klimt pisses me off. Art and Shit. The damn jeans, the same face, the shiny coins, and here I am. Me.

I am going down the stairs again. The Bohemian neighbour's flat is full of sounds. The air feels stale and there are just too many voices everywhere. Sitting on an iron fence, I am smoking as if my life depends on it. I need to get through the whole pack. People smile as they pass me by. I want to scream from the top of a cliff for them all to fuck off.

Why did I come here? To look for what? I am numb. I don't know what I am saying, but I realize from my lips that they are moving, and my eyes register nothing. There are sounds everywhere, rubber on road, flesh on flesh, and night on day. Somewhere in this haze, I will reach my bed and never wake up. I will wake up. I close the door to my room and lie down.

I cannot bat. Shula was beautiful, I learn. Shula as a huddled old woman with her head full of white hair, I see. And Mir, my father, what shall I wish for you? A slick Kalashnikov. I cannot do things just because they need to be done, or I would have kept on being in India with Maya.

I am Hamlet. I am the seeker trapped in the Inferno. I cry to the world. To be or not to be, that is the fundamental fucking question. I cannot even lose my mind.

Sure, this moment will pass, but it will leave behind its shitty residue, like all moments, like every moment. I seek nothing. I want no father. I want to be forced neither by moral authority nor by sweet love to become selves that I am not. I am crazy. I am a crazy.

'Leon, Can I come in, Leon?'

'Huh—okay.'

Jutta shuffles around the room, not looking at me.

'I knock before, but you were sleeping. I come because I want to get Klip out.'

Klip?

The cat. My head is blurry.

'Your door was not properly closed and Klip pushed in,' she explains.

I sit up. It's morning. Fat Klip hides under the wooden table before eventually meowing out with his tail held up straight; it brushes part of my toe at the edge of the bed. I bristle.

'You want coffee? I have extra at the table.'

'Sure,' I mumble.

Why not? More coffee. Ash in my mouth from the twenty cigarettes last night. I am floating.

The door shuts behind her. I stare at the tired big brown pieces of wood that are crafted for use around in the room; they must have come from the Burmese jungles, and now, here they are with me.

I hobble to the curtains and open the window. The day is bloody bright, as if to spite my mental state.

It is a day for picnics and a day to run away from everything. Like him. Did he leave with her on a sunny day?

At the table, I quietly sip. quietly sip. TV is on in German.

'Till when are you here?' Jutta asks.

I want to down the whole mug in one go and dodge her question. I am evasive, 'I should not have missed that plane.'

'Never mind.'

'Till when have I paid?'

'Tomorrow night.'

'That's it then. I will leave tomorrow.'

'Oh, I don't mean to ask like that.'

'No, honestly. It was planned before. I was going to leave tomorrow anyway,' I lie. And it is easy.

'How bright your last day in Berlin is! Cool but sunny, you must use it well.'

I nod.

It's not half past noon. I am walking to the underground station. I have no idea why. I have walked this road to the station these last weeks, still, it seems unfamiliar.

I get on the first line in, get off at the Zoo. I go out onto the road. A black man in a towering Wrangler ad looks at me. I march in front of the shops. See a memorial, feel irritated by the bright day and the homage in words and flowers.

I want to duck into the earth again.

I am not Leon, I decide. I will be empty of Leon. I will not think. I will not calculate. I will not speak. I will not be anyone.

I will be a nameless person in a city underground who is going nowhere. I am a nobody.

I am a NOBODY. Nobody at all.

✧

What Nobody Sees and Does That Day:

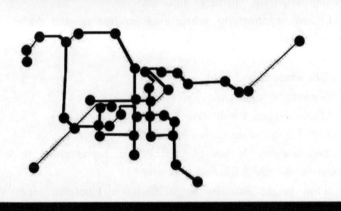

The city is a circuit of space, sign and subjectivity. Nobody is a madman. Don't follow him. He wanders for hours from one end of the city underground to the other, circulating mindlessly. All he sees are human marionettes. Nobody has sworn not to think, so he notices only what people look like, wear, carry and speak. He soaks in everything. It is a maddening day which yields absolutely no meaning. At night, he is collapsed—hot, sweaty, faint, painful—on a bench in Oskar-Helene-Heim station in Berlin.

✧

1:25 p.m. Streets.

Sees sun. Passes by a sleeping cat, a battered Mitsubishi Sapporo, psychedelic toys hung on a balcony. A Polizei man in uniform standing. Old women blowing noses and staring hesitantly/curiously at shop windows. Young men checking their reflections. Old men as if lost. Young women pressing ahead like battleships. A fluorescent Ford car. A Mercedes stopping as traffic lights change. People eating at the Imbiss. People having fish for lunch in the restaurant. Pinstripe variations on suits. Dresses obviously awkward. Nobody crosses as lights change again. People sit by mini-fountains with pretexts in the form of children, food or just weather-beaten folk smoking, dozing, pretending to read papers outside Wittenberg station. One man with 'loser' on his shirt reads the Welt Kompact. The ticket machine cunningly stands where it cannot be missed. Nobody does not validate his ticket. He goes into the womb of the earth and waits for U1.

U1 Uhlandstraße.

In a corner seat, Nobody sits and notices nothing, at first. Station passes. Women with popping eyeballs. A pair of lovers kissing. Bottle-blonde- wearing-off middle-aged women. Two sporty boys. Teenagers shouting at the last station. Nobody gets out and sees signs to a literature house and bookshop. He pretends not to have seen. Yet wanders right up to it, but does not go in at the door. Looks at Charlottenburg, surely affluent, cosy and arcane. Gets back into the station and waits for U1 Warschauer.

2:45 p.m. U1 Warschauerstraße.

People dressed comfortably, sloppily. Dozing and reading. A woman in folded up jeans, black foam jacket, round metal plate earrings, severe black glasses is reading with dark lipstick on her lips and a bag the colour of the fluorescent Ford. Some folk enter the tube and immediately glance around for corner

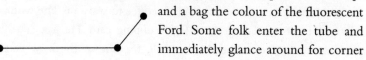

seats of carriages that are all gone; Nobody is in one too. Tube fills up at Kurfurstenstraße. A manly woman opposite stares at Nobody. The one sitting next to her is carrying Kemps rolls in her bag and does a crossword. A few seats away, a young girl with a Kefiyah scarf has a maroon jacket with a black hood on, green and white canvas shoes, black cord trousers and reads a thick book. People not doing books, papers or carriage TV sit with their eyes closed, some listening to music. A woman eats chunky Kitkat wearing mother-of-pearl pink shoes and reads the Welt Kompact. More people in. Nobody sits bolt upright to clear body space. A girl opposite in dazy hazy grey-blue stockings and short skirt carries biologie psychologie books, oversized headphones overcoming her head, tiny stud in pierced nose. Nobody peers into the next connecting carriage through the see-through windows and sees much the same, fewer people. The staring woman's jacket zip tassels are like Nordsee's fish logo. Nobody just gazes all around and tries with utmost force not to recall anything at all. Place next to him is vacant, but people prefer to stand. Nobody realizes that the pretend couple in ragged jackets and fat sloppy trackpants are actually ticket checkers. He shows them his pass instead of a ticket, they are surprised a little as if they expected him not to have one. They move to the next carriage, not finding anyone without a ticket still. The woman checker with cropped copper hair and a red windcheater fabric tracksuit is almost apologetic for checking. Another station and more people. A mother comes in wearing yellow trousers and a navy jacket with a kid aged less than five years, both suck on lollipops, not chocopops, eagerly, and talk in German. Nobody notices when getting out that there are glassy panels above the door, cameras?

Wander to S75 Spandau for Alexanderplatz.

The Warschauer Bridge has a ruinous underbelly full of train tracks. Nobody buys some more black coffee to wake up. The woman selling it insists he take a 10-1 free stamping card. He just takes it, it is easier than to refuse. Most of all, try not to think or recall.

At the Warschauer station, many green rabbits are stamped on the floor. Nobody stops and bends to peer at the green bunnies. An East Asian-looking guy sees Nobody peering at the green rabbits, and with amusement, violently jumps all over them. His manic jumping behaviour makes him seem a vagabond of choice. Nobody sees his fury dance and looks back at him while descending the stairs to the platform. The other guy smiles. Nobody gets on the S75. It's bigger and more accessible. More folks with families (kids in multicoloured socks and pink jackets), bags, two disabled vehicles. More scratches on window glass, saying variously, ZACK, TEKO, BDK, VSP, NUS, GDM, HMD and others. More women and more talk here. '928 ABH' is the vehicle number of one disabled guy. Nobody did not know that small disabled vehicles, too, needed number plates. Older conservative-seeming women wear soft leather, round-toe white shoes, jeans, pale jackets. An elderly couple compare their newspaper reading. Alex (Alexanderplatz) is here. An old, pale, limpid woman with bad teeth and hair on chin is poised in a wheelchair at the bottom of the stairs, looking up. When a large white guy asks if she needs help, she vehemently refuses.

Wander to U5 Honow.
  Going East. Back into U-bahn. Sees flower-sellers and buyers. A salami-seller eating bread, possibly with meat, eagerly. A man with blue jeans and green beret makes calls from a pink—fuchsia to be precise—public telephone. More people in U5, almost all desperately wanting seats, badly enough to ask co-passengers to remove bags. A guy stands beside, reading a book called *Die Gabe*. People seem upset by Nobody's glances darting all around. Quite a few times, they half-curiously half-strangely stare. A red and blue jacketed white woman wears an 'Om' in a silver locket. Two black

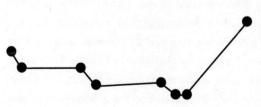

women standing near the door get off at Frankfurter Tor. There is a round camera at the centre of every seating segment in the train. A video eye in a yellow and black sticker is opposite and behind him. Nobody sees a lot of women with dyed hair, mostly blonde, and some horrifically dull shades of red. There are white shoes, and sometimes, white trousers, blue and red colours, jeans, big breasts, silver chains and lockets, some gold jewellery, back-combed '80s bouffant hair, metal-rimmed glasses, thin lips, patterned or hound's-tooth fabrics, and a definitely unfriendly vibe of barely concealed suspicion at times. A kid of less than ten sits opposite Nobody reading a book. Nobody senses a depressing dullness except for the chatter of a woman next to him. In the adjacent seating segment, a woman picks on her food and eats bits out of her sandwich. Most folk are drowsy in a late afternoon way. An Asian woman in her forties stands wearing a lilac top and unflattering jeans. No end to numbers in and out, no thinning of the passenger stream. The kid is reading *Artemis Fowl*. A guy wearing a deerstalker, sitting next to the chattering lot, reads a *Star Wars* book. Directly opposite him sits a man in black jeans and a 'muchmore' jacket, also reading with some engagement. Nobody feels his hands sweating like hell. No windows for fresh air. He also wants to pee. Coffee is a diuretic. Passing sub-urban greenery and scattered houses now. Sub is a perfect adjective for doing something subversive with words and worlds. The tube feels like an S-bahn even though it is a U-bahn. A large IKEA-type red and white complex passes by, it is signed 'Garten and Zoo'. Graffiti on every facing wall. Nobody makes out a 'Fuck You' and a 'Johnny Bravo'. Tons more people in at Wuhletal. Quite a few dressed in leather jackets. In maroon and beige, one woman's says 'College 69'. Two guys opposite in the middle talk as if to the gallery with a bravado in their demeanour. Tall rowdy kids in their teens in sneakers and half-shiny scrunched up combats shout as they exit at Kaulsdorf-Nord. Nobody is glad it is not night here alone. Endless stations pass by with an identical feeling of dead-end-ness, only some cosmetic dashes of colour here and there. Square, squat and lifeless buildings pass. Hellersdorf is a big exit station. The chatterer's friend is also off and she stares quietly into glassy distances. Nobody eagerly looks out for Honow that sounds like Hawai'i in his mind but resembles a desert strip. Chatterer fidgets with a bag and a small calendar. Someone's phone breaks the silence.

Honow and back.

Honow is a dead-end, and not just on the line. Nobody pays thirty cents for a pee and feels better. He could have not paid, but he does. Cycles, a pool, some pubs, a couple of bier-gartens, an apotheke and a hotel sums up the sight. A Rock-the-Nazis banner in pink. On U5 again. A big-built man in his late sixties, at least, with thinning white hair, beady eyes, leather file, and a Kaiser plastic bag forgets his paper and starts staring with some hostility at Nobody. He is really affected by Nobody's presence. Nobody looks conspicuously different from everyone else in this neck of the woods. A few stations later, the crowd gets varied. A young woman with knees torn out of her jeans and hair on way to becoming dreadlocks, a middle-aged woman in a cerise pinstripe suit; both attract lots of stares and sighs, especially from one Schröeder look-alike. One black guy at Wuhletal. At the graffiti stretch, Nobody catches the word 'Kazoo'. The windows of this carriage and all in view are clear, no scratches, no label tags, just lots of hand-smears. A well-dressed girl opposite with bad skin, hair falling over face, legs crossed, reads *Nächte im Harem*. Rusted dead-end tracks, houses upon houses. A nagging odour of lifelessness despite the few posters now and then. Sees a fat friendly guy with a moustache on the middle bench opposite—big black boots with yellow-black laces, grey socks, black torn trousers with white thread stitches, a jacket with large white checks on blue woolly stuff outside and red windcheater fabric inside, a bag, a beard, and a T-shirt with Garfield alongside the slogan 'I'm not completely worthless, I always serve [something unreadable]'. Most of him is covered in blotches of paint and whitewash. Train fills up. A baby with earflap cap and colourful get-up in a pram two carriages away plays with what appears to be a ticket for the tube. Some eccentrically dressed-up folk. An old man looks severely at a little girl in a light blue jacket and black skirt and shoes who reads a magazine as her legs partially obstruct his passage. Frankfurter Allee is a busy one. After Lichtenberg on way in, in Zone A, the crowd changes with skateboards common from Samaritenstraße onwards. Staring at people and things is a rule here. Three friends a seat away—two guys, a girl—one says the word 'Indisch'; Nobody couldn't care less. Adidas jacket girl opposite them stares non-stop. Schröeder fellow loses his focus, now that his party is gone. Woman opposite; large eyes, black and grey get-up, freckles, hair tied back, looks so bloody familiar, it's spooky. A policewoman complete with uniform and a charge-pad is waiting to get off at Alex. People are bored staring. Time to get off, Nobody tells himself. Spoke too soon, train is stuck somewhere and there is no movement. A few minutes pass. Driver makes an announcement asking for more time. People stare at the policewoman, her authority seems to pacify some real or imagined terror. Some stare at the TV screen, bored and resigned. Nobody feels like shit. Train seems askew, leaning a bit on one side. Both women opposite have mobiles in hand clasped like prayer beads. Tube moves again.

U8 Hermannstraße.

    This train does not have facing seats. At U8 platform, two pigeons play and a granny smiles at their wanders. Nobody wants to shoo them away. Not so much staring is at work now. Feels hunger finally. A French stripey sailor-jacketed woman reads a paper at the back of which is a picture of a naked woman. Opposite, two women sit  and talk. The Spanish speaking one wears a clock-hand brooch. A kid of about five is climbing the metal pole in the carriage. Soon, two of them are hanging upright from a grille looking for attention. Lots of traffic exchange in and out at Hermannplatz. A couple of fixer types, a tweed, familiar scratches on windows saying CREK, BHS and CASH, CASH, CASH. A

pushy, hungry and ruthless looking starlet is on TV. Two women and
one man; the one in black drapes herself all over the resisting guy.
End halt. Nobody is late getting off and is stuck inside the empty
train, doors close. Nobody reaches the train belly. Rings the alarm
and a driver with piercings lets him out from the tunnel inside.

S42 ring to Neukolln and to U7 Rudow.

Loud, crowded, but each to their own. The occasional
eavesdropper. Wait for U7. A teenager trying to one-handedly juggle
his big skateboard drops it over and over again. A baby cries, upset
over the sound? Nobody sees white Goths, Lebanese T-shirts. Feels
stared at. His favourite corner seat. Crowd reminds him of dull
bouffant red hair white shoe folk, though not as dead. One woman
stands wearing a headscarf. Nobody imagines how the big Honow
man would have stared at her. Some nodding old biddies. Stations full
of graffiti abbreviations—usually sharpish-shaped characters in blue
black, work of one group? Ad on TV of Cottbus University, study
there! Der Tagesspiel quite popular. All the white shoes make him

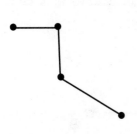

dizzy. Nobody hates white shoes that are not
sports shoes on anyone past their teens, at
most. A badly mascaraed woman in informal
cream suit, black sockless heels, wavy hair
and indeterminate ethnicity stares at him
periodically. Not just him, and with bad
vibes too. How many people having affairs,
cheating, avoiding and having something to
hide is he freaking out today with his constant gaze? Sees spindly-
legged old women with very short skirts. White and fading traffic
stays, others disembark slowly along. Rudow is another dead-end?
Not really, proximity to airport. Holiday Inn adverts, a girl rushing
for airport bus with baggage. Balconies with geranium baskets and
artificial birds on them.

U7 Rathaus Spandau.

A long ride in a cheery tube. Kids and bigger children talk excitedly. A woman carries a printed trouser suit in its transparent case. Another has a bicycle. A set of (grand)parents; him with umbrella, her with a headscarf, and the kid in pink with pearls and bows. London kind of badly dressed crowd. A guy with navy T-shirt, white fuck-finger forming the i of 'Sud-Berlin' on it. A ticket check at Blaschkoallees. The checkers look familiar. Short, smart Turkish guy caught with a problem. He has an argument but is walked off the tube at Grenzallee. Nobody wonders what next. The checker woman might have left him off, not so the man. Sud-Berlin gets off with his older mate who looks like someone from a café one night. At Karl-Marx-Straße, another Goth, skull on skirt, all black dress and spikes on each armband, doc martens. A Turkish woman with her kids gets on, older daughter rests head on mother's shoulder. Old monkey-faced white man with little spiky hair is staring at them over his paper. Then, abruptly gives up. Fairly unshaven, his right eye trails slowly over people and things, and then quickly returns on objects of interest. In the next carriage, two black guys

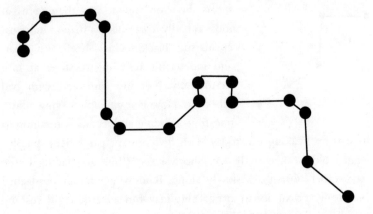

wear earrings in one ear. Goth is busy on an old mobile with an inch-long antenna. Books, TV, music, stares. Darker shoes, flatter hair. Gays and lesbians. Better trousers, bags, jackets, vibes. More busy and literary-looking fashionables. Orange and black spectacles look cool. Colourful and hip clothes on kids. Nobody sees a guy explaining something from the papers to his wife who appears gratified to be thus patronized. Two young girls run through the carriage between rows of people. A woman walks past with a tiger-print scarf, orange socks, red shoes, large bulbous red ring. A guy dressed in olive green one seat away looks super-bored. A woman chews her nails at the other end. Nobody's head hurts from this pointless soaking of the world. Past Wilmersdorfer Straße, crowd changes to older and more conservatively dressed people. Someone tries to sell the magazine *Notz* for 1.20 euro. No one listens. The American couple opposite finish their whispering to stare at the seller. He is poor and not up to it. His neck jerks a little when he walks off the tube. He has painstakingly combed his hair and carries an 'activ foto' crumpled plastic bag. A headscarf-clad woman texts away. Bespectacled man in grey-blue trousers and jacket rushes to get off, but the door closes; he waits with a rolled magazine. Yellow, red, green and black wires on the underground walls run madly along the glass panel in the door.

Rathaus Spandau, back in U7, Wedding from Jungfernheide.

Nobody buys the first thing he sees, once outside. An eis-crème at Florida Eis and a toast at the bakery. A sparrow gets trapped at the bakery inside the glass. He waits till it escapes finally. For more train madness. Not so many people now. Two guys talking in the facing seat, a woman with a top-crop of purple hair, an older man with bags, look up uncertainly when Nobody enters. People get on, get off. A guy smiles into nothingness, or possibly, his own reflection. Ads for Picaldi jeans and Hartnackschule. Purple top stands next to another curly head. Jeans, jackets and bikes abound. The carriage wallpaper is in pink and grey, it depicts Berlin symbols—the Brandenburg Tor looks like a comb and a hoe, and the other silhouetted monuments are like pistols of various kinds. Much younger now, the university crowd. Tolerant, self-focused and hopeful.

U6 Mariendorf.

A mix of older folk, younger students and a general chatter on the line. Nobody gets a bad seat. Some older women chew on a large berries. Two guys and a girl stand and talk. Jeans, leather shoes, long, neatly combed hair, hand in pocket and a Pilsner in the other hand. Loud speech and laughter. Slutty-looking woman chewing gum with open hair and make-up acts pert. The dude opposite has eyes manically peeled on a page that says 'Sex, Sex, Sex'. Sudden strong smell of detergent or cleaner. Nobody is tired. Alt-Mariendorf is like a little town near the station, a shopping and eating place, traffic, signs to Neukolln-Britz. Train in view to go to Tempelhof.

Tempelhof, S41/42 Innsbrucker Platz.

A woman walks up to Nobody. Sweater, two bags, short trousers, lots of hair, legs under pale withered tights, bad peeling skin. Leans over and says something to Nobody. He can't follow. 'I want Money. Money. Fifty cents.' He looks for change, then hands her some. She does not seem insane. Sitting opposite, she starts to violently comb her salt and pepper hair for a few minutes. It's oily and crackles with the static. She finally stops and puts an Alice band on, then starts to chew gum. What drove her to this? Mixed crowd in carriage, black, white, brown, Asian, Arabic. Nobody thinks he might have missed his station, but he hasn't. On his way to the S-bahn, Nobody gets into a lift with a woman in floral headscarf who has a little daughter in a pram and a small boy. There are also two bilingual Vietnamese French girls with a bicycle. The German voice announces 'Aushteeg' (austig) in a funny way. They laugh. Nobody wonders if he is psychically interruptive to these cheerful women. Sticker ads in the S-bahn. And windows scratched with SMK, ALM, 2F, 3L. Most people are getting off at Schoeneberg. A woman opposite wears multicoloured glass frames and leafs through FAKS Kunstprogram.

U4 Nollendorfplatz.

Not busy. Sees some gay guys busy with themselves. Couple of drunkards in the next cabin. Station arrives soon.

U3 Krumme Lanke.

Few people. Reading in carriages, dozing, gazing vacuously. At Wittenberg, a whole crowd is walking in; well dressed, well heeled, earnestly poring over the papers. The office returnees, late ones to the southwestern suburbs. Nobody notices that people here are excellent at avoiding lock-eye, like in London. A black guy makes 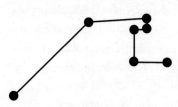 it in, panting, at the last minute. He's one of the ordinarily dressed. Nobody's palms are sweating non-stop. Next carriage, a bearded drunk stares a few moments at a bespectacled clean-shaven guy opposite who leans forward reading the *Economist*. A thought almost wells up inside Nobody, but then he winces, it is too much effort. His head and neck are painful. A well-dressed older man next to Nobody yawns.

᪂

Nobody is hot, sweaty, faint, painful—it is all a blur. I get off the underground train. Collapse on a bench.

I, Leon Ali, am lying shattered on a bench in Oskar-Helene-Heim.

I, Leon Ali, have exhausted myself and my senses.

I have been a Nobody rubbing myself on the fabric of the city the whole day; in its underbelly where the city ingests and digests bodies, I have been circulating like a diseased cell that cannot exit.

I chose to be Nobody because I wanted to feel nothing. I wanted to be futile.

᪂

It is dark. I lie as an ell with my feet near the ground and head on the wooden seat. I have been unconscious, I think. Then, it comes back. Vignettes of the day.

Everything starts to hit me. My body feels stuck in a violent jerking machine that is constantly moving, and I am being ferried and shuttled in an endless series of subterranean worms' bodies. Snake-like trains flicking their tails along the routes under the ground, clustered with people. I feel like I have been chewed up and spitted out. I ache in every muscle and joint, and my head is full of the air of other people's breath that I have been breathing the entire day. I experience myself as a part of other people's bodies, suits and dresses, hair and faces. But most of all, I exist in their stares and skin. I am under the skin of every one of the thousands of faces, only hundreds of which have registered. I cannot breathe, my lips are parched and my hands are trembling.

Moments later, the phone starts to ring. *Trrinng Trrinng.*

Shrill and Neurotic. Immediate and Unconsummated. This instrument is devilish. I do not count the number of times it rings. I simply let that sound flow into my own hell. And when the beast stops screaming, I comprehend that I am in pain.

My crumpled arms hurt. My head hurts. My legs hurt. My eyes hurt. The Pain is like a sensation on my tongue. Unlike everything else. It is Real. Palpable. Urgent. It demands something of me. I let the growing pain wash over me and I feel absolved. Just a little free.

In some measure of time that I have no capacity to grasp, I slowly get up. Sit hugging my knees. I blink several times and ball and un-ball my fingers into a loose fist. Then, I pick up the phone—what else can I do? The Moment Has Snapped and I feel incomplete and overindulged at the same time—and press buttons to return the call.

It was Keya. 'Who else?' says a voice I know.

9

Reconciliation

'Hello, Leon, where are you? How are you? I've been trying your number since the afternoon.'

Keya says she is concerned about me.

I tell her where I am. I mumble incoherently that I am nauseous, sweaty, dizzy, constricted. My hands shake.

'I'll be all right. I've had panic attacks before.'

'Breathe deep. Do you want me to come over?'

'No. The worst is done with. I'll be fine.'

She asks me what I have eaten and whether I slept yesterday.

'I am going to cook a meal. Come over, please. Get a cab. Shall I meet you at Wittenberg Platz?'

'Don't worry.'

'I absolutely insist.'

'I'll find my way to the flat.'

With effort, I haul myself up from the bench and slowly walk to the other platform. Leaning against a snack dispenser, I keep my eyes closed and try to see as little as possible.

I don't have the energy to go out onto the road. I get on the U3 back to her station and hail a cab.

She opens the door before I can press the bell. She fusses over me expertly. I sigh. I am dead tired.

'You are pale. Here, sit down and have a glass of orange juice.'

'You are being Florence Nightingale, you realize?' I weakly protest.

'You be a good soldier then,' she lays a hand on my shoulder, then suddenly dashes off saying, 'The onions! Thank God they are not burnt.'

I am instructed to take a shower. I like the idea. She hands me a towel, points to the soap, and turns the bathroom light on.

Why does she care? I amble into the bathroom and start taking off my clothes. I splash my face repeatedly with cold water and pour some of it from my cupped palms onto my head. Then, I step into the bath and let the warm water bursting from the shower soothe my body.

I stand there for some time.

'Leon? Leon? What will you wear?' she is back at the door.

'The clothes I was wearing.' I am embarrassed.

'Listen, they are probably soaking in sweat. I can lend you a big T-shirt. It's washed and newish. Should fit. If you don't mind. And you can wear your bottom clothes.'

She's really crazy.

'Leon? Do you hear me?'

'Yes. Yes, Keya. I'll wear the shirt. Hang it on the doorknob or something.'

'I'll leave it on a chair by the door. I'm in the kitchen, don't worry.'

I face the haggard wretch in my reflection and try to smile. Then, give up.

Keya has set chairs at a round table. There is white rice, paneer in a red gravy with onions, and raita.

'I wish I could have cooked a proper Hyderabadi biryani but I'm not that accomplished,' she says good-humouredly, 'I didn't know how much hot and spicy you could take, so I used paprika instead of Kashmiri mirch. The tofu looks hot, but isn't.'

'How can I thank you—'

'By having dinner.'

'You made all this.'

'It's easy. The tofu comes diced and fried at the store. The raita boondi and the raita masala are ready-made. I did combine the ingredients, slice and fry the onions and boil the rice,' she rattles on as she serves food on the plates.

I feel famished, but eat little. I can't seem to take the morsels in. I drink lots of water.

'Would you like a cup of camomile tea? I'm making some for me.'

'If it isn't trouble for you.'

'Drop the formality. I have to pour hot water over a tea bag. An onerous task indeed! And it's not like I met you last week.' She laughs. It is a funny joke too.

'Do you want to sit outside where it's fresh?' she asks me after dinner.

We step into the balcony. I breathe in the cool night air deeply. She switches the lights off in the flat and piles the dishes in the sink, then joins me, and we sit side by side on the chairs that we drag from inside.

'In a bit, the car park will close. Then, it'll be really quiet. I've often sat here watching the lime seeds fall in the dark.'

I let my head rest limp on the back of the chair.

I am silent for a long time.

Then, I own up, 'I can't tell you how I feel. I'm sorry. But I should have reacted better that day.'

She replies, 'Leon, I am sorry about being the Archduke Franz Ferdinand of the situation yesterday.'

I realize that it was yesterday; it feels long ago. How strangely she speaks. History for history. I consider her words. She has brought up history of an entirely different kind to explain this one. She was the Archduke Franz Ferdinand of the situation; I'm glad I paid attention in the History class to know that of the many causes of the First World War, the most immediate, the proximate, cause was the assassination of Archduke Ferdinand, which led to the ultimatum and the outbreak of war.

Always a war.

Maybe I am inexplicably quiet, for she adds, 'I precipitated it, I shouldn't have.'

'Why should you be sorry?' I blurt out at last.

'I don't know. I think it might be better if you did not have to go through this,' she softly answers.

'Keya, this is who I am. I refused to see. This is my story. You did the right thing. I feel the obvious—pain, anger and humiliation at being abandoned and forgotten.' It is difficult to say these words. I sound pathetic.

'You are one of many people who go through this.'

'I am still me.'

'See, today, I read up a lot on missing persons at the library. Do you know thousands, tens of thousands of people, vanish every year?'

'I can imagine,' I mutter.

'And there are different types of missing. Among adults, men are way more likely to disappear. You can think of people going away as on a continuum; some people disappear for a while, others never return.'

I am a statistic? Is that her point?

As if reading my mind, she says, 'Leon, I am not saying you are a statistic. I am only saying that there are reasons why people go missing. Many reasons. People mostly go away if they are unhappy. They want to escape unhappiness, accumulated stress and anxiety. Or if they want adventure. Or if they have been forced to disappear— like in Kashmir, where thousands have gone missing or disappeared without their loved ones knowing anything; or like here in Germany, where they were kidnapped and made to disappear during the Nacht und Nebel, the Night and Fog tactics, in Hitler's time. All that still happens around the world to political activists.'

'I understand what you are trying to say, even if I can't analyse it like you. I am sure there are reasons why people go missing. But I don't know what Mir's reason was, unless it was that beautiful woman, Shula.'

I feel a torment. 'I can't explain it. Mir having never been there is behind a mountain of little things in my life that are nothing significant in themselves, but add up to a...a...Oh, I don't know.'

'If I was never born… I mean, I must have been a responsibility, the thought of me. He must have desperately wanted to get away. It's like…like there are people who go missing, and then there is a thing called missing. To miss. What it means to be missing. It's not about the person who has gone missing for some reason, but the person left behind, who misses for no reason.'

'I am—' she begins, but I interrupt her.

'It is a letter, Keya. Supposing you got a letter. You open the envelope. And inside is a letter. But it isn't a letter. It's a blank sheet of paper. Can you imagine that?'

'That is bizarre. I never thought of it.'

'That blank sheet, sent to you on purpose, it could be anything, couldn't it? It's everything the person sending you couldn't put into words. They wanted to express, but couldn't, and they don't know why either. You have in your hands the best expression of their feelings, but it is a blank sheet of paper.'

I am repeating myself. She turns to face me and continues to listen in silence.

'That blankness leaves you no choice. You can't talk to an absence. It is a perpetual missing. If you never responded to it, it'll still be there. If you wrote on that blankness, you'd always be trying, trying, trying. Oh! It's terrible. There are no reasons. People give up on other people, and then find reasons after the fact.'

'Leon, I am not sure what to say. Anything anyone will say to you will be to think ahead, forgive and forget, think of others with a worse fate. To—'

'To try to be happy. I know.'

'To try to live in the present,' she completes. 'Only it's not so easy,' she contradicts herself.

'I gave up on Maya. I don't know why.'

'Maya?'

There is a muted light on the street.

'I hate myself,' I say, biting my lip.

'I'm with you, Leon. I mean, don't be harsh on yourself,' she whispers, sincere and awful.

'You don't know me. I am my father's son. I did to Maya what Mir did to Ammi.'

In anger last evening, I had promised not to add to Keya's storybook. Still, here I am. Recounting my betrayal of Maya.

I let my splintered and confused sentences spread around us.

When I have told her everything, Keya replies, 'I wish for you to be happy someday.'

'I want to be here by myself for a bit,' I say to her.

She gets up with a goodnight and slides the door behind her. Instrumental music floats out for a few minutes, then it is quiet. She must be asleep.

I sit alone in the balcony, a few square feet of space suspended in the air, and close my eyes against the vast endless skies that witness everything.

I never did justice to Maya. Did I do justice to Maya's story in the telling?

I don't know why Mir gave up on us. Do I know why I gave up on Maya? Isn't it because I cannot stay and confront a difficult situation? I find it natural to escape, to try and run away? Images of Maya assail me. I have an acute sense of guilt about her—I had deserted her. Maya had loved and trusted me; why did I have to run away from her like that? I dwell on that past.

Maya was my first love, someone I could never forget. She was a native of Bareilly; I often teased her for being from a town known for surplus cane and lost earrings in proverb and song. She had come to study English Literature at Hindu College, across the road from Stephen's. Tradition dictated that Stephanians look down upon Hinduites; we were posher, richer, smarter as a group. At inter-college functions, I saw this girl Maya win prizes for her college. I noticed in her a hunger for approbation that reminded me of my own predicament. I had chosen to hang out with the cool types to appear chilled-out; she had chosen to compete with and defeat the snobs. She was junior to me. I had seen her involved in many activities around the campus. It was quite a sensation when she achieved a record-breaking score in the first year university-wide exams. 'Did you hear? Some Maya from Hindu cracked the papers!' was heard on the grapevine.

By this time, I had already realized I'd never be part of the 'in' group, and was enough of a renegade to hang out at her college. It was a comedown, but I didn't care for my reputation with the high and mighties any more. I connected with the Hindu boys through sports, especially cricket. Everyone boasted how accomplished they were at the seduction and manipulation of women. I turned to Maya out of sheer curiosity. I imagined that she would be popular at her college, but found that she kept a solitary stance. I would see her sitting alone by the auditorium and studying in empty classrooms during the free periods.

I had no real conquests to my name and desperately wanted one. One day, on a lark, I went into a room where she was by herself, and we got talking. She seemed so sure of herself that I wouldn't have been surprised if her ambition was to become the Prime Minister of India! Her self-belief was sexy, and I was smitten. I took every opportunity to spend time with her. I would think of interesting things to say to her. We began to form a relationship.

Classmates assumed that we were 'going around'. I bragged to the hostel boys at Hindu that I had kissed—I mean, really kissed— their star peer; this was before I'd even touched her hand. People were not impressed. Instead of being jealous, they joked about me trying to convert a Hindu bombshell. 'You buggers can always tempt better,' they laughed. 'I can give you tips,' I laughed with them. I was not serious about Maya.

How could I be serious about Miss Perfection? She always mentioned how lucky she was and how far she'd go. I used to get irritated by this effort that came across in her personality. The only background I had on her was that she was from this small town in

Uttar Pradesh, and that she hated the big city Delhi that was false and gaudy and fast. She remembered her parents fondly and adored her elder brother who was a lawyer. It sounded like a cosy family. Yet, why did she have to be so obvious about how smugly happy her life was?

Who were my folks? she asked. I told her that I lived with my mother and my father was missing, presumed dead—I had never discussed Mir with anyone else till then. If I was fatherless, I surely wasn't claiming that other people's family stories ought to be unfortunate too; but the very next day after hearing about Mir, she had gone on overdrive telling me how grateful she was to have her parents be who they were. Why? My life wasn't denying or contradicting anything she'd felt about her folks; the smugness of her calm exterior irked me. Her emotions were never on display.

I lent her my notes from the senior year. She won more prizes. We met almost every day. I realized that behind her small town defiance, there was a defencelessness against the environment of the big city. By airing her opinions on everything and studying very hard, she was compensating.

I wanted to provoke her. Delhi shocked her, so I defended Delhi vociferously. Sex was taboo, so I went on talking of the need to break boundaries. I argued with her about her love of epic romances, about her dislike of cricket, her desire to top the course. Why? Why? Why? I'd constantly poke her, try to see if she could be cornered, to win her. I was being a bastard of sorts, but in my defence, I wanted her to share something of her real self with me. I wanted her to be vulnerable and passionate in front of me.

There came a time when I stopped relating my exploits with Maya to the hostel boys. I had begun to care for her. Now, I wanted to captivate her as she had captivated me. But she was always in control. I felt frustrated that I would never be able to penetrate her outward persona. I wish that had been the case.

One blustery rainy day, we had a huge quarrel; I wanted her to come with me to the movies and she was dead set upon going to take part in a practice session for something. We stood there at the college gates, drenched and engaged in a long staring match. I was the first to blink, turn around and leave. We didn't speak for days. I was hurt, but at the same time, delighted. This would free me, one way or another. Either she would capitulate, or I would be able to walk away, placing the blame on her.

After a week, she relented. I was overjoyed. Maya and I had moved on to a new stage in our relationship. I was not wrong. When we made up, she cried tearfully. After that, while she would still be the Maya that people knew with everyone else, with me, she became someone different. She began to tell me, bit by bit, her real story. It was a big win for me.

I felt that she was now truly mine. I got to know her life as it actually was. Her insecurities made her real. I told her that she and I would be the combination that would face the struggles of the world, both hers and mine. This is what love is supposed to be, I thought. It was what love had indeed meant to me then.

She showed me a scrawly pencil-and-pen map of the roads in and around Delhi University; she had made this when she was new in the capital city and no one had helped her. She would note and draw maps of roads she saw and try to piece it all together; it was so innocent. As Maya opened up to me, she told me that her mother was a depressive housewife and her father was a dentist with a small practice. Though he did all right, he was prone to bouts of alcoholism. She loved her parents, but there had been many difficult times, and they were sure to disown her if they discovered her affair with me. She was their main hope in life. Her brother had abandoned his legal studies, saying that he didn't want to be stuck in a notary's office. He had subsequently suffered an accident, turned to a religious cult, and refused to marry. This constant struggle between her parents and her brother had added more to the household misery, and Maya was glad to have escaped it by being in Delhi.

Her parents had sent her to study English Literature on the strength of her promise that after graduating with honours, she would get a well-paying job with the British Council or the BBC in Delhi. She intended to make good on it. They had allowed her to stay with other girls in a private hostel near the campus, and agreed not to look for her marriage until she was settled in a career. The more I learnt about her, the more I marvelled at how she had kept up her earlier blessed persona. I wanted to fall down on my knees and thank her in some way for being so special, for letting me into her life, for trusting me. Of course, I should have known that being the scarred bastard that I was, she would have been better off keeping the false face and the comforting stories.

I spent entire days and evenings with Maya, forgetting Ammi in the balance. Maya was a responsibility, Ammi was a responsibility, my life was a responsibility, the future was a big mess. I could only get a respite from thinking of all this in the company of the hostel guys and their rubbish talk. Making excuses to Ammi about staying away for filling application forms on a friend's computer at night, I would surreptitiously go with them to Majnu ka Tila for late night drinking sessions, and sleep on the dorm floor when back. Before long, even this comfort was denied to me.

In the middle of a raucous drink do at a back alley Tibetan bar in the Tila, where we swallowed momos and burned our guts with chang, their hooch, one asinine Physics fresher, Anuj Mishra, picked on me. He nearly choked when he saw me among the group.

'But you are not supposed to drink!' he exclaimed, between hiccups.

'What do you mean by supposed?' I tetchily retorted.

'Aren't you a Muslim?'

'If I feel like drinking, I shall drink. By the way, aren't you supposed to wear a sacred thread and grow a tuft of hair on your shaven head?' I had replied with acerbity. My money on the whisky was wasted, the alcoholic haze receded.

'Don't mind, yaar, I was curious. So I guess you eat pork too, then?' He was asking to be boxed. I struck a hand.

'Anuj, do you want me to get into a fight with you or what? I said, enough, okay?'

This was during an intense phase with Maya, so I was especially edgy.

Other guys intervened to stop me; Anuj was a puny wimp.

A Tibetan oldie turned up the volume on the TV that hung in a wall bracket above our heads. In the din, I still heard, 'Ali's going to marry that Hindu bombshell anyhow. Convert her—.' It wasn't funny any more. I was serious about Maya.

I thrashed the asshole Anuj, but it became a brawl, and I never went to those sessions again.

I was informed that Anuj the creep's revenge was to play carrom with his friends at the hostel on the game board, which would have Maya's name written on one of the corner holes. He would strike his plastic seed into that hole and rejoice.

There was no doubt that I had loved Maya the only way I had known then. We were hopeful of the world and trusting of ourselves; it was unbelievable. There was that time in Delhi when both of us were visiting Jawaharlal Nehru University together; we got off the JNU bus on a sunny winter afternoon and asked the driver for directions. He had pointed, 'Take that yellow brick road all the way...' We laughed like demented children—'yellow brick road'?! It was paved, bricky in a way, but certainly not yellow. I told Maya of the associations which, of course, the road did not evoke. We were happy; there were trees, sunny skies, but none of this was any good when I wanted to swim inside vodka to lose my soul. I loathed myself, condemned as I was, to be my own witness.

Maya. Maya. Maya. The night in Berlin cries out.

I lie crumpled in this chair on Keya's balcony, unable to escape any past, Mir's or mine.

I saw Maya as I had seen her under the shade of that tree on the day of the yellow brick road; she was warm and inviting, and life was all a dream. Yes, I had loved her. Loved her in that first and special way, a way in which millions of gapped moments could be seamlessly forgotten with a kiss and a look. It was mushy and stupid.

'Leon, I am not just an entity in your mind, I am a person too,' she would remind me when we argued over doing what I wanted. Had I understood what she meant? I kissed her forcefully and without warning as we returned from JNU. She was animated about something. I interrupted her to point out a lovely bird.

'Where?' she paused and peered into the tree, the sunlight bouncing off the mirror-work on her clothes.

I had pulled her close to me and maniacally kissed her hard on the lips.

She had broken from my grip and nervously looked around. 'Promise! Promise never to do that again.'

'Why? Don't you trust me?' my temples throbbed.

'I trust you, Leon. But we must not do anything before we are married.'

'Of course, I'll marry you.'

Our kiss went walking trenchantly along the yellow brick road. I stood stuck at the foot of the stairs, at the bottom of the well, at the edge of the fucking river, drowning in my guilt, jumping in the sea. I always had lies on my side. Wrong words.

I betrayed Maya. How did I knowingly hurt her so much?

Following the kiss Maya did not come to college for two days. I sent a message but she did not respond. I needed to see her. I walked the kilometre from the campus with a sense of trepidation, went up the stairs to the accommodation she shared with the other girls. I rang the bell with my heart beating in my throat. I knew that this was wrong, or at least risky in a big way. Male visitors were not allowed. I should not be there. I should not be trying to see her at home. But hell, I wasn't planning anything. For all I knew she might not be in, or her parents might have come to visit her.

As it was, she was on her own. She opened the door after several rings, a peep through the spyhole, and immediately vanished behind the curtain of the room with a brief gesture of one arm, indicating me to a sofa chair. I sat down and proceeded to gaze at the whitewashed walls, the cheap furnishings. There was a large cardboard-backed poster of a woodland, complete with a rustic cottage and a log bridge over a frothy brook. The scene depicted an idyll; nevertheless, I thought it a monstrosity. For one, the poster was florid and gargantuan, making everything appear out of proportion. The foliage came across as artificial and plastic. The bridge was no different, uniformly brown and neat. The overall effect was that of a studio set rather than the peaceful and remote woodland that it was supposed to represent. I cocked my head to examine the lower corners of the picture, searching for indications of a title or a signature; that was when she had walked in.

I saw her aslant and froze. Lifted up my head and looked at her. No, not at her; somehow our eyes had met, accidentally perhaps. That was the picture of a lifetime, one to remember a life by. If a movie were to be made, that would be the scene when the moment would freeze frame. It would be the still snap, the cover shot. It would be the soul of the story. It was my home, that picture. That moment, if it were a tunnel, would have led me to a happy life. That moment was my alternate history and my home. A wanderer would have stopped searching, music would have sprung up from nowhere. Yes, I had loved her. I could never love again as I loved her.

And I had let her go.

Maya was in a dotted red salwar kurta, no dupatta draped her bosom. She was just out of a bath. She had been unwell and unable to sleep. Late getting up, she was dressing when I had rung the doorbell. She wore no make-up. She looked like a wayward nymph. Her untied hair was wet and shiny. She had her earrings in her palm. As she put them on, I pointed out that one of the red glass beads was broken, touching her ear to say which one. Her kurta had wet patches from her dripping hair at the back. Her face was flushed. 'What brought you here?'

I tried to explain. I was there to see if she was all right. I also had to return a novel that I had borrowed from her. Mumbling this, I placed Scott Fitzgerald's *Tender is the Night* on the centre table. We looked at each other for a couple of seconds, her eyes black, mine brown. That was it. A conspiracy was afoot.

She went into the tiny kitchen to make tea; I ostensibly helped. The tea never did get made. She asked me to get the milk from the fridge in the living room, as she cracked elaichi in the pan of boiling water and peeled ginger with a knife. I returned to ask her which one of the bottles was hers—there were sections in the fridge. 'Girls are sensible about sharing,' I was saying, when I saw her from behind. The sight of her wet back, right where the bra was clasped, transported me to that first quarrel when she had stood drenched at the gate, refusing to come to the movies with me. I'd blinked first that time, because I could not bear to stare at her—the outlines of her body transparent in the clinging clothes. She must have divined my randy intentions even then.

I delicately touched her shoulder saying she'd get a cold from the dripping hair. She sprung around with an animal alacrity. I held her body in my arms—feverish, warm, frail. I drew her to me. She could not resist. I clasped her close.

'Leon, I love you. I love you. Promise me, you must promise me,' she repeated it like an incantation.

'I promise anything. Everything.'

We were carried away. I burned to feel her. She innocently threw her arms around me; I wanted to protect her. We kissed madly. We did not kiss like that even when we were more intimate in the months afterwards; awkwardly, we would kiss each other on the neck and face instead. I ran my fingers through her damp curls and over her small pink lips. I touched her through her bra and felt her flesh on mine. Her clothes were torn and mine soiled as we struggled in the throes of ecstasy. After that first time, a barrier had been broken.

She would ritually practise her attacks of modesty before yielding to my beseeching gaze and fervent pleas. I became bolder. I learned romance. I bought her a lacy bra and a triangular bottle of Charlie Red perfume, so I could both see and smell her to appreciate my gift; her breasts were soft in their prison nets. I became obsessed with her, and we started experimenting with our bodies every spare hour we got. My hands had found their destination inside her, and I could not stop wanting her, all of her. She was me and I was her.

We could not take off our clothes and revel naked—her flatmates were often around and she would be evicted if I came to visit routinely when she was alone—so we would find corners, closed classrooms and corridors, libraries, lifts; spaces where our bodies could touch and rub at will. That electricity of skin on skin was out of this world. In the winter, we would deliberately take autorickshaw rides after dark, where she would come wearing her shawl and I had my bag; we'd settle in the back and try everything. We'd go to the theatre, buying the cheapest student seats for plays in any language, and desperately fumble our way through the performance. Once, we were shunted out of the auditorium. It was enough not to just penetrate and get it over with. How I wanted to fully consummate my love, to believe in its truth!

But we never properly had sex. She was terrified of the consequences. She did not want to lose her virginity before marriage, and I had no choice but to respect this idiocy. I knew every inch of her body, I could draw its secrets with my eyes closed, I knew the meaning of her different smiles and frowns. Our relationship felt so right to me; it gave me the impetus to do well at college, to play better cricket, to dream of a happy life. I had it all with Maya by my side.

Then, what happened? A purple haze clouds everything. Why did things not work out?

Miserably enough, our growing intimacy had the exact opposite effect on Maya. She began to lose her endearing self-confidence, and it was replaced not by the initial innocent insecurities, but by a hardening sense of guilt and shame. She indulged our physicality, but she could not come to terms with it at a moral level. She wept and prayed to weird gods who put a distance between us. She felt that she had let down her parents, that she was the shame of her family. She stopped going for prizes, her studies were affected, she became withdrawn and morose.

Increasingly, whenever we weren't involved with our bodies, we were quarrelling because of some or other issue to do with our relationship. I would, wouldn't I, desert her in the future? Could I stay loyal? Would her parents accept a Muslim son-in-law, even if we bore them a grandchild? Would I get a decent job? Could I be able to hold off having sex for a few years? If not, what would we do if she got pregnant? Would I go away with another girl if I went to another city? Oh! it was crazy. She was such a fool. I loved her more than anyone and anything else. I would not have deserted her. But whenever she interrogated me, I would lose patience. I would snap at her, feeling hurt at her stupid lack of trust in me.

I failed to understand how much the physical intimacy meant to her, how she had already trusted me so much that it made her worried for the future. I was not mature enough to see that she required me to give the right answers that would assure her. She was troubled because I had become the centre of her concerns. While I could pursue other distractions and go out at any hour, she lived a girl's life in Delhi. She was away from her family and unable to share her anxieties with her housemates, who had advised her against the relationship. She became solely focused on us all the time. It was as simple as that. My inability to express my reactions in the right words had let me down. I would get annoyed at her doubts about us; the way she went into detail outlining every scenario that could go wrong made me wonder if I wasn't the blind one, unable to see my future infidelity and her grief. I hated being accused and blamed for her guilt and suffering. I did not want to be the cause of her downfall.

I pushed away my life and soul, my happiness, with my own hands. Before leaving for England I told her I no longer loved her. I could not handle the demands of a relationship. We were both unstable and insecure of our futures. Neither of us had proper families, we had no real role models. We were adrift and anchorless. I feared that she would want me to be a certain kind of person, develop an approvable identity.

But make no mistake, I had wanted to cut loose. I had broken up with unexemplary cruelty. There really was no good way to do this. I was burning me and my happiness as much as I was burning her. Surely, she could see that.

I don't ultimately know why I broke up with her the night before her final exams. I think I was insane with sensations that I could not name, fearful of futures that would waste me, terrified of responsibility. If I could be there again, I would do things a whole lot differently. But that's the 20/20 of retrospective vision.

Maya's prophecies have been vindicated in my betrayal. She cursed me—the loser, the swine, the seed of my father, compelled to desert women, the blood of cheats. Like Mir cheating my mother, I had cheated Maya. I am worthless self-pitying scum.

Did Keya understand? I told her Maya's story and she has pasted it in her scrapbook of tales. I don't need rescuing. I don't need redeeming. I need escapes.

I get up and go indoors. There is a humming whirr from the fridge. A faint light. Keya sleeps on one side of the fold-down bed. I tiptoe to the table and get my phone, then take a glass of water, and come back to the balcony.

Taking a mouthful, I hold it there, imagine velarizing an unknown oracle, taste the cold weight of the water at the back of the lower jaw, at the very end, the flesh beyond teeth; it reminds me of gargling, and I feel reminiscent of an old age I've not had.

Keya is right. Everyone has pains cut into their souls. The circulating underground today was full of real people. I had stared all day at them stupidly, proving nothing. I stare now at a dim starless patch of sky. I want to shed a tear. I can't bring one to my eyes. The monster that I am. My chest feels like a muffled bundle of crazy animals tied inside a large and rough jute bag; the burlap sack of my heart.

I want to talk to Maya at this moment. Years after the fact.

I flip open my phone. Switching it off, I dial several random numbers into it. Then, put the receiver to my ear and begin a conversation:

'Hello, Maya.'

'This is Leon. Remember?'

'How do you do your hair now? What perfume do you wear?'

'Okay, I am sorry, I had no right to ask any of that. Let me try again. How are you?'

'Right, I will speak of me then. I am fine. Well, to be honest, I feel terrible.'

'Why do I feel terrible, did you say? It is because you were right. I can't make sense of life.'

'Because?'

'Because I am insane. I'd have to be—for letting you go, and for still not having let you go.'

A father who abandoned me, a mother who does not need me any more, a love that I did not have the courage enough to bear, and now...well, now there is a whole new web. I pause.

'Giraffe.'

'Do you remember the way I said "giraffe" used to make you smile? You said it was all wrong.'

I am stuck in the past.

'I am sorry, Maya.'

'I did not say or do the things you wanted because I was afraid it would put me in an accused position. I was afraid of accusation and condemnation. You thought I gave myself too much license. You thought I needed crutches all the time. You were right.'

'I know none of it matters anymore, but I wanted to let you know that I mourned for you today.'

'I can see all the endless arguments we had for what they were—the filth of human egos in action. I'd said that I love you, but not as much as myself...it was disgusting.'

'Maya?'

I lower my voice to an absolute minimum. A car whizzes past on the road below.

'Maya, I hope you don't keep any of that bitterness in you.'

'I know that my words don't make you feel anything. I know that I lied to you and myself. But I am not presupposing a certain reaction again. I do not have an agenda.'

'I broke up for no reason. I had wanted to hurt you. There was discomfort, suffering and unreadiness. I hope I haven't ruined your life. I was afraid of the future.'

'Maya, we were infants. It was infancy as a condition in psychological life and relationships.'

'My cravings, like my fears, were so total.'

Shine a torchlight into something and people instinctively wince.

'But believe me, Maya, I still remember all the words you said to me, even the curses. And you are a missing. Just let me say it this once. I shall never say it again: I missed you in my life.'

'I no longer zip up and leave the room in conversations, as you once alleged. I listen, and I try not to be what I was. Of course, I fail.'

'Tell me something from your present life...'

I wait in silence for a time.

'I am in Berlin,' I say.

'Maya, I saw something. In a museum, I saw a woman hiding from her lover behind a pillar in the middle of the room, and him not missing her. Her peeping. Then moving to a column closer to him, him turning, and still not missing her, her being unable to wait. Her going over to him finally. Him realizing nothing. I thought the story sort of said something about relationships.'

'Yes, you are right. I am back to my crutches again. Unable to say anything I mean. What's more, my reading obscure books in London has made it worse.'

Planes jam into twin towers again in the balcony haze. I blot the images.

'Here is something real. I walked for miles one evening looking for an Indian restaurant here. I had a sudden need to eat a Hyderabadi biryani.'

'Do you still love jamuns the way you used to? I can see you buying them from the tokriwallahs in the summer and eating them. Your lips all purple.'

I am leaning on the railing.

'Had you a presentiment, Maya? Is that why you said I have the blood of cheats?'

'This is what it is—Keya says there are reasons for people to disappear. But after Mir left, there was an adulteress in his life, a Shula, whose husband is maybe in Kolkata. Someday I want to go and ask him for a photograph of her.'

'Who is Keya? you ask.'

'Keya is…is sleeping…in a room behind me. She's from Kashmir, but like me, she hasn't lived there. Collects stories like children collect marbles. She happened to me. Calla lily is her favourite flower. I feel terribly inadequate when I'm with her. I am not free of you. I am not free of Mir.'

Breaking into a smile, I say, 'Though Keya thinks I am free because I have a British passport. She envies that I am a man, too. Yes, she has taken a shine to me and she is—'

I pause.

'—different.'

'I spent today numbly circulating in trains under the ground, from one end of the city to another. I tried to drug myself on people to lose consciousness. I was Nobody.'

An ambulance, or maybe police, siren sounds in the distance.

'Why does Mir's affair with Shula matter to me? Hanh? I haven't even seen Mir. Maya, it matters because of you. I tried to verbalize it in front of Keya, but couldn't do justice to it. You, Maya, prove the worst of me. I am Mir, a selfish, contemptible man, who can't find himself and loses others. Maya, I want to be emptied of you.'

I flip the screen shut. Inhale. Slowly make my way to the bed. I'll have to sleep in my trousers and Keya's T-shirt. There is a pillow for me. As I lay my head on it Keya mumbles 'light'. The lights are already off, so I am not sure if she means close the curtains; I wait to hear more. But before I do, I'm fast asleep.

Hundreds of people are watching Keya. She is not wearing any clothes. There is a full moon. Dark butterflies hover in the sky. The fountain statue of the four women glints silver. The women in the statues have become magnified to a gigantic proportion. Keya is Lilliputian in front of them. She wanders around these megaliths seeking: which is 'Vistest'? She wants to ask someone which one it is, but when she opens her mouth, she cannot speak. She is mute. Seeing her sadness, one of the statues beckons her. 'I am yours,' it whispers with resonance. Keya is perplexed. How will she climb to the top of this woman? She lays a hand each on the legs of the giant, but her palms slip. She keeps trying. Slowly, she reaches the pelvis, then the navel, then the breasts and armpits, and finally the neck of the figure. The crowd below is invisible from here. She is bathed in a glowing light. She touches the large metal lip of the river woman statue. There is a butterfly perched there. Her hand brushes against the wings—soft, velveteen—then the wings expand and expand. It is a bat! She shrieks in horror and withdraws her hand. 'Are you Vitestula?' Keya asks. The statue is stock-still, but a cachinnatory voice booms, 'Shula.' Keya passes through a viscose stream and sees herself desperately trying to penetrate the statue which is now shrunk to the same size as her. Keya is not mute anymore, but she has nothing to enter the statue with. She cannot get inside the outline. Leon appears out of nowhere and stands wild-eyed behind her, watching silently as she struggles in trying to embrace and master the statue. A snake lies in a basket of berries and white-coloured chillies. She is stuck to the statue. A cloud of bats approaches from the horizon. She is paralysed with fear. No one will protect her. She vomits glass shards that form a congealed mass. Her teeth are melted in it too. Keya wakes up.

'Hope you slept well. I had awful dreams last night,' Keya says, as I open my eyes.

'Good morning,' my mouth feels stitched from the inside when I get up.

'Coffee? Tea?' she is a-brisk.

'Sure, anything.' My head hurts like there are explosions going off at random points in it.

Later when we have breakfast, which I help to make, I say, 'Thank you for yesterday. I acted mad. I won't be like that again.'

'No problem. By the way, here is a slice of cake. It's too many calories for me, but I bought it for you since you have a sweet tooth.'

'I don't.'

'Sorry?'

'I don't have a sweet tooth. I don't know why I lied to you when we first met.'

'You did?'

'Yes. I also have no massive inheritance to squander, and I do not wander, wonder, taking pictures. I worked in a Mayfair studio-cum-café for the last three years.'

'How charming!'

I am embarrassed by her affectedness.

'If you hadn't told me, I'd have taken you for the Sultan of Brunei!'

I am serious and it dampens her joviality.

'Keya?' I say, as she's scraping a burnt toast.

'I want you to know that I value what you've done for me.'

'Leon, I will say this briefly, for a change. I feel connected to your story, I am intrigued by the people in it—Mir and also Shula. Sorry,' she seems to think I abhor Shula.

'I don't hate Shula. I'm even considering going to the Kolkata address at some point, and asking her husband to let me see a photo of hers.'

She's quiet.

'Will you come with me?' I ask on an impulse.

'What?'

'I mean, when you have time and when you are next in India, will you help me piece the rest of the story together?'

'You know my answer. Of course, I will. I've just got to teach the rest of the term, mark papers, write more abstract articles on runaway arty people, as you put it that time—'

'There's no rush. I don't know when I am heading to India either.'

'But I do. Academic year-wise, I have time in August. My mother would like me to visit this year, and I was already thinking about it. So, I am quite certain I'll be there this August.'

'I'll be in touch with you.'

'And what will you do now?'

'Leave Berlin. Go somewhere else.'

'Not London?'

'Not yet. I'm going to observe the world and realize where I'm meant to fit.'

'Great. I think it's so wonderful. The way you up and do spontaneous things.'

'Keya, I never asked you this before. I wanted to. Tell me about your folks.'

'Tell you what?'

'What they do…Your father died young, you said; is it difficult for your mother to be by herself? Do you have siblings?'

'Well, here's a summary: my dad, who I was very close to, trained as an engineer from Kashmir. He wanted to be an architect but ended up being an official in Delhi. He never got over the trauma of leaving his homeland. My mom is also a salaried professional in government service. Her family migrated out of Kashmir a generation ago, so they're settled in the plains. My mother's brother and sister and their families also live in the same locality, and she has plenty of moral and logistical support. She couldn't manage it all by herself. I don't have any siblings. My parents had the whole overpopulation nightmare drilled into their heads!' she raps it off as if it were a recital.

'I hope you meet my Ammi someday.'

'I'd love to meet your mother, Leon…' she hesitates, 'though I'm not sure how you would be received by my people. If I say we're friends, they'd be nice but suspicious. If, supposing for the sake of argument, I hint at something more, they'd be ballistic. They're fairly difficult when it comes to Muslims. A cousin married a Muslim and she was excommunicated from society.'

'Oh!' How could I forget what India was like.

'Do they look for matches for you? Set up dates when you visit?'

'They can't dare say anything to me! They occasionally bring proposals to my mother and I tell her to give them a piece of my mind. I earn my living. I have my life. I am far from them. I will do exactly what I want!'

'What if you wanted to be with a Muslim? Or a Christian? It is a rhetorical question, mind you,' I can't resist posing the hypothetical question, and she takes it in the spirit of frivolity that I expect.

'I know you're not proposing, silly! They'd react the same as if I wanted to marry a black man or someone from a lower caste,' she says, air-quoting the last phrase with her fingers, and refusing tea with a shake of the head, 'they'd be horrified. White Christian foreigner type might do better.'

I pour more tea for me.

'Had he been alive, my father might have thought differently, I'd like to think. He wanted his daughter to light his pyre.' She is sombre. 'I am told he used to have close Muslim friends in Kashmir, and he got hell at home because of that.'

'Your father was also an engineer,' I say. 'Wouldn't it be totally crazy if your father had met Mir like I met you, or you met me. Whatever.'

It is an idle statement.

'Hang on! You never told me Mir was an engineer. You said he was a communist activist and a poet.'

'No one earns a living by being that alone, Keya! He worked as an engineer for an Anglo-German corporation, which is now bust. That's why he came to England. I told you that.'

'You said he worked. You didn't say he was an engineer,' she pounces. 'And he studied at the Regional Engineering College in Srinagar?'

'Yes. He studied and lived in Srinagar.'

'Incredible! My father also studied at the REC.'

I am amazed at how she takes up notions instantly. It's like when she got excited at the idea of passport bonfires. She is building a house of cards.

'Why is that ultra important? So many people study at a college without knowing each other,' I point out.

'But can't you see? Mir was a political activist, well-known on campus. My father Veer was not political, but I've always heard he had a lot of renegade Muslim friends. They…they might have known each other!'

Could it be? I ponder.

'Can it be? Isn't that an unlikely coincidence? We meet and then they know each other?' I question.

'Why is our meeting a coincidence? I meet dozens of new people every week. And I've met Kashmiris before. The only coincidence is that I marked you out in the queue and you left your phone behind,' she's even pouting.

'You marked me out?'

'Oops! Did I say that aloud?' she laughs. 'I was attracted to you. Which should have been obvious, right? And anyway, I'm attracted to lots of people every week.'

'Wow! you have interesting weeks—meet dozens of people, get attracted to many. What is it with teachers these days?' I mock.

'I do a lot more than teach. If you must jest, I am an Assistant Professor. It sounds better.'

She has forgotten about the calories and is gobbling the chocolate cake. I lift some on my fork too.

I reflect, 'You're right. They might have known each other. I'll ask Ammi when I see her. She never talks about Mir. But she might be persuaded to speak in general about those times. She, too, did her Bachelor's degree from the university there.'

'Do that! I'll see what I can dig from nosing around in my father's stuff,' she is excited.

'You have a long nose. You'll smell something.'

'You cruwl and widyqlus man,' she lightly raps my wrist.

I want to believe in myself when I'm with Keya. She makes a future seem possible.

In an hour, I am at the door, bidding her farewell.

I don't know when we'll meet again. It's best not to promise. She gives me her impressive-looking visiting card—Dr Keya Raina, her name embossed on it. 'It's got my email and other coordinates.' I tuck it into my shirt pocket.

She waves to me from the balcony as I leave. I keep turning back, trying to etch her into my memory. A light gust of breeze, her left hand holding her hair, the right on the rails which I'd gripped while exorcizing my demons last night.

'Don't miss your plane again!' she calls after me.

A Few Months Later

10

Tangled Histories

'Chips, Peas and Butty at couple o' quid; come one, come all. Chips, Peas and Butty,' the paunchy man in the apron is trying to attract customers from the 'Go Green!' rival, a hippie, who is fast selling her organic sandwiches with falafel, sprouts and guacamole garnish.

The curly-haired acrobat walks on stilts eating fire, a tarot reader is predicting a child's fortune while her parents look on. There are young men selling miracle pills, middle-aged women selling sterling silver jewellery, long queues for makeshift fairground rides and portaloo plastic cubicle toilets, trails of coloured powder in the skies. Teenagers hang around in groups wearing outlandish accessories on their necks and arms, rotund families eagerly mill about trying to get as close to the periphery of the launch as they can—the hot air balloons are about to be fired!

Ashton Court Estate in Bristol, wooded and wide, with deer park and a mansion, is the site of the annual Ballooning event, where tens of thousands of people come to have fun for three days in late summer. Keya stands with her friend and colleague Tanya; they are sharing a joke about the 'special shape' balloons as they are being inflated.

There are hundreds of balloons that can measure over a hundred feet each—most have rainbow colours and company logos, but there are also the huge rubbery things that are flamboyantly designed and often riotous. There are balloons that are the shape of a woman in a bikini, a large seated bulldog, a shopping trolley, a Scotsman in a kilt, complete with a big bagpipe. Tanya, from Edinburgh, is 'over-whale-ming-lee' delighted about the Scot, even though it's rather funny to see the udder-like gas propulsion attachment hanging between his feet.

The English sunset is a special beauty in early August, Keya thinks, as she surveys the luminous skies, pink and punk. As the balloons lift off, people clap and cheer. Some balloon baskets have the daredevil riders strapped to them, one goes aloft carrying a man seated on his bike. As he recedes into upper air, a mere dot of a fellow among the other outlines of drifting balloons, he is reflected in a slew of upturned pupils and echoed in the gasps of the stunned crowd.

'Tomorrow is the night glow. Oh, but you won't be here!' Tanya nudges Keya. The night glow is the much awaited finale, when pyrotechnic effects from the balloons rhythmically light up the skies at night.

'That's right. I'll have reached Delhi by tomorrow night. Flying in a metal balloon of a plane myself,' she answers.

'How lucky you are! I've always wanted to visit India.'

'And I, Inverness!'

They wander amid the human sea on their way to the exit. The car park is another mile from there, and on this walk they are joined by a man who tries chatting them up. They indulge him mildly, then hand a rebuff. Tanya has a casual boyfriend, an Italian and a lawyer. Keya doesn't fancy army types.

'So have you heard recently from the guy you met in Berlin, the one you were into?'

'He's finding himself. I get emails on occasion.'

'Will you be seeing him in India?'

'Not sure. Do you want a lift?'

'No, I'll be fine.'

'Have a nice break then! See you when I'm back.'

'You too. Bye!'

Keya pays the parking fee and manoeuvres her car out onto

the carriageway. She decides on a slight detour and drives by the Harbourside and College Green, up Park Street, and then past Wills Memorial and towards the Downs. She will be in Delhi tomorrow, and it feels pleasurable to savour the parting sights of the city that is her home now; she notes the boats and skater-boys, the laid-back summery vibe, the connexions to cigarette and slavery wealth.

At the Whiteladies Road roundabout, Keya turns left in the direction of Clifton Downs, a large open green space. A bee buzzes in through the slightly open window. To let it out, she rolls the glass down all the way and feels the breeze on her bare arms as they turn the steering wheel. She switches off the music, and parks by the side of a curved road overlooking the Avon gorge and the Clifton suspension bridge. Keya has given this stretch of the road her own place name—'the curve of the downs'; it is a beautiful vantage point where a narrow road hugs the side of a hill. Far down below, there is the Avon river flanked by its mudbanks, nesting between a neon-spotted carriageway scalloped on one side, and the black shrouded forests of Leigh Woods rising on the other.

The inky sky has few clouds, and the glitteringly lit, long, suspension bridge in the distance spans the two closest sides of what must have once been a gigantic rock. Keya shuts off the headlights, pushes back the seat and lies with her head low, eyes closed. It is restful urban meditation. She has done it before.

Infrequent vehicles trace their bearings along the loopy road. Hot air balloons flash inside her eyelids. She thinks of the times before aviation. In the ages when people had to walk across countries and, perforce, cross oceans in ships. When travel meant spending months with co-journeyers, forming relationships, trading experiences. When exile meant survival on stories and objects alone—carried and related over time. Tomorrow, she will fly across continents in a matter of hours; maybe the person seated next to her will not even exchange a word with her. Reaching the destination will be everyone's paramount concern, the journey an inconvenience. Keya formulates a statement: modernity was enabled by a mutation of speed.

The last few months have been busy and stressful. She resolves to pamper herself when in Delhi. Bright light shines upon her forehead. Leaning forward, she squints in annoyance, huh-uh? A car cruising in the opposite direction has her face in the full-on beam. She sees the green and fluorescent stripes at the side; it's a police car on a welfare round. The spell is broken.

There are more cars parked along the long curving road at maximal non-intrusive distances, angled away from each other. No one wants others to step into their private pleasures or regrets in this transient but real community of city-dwelling night refugees. Keya turns the key in the ignition and moves off.

Behind the expanse of the open greens are the large detached affluent houses with coloured lights from TVs flickering in the windows. On route to the gentrified areas—with their white pedestrian crossing markings and the yellow warning light globes that flash non-stop—she passes several stationary cars with feeble lights inside; groups of two or three, or more, people clustering. Who are these inhabitants of a city's underbelly? What are the shadowy folds privy to? Are they dealing drugs, swapping partners, making out, or are they, like herself, a mix of loners, lovers, poets, maniacs, students, aimless, addicted, deprived?

An intemperant sentiment reminds her of Leon. Lay-on Allee, the German street. She tunes the radio to BBC 4. Driving, she listens to a narration about women during the Cold War; it takes her thoughts to Shula Farid. Soon, she's home in her top floor flat.

The suitcases for travel are packed. She prints out her electronic ticket and keeps it beside her passport and wallet. Then, she puts on a music CD of *Main Hoon Na*—a recent blockbuster movie by a woman director that has her favourite star, Shahrukh Khan; a silly plot, but a lively soundtrack—and prepares a mélange supper using everything remaining in the fridge. She's going to be away for a month, so she's run down the stocks, but there's still enough to make a salad, a sandwich, and a soup, each one with unconventional ingredients!

Keya is dressed in blue jeans and a smart casual shirt. She locks her front door and drags the luggage downstairs into the waiting cab; he calls her 'My Dear', and in her sleepy overworked head, it sounds like 'Medea' of the myths. The darkness has conceded its joust to a faint light over the city. A haggard moon begs shelter from the passing clouds, pawning off its last pieces of silver to the day. By the time morning breaks clear, Keya is flying over the English Channel, dodging the sunbeams that ricochet off the plane's wings onto her window seat.

Two weeks later, Keya has had enough socializing and fun.

On every visit to India, it is nice for the first few days. She eats a variety of foods—from the crispiest dosas to the tastiest dhoklas— meets an assortment of relatives, buys new CDs and DVDs, goes to movies and dinners with old friends, and catches up with her mother.

Then, the downside appears. There is too much restriction on when, where and how she can be safely outdoors, constant harassment from ogling men, ridiculous bargaining. There are chasms between her and the people she once called friends, and a ubiquitous in-your-face materialism; moneyed middle class swagger plus a merciless indifference towards the have-nots. India feels as alien as anywhere else.

She has decided not to do any work on this trip, so she steers away from universities and libraries. There isn't much to do online either, as August is the quietest month for work emails from England.

Her sleuthing about Mir has yielded no results so far. Her mother's people have been to Jammu, but not Kashmir, for decades now; they support the BJP, some even the RSS, and blame the Congress-Left coalition for every national ill. 'Can you imagine, that corrupt and uncouth hick, Laloo Prasad Yadav, from Bihar, the most backward state, is the Railway Minister of the country which is ruled de facto by Sonia Gandhi, an Italian, a Papist?' Her father's relatives are too distanced and reticent to speak about the Valley. When they do, they don't fail to repeat: Kashmiri Muslims caused the problem. They did not speak to India, but sought an alliance with Pakistan. 'Tell me, if you have a problem in your home, will you discuss it with your family member or take it to a neighbour first? We Pandits are the victims no one cares about in our own country.' Veer had Muslim friends in Srinagar, but why should they care to remember the names?

An octagenerian uncle, on the verge of senility, unable to trust the vision of his cataract-clouded eyes, holds her hand to get her attention as he emphasizes: 'Pandit migration, Muslim terrorism, nothing matters. The most important thing is that Kashmir must remain a part of India.' An aunt impresses upon Keya the need to preserve her language and customs, even though she lives in the West.

It is a relief when children insist she play with them. No, not Rubik's Cube, please. And not Need for Speed. Very well then, the adolescents demand that she tell them about cars in England. She pauses. Hmmm...some are big and expensive, she saw two parked next to each other in a driveway with the number plates '2B' and 'NOT 2B'. A studious nephew breaks into a grin. His sister queries, 'What make were they?' 'Jaguars,' Keya replies.

When Keya probes her mother about her father's friends from university, Usha says she doesn't know anything. Her mother eschews politics; what is more, she came into Veer's life after he had emigrated.

'Can I see Papa's old papers?' Keya asks, as they emerge from a weekend Hindi play performance at a Mandi House theatre.

Usha looks surprised at her daughter's request.

Keya senses that an explanation is required. Briefly, and without mentioning Leon, she speaks of having lately thought a lot about Veer's days before coming to Delhi, especially his life in Srinagar.

'So that's why you asked me about his university friends?'

'Yes.'

'Is there something specific you are looking for?'

'Anything from his engineering or Shimla days. Whatever we've got.'

'There's an old briefcase with documents... I can get it down from the ceiling rack.'

After his death, Veer's ashes were immersed in the Ganges. In accordance with the smoky Brahmanical rituals, all clothes and personal belongings of the deceased are given away; otherwise, it may encourage the spirit to return to his place of dwelling, and deny him peace in the hereafter.

'What happened to the pen and Chinar leaf carving that I'd saved?'

'They're just as you left them when you went away to England. I didn't want them to be damaged, so I had them kept in the locker with the jewellery and finance papers.'

'Mom, I hope you don't mind my asking to see these things? I'll understand if you don't want me to—'

'Not at all, Keya. Why should I mind? He's...he was your father.'

'I am nostalgic about the past, it's true. And it's also that I want to know if someone I met is the son of a friend of Papa's.'

'Oh. Who is that?'

'You wouldn't know him. His name is Leon Ali. He's Kashmiri Muslim. His father was also an engineer.'

'Leon Ali—I haven't heard of him. But I think you should look at the papers in the locker, too. When I last went to pay the annual fee, I was arranging some property papers, and I found a letter there which had a Muslim name—not Leon though.' Usha frowns, concentrating.

'Mir? Was it Mir Ali?' Keya touches her mother's arm.

'Uh-uh. No. I can't remember the name. It wasn't an important document anyway. Your father never mentioned it. Judging from your excitement, I'm glad I didn't discard it.'

'You are a gem!' Keya can't wait to examine the briefcase and the locker. Then she suddenly remembers, 'Mom, you didn't remark upon the fact that this person, Leon, is a Muslim?'

'So what? Is he your boyfriend?'

'What if he were?'

'I'd say, do whatever makes you happy. You live abroad, so people expect less of you anyhow. And I am resilient to taunts—'

Usha raises her voice above the traffic din, '—I gave birth to you. I know that you've always been a headstrong girl. I tell the relatives who bring marriage proposals for you that they could better use their energy and intentions elsewhere.'

Keya lays a hand on her mother's shoulder.

'That is true. I am a *gone case*, aren't I?'

'That you are.'

Keya handles the thin foolscap sheets and the lined official paper covered in blue ink; there are quotes that Veer had scribbled from books, or notes that recounted the ordinary details of life. She recalls going with him—as a small fidgety child—to buy her first bicycle; an Atlas Goldline Super, she'd chosen it for their advertising jingle. He'd encourage her as the 'thinking one' or 'our intellectual', and buy her books by the dozen. Her memories of her father were not unique; every child with loving parents eventually confronts their death. But his death had been early, laden over with his exile, corresponding to a changed world—so it had become a boulder lodged in the corridors of age.

In the briefcase, she finds a copy of his Engineering degree certificate, a dated mark sheet, a photograph, a few letters from relatives and newspaper cuttings. She is convinced that the letter in the locker is the one she must have.

'You would have to come with me to the locker since it's in your name, isn't it?'

'That's right. I was thinking of taking you there anyway.'

'There's a nice Chinese beauty parlour next to the bank. I need to get a haircut and you could get a facial there.'

'You know what, I did promise myself some pampering. Let's go there tomorrow.'

'They can permanently straighten your hair. The frizz will be gone. It'll be manageable.'

'Mother, there you go with your remedies again! No matter how much you polish and scrub and treat me, I shan't transform into a straight-haired white-skinned petite doll.'

'How you interpret me! Well, forget what I said. You're beautiful as you are.'

'And I'll die before I use a Fair and Lovely cream!'

In the vault at the bank, Usha's safe deposit box is stored the sixth in the second row from the bottom. Keya lays aside the gold jewellery to take out the file, and riffles through it, goosepimples on her flesh.

Sure enough, she sees a small envelope that has been pressed razor-thin. It lies neatly hidden among the papers. It has been slit carefully at the fold and is intact. Her father's name is on the front and it misses the sender's name or address on the cover. There is a stamp from FRG Germany, and when she holds it up to see the smudged date, it reads 1988.

Keya has a rush of blood. Wiping her clammy palms on the sides of her skirt, she uses her thumb and index finger to gently pull out the letter.

Dear Veer,

I don't know if I can address you by this first name. I certainly feel like I can, given our common bonds, but I hope you don't mind my contacting you like this. I can't live without Mir… No, let me explain. I have been living in Berlin these last few years as the wife of an Indian diplomat. The only real happiness that I have ever known in my life came to me in the form of Mir Ali, who I met here in this same city. I love him more than I can imagine. I know that I ~~was~~ am married to someone, but I hope you will not judge me too harshly for that. I had my own reasons for choosing my actions. Mir and I meant the world to each other, and now, he is gone! I cannot for a moment believe that he has betrayed me, I would blindly trust him with my life. I don't know who has intervened (of course, you would know that Mir was always a political idealist), or what has happened. I worry day and night about what might have happened to him. I am not in Berlin anymore, but have been forced to be at this sanatorium in Germany. They are treating me for depression and God knows what else. It is true, I

*don't really know the difference between dreams and reality since he
has gone. He was my poem, my breath, my life. I have no reason
to be in a world where he does not exist... Anyhow, the reason
I am writing to you is that Mir had often spoken to me at great
length about you, especially in relation to his university days and
his time in Srinagar when you both were very close.*

*I can understand that it must have been difficult, but I think
time has dealt with the situation for you, even though this has
meant that you have not been able to see each other for some
time. I am sorry that I had to mail this to your address, but I had
no other way of contacting you, since I do not have international
phone access. I would be eternally grateful to you if you could
tell me anything about where Mir is. I know how Mir felt about
his homeland...Do you think he was driven to (or compelled to)
return to Kashmir for political reasons? I thought, if he is in
India, he might have contacted you in the last few months. You
must know that the situation here in Germany is changing by
the minute and no one can be completely sure of the future. On
top of that, I have been made a prisoner by my own mind, and
I am not allowed out of here. Even if Mir tried to contact me,
he might not know where I am. I beg of you to please help me
if you can. I can assure you that by helping me, you would also
be helping your oldest and most beloved friend who never forgot
you. I will wait with every post to hear from you and cannot help
but ask you, once again, to forgive me for this intrusion and also
to tell you how grateful I would be for your reply. I must end
this letter here as I cannot afford to let them (the people here)
see this. I am sorry, I almost forgot, but I know that you will
understand that you only have my deepest good wishes for your
life, family and work.*

Yours, with a great many hopes
Shula (Shula Farid)
1988. Address ...

The letter from Shula is a discontinuous and nervous plea addressed to Veer. As though formulated in haste, the contents are penned in a scrawly handwriting.

Keya re-reads the letter several times to see if there is anything else to glean from it. She lingers over words, trying to read between the lines. She checks the envelope again. She considers the implications.

Shula was requesting any possible knowledge of Mir's whereabouts.

This letter means that Agni was only partially correct, and that while Mir and Shula had been in love and perhaps eloped, other events had followed. So, Mir did not go away with Shula. Unless, of course, her father had known Mir's whereabouts and let Shula know, and they had been brought together again. But there was no way that she could know whether her father had replied to Shula.

From Shula's letter, it seems that Mir and Veer had been quite close in their youth, and while they had retained affections for each other, there had not been much contact as time had passed. This meant that her father had not shared this part of his life with anyone from his family. Could it be a past he wanted to forget?

Keya's thoughts turn to Leon. He had mentioned his mother Albeena's definite reluctance to speak of anything from the past. In fact, this obstinacy on her part had been a constant puzzle to him. Since Albeena was the only traceable person in the story, Keya cannot escape the conclusion that Albeena must know something that no one else alive or present does.

And yet, Veer had lived with his family right up until his death, never mentioning Mir. What did this mean? In any case, some facts are obvious to Keya at this point. Shula and Mir had been in love. Mir had vanished from Shula's life. Shula had been distraught, and to judge from the letter, also under some kind of treatment in Germany.

Keya can't help noting how this last fact contrasts with her own mental picture of Shula Farid. From Agni's account, Keya had imagined Shula as an adventurous and assured woman who dares to take a risk in love, but from her letter, she comes across as a scattered and dissipated woman who is hanging on to scraps of information about her beloved to retain her sanity. A beautiful and poetic adulteress, the bold norm-breaker, transformed to a nervy woman frightened by her circumstances.

Keya's half and hour in the vault is up. A peon comes to get her signature on a register. She carefully closes the iron door on her mother's jewellery and takes Shula's letter in its envelope with her. At the Chinese parlour, a new girl from Nepal shows Usha the back of her head in a hand-held mirror after the haircut. 'Do you like it? The waves?' she turns to Keya for an opinion as she enters. Keya inspects the artful concealing of the thinning hair on her mother's head, and says, 'Yes, that parting suits you, and so do the waves.'

'Did you find the letter?' Usha doesn't ask her any more than this. It means nothing to her.

To Keya, the letter proves that she and Leon are tangled up in each other's history.

11

Going To Albeena

The shirt clings to my armpits in the humid air. With my hair plastered by the sweat on my forehead and a bag in tow, I search for the pre-paid taxi counter at the Mumbai airport terminal. A man rudely elbows past me, grumbling with irritation.

'Excuse me, where is the pre-paid counter?' I stumble into a shop doorway.

The attendant appears from behind displays of luggage, chocolates, locks, water, 'Go out that way and it's on your right. This section is temporarily closed due to the renovation.' I buy a box of duty-free chocolates.

Metres away from the counter, I am surrounded by the private taxi drivers' offers, and the hotel and agency touts.

'No thanks. No thanks.'

I get a computerized slip of paper and settle in the cab that'll take me to Imran Tauzi's place in Andheri.

Imran is a friend of Uncle Siraj. He handles the Mumbai part of a joint business; contractor or shipping or export-import, one of those vague things. I'm staying at their place overnight. Tomorrow, I'll take the train to Ammi's ashram.

It's been three years—no, four—since I left India. I'm coming back to see Ammi. She's been increasingly concerned about me. Stupid Turan! After the 7/7 blasts in London, Ammi was mad with worry. I was, thankfully, in Greece at the time. Before I could call her, she rang the London landline. Turan answered and told her I'd been wandering in Europe for the last few months. She was so agitated: 'Leon, you never told me you went to Berlin! And other countries? Why? Where are you? You have not been working in London for three months! What are you doing? I am very very worried. Please come back for a visit. I want to see you.'

'Ammi, European travel is possible because of low-cost fares. Buying a ticket to India at such short notice will be expensive. And I have nowhere to stay in Mumbai,' etc. I tried to put it off, but she would have none of it.

She harangued me until I gave her a date. She had Uncle Siraj arrange for me to stay at Imran's place.

I was supposed to reach Mumbai last month, but then the big flood happened! Amazing, how the whole city just shut down with being waterlogged. I saw it on TV.

I delayed my ticket by a month, and good that I did, since I finally heard from Keya in the meanwhile. I'd sent her emails now and again and received short acknowledging messages back. After 7/7, she wrote me a long reply; reading it was like listening to her talk. Then, before I left for Mumbai, she called me on the phone from India and related stuff that blew my mind away. She had found a letter that proved our fathers had been friends indeed! And it was somehow comforting to know that Mir's dalliance with Shula was not that important in his life. Whatever the reason for his vanishing, it was not Shula!

When I told Keya I was going to visit Ammi, she said, 'Great! Go via Delhi.'

'It doesn't make sense, her ashram is a short train ride from Mumbai,' I explained.

Her response was, 'All right.'

I felt discarded. 'I want to meet you, Keya. Won't you come to Kolkata with me as you promised?'

'Do you still care what happened to Shula?'

'I'm not sure that I do. But she may have found Mir again. If

we go to Abhilash's place and see her there, we'll know for certain.'
'You're right. I'll contact him and try to arrange a conversation.
What is more, I am a bit bored here in Delhi. Let's catch up in
Kolkata. Let me know when you have an idea of the dates. We'll go
to Abhilash, and you can also fill me in on your summer in Europe.'
'I'll try.'
'What do you plan to do after that? When do you go to London?'
'Not sure. I might be interested in stalking you for a bit.'
She laughed.
'Just a bit then. Do.'

The cabbie asks me if it is my first visit to Mumbai.
'Yes.' It's been a long flight with a lengthy stopover, I don't feel
like talking. I'll tip him for tolerating my unfriendliness.
It's hot, smoky, noisy. I guess the A/C cabs cost extra for a reason.
I get off at Imran's large ground floor flat in a private colony. A
caretaker lets me in when I press the stylish umbo of a bell under
a gold name plaque.
Imran and his son Faisal are watching TV. The women and
children are in Lucknow for a nikah celebration this week.
I feel awkward in using their hospitality, even if overnight.
'Salaam, Leon son, welcome. Did you have a good journey?'
'Salaam, Uncle. Yes, I did. Thanks.'
'Arre, what is this uncle-shuncle? Call me Imran mamu. I'm
your Ammi's bhai-jaan's friend. Same as your Siraj mamu.'
I don't tell him that I've never addressed Uncle Siraj as Siraj
mamu either.
Faisal is a few years older than me; he works in the business
with his dad.
I'm tired, so they ask me to freshen up for an early dinner. I
present them the box of chocolates I bought at the airport and say
I'll leave tomorrow at dawn.
As the women of the house are away, they have the food

delivered from a hotel. They say their sunset namaz prayers and then we sit down to eat. I am asked many questions by the father and son.

'How are things over there in England?'

'What is their attitude to Muslims?'

'Did they trouble you after that bomb attack in London last month?'

I try to give replies.

'Are there attacks on mosques by those Nazis?' Imran asks me.

His son Faisal immediately corrects, 'Not Nazis, Abbu. In England, they are called Rey-shists.'

'Do the Muslims there go for Hajj; do they keep the roza?' Imran is inquisitive.

I am queasy, as I have never fasted at Ramadan myself.

Faisal looks at me, 'Will they ban the attire of our women, like in France, do you think?'

What do I know?

My answers don't seem satisfactory.

Faisal executes a skilful diversion, animatedly telling me about his trips to Dubai.

'What is the scope for me if I want to do business in Europe?' he inquires.

That haunting 'scope' again!

'I am clueless about business,' I say mildly, to their chagrin.

Not long after, the father goes on a tirade about the West, confusing America with England. His son tries to intervene, to no effect.

Imran comes off politics talk with the scary statement, 'India is smouldering. Ask any Muslim in Mumbai.'

When the heat is off, I feign an interest in the sizeable arras decorating a wall.

Over the dry-fruit-studded dessert, they ask me about Ammi, and inform me about Uncle Siraj's ongoing search for grooms for his daughters. I make sympathetic noises.

As soon as I hit the bed, sleep marches over in long shadowy strides.

During the crowded train journey to the ashram the next day, I doze; I am neither hungry nor tired, simply jetlagged. Belatedly, I make sense of the commotion in my compartment—the overhead ventilator has stopped working! People fan their sweat beads with rolled-up magazines and ask around for water. Fellow passengers correctly interpret my lack of perturbation and my fixed stares out the window as evidence of my wish not to be spoken to, so I am spared any talk. I sit oblivious to my surroundings, projecting ahead to what I would say to Ammi when I meet her.

On getting off the platform, I step straight into a burst of dark black smoke from the exhaust of a vehicle. I've inhaled poison and dust. Coughing and spluttering, I search my bag for water. Shit! I have left the Bisleri bottle on the train.

I hail an autorickshaw.

'Ashram or medical?' he enquires.

'Gandhi ashram—'

Before I can fix the fare with him, a portly man materializes, asking 'If you don't mind, can I share the auto with you? I am also going to the ashram.'

'No problem,' I sneak a glance at his small luggage. We can fit.

'I'll charge extra for two passengers.'

'I know what the fare is. You don't worry. Let us go,' the man addresses us both simultaneously. We set off.

He is a Youth Congress worker from Delhi who is coming to the ashram for a training camp. He's been here before.

'What's medical? The auto driver asked me ashram or medical,' I question him.

He points to groups of rowdy young boys hanging outside the PCO booths by the roadside. Some whistle and catcall after passing women.

'That is medical,' he sneers. 'There is a medical college here and numerous students who come to study medicine, but generally create a racket around the city.'

As if to prove his point, a couple of yuppie motorbikers cause a local cyclist to fall off his bike at an intersection. Let alone offering help, their pillion riders 'yoohoo' as they speed away.

Leaving the city behind, we go along a semi-forested stretch of road, and then turn into a wide green expanse of land with several single-storey buildings that are built to look like huts and barns.

'Here we are,' the driver halts.

The man and I split the fare and part ways.

The ashram is simple and well-organized. I report to a small room in the front building which serves as the reception. As I wait for Ammi, I notice the pictures of national leaders on the walls. I could be reading a chapter in a Civics textbook—there are Gandhian signs and symbols on everything: the charkha, a list of the eleven vows, and the seven social sins.

A khadi-clad man brings me a glass of water on a tray, then makes polite enquiries about my journey. I can hear prayers being sung, but before I can decipher the words, Ammi arrives.

I gasp at the sight of Ammi! She is so different from how I remember her. She has aged—she wears spectacles; she wears a brown rough-spun saree—her head is not covered. She kisses me on my forehead, hugs me and tells me how overjoyed she is to see me.

'Ammi, you look different.'

'Do I?' she smiles, 'May Allah bless you! You are still the same. My Leon.'

'You have a most pleasant son,' the man in khadi compliments Ammi.

'Thank you, Abhnaveji. I hope he can learn and be of use while he is here.'

Ammi ushers me to a meeting room with motherly affection and ado.

'Who was that guy? The one who bought me water and chit-chatted.'

'Abhnaveji is an eminent Gandhian scholar. He has written many books. He came back from Japan a few days ago.'

'Oh! I had no idea. I thought he was just someone who worked here. He looks so simple.'

'That's what's beautiful about this place, Leon. People don't have hang-ups about status. Everyone is equal. We strive toward an elimination of prejudice.'

'Wow! That means I've got to be good to everyone here. Because they might turn out to be millionaires or geniuses.'

'Because they are human beings.'

'Ammi, I know. I was not being serious,' I laugh.

'I can't believe that you are in front of my eyes. I was tormented about you. I am angry with you. Why did you go roaming in Europe without letting me know? Do you know how dangerous it is to be by yourself like that? Why did you leave work? You should have—'

'Ammi, relax. Don't start on all that again. You've scolded me enough on the phone.'

She pulls her chair closer to mine.

'Son, have you been eating properly? You are sallow—'

'I am perfectly healthy. It's the fault of the yellowish lighting here.'

'Do you smoke? Have you given up? I have requested you to kick that dreadful habit in every letter.'

'I hardly smoke, Ammi.'

'I hope you are not mixed up with the other stuff over there.'

'Sure, since I don't have a chance of convincing you with honesty, here it goes—your son is a smoker, a drug addict, an alcoh—'

'Shhh! Don't talk like a crazy. If you don't want me to pry into your life, I won't.'

'What kind of a mother would you be if you didn't pry? Go on, interrogate me to your heart's content. But make the most of it as I'm only here for a week.'

'Just a week. Why?'

'I'll tell you later. I want to visit Kolkata after this. And then, maybe travel around India.'

'Hmm. I hear so many young people travel around countries for no reason these days. It always surprises me, Leon. What is it that they are looking for? People travel to do jobs or to join relatives or go on a holiday, or for some reason. Why travel without a reason?'

'That's what I was doing in Europe this summer when Turan snitched on me. I was travelling around without a reason. It's this whole Gap Year concept.'

'I've heard of it. Some American students who came to the ashram were telling me. It's a Gap from what?'

'Gap from Life. From responsibility. From decisions. It's like you can be free.'

'I find that strange. To take a break from those things, you have to go inwards, not around.'

'You are old-fashioned, Ammi.'

'How do they fund it? How do you manage financially?'

'I don't know about others. I saved up for three years from my salary at the studio.'

'Even girls do it, isn't it?'

'Yes, and even aged people do it. It's simple, you go away and learn to see things afresh. Forget about past cares.'

She takes off her glasses and wipes them, distractedly.

'What happened?'

'Nothing. I was wondering why they haven't yet brought the tea.'

'When did you get those specs? They make you look like a Principal or a doctor.'

'It's not been long, under a year. I used to get headaches and the check-up revealed that I am long-sighted. They're not high power.'

'Your diet must be the culprit. You should—'

A woman, dressed exactly like Ammi, comes in with tea, toast and biscuits. 'Didi, thank you,' Ammi says to her.

Then turning to me, she instructs, 'Save the lecturing. Look, here's the tea. Go quickly, wash your face and hands in the adjoining bathroom. There's a washbasin there.'

As I splash myself with water, I realize my mistake. Damn! It was insensitive of me to discuss aged people who go away for no reason.

'Ammi, where will I sleep?'

'A man has taken your luggage to the dorm. It's a large hall with thirty beds. They'll assign you one.'

'And food?'

'There is communal eating in the dining area. Don't wear fancy trousers. You'll have to sit on the floor like everyone else.'

'Are there mealtimes?'

'Of course. And you must make every effort not to be late. Breakfast and dinner is between 7.00 and 8.00 in the morning and at night, lunch between 1.00 and 2.00.'

'Oh no.'

'Oh yes. Each ashram inmate has duties that in turn include cooking, cleaning, gardening, washing.'

'So it's like a big household?'

'In a way. Though our definition of the household would include people around us. We have visitors who come here for training camps. We also have duties in the village projects where we are involved.'

'I shared a ride here with one trainee. He was a Youth Congress worker. A big fellow. Showed me the medical student types in town. A nasty bunch.'

'Was it comfortable at Tauzi Bhai's place last night?'

'Yes, they sent you their regards. Does Uncle Siraj visit?'

'Once or twice a year.'

'Ammi, what do the trainees learn here?'

'They have classes on Gandhian principles, religion and morality, communal harmony, non-violent passive resistance. In addition, they come with us to the rural projects we run on sanitation, paper making, leprosy eradication. There's lots to do.'

'Do you miss Delhi? Our life there?'

'I miss you, Leon. But I am happy to be here. I find meaning in my work. And I know you have a life to live. There's no point being stuck in the past.'

Ammi is calm and thoughtful as ever.

'Son, have the other toast also. They prepared this tea and snack especially for you. It's an exceptional gesture. We never serve food outside mealtimes.'

'Do we eat in the same place?'

'The dining hall has separate sections for men and women. I'll also show you where my living quarters are—but you can't enter; it's better if you inform an office worker and they'll be able to call me.'

'I can talk to you when you're not working, that isn't forbidden, is it?'

'It's not a question of forbidden. It's the rules we have to live by. The discipline that is essential to work. You can talk to me any time you wish—I want to hear about your life in England, your work, your experiences. You can share my days, come to the prayers, visit the village, help me with the chores.'

'Good.'

It is a tough life in the ashram. I admire Ammi for enduring it. Nothing but commitment to moral principles can hold a person here. They have to clean the toilets, shower in cold water, get up at dawn, work all day. For the first couple of nights, I feel odd sleeping on a bed in a dorm, and not having my belongings under lock and key. But I see how it works—people are soft-spoken and kind, they do not disturb others; everyone is keen to help and assist.

Unaware of the extent of their generous concern, one morning I make an excuse about not feeling well so I can skip breakfast. I do it because I want to sleep late. It's terribly embarrassing when some people turn up—worried and anxious. Can they do anything to help? Should they get breakfast to my bed? Do I have fever? Should they send for a doctor?

I go with the ashram workers to a Dalit village. It is far removed from anything I've seen in the city slums. The low-roofed mud

dwellings have animals sharing space with people. Children chase
after vehicles. There are funny numbers and slogans on every wall.

'What are those?' I ask a trainee.

'The words? Those are the class and caste struggle slogans.'

'I know. I mean the numbers in chalk.'

'Oh, that. Those are polio vaccination records. Each mark indicates
something to the health worker.'

The children gather around me. I buy Glucose biscuit packets
from the tea stall and begin to distribute them.

It causes a mini-riot. Snotty sooty grasping fingers are all over
me—'I haven't got one! Give me one!'

I give up and hand them to one of the elder kids in the
group. 'I'll buy you as many packets as they want. You do justice
in handing them out.'

He's an incredibly sensible dude. He shouts at them and makes
them sit—they listen to him—as he distributes the biscuits in an
orderly manner.

At three rupees a packet, I buy most of the shop's supplies.

Seeing the happy little faces, I feel I've done good, but the other
social workers don't seem very impressed.

I try to be as involved as I can, for Ammi's sake. I spend time
listening to a tribal rights activist. He tells me how the tribal
communities suffer because they do not have individual land
ownership; their lands are taken away by the state and feudal landlords.
They don't get proper compensation, they are not treated with dignity,
and the development doesn't happen either, due to corruption and
lack of accountability.

'Land is the root of all trouble: wars, clashes, injustice,' I reflect
later with Ammi.

'It's not land that causes trouble. The earth gives us everything.
It's the emotions it arouses, the way we belong.'

I think of Keya and her work on exiles. I want to tell Ammi
about what I've learnt in Berlin, but don't know how to broach
the topic.

The day before leaving, I hatch a plan. Instead of beginning the conversation from Mir, I decide to begin it from Keya.

'Ammi, I've said much about my life in England and showed you pictures, but there are some from Europe you haven't seen.'

'Really, where are they?'

'Actually, there's just one. I forgot to show you this portrait I clicked.'

'Let me see it then.'

I seat her in a chair and hand her the photo of Keya, the best one, in which she is by the Neptune fountain in Berlin, in the golden evening light.

Ammi looks carefully at the picture, then at me for some clues as to the matter, and then again at the picture. Finally, she takes off her specs and tells me that she likes her.

'Well, she's not my girlfriend, if that's what you are thinking,' I say.

Ammi ignores my statement. She puts on her glasses again, peers at the photo, and asks me, 'Do I know this girl?'

I take my opportunity, and sit at her feet on a cushion.

'I have something to tell you.'

'What?'

'Her name is Keya, Dr Keya Raina,' I begin, 'she is a PhD and lives in Bristol in the southwest of England.'

'Raina?' Ammi's brows are knit in anticipation.

'I met her in Berlin.'

'Hmm.'

'You know I went there, but you don't know why. I went to Berlin to look for Father.'

Ammi's face is drained of colour.

'Why are you telling me this?' she snaps, 'You know that I do not want to talk of that past.'

'Please, Ammi. Please. Let me explain. I am not saying this to hurt you, or to unnecessarily dredge up a difficult past. I have a thing to tell you.'

I wait for a reaction. There is none.

She is still as a rock.

I try a different route and describe Keya's research project in Berlin, and how she helped me with getting access to some centres, though 'I found nothing'.

'And?' she asks. I can't be sure, but it's as if there's a trace of relief on her face at my words.

'Then Keya met this woman, Agnes, who has been living there for more than forty years, and she told her something about Mir.'

Ammi says she doesn't want to hear any more; she gets up, then sits down again, and waits for me to speak.

'Ammi, according to Agnes, Mir had an affair in Berlin with an Indian diplomat's wife. She was called Shula.'

'Leon, I don't care.' At the same time, a tear rolls down her cheek. Before I can reach over to wipe it, she quickly dries her face with the end of her saree, and adds, 'Inform me, Leon. Since you have come here to tell your mother what you think she ought to know, go ahead.'

Does she want me to stop? Should I? I pause and scan her face, but it's not clear, so I continue.

'Mir met Shula years after he left us. They went away somewhere, but he eventually disappeared from her life and she went into treatment from the sorrow,' I have it out.

'Did you meet her?' Ammi asks in an altered tone of voice.

'No, no,' I immediately respond.

'Then? How do you know this?'

'This is why I showed Keya's picture to you, Ammi. Keya is also from Kashmir originally. Hindu. Her father died many years ago. She was interested in my story, and looking through her father's papers, found a letter from Shula dated 1988 asking him whether he knew Mir's whereabouts, since they had been very close friends in Kashmir—'

'—Ammi? Ammi? Are you all right? Shall I get you some water?'

She grips the sides of the chair like she's fainting. I don't know whether I was right to force this knowledge upon her.

'No.'

I touch the folds of her saree at the knee, and clarify, 'Ammi, basically, Keya's father and Mir knew each other in Kashmir. That's why Shula wrote—.'

'I know,' she interrupts.

At length, she blankly stares at me, uttering, 'Veer. Veer Raina?'

How does she know? Before I can confirm or ask how she knows, she leaves the room.

I don't know what to make of it, and cannot speak to her till after dinner as she is called for her duties. Later that night, when I see her again, she is calm and composed. She sits next to me on a porch and asks for that photograph of Keya again. I hand it to her. She gazes intently at the picture for some minutes, lost in thought.

Then, she breaks the silence with the barely audible words, 'If I had a daughter, she would be like Keya.'

I don't know whether I am meant to have heard this. I look at her enquiringly, feeling curiously jealous for a fleeting instant.

'Leon, it is strange the way fate works, how you and Keya met in such a big world.'

I nod, questioning, 'How do you know about Father's friendship with Keya's father, about Mir and Veer?'

'I was their friend too, Leon,' she says.

I am taken aback at her matter-of-fact statement. Why had she never told me this? Did she really know where Mir was, after all?

'Do you have any remaining pictures of them? Of Father?' I hazard.

'No, you know I burnt them. Perhaps I was being naïve and selfish—'

'It's not that, it's just—'

She does not let me complete the sentence, saying, 'I will tell you everything you want to know.'

'I hardly know anything about any of this, other than what the letter from Shula to Veer conveyed.'

There is thunder brewing and big drops of rain come down on our heads.

We move indoors.

'Your father and I never should have married. We were too different. No, that is not correct. We felt strongly about the same things, but he was a very expressive man who always had a cause in his mind and on his lips. I could not communicate to him my agreement with his ideas. I was very quiet. Maybe he thought I never understood.'

'Why did you marry?'

'It's difficult. My relatives were keen for me to marry after my graduation. They already thought I had studied enough. Of course, I am lucky to have had that education, because of which I could later work and support myself. Mir had done very well in his Engineering and had good prospects. Everyone thought it would be a suitable match since we already knew each other.'

'And you?'

'No one asked me. But what could I have said anyway?' she sighs. 'It was so long ago; I could never have imagined that it would come up ever again in my life, and especially not in this way, Leon. Mir and Veer had a close friendship.'

'They studied at the same college together,' I state what I know, then add, 'Funny, they had such similar sounding names.'

'It was because of their names that they first got to know each other. People in their class would mishear their names. That is how they met.'

'How did you meet them?'

'I was studying at the main university, and I also worked as an assistant at the library. They often came, and once, we met in the canteen. It was rather strange to sit and talk with the two men, and I was very reserved, but because Veer's family and mine lived in the same locality, people did not mind. In fact, we were both from business families, and my relatives were casual acquaintances of some people from Veer's household. But there was a distance.'

'Because we were Muslim,' I say, before realizing that I already saw myself there. I was not even born then.

'That is true. We had different family situations. Veer's father would never have heard of anything between him and me,' she explains.

'So you loved Veer!' I exclaim.

I can't believe that it is my Ammi's life we are talking about. It feels unreal. Plain and simple Ammi in her rough brown saree and black-framed specs had once been young and in love. It's like a movie—Ammi in Srinagar amid flowers and trees, Dal lake and Nishaat gardens. My own mother!

'Bah, love! Is that how simple it is, Leon?' she says charily, though denying nothing.

'Mir was charismatic and inspiring, Veer more understanding—he helped me once with an assignment. I was doing a general degree. Their studies were difficult. They were learning how to build bridges, repair gadgets, make things work. I imagined how worthwhile it could be.'

'Your father Mir was the one involved in pamphleteering and political work. He was head of the students' union and a committed communist. He had a strong aversion to everything wrong and unjust. He would address the crowds with confidence, breaking into impromptu verses of his own. People loved his poetry and his idealist vision. In fact, both Veer and I admired him. Veer was like me in that way, quieter and less expressive, even shy. He and I did not speak much, but we knew we had a sympathy between us. Neither of us ever expressed it directly.'

'Didn't he ever say anything to you?'

'No, he could not. It would have been so bold,' she pauses, then sagely comments, 'We knew the difference between movies and life in those days.'

'Well, what else do you want to know?' she turns to me.

'You have not said anything about how things happened so that you and Mir got married,' I reply.

'I did have feelings for Veer, it is true. I went with a group of people to a friend's wedding and looked forward to seeing him there. We talked about things on a few occasions, neutral things, but we never declared our intentions. It would have been too much. As it is, Veer's father had forced him to study Engineering against his will. His heart was not in it.'

'And Father?'

'Mir enjoyed his studies, and managed to do well in spite of his political activities. He was full of life.' Ammi is wistful.

'Then?'

'Then what? Time passed. After his degree, Veer left for Shimla to escape being drawn into their family business. They did not like him being mixed up in politics; he even had to break off his friendship with Mir. He returned to Srinagar briefly when his mother died. He was a changed person.'

'After that, you lost touch?'

'We never did exchange letters or such. I don't know where he went, but later, I heard Siraj mention to someone that he had probably gone to Delhi to look for work.'

'Looks can say a hundred words, you did not need letters,' I lightly remark.

Ammi pretends not to hear. She continues, 'After a few months, when Mir got a job, my marriage was fixed to him, and soon, he was posted abroad with his company. I joined him after two years in England, and then you were born and he left. That is it, Leon. That is all,' she speaks with a finality, a resignation.

'Ammi, did you know anything about Shula Farid before now?'

'No, son, and as I told you earlier, I do not want to know. Why should we keep bringing up things from the past which make no difference in the present? He left me. And you. That is all.'

'He never saw me?'

'No.'

'He never contacted you afterwards?'

'No.'

'Do you think he was kidnapped? By someone, because of his political work. Was he a spy?'

'I don't think of such things. There can be endless speculations on someone's life and reasons, and one can be none the wiser at the end. Only he knew what he was up to. They searched for him and they found nothing. What else could have been done—'

Then I ask the question I have been burning to ask for so many years.

'Why did you never speak to me about this when I was growing up? Did you think I would not understand?'

She clasps her hands together and is silent, as if to brace herself. Then she sombrely admits, 'I did what I thought was right, Leon. Maybe I was wrong not to speak to you about it. Maybe I did not know what to say about any of this. Maybe I did not want to accept it, and speaking about it would have meant just that. Maybe I…' she stops.

'You thought he might come back,' I complete her sentence for her.

She says nothing.

'That's why you never married again and lived such a difficult life. Why such sacrifice for someone who deserted you?'

'Don't make me out to be a helpless victim. I never meant for you to get that impression. I lived my life the way I wanted to, and I have no regrets. I did not want to remarry. I did not sacrifice anything for anyone else. Do I seem unhappy? I chose to come here and live this life.'

'Ammi, remember, you used to always tell me how proud you were of me?'

'Yes.'

'It's you I should be proud of. I'm sorry to judge your life as a mere reaction to Mir's actions.'

At these words, she fixes her eyes on me, 'And nobody's life should be a reaction to anyone else's life ever, no matter who they are, and how much you love them. It is a lesson we must learn. We should not constantly search for pasts when there are futures that we can make. Maybe I am being harsh, but I think our unhappiness with memory is always of our own making.'

I feel small in front of her.

'Then do you think I was wrong to start this journey, this search for Mir and my history?' I can't help asking.

'It is not a matter of right or wrong. One does what one has to, given how one feels. I understand why you needed to do this, and it is right that you should live your life knowing the things that matter to you. I just did not realize your need to know sooner.'

'I had almost given up, and then I met Keya—' I say.

'How is she?' Ammi asks.

'She is...kindred. She's very bright and capable. Funny, strange, honest, helpful. She collects people's stories, she's bothered about the world. She cares. She gets excited about stuff and follows it through earnestly. She was amazed to find that our lives were connected. That her father and mine grew up together.'

'Maybe I will see her some day,' Ammi remarks. Then enquires, 'What other family does she have?'

'She has no siblings. Her mother is a government official in Delhi. She has support from her relatives in Keya's absence. Keya has been living in England for many years now. She moved there sometime after her father's death. She really adored him.'

'Veer is no more,' Ammi slowly intones. 'When did he die?'

'It was a tragic early death, some medical misjudgement. I don't know the details, I didn't know how to ask.'

Ammi seems melancholic. I patiently wait for a bit, not wanting to interrupt.

'Ammi?'

'Yes?'

'Keya and I are planning to go and meet Abhilash in Kolkata next week. She's in Delhi at the moment and will travel to meet me there.'

'Abhilash?'

'Shula's husband, the ex-diplomat. We got his address from Agnes, that woman in Berlin who knew Shula. We thought that if Shula returned to her husband, we could try to meet her. If not, we might get to know what happened, and if he knows anything else.'

'Has he said that he will speak to you both about this? You must allow for the possibility that he may not.' She is practical.

'I have not contacted him beforehand, but since Keya has been working on Indians in Berlin, we thought she could make it out to be a part of her research and ask him about his life there, or something. If he generally speaks to us, that's enough. Shula could even be there, or at the very least, we might be able to see her picture. Abhilash may know where she is if Mir met her again...' I list the various possibilities.

'If you and Keya think that this is what you ought to do, it is your wish. But remember that people don't always want to be found.'

'I don't mean to anger or upset you, I just thought—'

'I am not angry or upset, son. I hope that you can move forward with your life.'

'I will. And I'll remember what you said about not living one's life as a reaction to anyone else's, no matter how beloved.'

'May Allah bless you, Leon.'

It is already late and I bid her goodnight—she has to be up early.

The rain hasn't abated. Borrowing an umbrella from the watchman, I walk her to her building.

On the way back, I let myself get soaked.

12

Catch Up In Kolkata

*K*eya's step quickens on seeing me.

'It's wonderful to meet again. Look at you!' she shakes my hand, then throws an arm around my shoulder, for a second, in response to my abortive hug gesture.

'I smell of orange juice. The air hostess spilt it on me while trying to open a carton.'

'At least you didn't ask her for tea or coffee, or she'd have scalded you.'

'Not funny. See, I have these weird stains all over my clothes.'

It's the first time I have seen Keya in a salwar kameez.

'The stain could be confused for an arty design,' I make as if to detect odours, 'and you smell of faint citrus and airline tissue.'

She leans on my luggage, rather girlishly, saying, 'What made you experiment with facial hair?'

'I've not shaved for a few days while at Ammi's ashram. It's not exactly a convenient place for being dapper; no hot water, communal sinks.'

I feel odd with the focus on my bristle. I had no time to get ready, having arrived on the train to Kolkata in the morning, then coming straight to receive her at the airport.

'Leon, do you feel strange that we are meeting again? In another country at another airport.'

I don't like saying such things aloud. I want to say that it's good to be close to her.

She doesn't wait for me to reply, 'I mean, strange in a nice way.

Like happy strange. It's like you're not a name in an email line on my inbox or a voice on the phone, you're here in flesh and blood. I have much to catch up on, I'm sure.'

'Same here.'

'Give me a minute. I will call Hiren, the person who's arranged our accommodation, and confirm that we are headed there soon.'

Since neither of us have an Indian SIM card on our mobiles, she surveys around for a payphone.

'While you do that, can I get you something? A sandwich, tea?'

'Do, please. There was no food served on board. I'd like a Nestea from that stall and…umm…a packet of Kurkure. Thank you.'

I get the spicy snack and two steaming plastic cups of tea while she makes the call.

Coming back, she triumphantly announces, 'Yes. They've got a twin room for us at the university guest house—in case anyone asks, we'll lie about you being an academic. I also called Abhilash. As you know, he had agreed to meet us. He's fine with tomorrow. I assume that's okay with us?...'

'Sure.'

'So, I said "Yes".'

Taking the cup and balancing it between us on a bench, she avers, 'This is what we shall do. We'll get a cab and go settle at the guest house; then, if you want to sightsee—'

'No, I don't. I'm tired.'

'Suits me. I've been here before. In that case, we can rest in the evening and eat from the mess there. Tomorrow, we'll see Abhilash and—'

'I'm sorry, you came here because of me. I might be ready to go out later, if there's anywhere you want to visit.'

'Let's see. I am not going to have you feel like I did you a favour by coming here. I came here because of you—and that's not a favour. Do you understand?'

'Fine. But since you've been here, why don't you point the city out to me from the cab windows?'

'I'd like nothing better than to natter your head off,' she smiles, then dives into her laptop case, saying 'Where's the map?'

Keya in Kolkata. Keya in Berlin. Keya amazes me. Her zest for life, her sense of purpose in the little and big things. She's so different, so interested in other people, so able to deal with anything thrown at her.

'Shubodh, did you say?' she repeats the taxi driver's name.

'Subodh, Su-bodh. I am from Madhubani. These Bengalis here call me Shoe-bodh, but I am Subodh.'

'Okay, Subodh, we're going to Jadavpur.'

'Yes. Have you heard of Madhubani paintings?'

'Of course, they're famous. I've even got one. They're quite unique.'

I notice that the driver is thrilled at this. He and Keya talk about Kolkata politics and the status of Bihari migrants in the city.

'Where I live, all of us vote for Mamata's party.'

'So you're a Trinamool Congress supporter. Not a communist.'

'Definitely not a communist; they've ruined West Bengal,' he says.

Keya turns to me, explaining, 'The city is especially festive at the moment, due to the impending Puja. It is the biggest event of the year here.'

'I've heard of the Durga Puja. They make a big idol of the goddess and then immerse it in the water,' I respond, glancing at the parade of gods decking the front panel of the vehicle.

She follows my eye, 'Even communists here can worship gods. Quite a few are superstitious.'

'How is your research project? The one you were working on when in Berlin—Indian artists and exile.'

'Done and dusted for the time being,' she chirps, 'I spent the summer writing a draft manuscript. It kept me occupied until August.'

'That's why your emails were cryptic, like telegrams.'

'Partly.'

We are stuck in a traffic bottleneck. The driver puts on the radio.

Keya says, 'See those sweet shops, loaded with mithais. The sweets are so tempting in Kolkata. Especially the spongy white roshogullah dripping in syrup.'

The driver hears her and agrees.

She draws my attention to the stream of things outside the windows. There are billboards advertising cellphones, health retreats, insurance, newspapers, cars.

'Don't the statues of women workers here remind you of East Berlin?'

'Hmm. I didn't notice that,' I say.

Suddenly, Keya bursts into a laugh.

'What's funny?' I ask.

'Check out the back of that Gariahat bus—the maroon and yellow one—there, in that lane.'

I observe a bus precariously listing to one side and bursting with people crammed into every inch, many hanging from the doors. At the back of this trundling beast hangs a large fading tin board advertising a German luxury car: 'We couldn't make the roads better, so we just made a better car'.

It is a pathetic sight. I smile.

'India is the land of irony,' she comments.

'Here's the official area,' she checks names from the map and informs me of the landmarks.

The official area reminds me of New Delhi enclaves: the long broad boulevards, the flowerbed lawns, the High Court, Governor's House, Akashwani Bhawan, mosques, churches.

It is an entirely new way of travelling for me.

I notice people, places and things to avenge myself on them; when I'm upset, I ogle my surroundings to blank thoughts from my mind.

Keya notices her surroundings as if her life depends on it.

We pass the Strand, Shakespeare Sarani, Red Road, Victoria Memorial, the jewellers, confectioners, bathroom fitters. There are black folded umbrellas and bright yellow cabs, lambs marked in orange being led for slaughter across a street.

After a while, I wonder if it doesn't tire her to be so comprehending and mindful.

We've been in traffic for a couple of hours. The driver loudly honks at the red light. A traffic policeman glares at us as we pass. His attire is crazily bulky in this oppressive humid heat.

I am dozy with London dreams when we arrive at the guest house.

Hiren is a smart lecturer who cordially escorts us to the caretaker. I wonder how Keya knows him. When I get an answer from her—'We met at a conference'—I feel envious about these bright young things. My teachers at college were such bores. Maybe I should study further!

The caretaker says something in rapid-fire Bengali, takes payment for two days in advance, and hands us a key. When we sign in our names and separate addresses, he reacts by conspicuously handing over his charge to a junior staff. Is it because Keya and I are sharing a room without sharing a surname?

As soon as Keya and I are alone in the room—the first such instance since Berlin—she begins settling the bags in their proper corners. Why? We're leaving in less than forty-eight hours!

'You are a control freak, aren't you?' I jest.

'A good, wonderful control freak,' she winks, before flopping on a bed. 'This one on the left is mine.'

'Sure.' All the same, I go over and sit on the side of the bed that she's chosen.

She reaches out a hand towards mine. Our fingers and eyes interlock for a moment.

Then she's spry. 'I want to shower.'

When she's gone to the bathroom, I take stock of the situation. I need to tell her what I've learnt from Ammi before we go and see Abhilash.

How will I do this? What will I say? 'Your father and my mother used to have feelings for each other'—it sounds idiotic. Moreover, would it be right of me to impinge upon her image of her father?

No, she doesn't need to know about Veer and Albeena. It may unnecessarily hurt her mother if she mentions it to her family. I decide not to speak of it.

I'm standing by the wide aspect window when she comes out, dressed in fresh clothes, smelling of talc.

'The bathroom pipe leaks a little. Just letting you know.'

'Keya, listen, here's what I found—Veer and Mir and Ammi all knew each other.' It is best to be straight.

'Really? Your mother was aware of them?'

'That's right. Ammi told me they were friends. She said your father was a very helpful, sensitive person.'

'He was so wonderful. I wish he was alive. So you could have met him too.'

Before I can say anything, she asks, 'How did your mother react to everything? Did you tell her we are going to meet Abhilash and, possibly, Shula?'

'She doesn't want to know about Mir. She advised us that people don't always want to be found. She tried to get me to understand that no one's life should be lived as a reaction to anyone else's, no matter how beloved.'

'What wise words. I absolutely agree. I thought about your search a lot after we parted. It sounds cruel but it's true, you should move on and look ahead.'

'Then why did you not dissuade me from coming to see Abhilash?'

'Because I'm selfish. I am interested in Shula. Also Shula and Mir. The times they lived through were shot with political and social change. Shula, with her complicated identity and striving, fascinates me. I imagined her as a rebellious heroine, but her letter is penned by a broken woman. I want some day to write her story, her biography, if I get to meet her, and if she allows me. I hope that won't offend you.'

'Why should it? Shula is nothing to me,' I shrug.

It's begun drizzling. From the first floor window of our room, we silently see the red signal mast light slip behind the clouds, the tall palms leaning over a body of stagnant water.

'I spent the summer wandering places. Learning from life. I'm finding a way somewhere. I'm getting over my ghosts.'

'Like Maya?'

'How do you—Oh, yes, I told you.'

'I must confess. It's not like I was eavesdropping, but I couldn't sleep, and I heard you talk to her on the phone from the balcony that night in Berlin.'

I laugh.

Keya's expression challenges me.

'That was a charade. My phone was switched off. I was trying to have a conversation with an imaginary Maya.'

'That's crazy. You sounded in earnest. I covered my ears to not overhear.'

'It's true though. Later, when I emailed the real Maya with a long apology for those times, I got a succinct reply asking me never to attempt contacting her again. The gist was—You are forgiven; I'm happily married; leave me alone. It made me so happy. I wish I'd written to her earlier.'

'Meeting Ammi was good too. There are people who get meaning by improving others' lives.' I tell her about my encounter with the ashram inmates. About Ammi's life.

'I showed her the picture of you by that fountain.'

'What did she say?'

'She examined it carefully before pronouncing that she likes you. She thought you were my girlfriend.'

'Which I am not,' Keya states tonelessly.

Damn! Her face is turned away, and I can't parse her utterance.

'Are you...you are single, right?'

'Of course not! Don't you remember what I said about the dozens of people I meet and get attracted to every week!' She's enjoying it.

'Well—'

My sentence is interrupted by a sustained juddering that rattles the windowpanes and shakes the floor. Birds fly out from under foliage, shrieking.

'We're obviously next to a train station. There must be a commuter line behind the trees at the back of the building,' Keya says.

'I'm hungry. Let me sample the broken pipe in the bathroom while I shave and shower, and then let's get food,' I seize the initiative, for once.

We get the standard thirty-rupee thali from the canteen. I choose a non-vegetarian dinner; it's a treat for me after the bland vegetables at the ashram every day.

I shield my eyes as I squint at a plane humming in the sunny skies overhead. Keya and I have reached the address we have for Mr Abhilash Basu—the one Agnes provided in Berlin. We left the guest house with plenty of time in hand, given our experience with the traffic yesterday.

Abhilash's villa is in a quiet, affluent residential suburb. The front garden is blooming with colourful fragrant flowers of all kinds; the white wooden picket fence leads through a gate and along a gravelled brick-lined pathway to a door, where a dignified bilingual sign cursively spells his name. We ring a bell and are greeted by a uniformed servant, who politely leads across a front porch with screens into a reception room, informing us that his master would be there soon.

I am very jittery and my palms are sweaty. It's the feeling of taking an exam when I am not ready. I glance at Keya. She is supremely in command of herself, as if looking forward to a challenge.

We sit down. The contents of the large plush room radiate respectability. There is a cushioned leather sofa suite at our end, and around us, in the large oval space, are carved chairs, glass tables on wooden elephants' backs, a wine cabinet and a bookshelf. The entire floor is carpeted and a woven soft rug demarcates the centre. On the walls are decorations from distant places. From the high ceiling hangs a diamond drop chandelier; a grandfather clock chimes.

Keya nudges me to draw attention to a photo on the mantelpiece. Inside the bejewelled frame, there is the picture of a genial couple. Simultaneously, both of us stand up to scrutinize it. It appears to be clicked after a function or ceremony, because the man and woman are formally dressed. The green background doesn't give anything away; it might have been taken abroad.

A bespectacled Abhilash in a stiff navy-black suit is quite the senior official of the state. His arm is around Shula, who is noticeably shorter. Her chubby round face is pleasant. She wears a cream and red silk saree, after the Bengali fashion. They look happy. The date on the photograph is recent, from some years ago.

So this is it! What am I doing here?

'I'm not comfortable, Keya,' I own up, 'I won't know what to say to them.'

'Don't worry, I'll handle it. You needn't fret. Remember, we're pretending this is part of my work!'

She is obviously used to meeting and talking to people about their lives.

We return to the sofa, but before we can sit, Abhilash enters the room from the other end.

'Oh my! Why have you people not been seated yet? Please sit down, please,' he gestures towards the sofa and we sit, transparently apart.

'Hello! I am Keya—Dr Keya Raina—and this is my friend and colleague, Leon. I had written to you, Mr Basu—' Keya begins by handing him the bouquet of flowers she bought along the way here.

She omits my surname in the introduction.

'Welcome, Dr Raina and Leon—'

'Keya, please.'

'Keya. You may call me Abhilash. I've also lived in the West. Thank you so much for the flowers,' he seats himself and rings a bell, which immediately brings forth a reedy servant.

'Arrange these flowers. Now what will you have? Cold drinks, hot drinks? Hard drinks? In this weather...' he trails off, looking at me. The servant humbly waits.

'Thanks, Coke or Pepsi with ice would do,' says Keya.

'Same for me,' I add.

'Sure? Fine. Also get me lime juice,' he robustly commands. The minion hurries away.

'Let me see, so you are both academics in England,' he ends on a rising tone.

'Yes, we are scholars,' replies Keya, before I can open my mouth. 'I am interested in studying prominent exiles, and also Indians who were in Berlin at a historic time. I was informed about your being there before the Wall came down, and wanted to speak to you about your experiences.' She is the complete picture of an interested researcher, and even brings out a notepad and pen from her bag. She is lying with proficiency. I am amazed.

The obsequious slave offers us the drinks without meeting our gaze. Abhilash instructs him to turn the air-conditioning on.

I decide to be a spectator, as unobtrusive as possible. If I just watch them interact, I'll be able to slacken the tense whirring in my head.

Abhilash mostly addresses Keya and speaks; seldom does he nod or smirk in my direction to stress a point. I think he assumes that I am her boyfriend, chaperone, research assistant or such.

'So, Sir, Mr Abhilash, what was your life like in those days?' she asks, pen under chin.

'You see, Miss Keya, we are servants of the Indian government; we go abroad in the service of the nation and our work consists of furthering that purpose. We do whatever we have to in order to best perform our duties to the nation,' he talks on in response to her leading questions, and appears gratified by the interest Keya is showing in his life and work.

'If I may ask, what was your personal family background? As in, are you from an established family of diplomats? How did that shape your experience in the service?'

With an indulgent laugh, a quick look around, he says, 'Oh n-no, I am not a born elite. My father set up a modest textile factory, and with God's grace, his trade prospered; we became well-off, quite wealthy, in fact. My parents are not alive today, but they had this villa built before I was born. It was, obviously, a change to go from an entrepreneurial family to state service. I initially enrolled in Economics in Calcutta University to take up the business, but then soon decided I wanted to be a bureaucrat. That is life. Isn't that right?' He smiles and stares piercingly at us both, then continues, 'My Berlin job was one of my early postings and I learnt quite a lot.'

'You said it was an early posting, so age-wise, how come you are not in the service anymore?'

'I got tired of the luxury of that life—ha ha! Diplomats become useless people after a while. Unable to exist outside that cosiness. I took early retirement, and now serve on the boards of various organizations, here in Bengal itself. Actually, I wanted to work in my own country and with organizations of my choice. So, years ago, after spending nearly two decades in the service, I gave it all up.' As he ends the sentence, he demonstrates a letting go with the many-ringed fingers of both his hands.

'Did the Cold War environment in the city ever directly confront you? Did you ever have problems?'

'Not at all. We went there knowing about the situation in the city. Plus, we were on good terms with both Germanys. I was on the side of freedom; my side was the West. Of course, there were some defections, some Indian activists who made life quite difficult for us, but on the whole, we managed well.'

'Were there many Indian activists? Do you remember anyone in particular?'

'There were some,' he shakes his head dismissively. 'There are always some, but what can they do? They publish a few pamphlets, get a few idlers to sign ill-drafted bits of paper, and climb here and there, talk off the wall—ha! what else?'

'Do you remember any names?'

'Definitely not. You see, they were a nuisance and not really worthy of our attention.'

Keya goes on talking to him for a while, pumping him for information. At last, he remarks, 'You are from Kashmir, Miss Keya. I knew from your Pandit surname. You must surely know how these militants, these so-called activists, can unnecessarily trouble law and order in the pursuit of their own vain interests. The most important thing is the nation; national culture and national pride.'

Keya says nothing, immediately asking him another question about his career. She wheedles him for a long time, and I am bored listening to his self-righteous replies in which he routinely mentions the names of important politicians. He keeps on about Indian Culture and Traditional Values. I wonder if this is going anywhere.

'The most important asset is a nation's culture, its traditional values. In this, Miss Keya, the women have always made India proud,' he drones on.

He is of average build, medium height and dressed impeccably, even at home. His dryness and smug certainty is numbing me beyond belief.

I am almost asleep with my eyes open, when Keya finally enquires, 'What about the women? How did the spouses of the officials spend their time? What did they do? I am especially interested in the story of these women's lives.'

'Women have their own lives. They shop, attend functions, read magazines, watch cinema. I don't know what else they can do. If they have children, it is easier for them.'

'Mr Abhilash, I hope you will forgive me for asking, but I learnt in Berlin that your wife unfortunately became quite ill when you were there.'

I sit up to listen attentively.

'So, people remember me in Berlin. Aha! Well, what did they say, you must tell me first.'

'Just that your wife, Shula Farid-Basu, became quite unwell and you had to leave the city because of that.'

Abhilash pauses and scrutinizes Keya carefully, assessing something.

'It is true. Shula could not take the environment in a foreign city. In fact, she started to imagine things and the doctors were worried for her sanity. I did not want to put her through any more stress, so she was moved to a well-equipped facility in the south of the country, and I asked for a change of position on those grounds.'

'Shula—what a beautiful name.'

'Yes, my mother-in-law was a European Jew. Shula was, as you are aware, a Muslim, but I never cared that she had mixed blood,' he says with a flourish.

'I spoke to a friend of Shula's in Berlin, Agnes, Agni Michael. She remembered you and spoke highly of you. She told me about Shula's life, Santiniketan, Kolkata, Berlin—it was quite a journey. She also said Shula wrote poetry and painted.'

'Hn-unh. In those days, she did. There are diaries full of her writing in that desk drawer over there.'

'Do you mind if we get to know a little bit more about her? I do biographical sketches, as I'd said in my email. I'm very fascinated by her life and would like to write about her if it's all right.'

'Miss Keya, if you are so interested in her life, read it in her own words. Write about it. You know how women are. Uh…some of them. She always wanted to be written about. There are enough diaries.'

'Wonderful,' Keya is incredulous. This must be fabulous news for her.

'Of course, we would not dream of doing this without her permission,' she says.

Abhilash blinks at Keya, 'You have my permission. Her parents are long dead. She has no other relatives.'

His magisterial tone makes me sympathize with the poor adulteress for the first time. He makes her sound like chattel.

Keya, too, must be feeling the rush of blood. But she adroitly suppresses it as she requests, 'Can I take the diaries away to be copied?'

'Why not? In fact, you can take and keep them. My wife has wanted me to lose them, but I do not want to destroy them. Sentimentality, I suppose.'

He summons the servant again, and gives instructions to put the contents of the desk drawer in a bag.

The servant quickly carries out his task, while Abhilash asks us where we are staying in Kolkata; have we seen the city?

Soon, there's a brown jute handbag with stitched cloth flowers on the table in front of us. Keya steals an excited glance at me. It's mission accomplished for her. Maybe she doesn't see her joy reflected in my eyes—I've learnt zilch about Mir from this—because she directly becomes serious again.

'That is a lovely photograph on the mantelpiece. We were admiring it when you first came in.' Is she going to request a meeting with Shula?

'Thank you. I like it myself. It was taken on the occasion of our anniversary.'

'Is your wife here today?'

'No, it's a pity she isn't. Or she might have made you feel more comfortable. She never lets anyone depart without a meal. She is out with our daughter to shop for the Puja. It is the biggest event in the year for us Bengalis, as you know. Rather like your Shivratri. I used to have a Kashmiri friend called Dhar, Kiran Dhar; he was in the foreign service. Do either of you know him by any chance?'

'No,' we answer.

'He was very bright. Kashmiris are. Like Bengalis, you also have a very distinctive identity. But this man was related to the Governor of—' here he goes again, I think.

'Could we perhaps meet her another time. Maybe tomorrow?'

'Why not? If you wish. But she has never lived abroad, so I don't know how much she can tell you about exile,' he laughs. 'Unless you call living outside your own Bengal town an exile, heh-heh-heh!' he's amused at his whimsy.

'But, surely she has been to Berlin?'

'No.'

'Didn't you say some of her diaries were from Berlin?'

'Those are Shula's diaries,' he spells out, appearing puzzled.

'And Shula is your wife, isn't it?' Keya enunciates each word carefully.

'Shula was my wife.'

'Oh!'

'So this is—' we turn to the framed photo.

'Modhumita Chandan Basu, my second wife, the mother of my child.'

'I am so sorry, we did not know.'

'Never mind. I assumed you knew. Ah, that is why you were hesitating about taking Shula's diaries without permission. I see—'

'Where is Shula Farid these days?' I impulsively question. I can't control the unevenness in my voice. Is she back with Mir then? Did she find Mir? Contingencies bubble in my head.

'So he speaks! Mr...—er...Leon, you speak. I thought Miss Keya never lets you get a word in.' When he is done with the delight, Abhilash casually mentions, 'Shula is dead.' The words are devoid of any palpable emotion.

It is our turn to be shocked!

'Dead?' we rebound.

'When?'

'She has been dead for a long time. She died in that facility in Germany. Mental illness. Oh God!' he heaves a belated sigh.

I recall Shula's letter and realize that Shula died from the unhappiness of love, from missing Mir.

'We are so sorry,' offers Keya.

'Never mind. We all have our time to go,' he consults his watch ostentatiously.

We stand up to leave.

'Was there a Mir she ever knew?' Keya tries to ask in an offhand manner.

Abhilash halts, gazes at a mock-mural, saying, 'Hers was a curious life; she was different, very easily misled. You can write about her. But please don't mention my name. You can read of her life from her diaries. You seem to be genuinely interested in her story; I have known people long enough to be able to judge. I am happy to pass her memory on to someone like you. She lost her mind, and at the end, it was painful to see her like that. Always talking of strange things. In fact, though I married her for love, we didn't get along, so Miss Keya, your story might be quite interesting, am I right?'

'Could you please let us see any photos of her, or Mir?' Keya comes across as crafty now.

'I think I've shared enough. Now, if you don't mind, I have a lunch appointment.' Abhilash is dour.

We hasten away. 'Of course. Sorry for taking your time. Thank you again.'

He sees us to the front porch, and the uniformed servant leads us out the rest of the way. Keya clutches the jute bag and we flee the scene as fast as we can.

My breathing returns to normal only after we reach the main road. Why had we always assumed that Shula would have recovered? Abhilash would never tell us anything about Mir, even if he knew, and we agree that he probably did. He has given us the diaries to get rid of Shula's traces in his life.

Keya looks fatigued and broody, maybe from the exertion of playing her part. On the contrary, I feel a growing calm in my chest. When I went into the villa, I was uneasy. Shula's death has placed Mir beyond reach; she went mad from the missing. Ammi is right; people don't want to be found. Keya is right; they go missing for a reason. My life will not be a reaction to Mir's absence. Something will grow from the blankness of that fact. I had been wrong—the letter that arrives as a blank page is an invitation to a new start.

We spend that evening and the next day cooped up in our room, reading through every page of Shula's diaries. When we are done, I am deep in thought. Then, I notice Keya studying me tenderly.

She starts to say 'I'm sorry. I wish—'

I break in, 'I am completely in my present. Let us begin from here.'

13

Shula Farid's Unwritten Autobiography—Poets & Dreamers

Mir was a new beginning.

When I was with him, fairy tales paled. 'I love you' sounded and meant something different every time I heard it from him. When he called my name, 'Shula', I felt an overpowering sensation of surrender.

We found each other on a bridge.

I had stood there captivated by the eddies below, trying to focus on a swift-moving swirl, when a paper plane diverted my sight. Searching the air erratically, it landed on the water's surface. I looked up to see someone else distracted by the melting currents. Unbeknownst to each other, we had both been staring spellbound at the stream.

He came up to me, exchanged greetings, and enquired, 'Where is Xanadu?'

'I don't know,' I said.

'I'm sorry,' he replied.

He had evidently confused me for someone else.

Before he could walk away, I asked, 'Will you tell me?'

Mir was an underground man. It was fey to be involved with him. It didn't matter a whit to me.

Mir Ali—after the first few meetings, he told me his real name— was the man of my dreams. He was passionate, restless, eloquent, poetic. He was not weighted by authority, custom, or privilege. He brimmed with the sensations of life, ever ready to versify them. He was a fugitive because of his politics. I tried to understand his ideals, and I wanted to be his muse.

Abhilash and I had been living under the same roof for years; we led parallel lives within the four walls, but we were not together. Being the wife of a fabulously talented and self-assured diplomat, I did not have a life—I had a social life. I had to doll up and stand by his side at cultural programmes, celebrations, association and club dinners, meeting people, repeating courtesies. As the spouse of an official abroad at a sensitive posting, I could not take up any employment, and I was forbidden to play a part in any political activities, had I wanted to. We lived in the official quarters, so I could not entertain people at will. There were servants for the housework: the driver drove, the cook cooked, the maid cleaned. A gynaecologist had confirmed that because of an improper abortion previously, I could not conceive. Unlike my husband, I did not like watching ARD and ZDF with a glass of brandy in the evenings. Sometimes, I went out shopping, even to the pineapple and banana-starved East Berlin, for crystal and clothing, in our special cars with CC and D number plates that could pass easily through the checkpoints. I lived a charade. I had solidified into a person I despised.

Abhilash never displayed any passions. I had given up trying to pursue my art in public. I wrote poems when I was disturbed, my sketches landed on a shelf. He never discussed any of it. As long as I was a passable imitation of Mrs Abhilash Basu, he was satisfied; he didn't care what I really felt. A part of me felt duty-bound to continue the marriage, since he had selflessly nursed me through the breakdown in Calcutta.

While we were in Berlin, Ma-Baba died in a train accident in Bengal one winter. I was distraught for months. I painted my nails in the most garish colours. I copied an Escher and knitted wool—I barely knew reversing, could not purl, and the result was a miserable foot-long rectangle ridden with holes. I wept entire nights trying to put together a 2000-piece jigsaw puzzle of the Riesersee Alps. Abhilash took me to a bereavement therapist, locked the medicine cabinet at home, made overtures in bed. I was inconsolable. Soon, he lost patience and suggested that I join language classes, as a way of getting out of my surroundings for a few hours every day.

I resolved to intensively study a difficult language, choosing Russian, and insisted that I'd travel there and back unaccompanied. He gave in. Our wordless enmity resumed once more. Thankfully, Ma-Baba never witnessed the extent to which Abhilash and I had unravelled.

It was at this point that I met Mir on the bridge. Russian became my excuse. It was not an unthinking first love, it was an intoxicating letting go, heady and ripe. I felt liberated with Mir and his ideals.

Mir knew I was a diplomat's wife. I knew he was a revolutionary. He trusted me; I met a few of his comrades. He took me to the covert gatherings of communists and anarchists in cellars, where they had small hand-operated presses and big arguments. In 1987, when I first met Mir, they discussed not only the Cold War reality in Berlin, but also Chernobyl, Intifada, Gorbachev. My head swam after these sessions.

Then, in private, Mir would grieve over Kashmir, his beautiful and cruel homeland, where people suffered injustice. 'Like Berlin, my Kashmir is divided too.' He told me of the massive rigging in the Kashmir elections that year by the Congress and National Conference to prevent anyone else from winning. 'They deny us our future, Shula. The identity of my Kashmir is at stake. People are inflamed.' I was ignorant and unaware; I knew of the India-Pakistan wars, the religious divides. He said, 'There is a bigger, stronger, more powerful boundary than that between countries, or between religions—it is the Wall between those who can't live without power, and those who will die to achieve justice.'

We had to meet furtively. Mir was often in disguise. His overcoat could be stuffed, his glasses and his beard fake, his hair a different colour, but I could recognize him from his gentle voice and his astonishingly long fine fingers. He'd lay the barest tip of his hands on my skin, and I'd be joyously agitated. With him, I could feel as the wind and the birds, able to dash myself against any obstacle and see everything, all at once.

On the days we couldn't meet, we wrote poetry to each other. He composed one on the spinning waters that brought us together. I was inspired to pen 'Irregular Lines in Space and Shadows at Noon'. I noticed faces on pebbles and in the clouds. I realized that there were sparrows and zebras in this world. I saw miracles in the ordinary candle flame, and eternities in dried flowers, the apt immortelle. I discovered that I wanted to dance. Dance! With a fulfilled impenitence.

I used to call on a friend, Agni, to cover for me a few times when I was out late with Mir. When I saw her students dancing on stage, I watched carefully, and copied their moves when alone at home. My arms stretched out above my body, my hands moving like a wave of ribbons and my toes pointed straight, I danced. It was immensely joyful to partake in this simplest of pleasures. My body felt young, agile and lithe. Everything was a dream, every sensation divinely magnified: the crumble of a biscuit inside my mouth, the whirlpools in a cup of tea, the droplets of mist on the mirror, a child's cap placed a little to one side on his head—nothing was insignificant. The world quivered with life, I was in love.

One day, Mir and I had our rendezvous at the Berlin Zoo. As we walked together, we felt we were being trailed. A man in a deerstalker cap, with a cigarette hanging from his lips, kept watching us from the corner of his eye. We went from one enclosure to another, spanning the hopeless congregation of creatures. The orangutan appeared depressed, the tiger lay listless next to a lump of half-chewed meat, opening its mouth not to roar but to yawn, in a clear tank there floated three transparent jellyfish with silky gauze-veil threads that were intertwined in a muslin ménage-a-trois. We were on the verge of being cornered at the exit, when a busload of tourists made our escape possible. Running across the road, we got into a bus. There were no seats, so we stood under a crimped rubber roof and a pivot-swivel base; it was like being trapped inside an accordion. Mir informed me that he might have to go away for some time. I was red in the face as I mouthed 'Mir!' my breath failing me even in that smallest of words.

That was the day I said to him, I want to run away with you. Take me away. I'll be your comrade too. I'll cook while you plot. I'll be there when you need me. He explained that he had to go alone, but that he would come back. When we got off the bus, we climbed the dark and narrow stairs to a garret where he slept at night.

It was a small room with a rough wooden floor, an unmade bed, a 'Revolution is coming' poster on a wall, pamphlets, crumbs on plates, stubs, clothes hanging from hooks, big boots, and a few books near which was the blue file that contained the pages of poetry we had shared. He kneeled under the bed and pulled out a cassette player. I watched as he closed the window and put on an audiotape; he could not play it loud. It was the music of Kashmir. I sat on the floor with him and closed my eyes as I heard it. It made me think of water, boats with oars, and ripples reaching distant shores. The lilt was from several stringed instruments whose sounds lingered and intruded lovingly upon each other. Mir told me what a santoor sounded like, and how the girls in their costumes danced the roff arm in arm; he quoted a communist poet of Kashmir called Dinanath Nadim.

Through the dusty window, some light slanted in upon us. I saw it reflected as golden points in his irises, my image there. I narrated to him the tragedy of my life with Abhilash, my time alone in Calcutta, the baby I killed, my shattered dreams of being an artist, and my inmost turmoil from that failure. My voice trembled, tears came unbidden. He held me close like I was the most precious thing in the entire universe. He drank my tears, and said the green pools of love he cherished were not made to cry but to shake up the foundations of a man's heart and his world. The back of his arm touched my forehead at the edges of my face.

He said his life was unspeakably complicated. He had many identities, his passports were forged. He had left the woman he married when she was pregnant with his child. It was a necessary sacrifice. He had no choice. She would manage, she was capable. He had felt respect but not passion for her; she was dull and immune to the fire of his ideas. He never saw the child. It was easier that way. His life was a series of breaking-aways. Some he'd deserted, some, like his close friend Veer, had left him.

I shook with fears. Why could our paths not have been easier? Such was the surge of feeling we had, or perhaps the kind of creatures that we were, we did not feel guilt; we felt a yoking pain at the situation, but no regrets at what we meant to each other.

I could give up the world for him, and it would be a world well lost. He, I knew, was borrowed and doomed. Still, hungrily and eagerly, we spoke of the impressions we wanted to taste on our bodies together: rubbing newly fallen powder snow on the skin, playing in soft silted mud from the banks of a river that connects two countries, to climb to the top of a cliff on a windy night together, our bodies the part of a mad mind.

'Mir, let me belong to you, let us go away together,' I said. Instead of a reply, he put his arm tightly around me. His kisses brushed my face like a flowerful bough. He got up and spread the pages of poems all over the bed. Kneeling, he lifted me up to the bed, 'Instead of pearls and roses, I have dreams to share with you.' I arched with an excess of feeling. He let my hair loose and it fell all about me. Tenderly, he stroked my skin and gently touched my scalp with his fingertips. On the inside curve of the neck, in the fold of the elbow, by the waist, under the breasts, tips of my toes, the insides of my thighs and the back of my knees, he kissed me. Places on my flesh where I had never sensed a body's touch. One finger in his navel and the other in between his lips and teeth, I kissed his chest. We made love lying over the words of this world. He became a part of me like the waves of the sea. I was besotted. I was thrilled. It was generous agony. If there was no tomorrow, I could not care. I had awaited this sensation forever; it connected up everything in my life, and I felt a pure piercing happiness.

He wanted to estimate the precise angle of my shoulder-bone, and he counted with kisses the number of little moles on my body. 'Five,' he summed, 'on the front,' and then turned me over to complete the total.

He draped my long hair around him, and breathed my name over and over again—Shula! Shula!! Shula!!! The gathered words of the poems underneath calmly bore the weight of our pulsating flesh. We lay a long time in silence. Softly, I started to tell him how I found those birds fascinating, the ones which flew about randomly turning direction a hundred times, like wandering spirits of the skies, 'I forget what they're named...swallows? swifts?...one of the two. I saw them over a wood last year.' He pointed a finger in the air above us, 'Look!' He said he could visualize two of them flying randomly together. 'Randomly, yet together?' I tried to imagine. 'Yes, like a rare fortune,' he whispered, ' "A Randomness of Two", that shall be the title of a poem I will write for you.' At this, he immediately turned me to him, and with his lips pressed upon mine, forcing them open and close, he half-kissed, half-inhaled me.

I was happy. I was burnt. Maybe I even hummed tunes at home without realizing it. Because I did not love Abhilash, I did not feel guilty. It is true, I was cheating on him and he had never cheated on me. So what? He was probably fearful of public censure, maybe he could not love again. I wished he was a lying philandering common husband. But how could he be human and fallible? He had to be right and certain. Abhilash could keep his high moral ground and build tall imposing buildings of respectable grandeur on it, hoping to keep out vice.

Mir went away with a promise to return. I waited. In those days, the tea was always cold by the time the cup touched my lips. I was absent-minded. Abhilash did not say anything to me, but one evening, he dismissed the servants early and shut himself in his study. A loud German symphony played inside. I ignored it for as long as I could, then knocked. There was no answer at first. Some time later, he opened the door, he was in his dressing gown. Apropos of nothing, he said: 'Shula, I will never divorce you.' I understood that he knew. How long had he been aware? I couldn't find out. He did not confront or accuse me of anything.

My life became difficult from the very next day. I was under virtual house arrest. Abhilash refused me the vehicle, had someone constantly keep an eye on me, cancelled my classes. He started coming back on time from the office and suggested that we do something together.

'Like what?'

'We could go on a picnic. We could get a big canvas and paint together.'

I laughed hysterically.

'It's late for that.'

'It's never too late.'

'What would you say if I told you I have a headache?'

'Why, I'd give you a medicine to ease the pain.'

'And?'

'Find the best cure.'

'Abhilash, everyone in the world wants to immediately give a tablet to the person who says I have a headache. The person having a headache knows that they can take a tablet. They did not ask you for a tablet. They told you they have a headache. You understand? It is a feeling that they have.'

'I don't know how you came to be like this.'

'You broke me. Why don't you leave me?'

'I always played by the rules. Where do you want to go anyway?'

'I'll find somewhere.'

'Have you forgotten everything we meant to each other?'

'No.' It was true, I remembered loving him once.

'Life is not a fairy tale, Shula. There are realities to face.'

'I don't want to face any realities.'

'I advise you as a well-wisher, not a husband. This course of action will be your ruin. I don't want to say, I told you so, later.'

'Abhi, I know you mean well. But one cannot feel it without having felt it. I don't care if I am ruined.'

I was brazen. That was it. Abhilash did not say anything else.

Mir came back. I didn't ask where he'd been. I was under surveillance, so we could not meet. We wrote to each other. We agreed upon secret codes and signals. I lied to Agni about him being single. She saw how deeply I was in love. She helped us.

It was unbearable to be away from Mir; I did not feel total without him. Every doorbell and phone ring startled me, I could not sleep at night. Mir, too, could not live without me. I was a road, he said—open, wide, lost. I offered him no choice. In every scene, he saw me. I was his soul, I tugged at him awake and asleep.

His note said one day, 'Shula! The world writes me. You write me. Let me be forever yours.' We decided to elope. We would leave Germany and go to Vienna for a few days, while I got a fake identity. Then, from there, we would escape.

Mir and I wanted to run away from the world, but we could not go very far. As I conspired my departure, I realized it was a culmination, a dénouement.

I had made the excuse of being at a baby shower, and bribed the maid with my ring for when Abhilash called from the office. I picked a few clothes, money, jewellery, and my passport, and met Mir at the railway station. He was being helped by his friends. He was going to continue his activities with their organization in another country. I was not given any more details. If I proved myself, in time, I would be inducted into his work. 'And don't worry, I shall never fetter you. You can wear what you want and do whatever you wish. Run naked on a beach, I won't stop you, but double-cross me and that will be it.' I knew he was serious.

In Vienna, where we waited, we had unpunctuated days and nights. On a quiet pavement, as we passed under some blossoming trees, Mir shook the low boughs on my head and I was drenched in the pale pink petals of the falling flowers—I was something beyond happy, I was glad to have lived. 'I love you,' he said, and it meant the world.

As we walked through a pedestrian tunnel, I looked in my pockets for pen and paper to write a few lines of poetry stirring in me. Mir asked a passerby for a spare pen and tore a notice off a wall. On the back of this, over the dried glue stains, I wrote 'The Shape of Love': *A rough-hewn rock solid burning turning stone we call love/ Summer's sun and winter's fatigue/ Closing in upon its edged outlines/ Broken sometimes and fine dust maybe/ Love interrupts its own sublimes.*

The next day, I made sure to have paper and pen, but did not need it. That evening, I went over to an air vent set back from the pavement. Mir followed me. I said I was not about to do a Marilyn Monroe with my long skirt! I took out the blank unused sheet and tore it into pieces as tiny as I could make them. I then let them loose over the vent. The little fragments danced madly in the air. We recalled the bed with poems where we had first made love.

We went to Schloß Schönbrunn, a beautiful yellow palace with stupendous statues in the park. It was heartbreakingly pretty to stand there in the warm sunshine, and be able to kiss each other openly. Someone came up and asked us if we wanted a photograph taken; he could develop it within an hour. We had three taken. There was one of us both. Mir insisted on one of me alone. And there was a final one, at my behest, of Mir and me in silhouette, facing the palace, with our backs to the camera! The photographer was really amused at this last one; no one had ever before asked him to take a photo from the back.

We overheard the guides as they described the palace. I was captivated by Empress Sisi's story, and infatuated by the statue of Paris and Helen in the park. Paris holds Helen in his arms and they look at each other with lustful eyes—Menelaus's wife Helen, the

beloved of Paris, the woman who dictated the fate of Troy, the face that launched a thousand ships. The stone forms were flesh and I could not take my eyes off them. Then Mir showed me the hidden figure of a boatman who crouches under Paris and Helen; he can only be seen if you walk to the side and behind. It was the idyll of blissful desire and its unknown maker-doer: Paris, Helen and the Boatman. I carefully studied the face of the nameless boatman who makes the escape possible, and was still thinking about it when we slept that night.

At dawn, we heard a strident knocking on the door of the safe house where we were. There was no other way out. Mir peeked through the spyhole. They are armed, we are in trouble, he said. We clasped each other desperately, kissing last and long, till the latch gave way. He was dragged away, and I was roughly bundled into the back of a car where I was drugged with a kerchief. When I awoke, I found myself looking at Abhilash's face.

It hit me that Mir and I never got our pictures at the palace as promised by that cameraman.

'Where is Mir?' were my first words to Abhilash.

'Who is Mir?' he asked me in turn.

I looked around. I was not at home in Berlin.

'Where am I?'

'You are at a treatment facility for people with nervous disorders.'

'What?'

'Shula, you are sick. You were unconscious when I found you at home after you had been missing for a few days. We cannot take risks with caring for you at home. You need professional support.'

'Abhi, please, I request you. Let me go away from Berlin. I implore you.'

'You are not in Berlin. You are in South Germany. And you shall be here till the doctor sees it fit to discharge you.'

'But I am fine.'

'You are not fine. I have told you before that it is important to face reality.'

'Abhilash, I hate you.'

'Shula, you are my duty. As your husband and your only living relative, you are also my responsibility. I care for you and I am doing what is good for you. You must stay here.'

In the year that followed, I was kept under observation in a lunatic asylum. I insisted repeatedly that I was sane, but the burly American doctor and his many assistants would not believe me. Abhilash came to visit. He steadfastly refused to speak about Mir.

The more vehemently I protested at this, the easier it was for the carers to force pills upon me. I tried with little success to contact people in Berlin. I was allowed pen and paper, but forbidden use of the telephone. I managed to write a letter to Mir's friend, Veer, in India, begging for information about his whereabouts, but I did not receive a reply.

11 September

Mir my love! I am still thinking of our travels together.

23 September

I have not seen you since they took you away. I am powerless to escape from here. Things constantly happen to thwart every effort of mine…Strange men come and destroy the puppets that I have created. Pieces of painted characters are smashed and hurled against hard floors and stone walls. I can only watch. Grief is eating me. Every second, I am halved, quartered and sliced up inside. Could you rescue me?

25 September

You all. All of you.
So small.
The world's weight on itself,
And the fall,
And the end of it all.

30 September

And who is to say whether it is better to have cheated on a loveless marriage for someone you love or for someone you don't... I loved you. You are my soul-mate and my life. In the time that you have been in my life, I have felt like a person.

Abhilash never understood me. I want to write these words on all the walls of this room, so he can see it all the time—Abhilash, you never understood me! My husband is like the pathetic endlessly wound-up toy that keeps beating the drums on its lap, even when everyone watching has gone home.

I have no one, and he can make me suffer by not giving me my freedom. He can call me crazy, do what he wishes, but I am very sane. I know that Abhilash will force me in this struggle to the end. I am not sure he is capable of feeling anything at all.

10 October

Where are you? Make haste and come to me! Find a way, subvert something. I found a children's book of abridged stories here. Where is my fairy godmother? I am seized by the memory of old fairy tales. The books about goblins, witches, seven siblings... hundred leagues and sprawling castles. I constantly total the things I have to tell you when we meet. When? When? When? I will tell you about fireflies and the scallawags.

I am tired. They make me take chemicals for the cure.

12 October

Without saying anything, my husband gloats with an 'I told you so'. I think he knew it all along, and when we went away together, we were watched.

I wish we could have gone away. No governments would stop us, and especially you. We would not have to be furtive and depraved. Nobody could have loved as I have!

19 October

How you had once left a message for me on the Wall.

24 October

I want to be air, so you can inhale me.

Inside my head, squirrels chase each other—Down the rabbit hole she went, and found that Alice was not even her real name. Liars. They were all liars, every one of them.

I think of fairy tales. Red Riding Hood is running through the deep dark forest. She is dressed in red clothes and a cape. Her eyes are green and hungry. She meets no wolves. She runs. She is enchanted by the smells of the forest, the colours of the wilderness, the shapes of things, the sights of things, her own fast breathing and her beating heart. The unending forest, red and brown and black and green, has consumed the towns and cities. She hopes one day to reach the clearing at the centre of the world. In this clearing, she hopes to find HER. The cosmic seamstress who sits bending on the large sewing machine. She does not speak and she does not look up. She merely continues to move her feet, and her hands circle the large needle with a hole where the stitches continue to move forward unstoppably. When Red Riding Hood reaches there, she sees that the sewing machine is also a weaver's loom, and out of it, continue to fall folds of cloth. She wants to reach the seamstress at the clearing in the forest, and then ask to be remade.

She will wait for as long as it takes.

31 October

You brought in trains of questions with you. I had wanted to be your muse… It was beautiful. I was going to be a revolutionary. With you, I would live for the ideals…And then, what happened? Here I am alone, and gradually, everything has come a full circle.

6 November

If someone were to call out 'Shula' to me today, I might not

even answer. I just lie here waiting for the night to follow the day, sleep as much as possible and gaze into far distances. Abhilash tried to get me to see a new doctor, and I have been prescribed some medicines, but I refuse to take them.

I have always wanted to belong, I don't know why, and I have been rejected in a bizarre manner, so that I am not even sure of why what has happened did happen. You have vanished, and there is nothing that I can say or do that would bring you back. I have no means of communicating with you. I have no idea what has happened to you. I remember your fiery passion, maybe you were too dangerous. Have you been abducted, killed, and are dying at the hands of your captors? Do you think of me and of the possibilities of our love, as you are about to die? Might Abhilash be involved?

17 November

Is it all my fault?...Do you see the same sky at night as I do? I recall only your touch.

Today, I took sheets of paper with me into the shower. I stood under the stream of water and let my tears mix in the flood. One by one, I carefully wet each sheet of those pages and pasted them with water on the tiled walls, the glass partition, everywhere that I could reach...it was difficult. As soon as I would finish pasting one side of the wall, the drying pages would start to peel off from the other sides. Yet, there was a moment when the poems were all pasted around me, and I stood naked in the water, surrounded only by the clinging wet pages. I wanted to dissolve then.

30 November

What tells me that I cannot see myself coming from the distance as I sit here? I am left to myself as often as I like these days. But how will you find me? I heard the news on the radio, and have been thinking of you talking about all the big issues of the world, and how you wanted to change so many things. Everything is changing so fast. Who knows what is happening in the world? I am convinced that if you have gone or been forced to go, it must be for a greater cause. I remembered everything you had told me about your Valley.

7 December

Long smiles of the night
In my reflected self
Remind me of a place
Where nothing reconciles

I had a dream in which there were lotus leaves and dragonflies. I could smell flowers, and I pinched my arm to make sure I was not dreaming, but then I got up. Sometimes, I hate you for existing. I want to kill you for not being with me. I cry all the time and continually console myself aloud.

27 December

I had a cake for Christmas. Their medicines make me worse, and the more I scream and cry, the more they shh-shh and feed me their cures...I am insane with thoughts of my life and of you.

It's all still here. The winter is seeping into my soul. I feel terribly depressed. My world seems to have shrunk into a point in infinite space, and that point is you. I am suffering. Not a day goes by when the whole world does not remind me of how you are. I don't even know where you are. I strain to reach you on the other side. I cannot see or hear you. I cannot know you anymore. I want to be in your arms again. I feel only with you. Everyone else seems dry and dead. Only You. You.

I have stopped having dreams of you. I have stopped dreaming. They drug me to sleep, and I awake to the day. We were once together. Why did you not love me just a little bit more?

Do you sometimes suddenly turn around when you think of me?

This awful snowy winter. My body pains and my limbs feel dead. Will we ever meet again? I wish I could kill myself, but I stop with the fear: what if you are somewhere waiting to be with me again? What if you return one day and find that I have killed myself, and

have to go through what I am going through now?

I might in my spirit have walked into your dream, or as a thought into your waking life. I know that you are alive. For how could you be dead?

The way you watched me when I slept. How could I have slept when you were lying so near me? I would wake to the feel of your fingers tracing words in an unknown language over my bare skin. What did you write? Did you tell me something in those traces on the skin that I should have read and deciphered? All else is immaterial ruin. I love you.

3 January

I have been running a fever for some days now. I vomit almost everything I eat. There is a routine. They come in together through the door. Through his glasses, the burly man examines me again and says things. He nods as he always does, and pretends that I mean something to him. Then, I am left with my sins.

10 January

I am feeling dreadfully ill. It sounds so desperate, so helpless, so wanting. As I write, the table moves and the glass and jug clatter—I feel like banging them against the swimming wall. There, I have kept them on the floor and out of view. I want to scream, cry out, and when they come, I want to let go of myself in their arms and say, 'help me'. But I don't. I am resilient against them...

I am broken and tired, and the fever is making me want to kill myself. I want to die.

This damp cold shackles me. I want the sun. My forehead is burning. What if I banged it against a steadying force? I want someone to tell me that I am still with you, and all this is bad dream. The utter vacuum in my world picks me up with its huge hands and whirls me around, hits me against a wall, over and over again. My wound does not even ooze. Nothing happens in my world; the furniture does not talk. I feel cold and senseless.

25 January

Today, I was called into the senior psychiatrist's office. Apparently, the shocks are not doing the trick. He asked me to tell him how I felt. I spoke for a long time...

I told him that I feel formless. I feel like a non-solid person. I could walk into the solidity around me—the illusion of solidity—the spell of a black magic makes me formless and matterless. I said I wish that I had a better grasp of the situation but suddenly—no, not suddenly, but since you left, my form has evaporated. I can merge into any solidity. I walk into a room, and I walk into one such room every day, and from the ceiling are hanging thousands of threads...they hang halfway between the space of the ceiling and the floor. I walk into the room; I know that for my sanity, I have to be able to get a hold of each of these threads in my hands. I fail. I am never at peace.

The doctor merely shook his head. I was so happy one day.

3 February

Why do they say, descent into madness, like going down a well?

I have been having the most horrific dreams that centre on dead babies. I cannot get these images out of my head...I dreamt that some stranger takes me two floors below the surface of the earth, and there are large armies of people working in laboratories there, and most of them are unaware of what they are dealing with. In large separate rooms, there are carefully stocked severed body parts of infants; tiny arms and legs, heads and torsos. This underworld thrives on dead infants. I did not in the dream ask the stranger why I was being let into this secret. Because once I had killed too?... There were these massive realms of dead and cut-up babies two floors under the surface of the earth. Then, yesterday again, I dreamt that there were depressed infants, sitting in strange places such as shop checkout counters. They played with glazed pottery shards. People went about their business, and I was baffled by the sight of a depressed baby sitting near a checkout machine. No one else was

bothered by these babies. Something very wrong was on display. I saw a blood-soaked carcass of a dead infant hidden under my bed in a small tub. I saw babies slowly dissolving in acid from their legs up. As the rest of their body was turning into vapour, their face stayed intact till the end, streaked with tears of blood dripping from their eyes. I woke screaming. So violent and shocking are these dreams that I don't know how I will ever greet real children. My whole life came off its tracks, and I was wrecked...

I am depressed. I am not mad. I cannot anticipate thoughts of happiness. I am burdened with untied layers I cannot separate.

15 February

Life is despicable. Partitions, splits, breaks, tears. They see you. I tried to use my body as a mop. It was useless. I am not mad. You alone can prove this.

14

The Journeyers

I follow Keya's eyes to a kite drifting in the blue sky.
Our bags are packed, and we wait for the caretaker to return us the key deposit. Keya and I have decided to take the train back to Delhi. It is a day's journey.

We buy tatkal tickets, for a short notice trip, at the Howrah railway station. There is availability with reservation in A/C I tier. 'I prefer it,' I say, 'It will be relaxing and we can be by ourselves.' Declining the offers of the coolies, we reach the platform. I buy magazines at the A.H. Wheeler & Co. store, and get bottled water.

As we wait for the announcement of our train's arrival, Keya draws my attention to a coin-operated weighing machine by a pillar.

'Have you ever been on it?' she asks me.

'Yes, a few times, at the Delhi station, when we used to travel to visit my uncle at Eid.'

'Want to get a weight and a prophecy now?'

'Why not?' The machine is still as it was two decades ago, the upright tower of its body, the raised standing place, the flashing bulbs inside, the rotating red and white disc.

'It takes two rupees instead of one these days.' She inserts the coin and steps up. The ticket pops out in the slot.

When I've finished my turn, I question, 'What does it say about you?'

'I'm 54 kilos. My line is: You have self control, high tastes and self confidence. You?'

'I'm 65. It says: You are shy, ambitious, strong and tough.'

'Wow! What a pair.'

'Why do they have such a lot of foretelling stuff? Fortune cookies, crystal balls, palm lines, horoscopes? Guess it's difficult to accept that we are responsible for our own destiny.'

'It's a good diversion.' She adds, 'It's the nostalgia equivalent for the future.'

'How?' I'm not clear.

'It's a nostalgia for the future—for all the futures that won't be, because of the future that will be. Do you see?'

'Hmm.'

The train chugs in. We find our coupé, stow the bags. Before long, we are pulling out of the crowded station.

As we leave Kolkata, Keya looks pensive.

'A penny for your thoughts.'

'Me? Oh, I was just drifting. Thinking of what a journey this has been. And how it may conclude. As I told you yesterday, I have to be back in England in ten days.'

'I'm so glad you agreed to take the train with me instead of flying back to Delhi. I want to go to Kashmir before I return to London.'

'Because of Mir? What we read in Shula's diaries?'

'In a way. But also because of you. Remember, what you had said to me on the balcony that night in Berlin; that not only political activists, but ordinary people go missing and never return, that thousands of people disappear every year. Those are real lives. When I was wandering about in Europe this summer and trying to put it all together for myself, I realized that going missing is strange, because it is both a fantasy and an anxiety.'

'For the person left behind?'

'For anybody...When we first met, I told you I wander, wonder, take pictures. I lied, because that is what I wanted to do. To escape my reality. It is a fantasy to disappear, because we can step out of our identity and become someone else. Not between 9 to 5 when I could be a banker...' I smile at the thought, 'but every day and night. If I disappear, then I can reinvent myself anew. Like Mir did. I can pretend that what I left behind was worthless, and I am striving for something pure and true. Or I can pretend that I left behind something pure and true, and I need to be rescued by others I meet, like Shula did.'

'And the anxiety?'

'I think the anxiety is the more important part. It's the feeling that anyone can at any time disappear for reasons beyond their control.'

'Like be taken by death.'

'And also by force, by violence. The fact that it could happen to anyone we know makes it scary in a way.'

'That it is' Keya echoes.

'Because if they disappear one day, we may lose them forever. So if I love someone, I'd want to love them a lot to make sure I loved them enough. Or I'd just protect myself by not loving people too much, so I'm never that vulnerable.' I pause, 'I don't know. I'm rambling. Anyway, why did I begin going on about this? I've forgotten—'

'Kashmir.'

'Oh yes, so I want to go to Kashmir, if only for a day, to find a grave—any grave. Any monument to any unmarked person. I know there'll be hundreds of these in and around Srinagar. I'm going to adopt one as Mir's grave, and say a prayer for his soul there. I've hardly prayed in my life, but I'll make an exception. I'll lay him to rest in me.'

'And you want to do this in the city that meant so much to him, his hometown?'

'Sure. That will be my peace. I will then begin a new life and find my place in the scheme of things.'

'Have you thought of what you'll do?'

'I've thought and thought these last few months. When I see bright people like you, I want to study further. I might, eventually. As of next month, I shall belt up and plead with every editor in London town to take me on as a journalist, hoping someone will give me a chance.'

'Why journalism, Leon?'

'I don't have to get up early and be in office!' I joke. 'I've got a Literature degree. I'm way better at expressing myself on paper than in person. I'm interested in lots of different things. I like travel and taking pictures—what else would you recommend, to start with?!'

'How you've deliberated on the tiniest details. I can already imagine reading articles by you.'

'Another path I seriously thought about was taking up a cause. Working with a charity or something like that. Something humane and actual—'

'But?'

'But I'm not convinced, there's no point deluding myself. If I had the steering wheel to change the world, I wouldn't know which way to turn it! There are so many different choices. So many competing sufferings and stigmas.'

At this point, the TTE pulls aside the curtain and asks to see our tickets. He then matches our faces against our IDs and leaves.

'What else did you do in Europe?'

'That's it. I thought a lot.'

'What did you see?'

'Not much.' I explain, 'I don't see the way you do. I'm not that awake to my surroundings. Tell me, for example, what you see outside the window at this instant, even though it's tinted; try.'

Keya peers and replies, 'Okay, let me list as I observe—I see gravel, the mud, the sinewy tracks, the patches of green, clumps of grass, fields, the clusters of trees, and here! the scarecrow, the village roofs of thatch and asbestos, the grain stores, the pylons, the bales of rolled-up hay, the tillers, the harvesters, the animals, the waterholes, and the sky.' She pipes down, 'That's it.'

I slide up closer to where she sits by the window. I feel a weird sensation in my body. I look outside as she did, and I say, 'I see—the ground rushing like mad and the greenery in the distance moving slowly. The parallax. The sun. That's about it.'

She turns to me, 'Mr Journalist, you'll have to expand on that when you write for print.'

'Maybe they'll hire me to do the captions.'

She flashes her dimples.

'And this is why, I wandered through Europe but saw not much. When I was new to London, I went about walking through the city and looking at things. And sometimes, when I'm nervous, I intensely notice the details of my surroundings, to give my thoughts a break. Other than that, I notice stuff here and there, but I am nothing remotely as encyclopaedic as you are!'

'You had a busy summer?' I ask her.

'Very. I worked a lot and thought of you.'

'Thinking of me is work!' I laugh.

'Come on. Don't tease me. I worked. I thought of you.'

'You didn't write to me,' I complain.

'I didn't, on purpose.'

'Hmm. Why?'

'Well, I wanted to see if you'd still matter if I didn't communicate with you—and also, I wanted to understand you from the inside.'

'And how do my lungs bear up to scrutiny? I'm sorry, I said that to see the vexed expression on your face. I'll be serious. Go on.'

'It's silly, actually. I took down my favourite picture from a wall and hid it somewhere. Then pretended I didn't know where it was. Tried to sit in front of the rectangular mark on the wall where it had been. Imagining how it feels. Then trying to magnify that sensation a million times—'

She is strange. I adore her, I think to myself as she speaks.

'It doesn't make sense though, because it would be like eating madeleines for a week to turn a person into Proust!'

I look at her face; it is animated.

She mistakes my stare for incomprehension. 'Marcel Proust wrote this long memoir which was triggered—'

'Keya,' I protest.

'What?'

'You've got to stop misreading my eyes; why do you think I

won't get your references. If I don't, I'll ask.'

'I'm sorry, I'm not arrogant, you know. I just can't help spelling things out sometimes.' She's a picture of contrition.

'You don't have to be that sorry. Please go on.'

'I decided to broaden the example. I tried to think of things that people miss in their lives which affect them profoundly, like the lack of education, or health, or a home. But that wasn't such a good example, because one could, in a way, see the causes there. It is bad public policy, due to which people are uneducated or homeless—'

I hope this is going somewhere. Keya is off tangent, and I don't see what public policy has to do with missing and absence.

'So, I tried thinking of something closer. Something to make it inward. More substantial. I tried to locate the biggest missing in my life. It isn't my father, but it's his nostalgia of a home and homeland in Kashmir. I inherited a borrowed, second-hand exile. It's the carved wooden house with windows jutting out, one of many in an alley—named after a centuries-old Afghan ruler in Srinagar— where the buildings literally run into each other, with no space to spare. When I thought of that Kashmir, the house he grew up in... I felt closer to your sense of absence. I'm going on, and unable to convey—' She's obviously moved.

'I understand. I do.'

'This is why you should not assume that I was callous and didn't keep in touch. I wanted to feel you.'

'Come to Kashmir with me.'

'I—how can I? Can I?'

'You have ten days. Take two out, or three. We'll fly and save time. We'll be together, it'll be safe. I'll shield you if a bullet comes our way. I promise!'

'But, Leon, that would be wonderful. Can I really come along? I can't believe it. I could go to our ancestral home and see the rooms where my family used to live. And it would be impossible for me to go there alone, or even with my relatives. They are frightened to go back. That's the reality. You being a Muslim will be a plus—'

'And if the Indian army stops me for being a terrorist, then you being a Pandit turn useful.'

'How sorry it sounds!'

'Anyway, how good is your Kashmiri?'

'Not very. When my migrant cousins came, I hated them for being fluent.'

'Tsk-tsk! I'm quite all right. I met people in London and they call themselves Kashmiris, but they couldn't speak a word of the language.'

'Language is one of the many different ways of belonging. Speaking English doesn't make us British, does it?' she pounces.

'Not speaking it definitely won't. These people were from the other side of the Line of Control.'

'I think we're all multiply labelled people, and we ought to strive for better futures.'

'Multiply labelled people of the future—Keya, you do live in an Otherworld!'

'What I mean is that...culture isn't about belonging. It's more a longing.'

At this point, the on-board catering man in uniform with a smiley badge brings us our thermos flasks with hot water for tea, and the silver foil packed trays of food. He makes monosyllabic responses to our enquiries; we learn the state-run trains have privatized their catering; he's busy. We are hungry and attack the meal with gusto.

Over dinner, Keya explains to me the falsehoods she will employ in getting away from Delhi. She can't tell her family that she will go to Srinagar with a Kashmiri Muslim friend she met abroad; I'll sound like a terrorist. So, she'll pretend she's going to Jaipur or Agra, something touristy but safe.

That night, when it gets dark, we switch the lights off, stick the Velcro bits to secure the curtains, and lie next to each other, letting the soothing cadence of the wheels gently rock us.

'It feels like we have been voyeurs to every detail of Shula's

life these last two days.' She is referring to our marathon read of Shula's diaries in Kolkata.

'And what a life,' I say.

'That's it. I thought that happened only in books. And a hundred years ago. Shula really died of heartbreak.'

'Hmm. And Abhilash...'

'Why do human relationships inevitably involve pain?' she asks.

'I think the ones that matter can cause real pain.'

'And people still go on living, changing.'

'Do you think people change?' I've been curious about this question myself.

'Change themselves?'

'Well, themselves or others?'

'I think some do, and some don't. Or rather that some people believe in changing themselves, some try to change others, and some never ever change. Who meets whom makes the story of their lives.'

'You sound like Rumsfeld making his known-unknowns speech.'

'I do, don't I?' she giggles. I can't see her face in the dimness.

'Other-changer meets Self-changer, equals Perfect. Changeless meets Changeless, there's a Perhaps. Other-changer meets Changeless, sure Turmoil!'

'You make it sound like emotional blood-groups, Keya.'

'But don't forget, there are degrees of changeability.'

'Of course.'

'And we never know which one we are till we meet the next person.'

'And love, does that not change everything?' the answer is obvious to me.

'Love...' she hesitates. 'We love in different ways.'

'Are you saying some love better?'

'Not simply better or worse; when and how much.'

'That sounds calculating, doesn't it?'

'No, that's not how I mean it, Leon. Umm. Let me see. It's that some love intensely, and only once and for ever.'

'They do?'

'I think so. Then, some love intensely, but in succession.'

'I can identify with that.'

'Some love moderately. Sensibly. They seek the path of least resistance and avoid challenges.'

I think of Ammi, and add, 'Some love devotedly and will equal any challenges in their love.'

'And then there are those who love, yet manipulate with an awareness.'

'Keya, do you see what a fly on the wall would report? We're basically saying there are different kinds of people in this world. That's all.'

'It would be a very cold fly, chilled with the A/C. Like me. Brrr.'

'You're cold? They gave us blankets. Let me get the light.'

'Leon, shall I move to the upper berth? Are you sleepy? I need to get ready for bed.'

She snuggles under the blankets on the top berth. I lie down on mine. The moon beams on my face from the window.

'You should've slept down here,' I whisper.

'Why?'

'The moon outside.'

She doesn't reply for a minute.

'It's okay. Enjoy it for me.'

'I will. Goodnight. Dream well.'

'Leon, do you know why must there be a sun and a moon?'

'Because of day and night.'

'And alchemy,' she adds.

'Alchemy?'

'The lapis that turned matter to gold came from uniting the sun and the moon, figuratively.'

'Keya, you are otherworldly, and most unaware of it.'

I get no answer.

'Keya? Can I kiss you? I can't control the urge.' I feel a passion for her. And a fear of her reaction.

'I love you,' I whisper what I've felt for months. Then, follow it up with, 'Whatever the number of people you've been attracted to this week, you had better be single! I am not into complicated arrangements.'

'Shut up, Leon,' she leans over the side and drops her arm down. I reach mine up to touch her.

'Kiss me.'

Standing on the bed, I reach to where her head is. In the dark, I touch her lips with mine. For an uncertain amount of time, I feel erratic fires in every limb. I wish I could climb up there and sleep next to her.

'Keya,' I repeat, with fading breath.

'What's your favourite flower?' She is using my tactic. Words to calm sensations.

'You,' I say. 'When we first met, you'd said Keya was a kind of flower.'

'How you remember! I've never seen that flower. I'll find it for you.'

I am mildly jolted as the train comes to a halt at a platform.

'Goodnight. Dream well.' I slide back down to my bed and close my eyes. I want her in so many ways.

After some time, I hear, 'Leon? Are you awake?'

'Yes.'

'Please don't say anything to me until the morning now. I want the silence to be our confession.'

I try to stay awake in order to hold on to the way I feel for as long as possible. Finally, a big black ball of wool lead-coats my eyes. In my mind, I keep losing and retracing connexions, while being aware of the process, like waves crashing upon waves, but all of them connected with fine threads of Dhaka silk. Dhaka silk so fine that you can pull a ream through a tiny gold ring.

Next day on the train, we talk of futures.

'Keya, when we met, I'd said life is a residual phenomenon.'

'I remember,' she replies.

'I had meant that life is something we have to live in the presence of traces of things alive that are no longer there. Like wax from a burnt candle or ash from a fire. Things that surround us and trap us in the past. A past of places and people.'

'It is the remnants of fires that have burned in the past, and which we have to deal with in the present. But I've realized it is also the residue of a fertilizer that has remained in the earth, and on which the healthy root of a sapling nourishes.'

'I'm still saying that life's a residual phenomenon, but it is the residue of the earth that lives through things, and not just the fire that burns and passes.'

'Leon, you know how I came to collect stories, and why I like holding on to them?'

'Because you are interested in people. Isn't it?'

'It began with a tin toy bus I had as a child. There was a wind-up mechanical spring on it. There were painted passengers sitting in the windows, the driver, the conductor. All of the people looked different—a turbaned Sikh man, a bindi-wearing woman, a foreigner, a child—you get the picture?'

'Sure.' I could see a large red bus, something like the London double-decker, moving along a road with people of all colours, dresses, ages and types. Come to think of it, that was a good London bus for real, wasn't it?

'Well, I wanted to get to know the people in the bus. They couldn't speak to me about their lives because they were captured inside. I had to rescue them out of that painting. So, I broke the bus to bits.'

'Oh no!'

'I found springs, plastic and tin joints. Of course, I was admonished for my stupidity. But the point was, they were other people. If I wanted to understand their lives and gather their stories, I realized I'd have to imagine them from the inside.'

When we reach Delhi, I check into a hotel near the railway station for two days. She plans for the Srinagar visit, buying our tickets online. We spend time in the city together.

I take her to a place I grew up pretending didn't exist in the city: Old Delhi. I have hardly been here and she has never seen it either. We squeeze through the crowds in the insanely narrow alleys, go to a famous eatery tucked in a neighbourhood she would have difficulty visiting alone, we take our shoes off at Jama Masjid, watch the devout with curiosity, and climb the minaret to get a view of the congested heart of Mughal Dilli.

She takes me to the Planetarium on the grounds of the Teen Murti mansion where Jawaharlal Nehru once lived. We lean back in wonder and watch a show about the stars of the universe. In the middle of the day, we sit mesmerized under a dark sky of twinkling stars. I learn that the eclipse cycle of the sun and the moon is an interval of eighteen years, eleven days and eight hours; a duration that is termed a Saros. She says to me that the universe is a real world wide web, the biggest and the best: we're in it, so we think it real.

We stand in queue at the domestic airport the next afternoon; our flight to Srinagar departs in an hour. We're going for three days and have a small bag each. It is liberating to be heading there. I am sure she will observe every street, houseboat, shrine, garden, security barrier, soldier, bridge and mountain as we walk through the city and talk to the people. I'll find a grave. She'll see her home.

'Next, please,' the lady at the airline check-in counter calls.

We step up and say hello. We hand her our ticket printouts and passports.

'Keya Raina and Leon Ali, are you travelling together or separately?'

We look at each other and smile before simultaneously answering.